NIKOLAI RETURNS

BY

MICHAEL TANNER

TELEMACHUS PRESS

Cover designed by Telemachus Press, LLC

Cover art Copyright © Thinkstock/136691638/iStockphoto

Maps and illustrations by Danielle Klebes

Published by Telemachus Press, LLC
http://www.telemachuspress.com

Visit the author website:
http://www.michaeltannerbooks.com

ISBN: 978-1-938135-20-0 (eBook)
ISBN: 978-1-938135-21-7 (Paperback)

Version 2013.04.15

Printed in the United States of America

10 9 8 7 6 5 4 3 2 1

NIKOLAI RETURNS

PROLOGUE

Kurskaya Oblast, Russia, 1920

"Is this a sin, Your Honor?" the woman asked.

She gripped the steering wheel tighter as the man sitting beside her in the cab of the truck turned from his window.

"Don't call me 'Your Honor,'" he said.

"I'm sorry, sir."

"Don't call me that either. I told you, all that's over with now."

The woman sighed. "I'm sorry. I won't forget again."

"Don't. If they heard you say that back in Kursk, we'd both be sorry. It's 'comrade' or 'leader,' whichever you like, but the old titles are gone."

She sighed again and peered through the grime of her window at the open steppe country passing by in the dim light before dawn. Moscow was five long days travel from Kursk along this road and so it had always been called the Moscow Road.

Late spring rain stood in puddles in the fields that stretched to the horizon in every direction. The road was better now than it was during the *rasputitsa*—the "time of bad roads" after the snows melt—but just barely so.

She wiped her forehead and then pulled with both hands on the heavy steering wheel and downshifted the gears. The truck rumbled through a muddy rut. The reek of motor oil, old sweat and old leather filled the cab.

"But ... is this a sin?" she asked.

The man rubbed the back of his gloved hand and shrugged. "Depends on your point of view, I imagine. But it doesn't matter."

"They haven't done anything."

"We have orders and that's all we need to know."

She nodded. Yes, that was true. Orders were orders. But why did this matter for the Revolution? That's what was bothering her. Something about this didn't make sense.

"And I won't enjoy it, if that's what you're thinking," he said. "But it's necessary. It has to be done. One day you'll see that."

"I suppose you're right."

Then she remembered the others traveling with them. "But what about them, Comrade Leader?" She cocked her head toward the open bed behind the cab where six men sat quietly on wooden boxes.

The leader looked back through the window. The men were staring out at the empty landscape while the truck bed heaved to and fro. "Well, you know …" he said. "Too many years at war. After a while that starts to eat away at a man's soul."

The woman shifted into a lower gear and the engine whined.

"Anyway, if they enjoy this … that's not our business," he said. "Our business is to get this done. If anything goes wrong, we won't want to go back to Kursk, believe me."

"Yes, sir."

"And don't worry about the men. They're quiet enough this morning."

She remembered their bloodshot eyes when they arrived at the truck in the dark. "Oh, I think they'll be quiet for a while," she said, tapping her neck with her forefinger below the right ear, the age-old peasant signal to ditch the tools and duck behind the nearest shed with a bottle.

The leader leaned back in his seat and laughed. "Well, for once I guess that's a good thing."

As the truck bounced through another rut, the woman looked to the east and saw a pale pink and blue glow in the sky. Dawn had come.

"How far now, Comrade?"

He scanned the fields outside his window. "Five versts, maybe less," he said, measuring the distance in the old Russian way.

She pursed her lips. This was good, very good. The road was drier out here in the country and they were making better time now. They should arrive on schedule, maybe even a little early.

As she rolled down her window, the sun broke over a band of clouds above the horizon in the east and shafts of yellow light streamed up to the heavens.

~~~~

Half an hour later the truck pulled up in front of the high red brick wall surrounding the Korennaya monastery and the woman switched off the engine. The wooden doors that hung in the arched front gate were open and she looked through the gate and down the straight, wide brick walk, past the workhouse and dormitory, to the front doors of the gleaming white church with sky-blue domes standing on the highest bluff over the Tuskar River. A breeze rustled the leaves of a row of poplar trees along the front wall. The trees had the bright green color of spring.

In the morning quiet, the men in the back started to come to life. One lit a cigarette and another cleared his throat and spat on the ground. A third man, with a drooping black mustache, pounded twice on the cab window.

"*Tovarisch*," he said to the leader through the glass, his brow raised and palms upturned. "Now what?"

"Now we wait," the leader said.

~~~~

While the morning sky lightened, a lone figure, wearing the clean garb of a novice, hurried along the brick colonnade from the dormitory to the old church. He was late again for matins, the third time in a week, and this time the prior was sure to notice.

He knew how important it was to follow the rules—to be obedient—and he tried to be on time, oh how he tried. Each night his last prayer was to be on time the next morning. But his best, deepest sleep always came in the hour just before dawn, turning his eyelids to lead.

By the time he slipped into the stained glass-colored gloom inside the church, the monks were already in their places and singing their morning prayers.

3

Each day at dawn the monks of Korennaya assembled in the old church on the riverbank. Following the rule laid down by St. Basil in the fourth century, they stood shoulder to shoulder in rows facing each other and for an hour filled the sanctuary with their songs chanted in Old Slavonik, the ancient tongue of the steppes, now long forgotten outside the Holy Mother Church. As the novice took his place in the back row, with the smell of incense in his nostrils, they began the Archimandrite Sophronios—the glorious Prayer at Daybreak:

> *O Lord Eternal and Creator of all things*
> *I have no life, no light, no joy or wisdom:*
> *No strength except in Thee, O God.*
> *Grant unto me, the worst of men*
> *To love Thee as Thou hast commanded*
> *With all my heart, and with all my soul*
> *And with all my mind, and with all my strength;*
> *Take me not away in the midst of my days,*
> *Nor while my mind is still blind*
> *But when Thou shall be pleased to bring my life to an end*
> *Forewarn me that I may prepare my soul*
> *To come before Thee.*

For a moment he closed his eyes. There was no better proof than this sublime music that the breath of life in these holy men had come from beyond this world.

But today his mind wasn't just on the music.

His head throbbed and his stomach churned. He felt feverish and faint. The flu he'd been fighting for a week and thought he'd finally shaken off had returned in the night, with cramps that gripped his insides.

Dear God, not now, not again. It's bad enough to be late, but now this. The latrines, he had to get to the latrines.

And so he backed out of line and made his way out the front door to the stone steps where the morning air on his face momentarily refreshed him. He dabbed his brow with his sleeve and started down the steps toward the common.

Then he stopped short and sucked in his breath.

There, parked outside the front gate, was a truck, an old military truck from the look of it. Its coat of field gray paint was splotched and faded and its front grill was missing so that he could plainly see the radiator tubes. Half a dozen men, each with a rifle, stood nearby, smoking and talking. In an instant the pain in his head and stomach was forgotten.

No man on God's business needs a rifle. The father abbot, he must find the abbot!

~~~~

While the woman waited with the leader in the cab, a lone figure came out the front door of the church, paused and looked in her direction, and then ran down the steps and across the common.

They'd been seen.

The monks' voices carried faintly through the open door of the church and across the common. The leader leaned out his window and listened.

"Beautiful, isn't it," he said after a moment. "A bit melancholy, but beautiful."

She nodded as she poured a cup of tea from a bottle she'd kept beside her on the seat. Did he really enjoy the music? Those animals in the back could never appreciate it, but this man ... maybe.

She passed him the cup and he peeled off his leather glove to take it. A raised scar ran from the stump of his forefinger down to his wrist. She'd seen it before, on one of the few occasions when the leader removed his glove, but she'd never asked about it.

Well, why not now? He's not like the other officers and, besides, no one is listening.

"The Germans, Comrade Leader?" she asked.

"What?"

"Your hand—did the Germans do that?"

He set the cup down on the dashboard and flexed the fingers he had left. "No, not the Germans, or even the Austrians—they wouldn't have let me off so easy. No, this was a little present from my men. A bayonet."

"Your men did that? Why?"

He picked up the cup. "You've never seen an army go to pieces, have you?"

She shook her head.

"Well, you know engines. Think about an engine, think about one running so hard and so long it finally blows apart. That's a fairly good picture of it. And when an army comes apart, people get hurt."

"But why you, why that?"

He flexed the hand again and studied the scar. "After the Czar was gone, most of the men just gave up. They were tired of fighting, tired of mud and tired of their officers—especially the officers. They were just making a point for me, letting me know they didn't have to take my orders anymore." He blew on his tea and took a sip.

She thought of the men relaxing around the truck and shuddered. The leader had been one of them, promoted from the ranks, and if men like these would do that to him, what might they do here? She hoped the leader stayed healthy today.

~~~~

When he reached the top of the steps outside the abbot's private quarters, the novice paused and steadied himself against the heavy door. This was a terrible intrusion, but surely the old man would understand. There was so much at stake. He took a breath, gripped the handle, and pushed.

But when he entered the room, his tongue failed him. "F … Faa … Faaaaather," he stammered.

The old abbot was on his knees at the foot of his bed and he looked up with moist eyes. The novice swallowed and concentrated, willing the words to come out.

Not again, not now. Please let me speak.

"F … f … forgive me. So … so … soldiers."

The old man blinked twice. "Soldiers? Soldiers where?"

The young man pointed toward the common. "Th ... the g ... gate."

The abbot lowered his head onto his chest and closed his eyes for a long moment. The young man glanced around the room. It was his first time in these quarters and he was struck by their simplicity. Why, other than a worn floor rug, they were no different than his own. There was only a bed, a wood table for the night bowl and a chair. This, for a man to whom was entrusted one of Russia's great monasteries, a place to which pilgrims journeyed from every province to venerate its holy icon and experience the healing powers of its spring water.

The abbot opened his eyes and crossed himself. He held out a bony hand.

"Help me up," he said and the young man gripped the hand and pulled him to his feet. "How many soldiers?"

The young man concentrated and spoke slowly. "Six ... s ... seven. And rifles ... th ... they have rifles."

"Did you speak to them?"

"No, Father. I c ... came here."

"Then you did well," the abbot said, patting the young man's arm. The lines on his forehead were deeper than the novice remembered.

"Father, has it c ... come? Has it s ... started here?"

The abbot sat on his bed and reached for his boots.

"I pray not, but if it has, it's God's will that it should. Never forget that, whatever happens today." He stood and looked into the smooth, troubled face. "God's will is God's will, whether we like it or not. I just pray it's not too late for these men."

~~~~

Matins ended an hour after dawn and the monks began to leave the sanctuary in twos and threes. Some strolled across the common toward the workhouse while others walked along the arched brick colonnade that followed the slope of the bluff down to the river and a spring that flowed from the decayed remains of an old tree. Others lingered in the garden planted with willow and pear trees that followed alongside the colonnade.

7

The leader took a final swallow of his tea. He never touched liquor, but maybe that's what he needed now.

Well, let's get on with this.

He knocked on the window and stepped out of the cab. The men crushed out their cigarettes on the ground and gathered at the rear of the truck. He drew a revolver from a holster under his coat and waved for the men to follow him through the gate. Each man shouldered his rifle and picked up a box from the bed of the truck and set off after him. One of them also carried a small leather satchel. The woman stayed behind with the truck.

The men followed behind the leader in a ragged line across the common and up to the church where they laid the wooden boxes gently on the steps. Then the man with the satchel pried open the top boards of each box with his knife, drew out the contents—packages of amatol, a mixture of ammonium nitrate and TNT—and placed the packages in rows on the steps.

The leader watched him work. He was good, the best sapper the leader ever had, careful, and not a loudmouth like some of the others. He knew his business well from all those years on his belly on the Galician front blowing Austrian and German wire. How many sappers had blown themselves up along with the wire in those days? The leader couldn't remember them all anymore.

One by one, the sapper checked the packages of explosive to make sure the bumping and jarring on the road hadn't spoiled the mixture. When he finished with the last package, he looked up and nodded to the leader. Then he opened his satchel and pulled out a strip of brown leather with stitched pockets that resembled an oversized bandoleer. Each pocket cradled a lead azide detonating capsule.

It was now full light and dozens of monks and visitors were out on the common in the soft morning.

"Comrade," one of the men said and when the leader looked up, the man pointed to the common where two figures were running toward the church. The leader smiled.

Convenient, very convenient. Now he wouldn't have to waste time searching for the old man.

When the abbot and the novice reached the church, they stopped at the bottom of the steps. Their boots and the trains of their cassocks were wet from the grass on the common.

The abbot was breathing hard and he raised his arms up. "God be praised," he said. He paused, took another breath, and then spoke again, this time in a stronger voice. "My son, you must not do this, I beg you. You will regret it all your days. Your children and their children will regret it."

The man with the mustache produced a length of rope from his pocket, pushed the abbot to his knees and tied his hands behind him. He gave the last knot a jerk and the old man winced.

"Not so tight," the leader said.

The man snorted but leaned down and loosened the knot. Then the leader noticed the woman walking across the common toward them. The sunlight striking her hair gave it the color of burnished copper.

She ought to stay with the truck, she knows that. But ... it's good she's here. Strange, she's just a peasant girl—well not really a girl anymore—but I can talk to her.

"Will you answer me, my son?" the abbot said and the leader turned away from the common to face him.

"There's nothing to say."

"Praise God, there's everything to say."

"Not to me."

"Why do you do this?"

"You know why. This place and everything in it are relics, things of the past. They must go."

The abbot shook his head. "You misunderstand me. I'm not speaking of these buildings, of all these bricks and stones. I speak of you. The book is open and your page has yet to be written."

He started to rise, but the man with the mustache grabbed his shoulder and pushed him back down to his knees.

"What are you talking about, what book?" the leader said.

"The book of life. Whether your name will be written in it is your choice. Don't do this."

A smile spread across the leader's face. "What's this nonsense, a riddle, for more time?"

"Is it nonsense to fear for your soul?"

The leader shoved his revolver back into its holster. You're losing control. Everyone is watching and you're losing control. No more talk.

"That's enough."

"My son, I'm talking about God's Word," the abbot said. "Don't let the book close without your name in it."

The leader turned and strode up the steps. "Gag him," he said to the man with the mustache. Then he motioned to the sapper. "It's getting late."

The sapper pointed to a row of charges on the top step. "These are enough for the church. They can start there."

"You heard him," the leader said to the men. "Remember the placements we showed you. We have none to waste."

At his command, each man picked up a charge and began to walk slowly to the chosen points along the thick walls. The charges were shaped to focus the blast for maximum power.

When the charges were tamped into place along the base of the walls, the sapper gently pushed a capsule from his bandoleer into each one. To each capsule he attached the wire that would carry the detonating current. When all was ready, he moved back to the middle of the common where he screwed a wooden handle onto the detonator box. The leader and the others stood around him.

"Ready," he said.

The men, the abbot and the novice, the woman, they all had their eyes on the leader.

Do they think I won't do it, that I'm not up to this? Well, what choice do I have?

"Do it," he said and the sapper turned the handle with a twist of his wrist.

In an instant, orange light flashed and a shockwave ripped through the still air. A roar spread out from the base of the church and reverberated across the common and out onto the steppes. The leader dropped to the ground. He was back at the front, cowering in the dirt for cover from the inferno of an enemy bombardment. Only now, the deep, hollow percussions of the shells launching from heavy guns hadn't been there to warn him to steel himself against the violence that followed.

As the shockwave passed over the common, the church walls collapsed on themselves with a rush of air and a cloud of dust that billowed up to the sky. Monks, pilgrims and even some of the leader's men fell to the ground and covered their heads. Chunks of masonry rained down as five hundred years of loving craftsmanship were obliterated. Even the man with the mustache stared with his mouth open. The novice wept.

As the dust spread out over the walls, the sapper stood up and brushed off his jacket.

"Which one now?" he asked.

The leader turned to the abbot who stared back at him with hollow eyes. "The workhouse," he said and the sapper motioned to the men to pick up more charges.

~~~~

By dusk Korennaya was no longer a great monastery. Only the stable, one of the dormitories and sections of the south wall were left standing. Around these lay piles of rubble. Brick and plaster, blasted to fine powder, hung in the air and coated the trees, giving the appearance of a late spring frost. The great arched colonnade from the church down to the river was gone and pieces of the columns and the painted vaulted ceiling constructed centuries ago by Italian masons littered the garden amid broken trees.

After the last charge was used the man with the mustache pointed to the abbot.

"What about him?" he asked the leader.

"Untie him."

"And then?"

"And then nothing. We're finished here."

"That isn't our order, Comrade," the man said.

"That's my order."

"They won't like it."

The leader pulled back his jacket, revealing the butt of the revolver in its holster. "They won't like it if you refuse my orders."

The man twisted his mouth, but then he let out a long breath, pulled the abbot to his feet and loosened the rope.

"Will we come back tomorrow, Comrade Leader?" the sapper asked.

The leader swept his eyes over the ruins. The point had been made well enough, hadn't it? By God, even those jackals in the Kursk soviet, whence his orders came, must agree with that. Night was coming—a long night—and it was time to go.

He shook his head. "We've done enough. Let's get back."

~~~~

The woman was waiting in the cab with the engine running and she watched the leader climb in and close the door.

He looked older and it wasn't just the dust in his hair.

She held out the bottle of tea to him, but he pushed it away. She put her hand over his and squeezed.

"We've sinned today, Your Honor."

"Yes."

"Now how do we set it right?"

PART ONE

CHAPTER 1

৵

1990s

A burst of light blinded me early in the morning.

This was like no light I'd ever seen—pure, stark white, otherworldly white—and it burst around me like the flash from a great camera. It came from everywhere and nowhere and in an instant my eyes were as dead as if I'd taken a long look straight into the sun.

In the moments that followed I stood still in the darkness, in the drizzling rain, struggling for an explanation, trying not to panic.

Stay calm, stay calm. Whatever this is, it'll pass.

But there was no way I could stay calm. My throat tightened and my breath was short and shallow. In those first moments I wasn't sure which was worse, losing my sight or hearing what I had heard just before the flash.

Surely that hadn't been real—it couldn't have been real.

Yet something was now real enough to make me violently ill. My head was pounding, sweat rolled down my face, and my arms and legs trembled. Waves of nausea rolled over me.

Just before the flash, my friend Styopa and I were on a footpath in a stand of woods near Semkhoz, a village about an hour's drive northeast of Moscow. The green pine and birch trees had hidden us from the road and the ground cover of needles muffled our voices.

But we were in plain view of anyone who might come along the path.

The last thing I saw was Styopa running out of the woods, back toward the car. As the sound of his footfalls died away, a storm raged in my head. What had happened here? A bomb, a grenade? Surely not—there'd been no sound or shockwave and other than the sickness in my stomach and my trembling limbs, I wasn't injured.

Or was this an hallucination, or some bizarre brain malady that had hijacked my senses? Maybe my brain had just gone haywire, making me see and hear and feel things that weren't really there.

But my instincts told me that wasn't the answer either. I could hear and feel the cold rain and smell the loamy scent of the woods, and generally speaking, my wits were still with me.

No, whatever this was, it wasn't just in my head. Something—or someone—had done this to me.

Then Styopa was back at my side. "What are you doing? You're the one who's acting crazy. We can't stay here!"

"I can't move, I can't see," I said. And although I couldn't see his face, I could well imagine his reaction. Styopa was my old pal from the war in Afghanistan—and now my business associate—and I knew him like a brother.

"What are you talking about? We need to go—now."

"I'm telling you I can't see."

"Kolya, if this is some joke …"

"There was lightning, you saw it."

"Ok, so? It's raining."

"I think it hit me, did something to my eyes."

His strong hands felt up and down my arms and legs and then he passed his fingers through my hair and around my neck. "You're not hit, you're ok."

"I'm telling you it must have hit me."

"That's nuts. You'd be burnt up. It didn't come near us."

"Look," I said. "I can't see a thing and if you don't help me out of here, somebody *will* see us."

We were taking a terrible risk every minute we stayed in those woods. He grabbed my arm and pulled me along the path, back to the road. Along the way I tripped several times on the uneven ground and tree roots. Whatever was wrong with my eyes was no joke. After the third stumble, I sensed he was more worried than angry because he wasn't pulling me so hard and he eased his grip on my jacket.

When we came out of the woods he told me the car was still parked where we'd left it, on the side of the road, off the pavement and in the grass. The country road was quiet and that was a relief, but I knew it must be getting lighter and someone was sure to come along soon. We had to leave.

As the minutes passed without my eyesight, the fear that I might live out the rest of my days in darkness began to tighten its coils around me. My chest ached and I couldn't get a good breath. I wanted to scream.

Styopa led me around to the passenger side and opened the door and I smelled the leather of the seats. It dawned on me then how foolish we'd been to bring that car, Styopa's sleek new silver Mercedes, because in those days in Russia people noticed a car like that. But he had insisted on bringing his pretty new toy.

He folded me into the front seat, closed the door quietly and then climbed into the driver's seat. He started the engine and turned the car around on the road, back toward Moscow.

As we picked up speed, I leaned back in the seat and tried to stay calm by remembering the details of the car, the polished wood trim, the camel-colored seats, and Styopa's Afghan War service medal dangling from the rear view mirror. Strange, but I could picture it all so clearly—except for the colors. I couldn't see the colors.

Is that the first thing you forget when you go blind, the colors? My God, what will I do if my eyes are ruined?

When Styopa said we had crossed the outer ring road, bringing us back into Moscow where we could blend into the early morning traffic, I relaxed a bit. My throat loosened and my breathing was easier. Moscow weather in September can be tricky and even though it had felt like high summer for the last few days, that morning had turned cold, so cold we had to tramp back and forth in the woods, flailing our arms, to stay warm. Now the heater was running on full and the car was hot and dry. My window made a soft 'whrrr' sound when I pushed the button to lower it and the cold wind stood my hair straight up in front and chapped my cheeks. The car slowed and the chirping of hundreds of sparrows told me we must be passing the trees along Prospekt Mira.

"Ok," he said. "I'm listening."

I swallowed to fight off another wave of nausea. "For what?"

"An explanation."

"I wish I had one."

"I'm not kidding, Kolya. People don't just go blind—like that." He snapped his fingers.

"So you're a doctor now?"

"It's not funny."

"You saw the lightning."

"Yeah, I saw it, but it didn't come near us. It had to be a klik away."

I rubbed my eyes and blinked. I shut them hard and opened them again. Still nothing—just darkness, black darkness. What if this is permanent? How can I live like this? The coils tightened again and tears came to my eyes.

~~~~

We arrived at Mokhovaya Street and Styopa pulled into the car park for my block, stopped at the security booth and spoke to the attendant, and then parked in one of my spaces on the ground level. He helped me out of the seat and up the stairs to the door of my flat on the third floor.

My block of flats was one of the best in the city—the best new construction with all the latest appointments—but the stairs had that same dank odor of neglect as in every cheap soviet-era block in Moscow. I'd complained about it often to the maintenance staff, but now the smell welcomed me home.

Styopa opened the door with my key and led me across my parlor to my leather chair near the window and lowered me into it. I tried to remember the place—my lacquered wood table and matching book cases from St. Petersburg, my favorite rug from Azerbaijan, my leather divan. I could see it all in my head, but still not the colors, not even the red and gold geometrics of the rug. I saw it all in just black and white.

I leaned back in the chair and he pulled off my shoes and dropped them onto the floor. I heard him go into my kitchen and I listened to him moving about, opening cupboards, dropping things on my new stone countertops.

My kitchen had all the best and newest stainless steel and chrome appliances from Germany and Finland, even a machine that could heat water for tea in seconds to just the right temperature. I'd been proud that those little gadgets had cost more than a month's wages for a workingman in most places in Russia.

Then Styopa dropped something again and I heard him swear. "Where's the sugar?" he called to me.

"On the shelf, in the blue bowl."

I was thinking more clearly now, and my breathing was better. I suppose I was getting used to the darkness. I remembered what I was told in those woods. I needed time, time to process that. Maybe time alone in the dark was just what I needed.

Then I heard someone nearby. "Here, take this, it's tea," he said as he took my hand and led it to a hot cup. I grasped the cup with both hands. "Go ahead, drink it. It'll help calm you down."

I heard him pick up a chair and bring it over and sit down in front of me. The wood creaked when his weight settled onto it.

"I am calm," I lied and I sipped the hot liquid. It was thick and strong and if there was sugar in there I couldn't taste it. I grimaced. Was he trying to give my nerves another jolt?

I set the cup down on the floor and rubbed my forehead. "I can't believe it. We're going to jail for sure."

"Nobody's going to jail," he said. "It was an accident. I admit I wanted to shake him up a little, ok? I admit it."

Then he stood up and I heard him walk back into the kitchen, pick up the telephone and a moment later speak in a low voice. The window next to my chair was open and I could hear the traffic on the street below. The sounds were clear and sharp. Hanging on the wall across from my chair, over the divan, was a painting of the snow capped peaks of the Ural Mountains, where Europe ends and Asia begins. It was a big painting in bright greens and blues that covered most of the wall. At least I assumed it was there—it was there when I left the flat that morning. I'd bought it on a trip that summer to Yekaterinburg. Maybe if I'd stayed out there and gotten myself lost in those mountains I wouldn't be in this mess now.

Styopa hung up the phone and came back and sat down in front of me. The chair creaked again when he leaned back. "I've got to go. The colonel wants the details."

"Then go," I said.

"You want anything?"

I shifted and sat up in my chair. A moment passed. "Bring Ksusha when you come back," I said.

The chair legs slammed down onto the floor. "Are you out of your mind? We can't let her in here now."

"I want to talk to her."

"If you want a pretty girl, we can go to a club when you're feeling better, but she's not coming here—period."

"Then I'll call her myself." I started to get up, but he held me down by the arm.

"Sit down, you fool. You'll just fall and break something."

"Either you bring her here or I'll get her on the phone."

"No."

"Look," I said in my most reasonable-sounding voice. "I won't say anything about this morning—about what happened. I won't. But I need to talk to her."

There was more traffic on the street. A motorist gave a long blast on his horn and shouted out a greeting.

"Please," I said. "It's important."

A long moment passed before he answered.

"I'll think about it," he said finally. "Anything else?"

"Yeah, this," I said and I held out my hand.

I heard him go back into the kitchen, open a drawer and turn on the water. He came back and took my hand and rubbed it with the wet cloth, on both sides, in between my fingers and in the crevices of my nails. Then he went back to the kitchen and turned on the water. I could imagine the water, pink with blood, squeeze out of the cloth, pool in the sink and wash away down the drain. He turned off the water and a moment later the door to the flat opened and then closed.

~~~~

After Styopa left I brooded, listening to the traffic grow heavier and louder and feeling generally sorry for myself. Later I fell asleep for what must have been many hours because when I woke, the muscles in my neck and back felt like metal rods. My eyes were still dead and my mouth tasted like sand and so I started to pull myself up to grope my way into the kitchen. Then I heard a sound nearby and I slumped back into the chair. A fragrant hand touched my forehead and my pulse jumped.

"Ksusha," I said.

"I've been watching you sleep."

I'd know her scent anywhere. Not her perfume, just her. "You should have gotten me up. How long have you been here?"

"Not long."

"You know what's happened?"

"Styopa called. He didn't say much, just that there's something wrong with your eyes."

"I can't see," I said.

"Kolya, let me take you to hospital. You can't just sit here."

"No."

My back muscles were still aching and I shifted in the chair. I wasn't ready to leave the flat, not yet. I had things to sort out.

"I need to talk to you, tell you something."

The wooden chair creaked ever so slightly when her weight settled onto it. The walnut clock on my table chimed twice. Two o'clock in the afternoon. It seemed much longer since that morning in those woods at Semkhoz.

"Do you remember the things my grandmother told me?" I asked. "You know what I mean."

"I thought you didn't believe in that."

"What if it's true, what if this is it?"

"Is that what's happened to your eyes?"

"I don't know, it may be a sign." My throat started to tighten again. I leaned over and felt along the floor for the cup of tea. I found it and took a drink. It was cold and bitter, but it soothed my throat.

"Why do you say that?" she asked.

I wished I could see her face, read her expressions, get some idea of what she really thought.

"You won't believe it."

"Tell me what happened."

I took a breath. Putting it all into words would make this more real, more concrete, less like the bad dream I wanted it to be. But I had to tell someone and Ksusha would understand.

I couldn't tell her the whole story, who had spoken that morning or why, but I told her the words that had been spoken to me just before the light flashed.

When I finished, she was quiet for a long time. Then I heard her stand and walk to the window.

"Well?" I said.

Still she didn't answer. She came away from the window and sat down again. The chair creaked. "It all makes sense," she said. "It all makes perfect sense."

"Maybe so, but it's impossible. I can't do it."

"It's not impossible, nothing's impossible."

"They'd put me away just for talking about it."

"Maybe in the old days. But things have changed."

"Not that much. And what about the colonel? He'll never let me go, never."

"You can't worry about him," she said.

I laughed. "You don't know him."

She took my hand and held it in both of hers. Her touch was warm and dry and marvelous. "I know this—if you're right, it's wonderful, Kolya, wonderful! You must do it—you must."

I took another gulp of cold tea. She was right, of course. She was just telling me what I already knew, but getting up the courage to do the thing, with or without my eyes, was the problem.

"I've got to think," I said.

"I can come back later if you like."

I nodded.

"Ok, then, tonight. We can talk more tonight."

Then I heard her go to the window again. "Before I go, there's something else," she said.

"Yes?"

"You know what it will mean if you don't do this."

My pulse jumped again and the sick feeling in my stomach came back.

"I know."

"Then can you take the chance?"

She touched my cheek and a moment later the flat door opened and closed and I was alone—alone to think and remember.

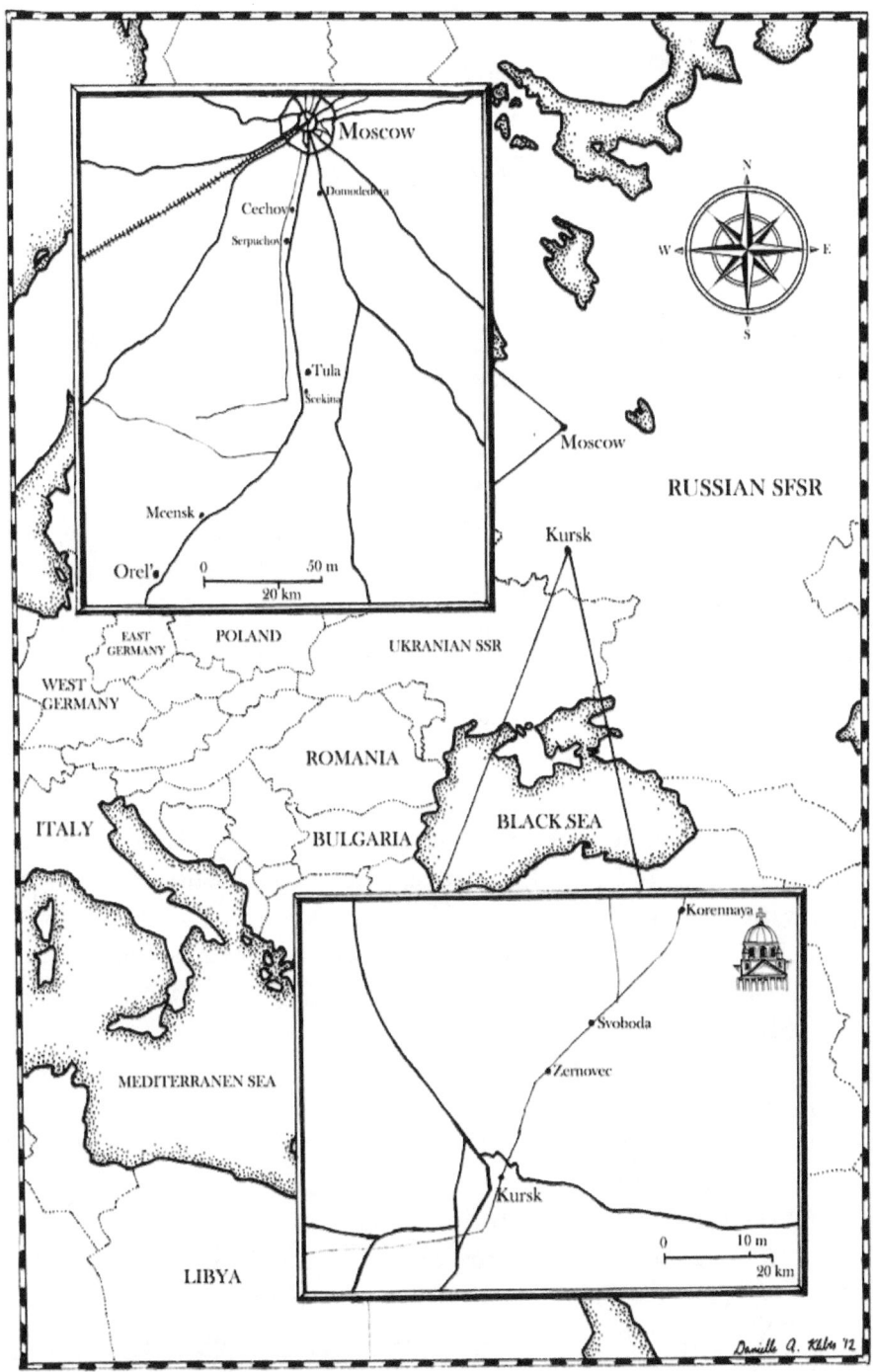

Moscow

Cechov
Domodedova
Serpuchov

Tula
Scekino

Mcensk
Orel'

0   50 m
  20 km

Moscow

RUSSIAN SFSR

N
W   E
S

Kursk

EAST
GERMANY   POLAND
                        UKRANIAN SSR
WEST
GERMANY

ROMANIA

ITALY
          BULGARIA   BLACK SEA

                                        Korennaya

                                        Svoboda

                                        Zernovec

MEDITERRANEN SEA

                        Kursk

                              0   10 m
LIBYA   20 km

Danielle A. Kible '12

23

CHAPTER 2

❧

O n the day I turned fourteen the armies of the USSR crossed our
southern frontier into Afghanistan. For a time, the news from
down there in the papers was very good and I read all the stories I
could find. It was all so exciting. One evening that following summer,
I was sitting at the table in our dacha's garden with my father and Deda,
my father's father. At the first lull in their conversation, I spoke up.

"Misha's uncle's in the motor rifles and now he's in Afghanistan,"
I said.

Our faces had grown indistinct in the dusk. Deda was peeling an
apple and he looked up at Father.

"He's sure he's there. He has a letter," I said.

Deda folded his knife. "Misha can only guess he's there. You
know that."

"No, he's there. They got a letter this week. It had all the clues.
They're sure he's there." I wished someone would send letters from
the war to me.

"He shouldn't talk about that," Father said. "And neither should
you."

"Even to you?"

"Even to us," Deda said.

"Nobody can hear us out here."

"That's enough, Kolya," Father said. He folded his thick blacksmith's hands on the table.

"He'll show it to me tomorrow. I'm sure it's true."

"If he has a letter with things like that in it, he should keep it to
himself," Father said. "It sounds like the censors wouldn't like it."

"Well, it got through. And, anyway, he's only told a few of us."

"Just a few of you?" Deda said.

"Me and Zhenya and Oleshka."

Father raised his eyebrows at me. "And how many have you and Zhenya and Oleshka told?"

Fireflies darted and flickered among the rows of gooseberry and currant bushes. The day had been hot and the air was rich with the smell of grape, lilac and bird cherry and ripening tomatoes, cucumbers, peas and turnips. Our dacha was just a simple cabin of logs chinked with concrete, but it lay in a charming spot in a stand of white-trunked birch trees on the outskirts of Kursk along the Moscow Road. Our back steps looked out over land farmed by a collective—undulating fields that became a great roiling sea of coal-black soil each spring after plowing.

Then Mother set the samovar for our tea down in the middle of the table with a thump. "No more talk about that, Kolya."

"Misha says they won't even need their winter uniforms," I said.

She stacked our dirty plates at one end of the table. "Misha seems to know an awful lot about it—too much it seems to me."

"Kolya," Father said. "Let's go look at the fire." He'd put more wood in the forge before we sat down to eat and it was getting time to stoke the coals.

"Good, you do that, go look at the fire," Mother said. She picked up an armful of plates and went back into the cabin.

"What's wrong with her?" I said.

Father shrugged. "I think you've upset her."

"Me? What have I done?"

"You brought up that letter," Deda said.

"Why does that upset her?"

"One day you'll understand," Deda said. The light from inside the cabin glinted off the Medal for Bravery pinned to his jacket. It was a beautiful silver disc with red lettering hanging from a scarlet ribbon. He received it after the Battle of Kursk in the Great Patriotic War.

Then Babulya, my grandmother, waddled out of the cabin carrying a plate of cakes and set it down next to the samovar. Mother came back with a bowl of sugar and a pitcher of milk.

"What do you say, Nana?" I asked.

"About what, dear boy?" Babulya said.

"About the letter, Afghanistan, the war."

She took my chin in her rough hand and looked into my face. "You have nothing to worry about."

"So there you are," Deda said to Mother and laughed. "If Babulya says so, there's nothing to worry about."

Father winked at Deda. "We should tell the Politburo."

"It's nothing to laugh about, either of you," Mother said and Father sat back in his chair and drummed his fingers on the table.

"I said Kolya has nothing to worry about. I didn't say anything about those fools in the Politburo," Babulya said.

"Oh, Babulya, please, don't talk about it," Mother said. "Kolya won't go."

"He'll go if he's called," Deda said. There was no more laughter in his eyes.

Father reached over and patted Mother on the arm. "Sveta, nothing will happen, you'll see. How long can a few goat herders stand up to us?"

Mother pulled her arm away. "A short war? Aren't they all supposed to be short when they start?" She stalked off into the cabin. Deda stared out across the fields of the collective. In the distance stood the faded white walls of one of the chapels of the old Korennaya monastery. The collective used it to store seed and tools.

"You'll go if it's God's plan," Babulya said.

Deda rolled his eyes. "Babulya, don't say those things to the boy."

She turned and pointed a gnarled finger at him. "And I'll thank you to stay out of this, Viktor Mikhailovich. You of all people have nothing to say about it."

"Plan for what?" I said.

"Kolya, the fire," Father said.

"What plan?"

"Babulya's teasing you," Father said.

Babulya shot Father a hard glance and then turned back to me. "One day—you'll understand."

She picked up the last of the plates and went back into the cabin.

Father stood up from the table. "Kolya, the fire," he said and he walked away toward the forge.

CHAPTER 3

𝕥

*T*he next day we were back in our flat in the city.

To a young boy, Kursk was a fine place to grow up. I played in its parks, watched parades in the city center and built forts in the woods around our dacha. It's a raw city sprawling near the edge of the Russian steppes at the confluence of the Seym and Tuskar rivers, five hundred kilometers south of Moscow along a straight line to the Black Sea. Founded by nomads in the eleventh century, it was destroyed by Tatar invaders in 1240 and rebuilt in the sixteenth century as a trading post on the fringes of the Muscovite principality. In the late twentieth century it was a city of big, noisy plants, broad boulevards and blocks of flats as numerous as blades of grass. My family and half a million other souls called it home.

Late in the afternoon Deda burst through the door with a wide grin.

"Look, look at this! You won't believe it!" he nearly shouted.

In his hand was a piece of paper he held up for us to see. Babulya, Mother and I gathered around him. He sat down at the kitchen table, but then sprang back up.

"Do you remember when I put in for the new flat?" he asked Babulya.

She thought a moment. "You mean when Vanya and Sveta were married?"

"That's it. Look, it finally came through. It says four rooms."

He held out the paper and Mother snatched it away from him. "It's not possible," she said as she studied the print. But as she read I could see from her face that this strange paper was starting to work its magic on her too. She smiled.

"It just came in the mail," Deda said. "There was no warning. Today it was just there. After all these years, who could imagine!"

Mother was reading the paper closely. "It's from the administration of housing," she said. "And it says Deda's request for a new flat has been reviewed and a larger unit is now available. His application is therefore approved."

She turned the notice around, showing us the print. Then she read on.

"We've been assigned to flat number 35 at 14 Parkovaya, occupation to begin on the fifteenth of this month." She looked up at us. "It says this flat has been assigned to a family who will move in at the end of the month."

Babulya clapped her hands and she and Mother hugged each other.

"Fantastic luck," Deda said.

"It's a blessing, not luck," Babulya said to him.

"Whatever you say. We'll take it."

A flat of four rooms was a blessing indeed—and very good luck. Of course, that included the kitchen, but it meant a bedroom for Deda and Babulya, a bedroom for Mother and Father and the parlor for me. Our little three room flat was starting to feel cramped already.

"The fifteenth is just six days from now," Mother said. "Can we be ready to move in six days? I mean, think of everything we have to do, all the packing."

Deda grabbed the notice back from her. "Of course we can. We have a fine new flat and we will take it. Besides, look at what it says, do we have a choice?"

"You never told me about this," I said.

"I forgot about it," he said. "I put in the papers before you were born. I asked about it a few times, but I thought nothing would ever come of it. I just forgot." He laughed and slapped his thigh.

"Number 14 Parkovaya. Do you know this place?" Mother asked Babulya.

She shook her head. "No, but we must see it right away—tonight."

Deda punched me on the shoulder. "Get ready, boy. We are moving!"

~~~~

We couldn't wait to share our news with Father. He worked in the sugar plant making and repairing the tools the floor workers used to move the sugar beets along the big conveyor belts through the washing and slicing machines and into the cooking vats. When we heard his key in the lock that evening we all crowded into the hall to greet him. His face showed his surprise at finding us huddled there together.

"What? What has happened?" he said.

Deda held out the notice. "This."

Father took it and after he'd read a few lines he smiled, and we all laughed again and hugged each other.

Father agreed we should go that very night to see our new home and so we set out as soon as he bathed and changed his clothes, while there was still daylight.

~~~~

Finding the new flat was no trouble at all because it turned out to be just a short tram ride away. And so, within the hour, we were standing in front of the block at number 14 Parkovaya admiring what we saw. It was one of the older blocks of flats—only nine floors instead of the standard fourteen floors of the newer buildings—and instead of gray, pitted concrete, it was built with white bricks. Out in front was a copse of trees with shiny metal benches underneath.

"A good place to watch our new neighbors, eh?" Deda said to me. "Who knows what we'll see."

Over the next few days Deda and Father went to the housing exchange to sign the necessary papers and then to the police to show our city residence permits. Everything was approved without any of the usual "technical" problems that can come up when dealing with the housing officials.

"I told you this was a blessing," Babulya said.

After the final approval, a woman from the exchange met us at the flat with a key and we spent the next hour inspecting it room by room. The notice had been accurate in every respect—there were two bedrooms, a kitchen, a toilette and a big parlor that would do nicely as a bedroom for me. And it even had a telephone. It was all too much for us.

When the time came for the move, Father hired a truck and we loaded our belongings for the trip to 14 Parkovaya.

~~~~

It was on that first day in our new home, while we were unpacking, that Mother called to me to come look out the parlor window.

"Kolya, look at this. There's a cage back here, with birds in it," she said.

I came to the window. It was a sunny day and I squinted at the empty lot behind our block. It was dotted with trees and next to one was a cage filled with what looked like pigeons or doves in shades of white, grey and black. There must have been twenty or more.

"I wonder whose it is," she said.

"Can we go down and look?"

The cage was a wooden frame with three of its sides, its top and its door made of wire mesh. The fourth side was a shelter made of wood. It looked big enough for me to stand inside, with room to spare. The birds rested on pegs or hopped and pecked along the floor.

Mother tousled my hair. "It belongs to an old troll who'll feed you to his birds if you go near them."

I laughed and reached out to try to tousle her hair, but she backed away out of my reach. "You have to be quicker than that," she said.

Then Father came out from the bedroom. "Sveta, Kolya, what are you doing?"

"Father, look at this," I said. I pointed into the empty lot.

He came up to the window and frowned. "We have work to do. Have you finished with the dishes?"

"It's a cage, full of birds. Let's go down and see it."

"I don't care if it's full of elephants," he said.

"Aw, but …"

"Kolya, the kitchen," he said.

"You can go later," Mother said. "It won't go anywhere. Father's right."

Father nodded and went back into the bedroom.

For the rest of the day I watched the cage from the window until the last of our things had been unpacked and put away and Father had finally given me his permission to leave the flat. I bolted down the stairs and into the vacant lot.

On close inspection, the cage was an even better home for the birds than it looked from our window. Someone had put out bowls of water and seed and had laid down a layer of clean newspaper in the bottom of the shelter. It was all done very nicely, with the corners of the paper folded to fit the space exactly. And the construction was good too—sturdy boards with mitered joints. This was the work of someone who knew carpentry and wanted a good, safe home for these creatures.

But who? No one had come near it all day.

~~~~

Over the next days I watched the empty lot, hoping to learn the care-taker's identity. But whoever he was, he came either very early or very late because even though each day the water had been changed and new seed put out, I saw no one.

As the days passed, I started to imagine the reasons the caretaker wouldn't show himself. Maybe he was so hideously ugly he couldn't show himself in daylight. Or maybe he was the leader of a sinister criminal organization, or a network of international spies, and he used the birds to carry messages to his confederates. The possibilities seemed limitless.

But then, on the fourth day after we moved into the flat, the care-taker suddenly appeared, in plain sight in the middle of the afternoon.

I confess I was disappointed.

This mysterious person—grist for so much thrilling speculation—was just a boy like me, maybe a year or two older. He was standing in the middle of the cage with a big grey bird perched on his arm. I ran down the stairs and into the lot and then came up quietly and stood outside the wire, doing my best not to make any noise. A moment later he turned and spoke to me.

"You must like birds," he said. "Or you don't have anything to do."

"I have plenty to do," I said.

"Then why are you just standing there?"

"Um ... well, I've never held one like that."

"Want to try?"

"Ah ... sure," I said.

He nodded toward the cage door. "Come on in. Just don't make any quick moves. They need to get to know you."

I hesitated.

"Go on. It's ok. You're a lot bigger than they are."

I opened the door slowly and stepped inside. At first the birds flapped their wings and hopped from perch to perch. Feathers floated in the air. But I stood my ground and soon they quieted down.

"Are they all yours?" I asked.

"Mine and my dad's. But ... well, I take care of them now. I guess that makes them mostly mine," he said.

The bird was resting on his forearm.

"Could I learn to hold them like that?"

"Sure," he said. "Stretch out your arm."

I stretched it out and he placed his arm alongside mine. The bird stepped across and stood on my wrist. It was heavier than it looked and its head bobbed up and down. Then it relaxed and went into a kind of trance. It gripped my wrist with its claws.

"How long will he stay like that?" I asked.

"It's a she. As long as you let her."

I ran my fingertips over the wing. "Her feathers are really smooth."

"The top ones are the smoothest. That's how they get lift. The air moves faster over the smooth feathers and it gives them lift, like a jet wing. The others are smooth too, but not as smooth as the top ones. There're different kinds of feathers, you know."

"No, I didn't know that."

"Well, there are."

He reached over and spread one of the wings against his palm. "These close to the body are the lesser coverts. And down here are the middle coverts and out here are the greater coverts." He moved his finger along the wing. "Out here are the secondarys, and here are the tertials, and these are the primaries."

He seemed to know what he was talking about.

"Where did you learn all that?" I asked.

"From books. I have lots of books."

"Ever let them out?"

"Sure. They're made to fly, aren't they?"

"Well, I know, but won't they fly away?"

"They always follow the lead bird—that one there," he said, pointing to a big, dark bird on the cage floor.

"And they come back?"

"This is where they eat. Why would they leave a place where they eat? They're not stupid."

"I didn't say they were."

"People don't understand them. They kick at them or throw things. They're the stupid ones."

I knelt down and the bird jumped off my arm onto the floor. "Well, I don't think they're stupid. Anyway, thanks for letting me hold her."

"Sure."

"Well, I guess I'd better go."

He nodded. "I'm Sergei."

"I'm Kolya. We just moved into number 35."

"I know, I watched you. We're in 22."

"Let me know when you're going to let them fly," I said.

He shrugged. "How about now?"

34

"Sure."

"Stand over there."

He bent down and stretched out his arm and the lead bird jumped on. Then he opened the door and stepped out of the cage with the bird on his arm. He left the door open and walked out into the open away from the trees. He raised his arm and the bird leapt off into the air, climbing swiftly. Then, one by one, the other birds hopped out of the cage and flew up to join the lead bird, following behind him. As more birds joined in, the growing flock spiraled upward and upward until it was so high overhead you could barely pick out one bird from another. With their wings outstretched, they sailed in the wind in a wide circle above us. I watched with my neck craned all the way back to my shoulders.

Then, after a time, he raised up his arm and the lead bird brought the flock swooping back down into the cage.

Well, not quite the whole flock.

As the flock neared the ground, a small white bird peeled away and made straight for an open window on the first floor of our block and disappeared inside.

"Oh no, not again," Sergei said.

An instant later I heard a scream from inside the flat.

A plate window gave us a clear view into the flat and I saw the white bird hop along the tops of furniture from one end of the room to the other, its wings flapping.

"What'll we do?" I said.

Then another scream cut through the still afternoon and a woman came into view through the plate window. She wore a purple house coat and her hair was tied up on her head in a purple scarf. She gripped a short broom with both hands. The bird flapped back across the room again and the woman took aim and gave a full body swing with the broom. She missed. The broom whiffed the air and she spun off balance and out of sight. I heard a thud through the open window and then Sergei's full-throated laughter.

"Haw, haw!"

The bird, its wings flapping, was still trapped inside and it crossed the room again. The woman climbed to her feet and swung again. She missed again, or I should say, she missed the bird again. This time the broom head swept a row of photos and a lamp off a table. I heard a crash and Sergei was now bent over in laughter, holding his side, struggling to breathe.

"Haw, haw, haw!"

The poor captive darted across the room again and this time smacked into the glass of a small window on the other side of the plate window. It pummeled the pane with its wings as the woman took aim with her broom for what would have been the *coup de grace*.

With Sergei's desperate laughter in my ears, I jumped to the window, gripped the sash and pushed it up. The bird shot out, barely missing my head, and I fell back onto the ground. The woman's head popped out and she glared at me with flaming eyes.

"Hooligans, criminals!" she shouted. "I'll call the militia, I swear I will!"

Sergei was almost choking. "Ko … Kolya … haw! haw! … this way," he managed to say.

"You'll pay for this, you will!" the woman yelled. "I swear it, I swear it!"

I scrambled backward on my palms and heels as she let loose a burst of profanity. I jumped to my feet, pulled Sergei up and we ran as fast as we could around the side of the block.

"Come back here!" she hollered as we rounded the corner. "A bird through an open window is bad luck and NOW look!"

We didn't stop running until we collapsed onto the benches in front of our block. Sergei was coughing and trying to catch his breath. He slapped me twice on the shoulder and finally stretched out his hand to me. I took it and we shook.

"Y … you can play with my birds any time you like," he said before another spasm of laughter took hold of him.

"Haw, haw, haw, haw!!"

Chapter 4

*n September after we moved to Parkovaya, my parents enrolled
me in a new school, Work-Polytechnical School No. 6. Five hundred pupils were enrolled in W-P 6, all of us stuffed into four rambling
wooden buildings around a courtyard six blocks up Parkovaya Street
from my flat. Across Navrozov Street from the back side of W-P 6 was
the tractor factory that covered two city blocks and gave everything
around it a faint odor of diesel. I joined a class of twenty other boys
my age.

Each morning at eight thirty we assembled in the courtyard for
attendance call and announcements before we were dismissed to our
classes. My classroom was on the third floor and from the window
beside my desk I looked down on the front gate of the tractor factory.

W-P 6's mission was simple—to give us the basic instruction necessary for us to become useful servants of the state, nothing more.
Most of us prepared for one of the skilled trades and I trained in gaso-
line and diesel engine mechanics.

Sergei was in his last year at W-P 6, two classes ahead of me. We
walked to school together in the mornings, but he stayed later most
afternoons for drill and physical training. I looked after his birds in
the afternoons, cleaning the cage, changing the water, and leaving out
more seed.

One afternoon I noticed one of the birds had a sore on its leg and
so I went to tell Sergei about it that evening before supper. I arrived at
his flat and pushed the buzzer. It made a twittering bird sound and a
moment later his mother opened the door.

"Well, Kolya, I should have guessed it was you," she said. "I'm
afraid Sergei can't come out. He's busy right now."

"Hello, Kaari Georgiyevna," I said. "I'm sorry, but I think one of the birds is hurt. I won't stay long."

She eyed me for a moment and then opened the door wider and stood to the side.

Sergei's mother dyed her hair bright red and I'd heard some of our neighbors in the block say it was no surprise she had red hair because her people were gypsies. They said she came from Hungary or Romania or one of those places where gypsies come from. I never understood the connection between being a gypsy and having red hair, but I supposed there must be one. Her given name, Kaari, sounded like it could have been a gypsy name, but I wasn't sure about that either because I'd never met a gypsy. She was a slender woman with soft dark eyes and she was always nicely dressed in slacks and colorful sweaters. She was nothing like the gypsies I saw later in Moscow who never bathed and roamed the metro in packs and, if you weren't careful, would surround you and run their grimy hands over your clothes and through your pockets.

Kaari Georgiyevna closed the door behind me and I kicked off my shoes and followed her into the parlor where Sergei was sitting on the floor. A composition book lay open in front of him. A newspaper lay open on the divan and the door to the bedroom was closed. It might have been my imagination, but I thought Sergei frowned when I came into the room. Kaari Georgiyevna went into the kitchen.

"I think one of the birds is hurt or maybe sick," I said. "There's a sore on her leg. It looks bad."

"Which one?"

"The little speckled one."

He nodded and cleared his throat. "Yeah, I saw it yesterday. She probably scraped it or something. She'll be ok. Thanks."

"Sure."

Did he just frown again?

I stood there a moment but he didn't ask me to sit down. Then I noticed the open pages of the composition book were filled with what looked like math problems.

"You're doing math problems?" I asked.

"Um ... yeah, a few."

I nodded. "Why?"

"I'm ... I'm, ah, you know ... practicing."

"Practicing? For what?"

He cleared his throat again. "The entrance exams."

Then it was my turn to frown. "Exams? For what?"

"For university—what else?"

It took a moment for that to sink in and when it did, I almost laughed. But I caught myself in time.

"Really?" I managed to say.

"Don't look so surprised. Lots of kids are taking them this year."

"I know, but ..."

"I have enough time. They aren't until spring."

I knew when the exams were given. The dates were printed in the newspapers.

"Come on ... what is this really," I said.

His frown deepened. "I just told you. You don't believe me?"

I coughed to keep from laughing. "Sure, it's just that ... look, even some of those rich creeps from the *phys-mat* schools can't pass those exams—and they take the courses the tests are on."

"Well, maybe they don't study enough."

"I guess."

He still hadn't asked me to sit down. "So ... you would go to university here in Kursk?" I asked after a moment.

"Probably here in Kursk, but if I get really good scores there's a chance I could go to Moscow."

That did it. The notion that any of us from a W-P school could ever go to university in Moscow was too much. "Be serious," I said. "Those things are impossible and you know it. They test on subjects you've never had."

His face darkened and he started to say something, but then Kaari Georgiyevna came out of the kitchen and sat down on the divan next to the open newspaper.

Sergei waited for her to sit. "I'll be ready, you'll see. I have a tutor."

"Sergei's making excellent progress," Kaari Georgiyevna added. "We're very proud of him."

"A tutor?" I said.

"That's right," Sergei said.

"Well, how much does *that* cost?" I said, regretting it as soon as the words were out of my mouth. It was bad manners to ask what things cost.

"It's worth it," he said.

"Well, what about your service?"

"He'll get a deferment," Kaari Georgiyevna said.

"It's almost automatic for university students," Sergei said. "The state needs trained engineers, you know. There's a shortage."

"A shortage?"

"It's true," he said. "So they're starting to let more pupils into university."

By that time it was clear they weren't going to invite me to sit down and so I decided it was best to let the whole thing drop. "Ok, well, that's … that's good. Good luck," I said.

Sergei closed the composition book. "Look, don't say anything about this."

"What do you mean?"

"Around school, you know, don't say anything."

"Oh, *horoscho*, I won't say anything."

He slid the composition book under the divan and stood up. "Anyway, I've done enough for today. How long before supper?" he asked his mother.

She looked at her watch. "Another hour or so."

He turned to me. "Julia's dancing today at the *Dom Kultury*. Want to go watch?"

~~~~

The *Dom Kultury* was the hub of activity in the neighborhood. There was always a lecture or concert in the auditorium on Friday night and on Saturday afternoon the Young Pioneers drilled on the square out in front. When the girls' dance troupe from W-P 6 practiced there, Sergei usually went to watch his girlfriend, Julia. I didn't know much about dancing, but Julia looked very good to me. She could kick up her long, shapely legs almost to her chin. I tried that once and pulled a muscle.

On the way there we stopped at one of the kiosks on Parkovaya Street. A girl, a pupil at W-P 6, was working inside and the shelves behind her were lined with green and red bottles of water, wine and vodka, packages of cigarettes, sweet treats and sandwiches. Sergei stepped up to the window.

"Chocolate, the brown crumbly kind," he said.

The girl wrinkled her nose. "You're the only one who likes that."

He dug into his pocket for his money. "It's for my dad."

She reached up to the top shelf and pulled down the package wrapped in shiny paper. "Tell him he should try the white. It's better and not so expensive."

"He likes the brown—it's his favorite."

She shrugged and handed him the package through the window and he gave her a five ruble note.

"You want anything?" he asked me.

"No, I'm good."

The girl gave him his change. "If your dad likes it so much, why doesn't he ever come get it himself?"

He slid the chocolate into the inside pocket of his jacket. "He can't."

"Why not?"

"He's ... he got sick. Last year."

"Oh ... sorry."

"It's ok, he's getting better now," he said.

"Well, tell him to try the white."

"It wouldn't do any good," he called over his shoulder as we headed up the street.

When we got to the cultural center, the stage attendant told us the dance practice for that afternoon had been cancelled. That was too bad because I was looking forward to watching Julia's nice legs at work.

I leaned back against a wall. "Well, I better get home."

Sergei leaned against the wall beside me. "As long as we're here, we might as well have a smoke."

"I can't, I don't have any," I said.

"You can have one of mine."

"No thanks," I said and he laughed.

Sergei liked to smoke *papirosi,* a nasty kind of cigarette that was half tobacco and half cardboard tube. Deda smoked them sometimes and they left his clothes and hair smelling like burnt cardboard. Sergei fished a package from his shirt pocket and offered me one. I shook my head.

"Go on," he said, holding out the package to me.

"No, thanks."

"Well, that's all I have."

"Then you smoke. I'll just wait."

"Ok, suit yourself."

We went down to the latrine in the basement where I always went for a cigarette. The place was so foul-smelling I never worried that Father or Deda would come looking for me down there. Sergei lit up, took a deep drag and the end of the smoke brightened.

"They're good when you get used to them," he said, exhaling smoke through his nose and mouth.

"If you like sucking on a torch," I said and he laughed again. He took another drag. The latrine was quiet.

"Julia seems like a good girl," I said.

He nodded.

"Are you making any plans, you know, serious plans?"

His smoke had gone out—it was hard to keep the cardboard lit— and he struck another match and puffed away. "Not yet," he said after he'd gotten the smoke lit again. "Not until I see what happens about next year."

There he went about those exams again. "Are you really going to take those?" I asked.

"When I'm accepted at university, then I'll make plans with Julia. You don't believe me, but you'll see."

"So you're going to marry her, right?"

"I didn't say that."

"You said you'll make plans. What other kinds of plans are there?"

"You ask a lot of questions, you know that?"

"How do you know she's the one? How do you know?"

"Why do you want to know that?"

"I don't know. I might have a girl one day."

"When you get a girl, then ask me," he said.

"That could be a while."

"Then you don't need to know now."

"You want to marry Julia, right?"

He sighed. "She's a clever girl. She'd be a good wife."

"How do you know she'd be a good wife—she's just a girl?"

"I just think she would be."

I turned and faced him. "But ... she might be an awful wife. How do you know she'd be a good one?"

"Well, for one thing, she doesn't ask a lot of stupid questions."

I had one more question to ask—of a more personal nature—and I was trying to find the right way to ask it, but then I heard footsteps on the stairs.

"Somebody's coming," I said.

Sergei threw down his smoke, crushed it out on the floor and kicked it over into a corner. It was too early for Father to be home and I didn't think Deda would come to the center looking for me without Father, but I could never be sure.

We swatted at the air to get rid of the smoke as the footsteps grew louder. Then a lone figure came into view on the stairs—and I groaned.

It was Yuri Matyukh, a neighbor from one of the blocks down the street from ours. He was five years older than Sergei.

This was truly rotten luck.

"Well, hello *Kotik*," Yuri beamed at Sergei. He ignored me.

He shuffled over to Sergei and draped a thick arm around his shoulders. "What's the trouble, your little cow girl friend not here today?"

Sergei tried to move away, but Yuri held him around the shoulders.

Then Yuri sniffed the air. "Is that smoke I smell? Have we been smoking?"

Sergei didn't answer.

"I'll bet your mommy wouldn't like that—would she?" He squeezed Sergei about the shoulders and Sergei grunted.

"Well, I'll tell you what. I won't say a word, I promise. Just give me one, *Kotik*, and we'll keep this just between us. How's that?"

'*Kotik*' means 'kitten,' but I'm sure Yuri didn't mean it fondly. He stood there, grinning that malevolent grin with his free hand held out. Sergei didn't move.

"Come on," Yuri said and he snapped his fingers twice. "Let's have it."

Sergei pointed to the crushed butt on the floor. "That was the last one."

Yuri looked at the floor and then back at Sergei. And now he wasn't smiling anymore. "Really? The last one?"

"That's right."

Yuri scratched his head. "You know, something tells me you're not sorry, not sorry at all. But let's see if you'll be sorry about *this*."

He slid behind Sergei with one liquid move, grabbing both arms and pushing the elbows together. Sergei cried out.

"Are you sure that was the last one, *Kotik*?"

"Agggah! Stop!"

"Stop? Why should I stop?"

"You're breaking my arms!"

"Then tell me what I want to hear." He pushed harder on the elbows.

"AGGGAH! Ok, ok! I'll give you one!"

Yuri held his grip, his lips practically touching Sergei's ear. "Sooo, you do have one. I thought so. And you told me you didn't. Now what am I going to do about that?"

He pushed on Sergei's elbows again, this time so hard they nearly touched. Sergei screamed.

As my friend suffered this abuse, I stood there watching, not knowing which I felt more keenly, my loathing for Yuri or my disgust with myself for doing nothing. I knew I had to help, but my feet felt stuck to the floor. Yuri was my senior by seven years and he had done his military service. There was no telling what he could do to me.

But I couldn't just stand there. And so I reached into Sergei's pocket and pulled out his smokes.

"There's one left," I said, holding out the package. "Take it." Yuri looked at me for the first time, but held his grip on Sergei.

"Ahhhh!!" Sergei cried out again. "You're breaking my arms!" He looked like he was close to tears.

"Take it!" I yelled.

Yuri held Sergei for a few seconds longer and then pushed him aside. He pulled himself up to his full height in front of me. I hoped he didn't see my legs shaking. Then, like a strike from a snake, his hand shot out and snatched the package away from me. He pushed me back, but I managed to keep my balance and stay on my feet.

He fingered the last *papirosu* from the package, produced a lighter from his pocket and took his time lighting up. He took a long puff and then, with the smoke dangling from his lips, turned and gave Sergei a shove with both hands, sending him sprawling onto the floor.

When Sergei landed, the chocolate bar popped from his pocket and Yuri stomped down onto it with his shoe. The chocolate spewed out from the edges of the wrapping.

He stood over Sergei and pointed a finger down at him. "Don't ever lie to me again, *Kotik*. Ever."

And without a word to me he turned and walked up the stairs.

Sergei sat up on that cold dirty floor and watched him go. It was several moments before either of us spoke.

"How long has he been doing that?" I asked finally.

He pulled himself up and picked up the package of chocolate. "I don't know, a while."

"When I get bigger, I'll fix him."

He brushed off his pants. "You're big enough now—just look at you—and anyway, he's not so bad."

45

"Not so bad? Are you crazy? He's a snake, a weasel."

"Not all the time. I've known him a lot longer than you have. You don't know what he lives with."

"I don't care. He's just plain mean, that's all. One day I'll get him."

"No you won't."

"You watch me."

He tossed the chocolate into a trash bin. "You don't know what you're saying. Let's just get out of here," he said.

When we came up the stairs there was no sign of Yuri. I told Sergei goodbye and went home.

CHAPTER 5

I went to see Sergei at his flat straightaway the next morning. He let me in and I followed him into the parlor and this time he asked me to sit down. The newspaper was open on the divan again, in the same spot as the day before, and the bedroom door was still closed.

"Your arms alright?" I asked.

He stretched them backward and forward. "A little sore, but they're ok."

"That's good."

"Listen, about yesterday, I know you were just trying to help," he said.

"I meant what I said. He's a rat."

"Well, forget about that."

"Forget that he's a rat? I don't think so."

"Forget about what happened yesterday." He dropped to the floor and pulled a box from under the divan.

"Fine with me," I said. "If that's what you want."

"It isn't important, it isn't."

"Well, if you say so," I said. He kept looking at the floor, not at me.

"I do say so," Then he looked up and smiled. "Let's have a game." He opened the box.

"Sure, why not," I said.

We sat on the floor and set up the black and white wooden chess pieces on the board and in no time we were engrossed in the strategy and tactics of our game. Sergei moved his pieces swiftly across the squares, but I had to take my time with each move. After the opening moves he launched a sly attack with his knight and I was concentrating on the board, trying to see what was coming next, when the bedroom door opened.

I looked up and I'll never forget the sight.

The figure standing there wore a ragged robe and slippers and couldn't have weighed more than sixty kilos. The skin on his face was so tightly stretched that it looked like rubber. And his hands—his only other exposed flesh—were thin and angular with blue veins and long blue nails and skin the same sallow color as his face.

He looked like a walking corpse.

I tried to hide my shock, but I'm sure it showed. This was surely what the final stage of life—if you could call this life—must look like.

The ghastly figure padded slowly into the room and sat down on the divan next to the opened newspaper. I watched him without saying a word.

"There, that's good," he said after he propped himself up with a pillow. His voice was surprisingly strong.

Then Sergei coughed. "This is my father, Mikhail Petrovich," he said to me.

He turned to his father. "This is Nikolai. Everybody calls him 'Kolya.'"

I stood up. "Hello," I said.

Mikhail Petrovich leaned forward and offered me his hand and reluctantly I took it. He had a firm grip and he held my hand a bit too long and I hoped whatever he had wasn't catching.

"Hello to you, Kolya." Then he let go of my hand and peered down at the chessboard. Sergei's last move had gotten me onto the prongs of a knight's fork and after my next move I would lose either my rook or my bishop.

In spite of his wasted appearance, Mikhail Petrovich's eyes were clear and focused. He looked up from the board at me and smiled, showing me a mouthful of metal teeth. "So what's next?" he asked.

I sat down and studied the board. "I guess I'll lose one of them," I said after a moment.

Mikhail Petrovich laughed. "Of course you'll lose one of them. The question is which one. Which one to let go?"

I swallowed and concentrated on the board. I wanted to sound clever and I tried to remember what I'd once read in a book about the game. "The one I won't need," I said.

He laughed again and I was beginning to feel really foolish.

"And which one is that?"

I stared at the board. "The bishop," I said.

"Ok, show me."

I moved my rook to safety and Sergei promptly captured my bishop with his knight. With the next few moves I tried to retaliate, but soon it was clear I needed my bishop to fend off the kind of diagonal attack Sergei had planned against my king. A few more moves and the game was finished. Mikhail Petrovich grunted and sat back on the divan and picked up his newspaper.

"I guess I'm not a chess player," I said.

"Humph, that's easy to see," Mikhail Petrovich said.

Sergei opened the box and we started to put away the pieces.

Then Mikhail Petrovich put his paper down. He leaned forward. "Look ... ah ... I didn't mean it that way," he said. "I just meant maybe this game isn't for you."

"I can practice."

"Maybe, but one day you'll find whatever it is you're good at, whatever you're meant to do."

"How does he do that?" Sergei asked.

Mikhail Petrovich shrugged and picked up his paper. "Pay attention to things," he said. "It'll come along."

"You sound like Babulya," I said. "She says there's a plan for me."

Mikhail Petrovich frowned.

"Well, that's what she told me," I said.

He shook his head. "Look at me. You think there's a plan for me to end up like this?" He pointed a long finger at his face.

"I ... I don't know," I said. I felt an itch in my collar.

"Of course there isn't. This just happened and now I live with it. That's life, not some plan." He looked at me with his black eyes.

Sergei coughed again. "Well, I know what my plan is—to go to university," he said.

Mikhail Petrovich sat back and smiled. "Then no more games today. Time for the books."

CHAPTER 6

֍

Every year on the first of May the people of the USSR celebrated International Labor Day with speeches and parades and parties. It was my favorite holiday.

My parents invited guests to our flat for the celebration and Mother and Babulya always laid out a fine spread of food—salami and pickled cucumbers, red beet salad, salted herring, potatoes, fresh bread with dishes of butter, marinated mushrooms, smoked salmon and for that special day, red or black caviar. There was so much food there wasn't room to sit at the table.

Our guests always stayed late into the night, eating and talking and eating again, and drinking all the while.

On International Labor Day in Sergei's last year at W-P 6, the whole school went to the city center to watch the parade. We assembled in the courtyard in the morning and then walked over to Lenin Street and caught the trams for the ride up the broad, straight boulevard, past the tank monument, to Red Square.

The boys wore red armbands and the girls had red ribbons tied up in their hair. Our teachers gave each of us a little flag to wave. I wore my best clothes. Everyone was laughing and talking.

The trams let us out two blocks from the city center and we walked to the big paved plaza we called Red Square. There were many other people walking toward the parade and soon we were part of a huge, swiftly moving crowd.

I found Sergei and we pushed ahead to get a good spot. When we reached the square, he pointed to the raised seating platform for the Party officials and other dignitaries.

"There, that's the best place," he said. "We can see everything from there."

"Just make sure I can see the governor," I said.

"Don't worry, you'll see him."

Red Square is two city blocks long on each of its four sides and all of the most important buildings in Kursk front onto it. The city administration building, massive and grey, faces east and my favorite structure, the offices and residence of the oblast governor, face south. With its twelve tall columns, each topped with an ornate capital, and its finely-detailed frieze decorated with gold leaf, the governor's residence was the jewel of the city.

And there, in front of the residence, stood Lenin, six meters tall, in stone. The sculptor had caught him in mid-stride with his right arm raised with fingers extended, his eyes fixed on a point in the distance. It was a familiar pose for Comrade Lenin and I saw it in statues and portraits of him everywhere. I think it was meant to show he saw things the rest of us didn't see.

The seating platform faced the square in front of the governor's residence and it was decorated with red banners and flags. Officers from the army garrison and city officials were already taking their seats.

Sergei and I found a spot on one side of the platform. I wanted to get a good look at the governor when he stood to review the parade. I had seen him once before, at the last May Day parade, and I remembered him standing very tall and straight in his fine, dark overcoat, reviewing the troops.

On the other side of the platform a band was tuning its instruments and all around the square people talked and shuffled and waited, everyone watching Lenin Street to the west where the parade would start. Many people drank tea and ate treats they bought from the kiosks and street vendors.

The day was cold, but the sun shone brightly through a few high, thin clouds. Excitement was in the air. It was a grand day.

Precisely at ten o'clock, the band started playing and the crowd got louder and people began to stand on their toes and to jump up, looking over the heads of others toward the west.

"Here he comes," Sergei said, poking me with his elbow.

I turned and saw a phalanx of men walk briskly out the front door of the governor's residence, around the statue of Comrade Lenin, and up the stairs on the side of the platform. The governor led the way with many officials and army officers wearing colorful ribbons and decorations on their overcoats trailing behind him like the tail of a glowing comet.

The governor looked to be the youngest man among them and he wore only a single gold star hanging from a red ribbon pinned to his overcoat. But everyone he looked at stood a little straighter or reached up to smooth out a wrinkle in the suit or uniform. When he sat down, one of the officials held his chair for him.

It must be wonderful to be so important.

For a few minutes the governor sat and watched the crowd while the band played. He looked relaxed as he chatted with the officers and Party officials sitting around him. Then the music stopped and he stood and stepped forward to a microphone.

"Comrades, good morning! I welcome you!" he said.

His voice was clear and sharp and it crackled across the square from loudspeakers.

"Today we celebrate another year's advance toward world socialism. Be proud of your achievements—the achievements from your labor!"

The crowd cheered and then the governor spoke about the great sacrifices our country had made in the past and the challenges we would face and overcome in the future. Most of it I had heard before in other speeches, but I listened anyway. When the speech ended the crowd clapped and cheered again. Sergei and I waved our flags high in the air.

Then, as if on cue, faint sound came from the west. At first it was just a low rumble, but quickly it grew and I recognized the drone of approaching vehicles.

A moment later the lead parade vehicle—an open military car with two officers seated in the back—came into view over the rise on Lenin Street. It raced out onto the square and stopped. One of the officers stood and saluted toward the governor and the governor and the officers and officials on the platform waved back to him. Then he sat back down and the car sped across the square as the first of row after row of trucks, mobile artillery and other vehicles appeared in a column from the west.

Soon the square was filled with the growl of powerful engines—so much noise that Sergei had to shout into my ear for me to understand him. Everyone around us was cheering and the crowd was alive with the motion of flags waving back and forth.

Next came formations of soldiers and I could feel it in my stomach as thousands of boots struck the pavement in perfect cadence. I waved my flag high over my head as I yelled and whistled.

After the soldiers, a detachment of Young Pioneers, looking especially smart in their white shirts and red neckerchiefs, marched out onto the square with rifles and flags. They advanced at quick time in line formation and at close intervals and then executed a deft series of facing movements and two perfect countermarches. The crowd cheered.

"Pretty good," I shouted at Sergei.

"Next year that could be you," he shouted back.

I thought it would be wonderful to be marching in the parade with everyone I knew watching and cheering for me.

It took nearly two hours for the parade to pass us and when it was over, my voice was hoarse and my legs were aching. But I felt wonderful. I was proud of my country and its power. As we made our way back to the trams, Sergei and I walked together. With the crowd thinning, it was easier to talk. His hands were stuck deep into his pockets.

I'd been worried all morning about what I should say to him.

"Ah ... listen," I said finally. "I'm sorry. I know you studied hard."

He kept looking straight ahead. "Maybe I should have listened to you."

"Naw," I said. "I never would have tried. At least you tried."

"I guess."

"You can take them again, I mean, after you get back."

Without a university deferment, his *poveska*—his induction notice—would arrive in a matter of weeks, summoning him for his two years of service.

"Maybe, I dunno," he said.

We climbed onto a tram and found an empty seat in the back.

"You'll let me know how it's all going, won't you?" I said.

"If you like."

"Sure. I'll write to you too."

"Most of it will be pretty dull," he said.

"I want to hear it all. Don't leave anything out. I mean, you know … don't leave anything out you can talk about."

He gave me a quick smile, the first one since he'd gotten his notice about the exams, and he leaned close to me. "Well, Father and I have worked out our code. It's pretty good."

"Are you sure that's a good idea," I said. "Don't get caught using one of those."

He shrugged. "It's no problem. The censors don't care—unless you're in the Rocket Forces or some special duty like that, or unless you try to pass something that's really secret."

"Well, ok," I said.

He looked over his shoulder and then leaned closer to me. "I'll tell you what it is—but you can't tell anybody."

I looked over my shoulder. "I won't tell."

"Not even your parents."

"I promise."

"Or your grandparents."

"Nobody," I said.

"You swear it?"

"I swear it."

He held out his hand and I gripped it. Then he looked over his other shoulder and dropped his voice. "You're in it."

"Me? Really?"

He spoke in a low voice. "The clue'll be in the last part of the letter. If I ask about Julia, it means I'm posted inside the country. If I ask about you, it means I'm posted somewhere abroad."

"And … what about the war?" I asked.

"If I ask about the birds, I'm in Afghanistan."

I let out a long breath. "I hope that doesn't happen."

"It probably won't. There aren't that many of us down there, and they say it won't last much longer."

"That's good," I said.

Then the tram came to our stop and we got off, along with dozens of others from W-P 6.

"It's a good code," I said while we walked back to the block. "They'll never figure it out."

"Father helped, but it was mostly my idea," he said.

"And your mom?"

He shook his head. "She won't talk about it."

"Well, anyway, you won't have to worry about the birds. I'll take good care of them."

"Thanks, that'll help," he said.

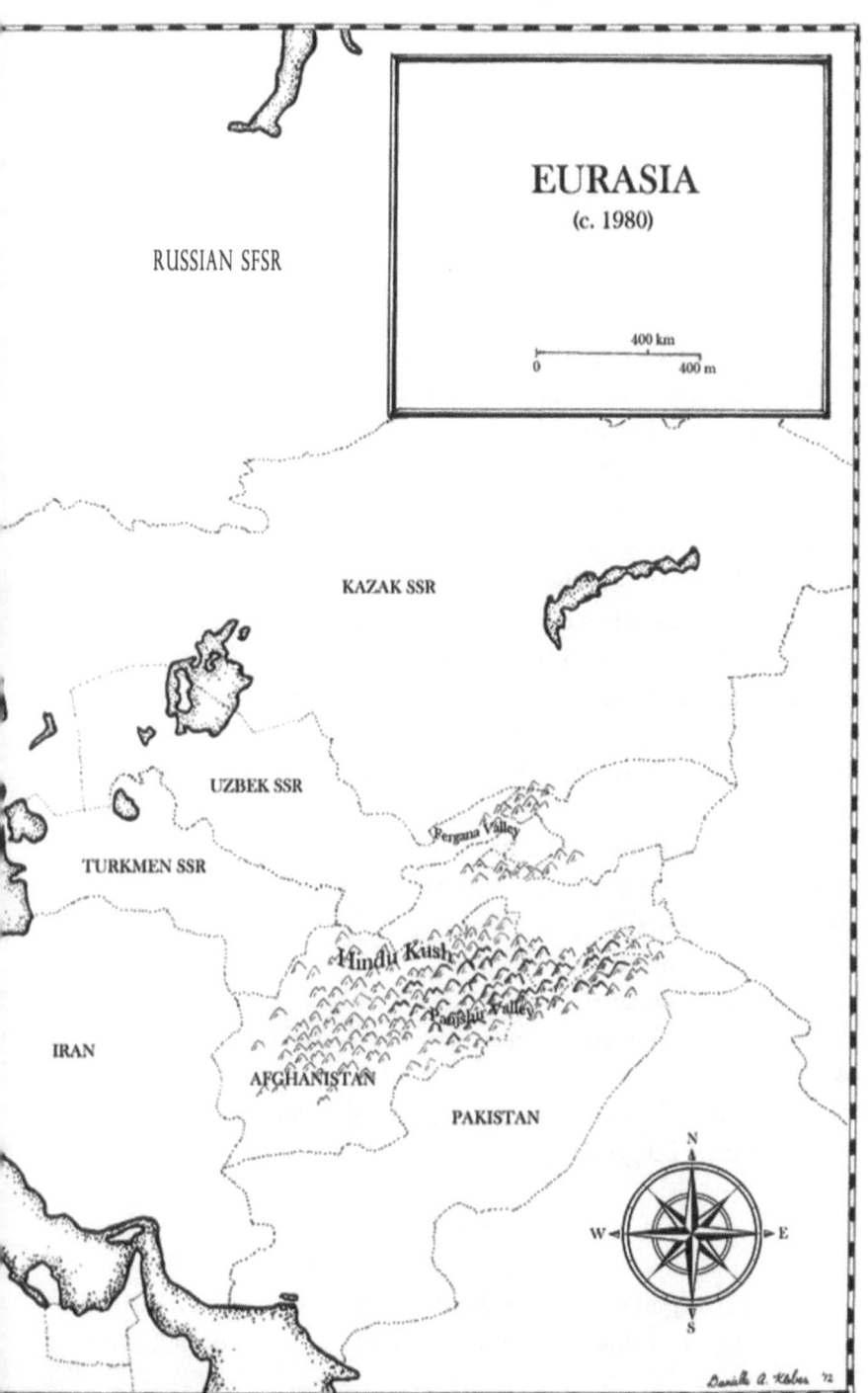

EURASIA
(c. 1980)

400 km

0   400 m

RUSSIAN SFSR

KAZAK SSR

UZBEK SSR

Fergana Valley

TURKMEN SSR

Hindu Kush

Panjshir Valley

IRAN

AFGHANISTAN

PAKISTAN

N
W   E
S

CHAPTER 7

ᣟ

S ergei kept his word about writing to me. Every other week, and sometimes more often than that, a letter arrived. He was right when he said most of it would be pretty dull stuff—about the food and the drills they put him through—but it was good to know he was alright.

And he was wrong about the censors. Every one of his letters had words and sometimes whole lines cut right out. One had so many holes it looked like a doily when I held it up to the light.

Then one day, it came. It was like every other letter, the same old Sergei, the same plea for me to write more often, but at the end was the question: "How are my birds doing these days?"

I wanted to crawl under my bed and stay there. I knew I had to tell his parents, but for two days I kept quiet about it.

"You have to tell them," Father said.

"Maybe he's already told them himself," I said.

"What if he hasn't?"

"Why does it have to be me?"

"I'll go too if you like."

"What if I wait until the next letter—to make sure it's not a mistake."

"Kolya," he said. He put his hand on my shoulder.

"Ok," I said. "I'll go tonight."

~~~~

After supper I dragged myself out the door and down the stairs to flat number 22. But when Kaari Georgiyevna met me at the door I knew my friend had been the bearer of his own bad news. Now those soft eyes regarded me through dark circles.

I held my letter out to her. "You'll want to see this one too," I said.

She pushed it unread into the pocket of her housecoat and then folded her arms across her chest as if to ward off a sudden chill. "Come in. I just made some tea."

"No, thanks, I can't stay. I … I just wanted to bring you that."

She nodded. "Just as well—Mikhail Petrovich went to bed early tonight. He'll be sorry he missed you."

"I can come back tomorrow."

She nodded again. "He'd like that right now."

I turned to leave, but then she reached out and took my arm. "Kolya, you talked to him—about his code, I mean. You talked to him about it, didn't you?"

"Just once. He told me not to say anything."

Her eyes were bright. "Could it be a mistake? Maybe we didn't remember it right."

I looked down at the floor and then back up at those eyes. Should I lie to her? Would that help?

I shook my head. "I'm sure he said the birds meant Afghanistan."

She chewed her lip for a moment and held onto my arm.

"He'll be ok," I said. "He's clever, a lot more than most of them out there."

"But he's not big like you. That's what you need in a place like that, to be …" She looked down at the floor and covered her mouth with her hand. She let go of my arm and shut the door.

~~~~

As the months went by, Sergei's letters kept coming and in spite of the censors' holes, I could tell he was in decent spirits. The weather wasn't so good, but the food was, and he was getting plenty of exercise in those mountains.

"You won't recognize me," he wrote. "I'll be able to take you on with no trouble."

~~~~

Then one afternoon I found Mother alone in our kitchen. Her cheeks were red and wet and a strand of her brown hair hung across her forehead. She was just thirty-eight, still with the figure of a young woman, but already there were wisps of grey at her temples.

"What is it? What's wrong?" I said, but already I was fighting back my own tears.

She wiped her cheek with the back of her hand and then hugged me. "Kaari Georgiyevna was here today," she said.

"Yes?"

I looked into her eyes and then slumped into a chair.

"No ... no, no."

More tears rolled down Mother's face as she handed me an envelope. "She brought you this."

I took the envelope, opened it and read the notice inside. It said that "with regret" Sergei's family was notified that he had "perished fulfilling his duty to the state."

"Oh, no," I wailed. "No, no, no."

CHAPTER 8

❧

Without my sight I couldn't judge how much time had passed since Ksusha left me or how long it would be before she came back. I dozed again and when I awoke and my head cleared, I thought back over the events of that morning in the woods and why I now sat in darkness. Had that all been a dream? It seemed so now, except for the undeniable fact that I couldn't see. That was certainly no dream.

Then the door to the flat opened and closed and a moment later Styopa spoke to me.

"Well?" he said. "Are you going to show some sense and let me get you some help? You haven't moved all day."

"I told you this morning, I want time to think—here, not in some hospital room."

"You're being a fool, you know."

"Ksusha came by," I said. "Thanks for telling her."

"You're welcome. Now forget about her and let's get you out of here."

"Bed," I said. "I want to go to bed."

"They have all the beds you'll need."

"My bed."

I heard him go into the kitchen and open the refrigerator. A moment later he closed it and came back to me.

"You have plenty of food. What do you want?" he said.

"Nothing," I said. I was voraciously hungry, but not in my body—something Styopa wouldn't understand.

"Ok, then," he said. "Come on, let's get you up."

He pulled me to my feet, led me into my bedroom and laid me down. The window was open and I lay there for a long time listening to the traffic on the street below and faint music coming from the open window of another flat.

PART TWO

CHAPTER 9

As my last year at W-P 6 drew to a close, my time for military service was fast approaching. I made no plans for the future because the state had made them for me. One evening at supper Deda picked up a length of salami from the table and pointed it at me.

"Remember—if we send you one of these, don't eat it—save it," he said. "It'll be like money, better than money. You can trade it for things you'll need."

"Deda, please, don't—" Mother pleaded.

"Why should I keep quiet?" he said. "Should we pretend this is not going to happen? That's nonsense. There are things I want to say to the boy."

"I'll remember," I said.

"And the officers," he continued. "Remember what I said about officers."

"Stay away from them."

He put the salami down. "Don't trust any of them, especially the young ones. They might try to act friendly, but they don't mean it. All they care about is looking good for the higher-ups and they'll use you to do it."

"I'll stay clear of them," I said.

He picked the salami back up. "But trading is the key, boy," he said. "They'll never give you everything you need—get used to that. You'll have to trade, especially for good boots. Pay attention to your boots. It's better to have them too big than too small. Too big and you can stuff paper into the toes. But too small and your feet will be like sausage. The others will be worried about their tunics or their trousers. Let them. You find someone whose boots don't fit and trade."

On and on these admonitions went in one variation or another at every meal that winter and spring.

Then, on the fifth day of June, my long awaited induction notice arrived in the mail. Father handed the envelope to me unopened and I tore off the end and drew out the single sheet of paper inside. It was a simple, harmless-looking form letter, three sentences long, from the Organizational Directorate of the Military Districts. But when I finished reading it, I was sure my eyes were playing tricks on me.

"What's wrong?" Father asked as I looked on the back of the sheet and then inside the envelope.

"It's from the Moscow District," I said. "It says I report in two weeks to Moscow."

"What? That's impossible. Let me see it."

I handed the sheet and envelope to him. "That's what it says—Moscow."

He stared at the notice for several long moments and then looked on the back side and inside the envelope. "This can't be right," he said. "We live in Kursk, we're in the Kursk district. Why would they send you to Moscow?"

"I don't know," I said.

"What about your friends from school, are any of them going to Moscow?"

"I don't know—I don't think so."

He turned his attention again to the notice and his brow wrinkled. "This can't be right, it can't be."

We all read the notice again many times, searching for clues to its meaning, but of course there were none. That I should report for induction in Moscow and not in Kursk was simply inexplicable and try as we might, we could think of no sensible explanation.

~~~~

"They must have some special duty for you," Mother said at supper the next day, but Father shook his head.

"It doesn't say that. It just says 'report' like they all do," he said.

"Well, we need to find out," she said.

"No, we don't," Father said and then Mother sat down next to him at the table and took his hand.

"Vanya, we need to try," she said. "For Kolya, we need to try."

"Find out what?" Deda said.

"The reason, of course."

"You'll do nothing of the sort," Deda said. "You'll just make trouble."

"What are you thinking?" Father asked Mother.

"We go to the induction center here and show this to them. They can explain it, you know they can," she said.

Deda let out a deep sigh. "You think they'd tell us even if they know?" he said. "And what difference would it make anyway? They'll never change it."

He was surely correct about that. The authorities in Kursk would never interfere with an instruction that involved Moscow.

Mother dropped Father's hand and stood up. "So you won't help then," she said. She went into the kitchen.

"Sveta," Father said. "Please ... we'll just make trouble for the boy."

~~~~

Early the next morning Mother shook me awake by the shoulder. "Kolya, get dressed, we're going," she said. I propped myself up on my elbows.

"Going where?"

"To the induction center." She was already fully dressed and drinking her morning tea. I looked around the dark flat. No one else was up.

"Are you sure? Deda and Father won't like it," I said.

"I'm not worried about them. They can sit around here on their hands if they want to, but we're going to get some answers. Now get moving."

I rolled out of bed and reached for my pants. It was clear there was no point in arguing. I dressed and ran a brush through my hair and then we left the flat for the tram into the city. An hour later we arrived at the induction center on Mozhayev Street, its door still tightly shut and locked. We each pressed an ear against the heavy door and in spite of the building's deserted appearance, we heard noise from inside. While I stood to the side, Mother knocked on the door until eventually we heard it being unlocked from the inside and an officer stuck his head out. He was chewing on his breakfast. He looked at me, then at Mother.

"What do you want?" he said. "We're not open. Can't you see that?"

"I see that, but we have a question, an important question," she said.

He leaned toward her and spoke very slowly. "Did you hear me— we're not open."

She held out the notice to him. "Read this ... please," she said.

The officer looked over at me and then back at Mother who continued to hold out the notice. After a moment he let out his breath and took it. He unfolded it and took a pair of reading glasses from his pocket, put them on, and then read the notice.

"So?" he said when he'd finished and looked up. "He reports in ... ten days. Come back then."

Mother tapped the sheet with her finger. "But look where he goes," she said.

The officer looked down at the page again and his eyebrows went up slightly. "Moscow," he said and then he shrugged. "So?"

"But he lives here in Kursk. Why does he report in Moscow?" she asked. The officer folded the sheet and handed it back to her.

"I have no idea. Ask them when he gets to Moscow."

"That's no answer," she said. "I could have told him that. We want to know why."

He put his glasses back into his pocket. "Look, lady," he said. "There's nothing I can tell you except just do what it says. If it says 'go to Moscow' he should go to Moscow."

"Are there any other boys from Kursk reporting there?" Mother asked.

He shrugged again. "I don't know, I don't think so, but that doesn't matter. It says what it says."

"But what if it's a mistake," she said.

"What if it is? He needs to do what it says."

Mother put the notice back in her bag and crossed her arms across her chest. "And that's all you'll tell us," she said.

"That's all I can tell you," he said.

She stood there a moment, tapping her toe on the pavement. "Alright then, thank you. You've been … very helpful," she said.

He closed the door and we started up the street. But then he opened the door and called after us. "If I knew something, I'd tell you—but I doubt it's a mistake." Then he pulled the door shut.

Mother and I looked at each other. "Annoying little man," she said. She draped an arm around my shoulders and squeezed.

~~~~

And so the time came. At suppertime, nine days after my induction notice arrived I sat at the table in our kitchen drinking tea and eating a supper of soup and cheese sandwiches Babulya had prepared for me. A plane ticket to Moscow would have been much too expensive and so we had agreed I would go that evening by train.

Mother and Babulya sat across the table watching me eat. I told Babulya the food was good and Mother asked me again if I had my train ticket and the instructions for Moscow Father had written out for me. Then she placed her hand over mine.

"You're good with figures," she said. "There might be an office job for you, maybe in Moscow."

"Yes, I'll try for that."

"Promise you'll try for a job like that," she said, looking into my eyes. "Promise."

"I promise." I squeezed her hand. Every mother of every conscripted boy had the same hope, for a safe, easy job and a posting within the borders of the USSR, even a posting in Siberia.

"Write to us, dear boy," Babulya said. "We know you can't tell us much, but write."

"Every day," I told her and she smiled. "Well, maybe every other day," I said.

"I'll pray every day you ask about the chapel," she said. It was she who had insisted that a reference to the old Korennaya chapel would mean I was somewhere safe.

"I'm sure I will," I said.

Father had gone to hire a car to drive me to the station and he arrived as I finished my soup.

"It's time," he said. "Deda's waiting in the car."

I rose from the table and Babulya straightened out the collar on my old jacket. My clothes would be taken from me when I was issued a uniform and so I wore old ones, but she had seen to it that they were clean and mended. Mother handed me a paper sack packed with cheese and bread for the trip and soap for washing the next morning. She reached her arms around me in a tight hug she held for a long time. Then I pulled away and followed Father out the door and down the stairs.

~~~~

The train to Moscow departed every evening at ten o'clock. Father parked on the street near the station and we walked the short distance to the platform. The night was cool and crowds of people stood in queues on the platform to board the cars. Another queue had formed in front of the station kiosk where people were buying bottles of water, newspapers and snacks for the trip. An old woman sitting next to the kiosk was selling pickles and boiled potatoes.

"Go on, move off," the man in the kiosk said to her. "I have the permit here."

She picked up her baskets, moved a dozen meters down the platform and sat down. The man in the kiosk glowered at her.

Porters pulling carts loaded with stacks of luggage moved back and forth along the platform picking up luggage in one spot and setting it down in another. Some people stood about quietly, while others talked and laughed and waved to travelers through the car windows.

Father had bought me a ticket for a sleeping compartment so I could get some rest on the trip. We found my car just as the attendant gave the on-board signal. I turned and hugged Father and then Deda and then boarded. It was good there wasn't much time for talking.

I moved down the corridor inside the car, stopping at each compartment and checking the numbers above the door against my ticket. When I reached the open door of my compartment, I was pleased to see I would be alone on the trip. In those days it was common to share a sleeping compartment with complete strangers, but mine was empty. There were four bunks, two on bottom and two on top. I sat down on a lower bunk and settled back against the wall. Then Father's face appeared in the window and I sat forward and waved to him.

"All ok?" he asked. The glass muffled his voice.

"It's good. I'm alone."

"Perfect. Now get some sleep."

The attendant appeared at the door, her arms piled high with pillows, sheets and blankets. She was an old woman wearing a blue uniform and she tossed my bedding onto the bunk above me.

"The toilette's in the rear," she said. "Do you want tea?"

"No, thanks, no tea," I said and she moved on to the next compartment.

Then the car lurched gently into motion and the platform began to move slowly backward, past the window. Father walked and then ran alongside my window, waving, as the car gained speed. I waved back and smiled and then suddenly the car reached the end of the platform and he was gone.

The lights of Kursk moved past my window and soon we left the city behind and headed out into the open country. The city lights receded and then there was nothing outside the window but the dark emptiness of the steppes.

As I settled back again onto my bunk, the muscles in my neck and shoulders throbbed.

Probably just the strain. But Father was right—now I should rest. There would be time in the morning to think about what was ahead.

I propped up my feet and let my mind go blank. I swayed back and forth with the movement of the car as we rolled through the steppes past Zolotukhino, Zmiyevka, Orel and then Mcensk. By the time we left Mcensk, it was the middle of the night and I switched off the light and let the car rock me to sleep.

~~~~

I awoke often over the next hours as the train slowed and stopped, wheels squealing, at Shchekino, Tula and Yasnogorsk. At each stop the bluish platform lights shone in through the window, illuminating my compartment. I was dimly aware of voices and footsteps in the corridor outside my door. Then the car jerked again gently into motion, throwing my compartment back into darkness and I slept.

~~~~

Near dawn the car attendant knocked on my compartment door.

"Kursk Station, Moscow, one hour," she called out in a loud voice. Then she knocked at the next compartment. Her voice became fainter as she moved down the row of compartments, knocking on each door. I heard people forming a queue in the corridor to use the toilette. The air in my compartment was hot and stale and my window was stuck shut so I slid back my door and stepped out into the corridor. A man stood there, smoking a cigarette while he gazed out the window at streets and buildings gliding silently past us in the early morning light. The windowpane was down and morning air blew in. His face was lined and he hadn't shaved.

"*Dobroe ootre*," he said.

"Good morning," I answered him. I was still groggy from sleep and I didn't feel much like talking, but the cool air from the window was refreshing.

"This is Moscow?" I asked, nodding toward the window. He shook his head.

"Not Moscow—Shcherbinka. Moscow in a few minutes." He reached into his pocket and pulled out a package of cigarettes and offered me one. I took it and he lit it for me. It was all tobacco and it tasted rich.

"Thanks," I said.

"You're very welcome." His compartment was next to mine and the smell of cooked food wafted out.

"What did you think of the excitement last night?" he asked.

"Excitement?"

"Yeah, when we hit somebody—or something."

"I don't know anything about that," I said. "I guess I was sleeping."

"They're not sure what it was. The engineer said it was a man. But … well, by the time he got us stopped and we went back to look, whatever it was, was gone."

"Where was this?" I was smoking his cigarette and I thought I should at least be polite.

"Dunno exactly, somewhere north of Malinovka."

"I boarded at Kursk."

"Then you were on board," he said.

"I didn't hear a thing."

"Good for you, you must be a good sleeper."

"I didn't think so last night," I said. I rubbed my neck and shoulder. They still ached.

"Well, there wasn't much to see, but it was good to get off and stretch the legs."

"You didn't find anything?" I said. He shook his head again.

"Nope. We looked for half an hour, but nothing."

"Where could a man go in the middle of the steppes in the middle of the night?" I said.

"A good question. I asked it myself. Maybe the engineer just wanted a little break and made it all up." He laughed and tapped his forefinger against his neck below his right ear. "Just to settle the nerves." He winked at me.

By that time we were coming to the outskirts of Moscow, passing clusters of people waiting at street corners for buses and trams. Others trudged along the streets, heads bent down, heading to their jobs or to join the early queues for the markets and shops. The car shuddered under our feet as it slowed.

"This is a great city," my companion said.

"It's my first time."

"Oh, then you should see the sights; the Kremlin, the view from the Lenin Hills—and all the other things; they're wonderful."

"I won't be here long enough for that."

"You can come back. Moscow has been here for eight hundred and fifty years. It'll wait for you."

"You work here?" I asked. He took a last pull from his cigarette and flicked it out the window.

"Work, no; pensioner, I live here."

"I guessed you came from the south."

"Why would you say something like that?" he said. He jammed a hand down into one of his pockets.

"I didn't mean anything. No real reason I guess, except you're coming from there."

"My boy married a girl from Orel. Why he would choose to live in a place like that I'll never understand, but I go there to visit."

"I see," I said. The queue for the toilette was getting shorter and it was time to take my place in it. But my companion reached out and touched my shoulder.

"This isn't just a place," he said. "It lives, it has a soul. You could burn Orel down and rebuild it anywhere and it wouldn't matter. It has no soul. It's just bricks and pavement. But Moscow is a living thing. There's no place like it in the world."

I wondered how many other places in the world he'd actually seen.

"I've always lived in Kursk," I said.

"Never been there. Does it have a soul?"

"I've never thought about it that way."

"A place has a soul if it draws you there. There must be a place that does that to you."

Now I was ready for this conversation to end. It was as if this stranger knew things about me.

"I ... I've never been away from Kursk," I said.

"Is that so? Never? Then this really is a special trip for you, yes?" A gust of cool wind blew in through the open window.

"You could say that," I said.

He looked up at the sky. "There'll be a storm later. It'll cool things off late in the day. Make it perfect for walking."

"Not for me, I'm afraid."

"Walking is the best way to see the city. You look healthy enough for it."

"I report today for service," I said.

"Oh, I see." He looked out the window. "I did my service in Poland. Can you imagine, me—a tank driver?"

"Maybe I'll get tanks," I said and he laughed.

"You should hope not. All of Poland is about this big," he said, holding up his hands in the shape of a small rectangle.

"Well at least you learned to drive," I said and he laughed again.

"I haven't had many tanks to drive these days. No, no, you don't want tanks. You want the *decantniki*."

"The Airborne Forces? Why?"

"My brother's boy just finished with the 104th Guards. All in all it was good duty."

"It's been pretty hot for them, hasn't it—in the war, I mean."

"True, for some, but his regiment spent the whole time in Kirovabad. He came home without a scratch."

"Airborne—I don't know," I said. "I've never been in a plane."

"Neither had he and, besides, you won't be doing the flying. You can ride in the back of a truck can't you? Well then, you can ride in the back of a plane."

"My chances of getting into one of their training regiments are pretty slim," I said.

"True again, but better since you're reporting here."

I watched over his shoulder as the car attendant moved down the corridor carrying a tray filled with cups of morning tea. There were maybe a dozen glass cups in metal holders. The tea was dark, almost black. She dragged one leg and when she reached my compartment, she caught her foot on the heating pipe that ran along the corridor floor and pitched forward, sending the tray and cups crashing to the floor in a jangle of metal and glass. Heads popped out of compartments up and down the corridor. Tea soaked the carpet and splashed up on my companion's trouser leg. He looked down at the woman, then shook off his leg and withdrew into his compartment, sliding the door shut behind him.

"I'm sorry," the old woman said to me, her eyes down.

She straightened her jacket and crouched down on the floor, wiping the corridor wall with her sleeve. Lucky for her the glasses were stout and none had broken. I watched her a moment and then crouched down and gathered up the glasses.

CHAPTER 10

❧

We pulled into Kursk Station at seven o'clock. From there I rode the metro to Mayakovskaya and then I walked the three blocks to the induction center. Father's written instructions for this were clear and correct in every particular and I arrived at the center just before eight o'clock.

The inside of the center was a bare hall furnished with long wooden benches arranged in rows. Six officers sat along one wall behind a long table. Typewritten lists of names were lined up on the table top. I handed my induction notice and identity card to one of the officers, a major.

"Razkazov," he said as he looked at my card. He laid my papers on the table and reached for one of the lists. He folded back several sheets and then ran his finger down the page until he found what he was looking for. "This you?" he asked, holding the sheet out to me. I looked and there was my name, even my address in Kursk.

"Yes, Comrade Major. That's me."

"Ok, sign beside your name and go have a seat," he said.

I signed and he handed my papers back to me and pointed in the direction of the benches. I hesitated a moment and he looked up.

"Yes?"

I hesitated another moment. "My name, Comrade Major."

"What about it?"

"Can you tell me why I'm here? I ... I don't live in Moscow."

He looked down at my name on the sheet and shook his head. "How should I know? The lists come from the Directorate. You'd have to ask them. Have a seat," he said and he turned to resume his conversation with one of the other officers.

"Thank you, sir," I said.

I turned away from the table, but there would have been little point in following the major's instruction to sit down. There were hundreds of boys already in the hall that morning, most of them standing up, talking and milling about. Many acted drunk, talking loudly with slurry words, and their clothes were torn and dirty and their faces were bruised. The room smelled like sweating bodies. The officers behind the table paid no attention to them.

I walked up one row and then down another looking for a place to sit, a place where I wouldn't be knocked into or forced to listen at close quarters to a lot of boisterous drunk talk. It wasn't easy to find. I was about to take a spot next to a boy who was stretched out and snoring when I noticed a pair of clear pale eyes watching me from the opposite row. I nodded to him and he nodded back.

"Not so pretty, is it?" he said and I smirked. He gestured with an open palm to the bench next to him and I sat down.

"I watched you come in," he said. "I guess this wasn't what you expected."

"I don't know what I expected."

"Well, don't worry about them. They'll quiet down when things get started."

"Soon, I hope."

He glanced down at his wristwatch. "Oh, anytime now," he said.

"I'm Razkazov, Kolya."

"Oleg Krepko," he said as a boy sitting two benches away from us collapsed onto the floor.

"At least down there he can get some sleep," Oleg said.

"We'll be here that long?" I said.

"Most of the morning. Maybe all day. As long as it takes."

"They don't look too happy," I said, nodding toward the officers behind the table. Most of them stared stonefaced at the room.

"Would you want that job, every morning the same thing, a rabble like this?" Oleg said.

"I can think of worse things."

"Well, maybe. Anyway, they'll start to get rid of us soon. Just hope you're picked early."

"Why's that?"

"To get out of here, of course," he said. "And to get some dinner. They won't feed us in here." I'd finished the last of Mother's bread and cheese on the train hours ago and was hungry again.

"And the doctors are better with the injections in the morning," he added. "They're in a hurry in the afternoon and that can hurt."

"How do you know all this?" I asked.

"My brother did his service at one of these places. He's out now, back home with my folks in Tartu."

"Tartu?"

"Estonia. My dad was a military man, attached to the airbase there. You?"

"Kursk."

"Really? Why are you here?"

"I'd like to know, but nobody can tell me anything."

He nodded. "Well, it's probably lucky for you."

"Why's that?" I said.

"Better assignments. In Kursk you'd probably get stuck in some broken down motor rifles regiment."

"Is that why you're here?"

"My dad arranged it," he said.

Then one of the officers stood up from behind the table and blew on a whistle and the noise in the hall died away.

"Ok, now it begins," Oleg said.

The officer shouted out that there would be no more talking and to make sure we followed his order, four tough-looking sergeants entered the hall and began to walk up and down the floor between the benches. One boy was still whispering and when one of the sergeants slapped him solidly on the back of the head, even the drunks straightened up. A few minutes later another officer rose from behind the table and began to call out names. He read from one of the lists without looking up and when he had called out about twenty-five names, he put the list down. He told the boys whose names were called to stand and line up at the doors at the rear of the hall. After they lined up, two more sergeants appeared through the doors with their pistols drawn and led the boys away. Then the process started again.

As the morning wore on, Oleg and I waited.

Late in the morning, two officers wearing different uniforms from the officers behind the table came into the hall. They walked slowly up and down the rows looking us over. One of them stopped in front of Oleg, asked to see his papers and then told Oleg to follow him to a corner of the room. I watched them talk as the officer with the whistle rose again from his seat behind the table and called out more names. After several minutes Oleg pointed at me and the officer motioned to me to come over to him. I came and stood in front of him at attention. He dismissed Oleg.

"Documents," he said and I handed him my notice and card. He studied them a moment.

"You live in Kursk?" he said. He looked me in the eyes.

"Yes, Comrade Captain."

"What are you doing here?"

"The notice says to be here."

"I can see that, but why?"

"I was hoping you could tell me," I said.

"Me—how would I know?"

"You or one of the other officers, Comrade Captain."

"I have no idea," he said. He stepped back and looked me up and down. "You're a big one aren't you? What, one hundred kilos?"

"About ninety-five, Comrade Captain."

"Umm … you can lose some of that. But you look fit and sober."

"I am sober, sir," I said.

"The hair might be a distraction though. Any medical problems?"

"None, sir," I said. He handed my identity card back, but kept my induction notice.

"Well, our medical people will find out. Wait here," he said.

He walked over to the table and showed one of the officers my notice and that officer showed it to another officer who looked again through the lists. The three of them turned to look at me and then talked together for several moments and then the first officer behind the table shrugged his shoulders. The captain came back to me.

"You know who I'm here for?" he said.

"Yes, Comrade Captain, I think you're with the Airborne Forces."

"Correct. Your friend there is willing to try one of our training camps. Would you like to come with him? There'll be hard work ahead, but if you make it, you'll be a soldier."

"Yes, sir," I said. "Thank you, sir, I'd like that."

"Then come with me."

And that was my induction into military service. Later that night Oleg and I and thirty-three other boys sat strapped into our seats aboard an Ilyushin IL-76 transport jet as it lifted off from Kubinka airfield for the long flight to a training camp in the Fergana Valley in the Uzbek republic.

CHAPTER 11

W̲e touched down in the Fergana Valley the next morning at
first light. After two nights of travel with little sleep, I felt
weak and disoriented and I needed a shower.

The transport door swung open and we emerged, stretching and
yawning. I found myself standing in the middle of a broad, dusty valley that was empty in every direction except for the airstrip and the
collection of squat buildings of the training camp surrounded by a
wire fence. A range of mountains with white tops and slopes in deep
purple shadow rose up to the southeast.

When we were out of the transport, our escorts—veteran airborne troopers—formed us into ranks on the tarmac. From there I
got my first good look at the camp that would be my home for the next
four months. Even at that early hour, it was in full motion. Recruits
marched in formation along the perimeter wire while others sweated
through exercises. This was a place where boys like me learned to
survive. Every four months the graduates of this academy, with their
lethal new skills, departed to join one of the active duty regiments and
in their places a fresh cadre arrived and the training cycle began again.

As we formed into ranks, the engine of an open staff car cranked
to life outside the only two-story structure in the camp and two men
walked briskly out the front door and swung themselves into the front
and rear passenger seats. The whine of an aircraft engine announced
the arrival of a second transport, an Antonov An-12, which banked
for its approach, touched down on the airstrip and rolled to a stop next
to our transport. In minutes it disgorged about fifty boys who lined up
on the tarmac beside us.

Then the staff car stopped at the edge of the tarmac and the two men stepped out. They wore crisp, mottled fatigues, boots and bright blue berets. The taller man, an officer, looked us over for several minutes while we watched him and waited. Our escorts came to attention and saluted. Some of us recruits attempted a belated salute, but it was a weak effort.

Finally the officer spoke.

"Good morning to you. I am Colonel Gerasim, the commander of this camp," he said. "Welcome to the Airborne Forces."

His face and neck were lean and muscular and his skin was almost bronze. He looked young to be a colonel.

"Your training begins now and I have just one piece of advice for you," he continued. "Learn what we teach you and learn it well—it'll make you good soldiers. After that, most of you will join one of our regiments in Afghanistan." He paused a moment.

"Those of you who cannot complete our training will be sent to join a motor rifles unit and from there probably to Afghanistan," he said and then he paused again. "I've been in those mountains and I can promise you'd rather be there in one of our units, knowing what we'll teach you. What you learn from us will keep you alive."

None of us had spoken a word.

A light breeze was blowing and a fine layer of dust covered my shoes and trousers. Then one of the boys from the Antonov fell out of ranks onto the tarmac, dead asleep. He woke up when he hit the pavement, as two escorts pounced on him, grabbed him by the wrists and yanked him to his feet. The colonel watched with an expression of indifference while the boy steadied himself.

"Where you're going that could get you killed," he said and then he paused again for a long moment. I was straining to hear every word.

"Some of you haven't slept for a day, maybe two days. You'll get used to that. There are no soft beds in the mountains and if you sleep up there, you won't need to worry about the bandits—your comrades will shoot you."

The sun was climbing in the sky above the mountains in the east. The day was already warm.

"But there'll be time to talk about that later. For now, let's get you looking like soldiers. Dismissed," he said. All of us, escorts and recruits alike, came to attention and saluted and the colonel climbed back into the staff car. Our escorts lined us up in two columns, each two men abreast, and we marched double time to the camp.

Once inside the wire, we stood in one queue after another for hours while our induction papers were checked against more lists, our hair was shaved off, and we were issued uniforms and equipment. The quartermaster told me to sit and lift up a foot and he held a boot up next to it for sizing. When I tried the boots on later, they fit perfectly. Deda would have been pleased with that.

After we got our uniforms, they divided us into companies and we marched to our barracks where I met the man who was to have absolute dominion over me for the next four months—Sergeant Valery Pryamilov.

"Proceed inside and choose a bed!" the sergeant barked. "Place your uniform and equipment in the box at the end of your bed and stand at attention beside the box. Do it now!"

We ran inside, each of us scrambling to choose a bed and stow his gear. Oleg and I took beds next to each other at the end of the row. The room was nothing but wooden walls and a wooden floor with a shower and latrine at the end. It was empty except for two rows of metal beds, each bed fitted with a mattress and bedding in a pile on top. A grey, metal locker lay on the floor at the foot of each bed. The room looked like no one had ever lived there.

I threw my gear into my box, but before I could arrange it properly, Sergeant Pryamilov followed us inside and yelled out "Attention!" I found a place at the foot of my bed and stood rigidly straight while the sergeant walked up and down the row of beds, telling some of us to stand straighter or at a different spot.

"Look carefully at where you are standing," he said after each of us was in his proper place. "That is where you will stand at every inspection, not a centimeter different."

He stopped and grabbed one boy's box and dumped the gear out onto the floor.

"Wherever you come from, whatever you were doing two days ago, forget it. This is your world now, this camp, this barracks, this life—nothing else. Forget everything else. Focus on what you're here to do. Things will go easier."

He stopped to peer into the box of the boy next to me and then he dumped the contents out onto the floor.

"Keep your box in proper order," he said. "If your effects are not in proper order, you will go on punishment detail. Do you understand?"

"Yes, Comrade Sergeant!" we all shouted together.

"Your spare uniform will go on the left side of the box. Your equipment on the right side. When weapons are issued to you, they will go in the rack by the door." He paused to look into my box and then he continued down the row.

"You will wear a clean uniform at all times. You will wash your uniforms every other day at the wash house. You will shower every day and clean your teeth every day. If you fail to do these things you will go on punishment detail. Do you understand?"

"Yes, Comrade Sergeant!"

He dumped another boy's gear out onto the floor.

"Reveille is at 06.00. You will have ten minutes to make up your bed and form up in ranks outside for exercises. If you're late you go on punishment detail." He paused.

"Do you understand?"

"Yes, Comrade Sergeant!" we all shouted.

On it went. He gave us many more instructions then and later in the day and the penalty for failing to comply was always the same—punishment detail. He didn't tell us what punishment detail would be, but I was sure it wouldn't be good.

I was afraid of Sergeant Pryamilov from the start and from what I learned about him in the coming weeks, I had good reason to be. He was a *starschina*—a top-rank, extended-service noncommissioned officer—who had done two tours of duty around Kabul with the 103rd Division. I came to know him as a hard man with a hard heart.

The only good thing about that first day was the food. Dinner was served at 13.00, supper at 18.30, and at both meals there was good, fresh bread, heaps of meat and noodles and hot, strong tea—plenty to fill us up in the fifteen minutes we had to eat it. By dinnertime I was starving and I devoured every scrap.

That night, when the first day was finally over, I fell into my bed. So much new information had been thrown at me that it was impossible to process it all. My brain randomly replayed one image from the day after another, like a broken slide projector, until finally, relief came from dreamless sleep.

~~~~

The second day began at 06.00. A whistle pierced the morning quiet and I awoke with a headache to see Sergeant Pryamilov, fully dressed in new fatigues, walking up and down the row of beds, shouting and smacking the feet of any boys who weren't moving with a wooden rod.

"Get up! Up! Get up!" he yelled. "Form outside! Ten minutes!"

I staggered to my feet and fumbled into my tunic and trousers and then pulled on my boots. The boys around me leaped from their beds to the floor. I was second in line to do my toilette, then I made up my bed and ran for the door. As I left the barracks, I checked my watch; it was 06.08. Outside, as I came down the barracks steps, I saw the sergeant waiting, looking fresh and alert. At 06.10 we were all in ranks.

"Some of you look to be in very poor condition," the sergeant began as he strode back and forth in front of us. "We'll change that, beginning now. We'll start with two laps around the camp. The first five of you to finish the first lap can sit out the second lap. Anyone who does a lap in more than fifteen minutes will do three more. Now go!"

He blew his whistle and we started forward en masse. Judging by the quickness of our pace, I knew we were all determined to run only one lap. I know I was. The distance around the camp was, I guessed, two and a half, maybe three kilometers, but I was in no condition to sprint half that distance and most of the other boys looked to be in worse shape than I was. But sprint was exactly what I did, the prospect of running just one lap around the camp impelling me forward at near top speed. And although I ran as hard as I could, I finished the first lap well back from the lead—and badly winded.

"Two more laps and the first five sit out the second one!" the sergeant called out as we passed the starting point and he waved us around the camp again. I swore and kept running as my chest started to burn. Oleg was one of the first to finish and I saw him squatting on the ground, looking like he wasn't winded at all, enjoying his rest. I had fallen for the sergeant's little trick, but I ran on, hoping to be one of the first five in the next lap.

I wasn't. I finished ten back from the lead as my chest burned hotter and my legs ached.

"Two more laps and the first five sit out the second lap," the sergeant called out as we passed the starting point again. On I ran, dizzy and nauseated as my boots dragged the ground, stirring up little clouds of dust. I was in agony, but still I ran, thinking of nothing but the pain.

I ran five laps that morning and when the sergeant finally told us to stop, I leaned over and heaved up what remained of my supper. Many of the others did the same and the sergeant watched us with a face showing his disgust.

"I thought so," he said. "How do you expect to run up and down mountains in thin air if you can't run a few short laps down here on level ground?" He shook his head. "We have a lot of work to do."

I knew he was right, but I could barely listen, so intense was the burning in my chest and in my throat. One boy fainted, but he revived when the sergeant poured water on his face from a bucket he had ready.

"Get up," he said and the boy wobbled to his feet.

After that the sergeant led us for an hour in exercises that stretched and pulled every last one of my muscles to its limit. This was going to be a long summer.

Later in the day I admitted to Oleg how stupid I'd been about the run that morning.

"I wasn't very clever today about that," I said.

"No, you weren't," he agreed.

"I'll slow it down tomorrow."

"Slow it down a little, but not too much. I watched you—you're in ok condition. Just figure out where that puts you in the company and pace yourself."

"How did you get so quick?" I asked and he shrugged.

"Practice. There's a river running through Tartu and every day I ran from our flat through the city and back—out on one side of the river and back on the other."

"You did that for fun?"

"Hardly."

"Why then?"

"So I wouldn't do what you did this morning," he said.

On the morning run the next day I tried to follow Oleg's advice. I watched the others and paced myself just ahead of the boys I thought I could beat. I discovered Oleg was right—at that speed I could conserve my strength but run fast enough to do just three laps around. That was better than five. I was making progress and by mid-summer I had enough endurance and speed to run just two laps around each morning. Each of the other boys eventually found his proper place in the company for the run too. Those in the worst condition ran the most laps. Sergeant Pryamilov knew his business.

After morning exercises each day there was breakfast and after breakfast, political lectures. Then we marched and drilled. Behind the barracks was a square of asphalt where we assembled and marched and drilled, back and forth, for hours every day. Sometimes we carried weapons and field equipment and sometimes not, but always it was the same back and forth in formation to cadence called out by the sergeant. We must have marched a hundred kilometers on that square that summer and by September I knew every crack and hole. Some of the boys complained about the marching, but I accepted it as just part of becoming a soldier. Besides, if we weren't marching, the sergeant would surely have us doing some other disagreeable task.

After supper, in the long summer evenings before lights out, we had a little time to relax and talk. After just a few weeks, it felt like I'd known the others for years. There was Roman Davidov from Moscow and Dima Ginyavsky from Stary Oskol. Maxim Kurdin and Sasha Nabasov came from the same *oblast* in the Ural Mountains region, Max from Chelyabinsk and Sasha from Sverdlovsk. We talked and shared stories about everything—families, girl friends, things we would do when we got back—anything on our minds. It was the pointless kind of small talk that boys separated from home for the first time make, part homesickness and part braggadocio, but it helped to pass the time. I especially liked Max's stories about the Urals because I'd never seen a mountain before I came to Fergana.

"Well, you wouldn't really call them mountains," he said. "I mean they're not like where we're going. But they're good for camping."

"What about wild animals?" I said. "You know, bears and wolves."

He nodded. "One time a pig ran into our camp—out of nowhere, there it was," he said.

"I mean a real wild animal," I said.

"That one was real enough for me."

"And then what?" I said.

"I swung at him with a skillet and he took off."

"If I was a pig I'd run from a skillet," Oleg said.

Sasha had been listening to Max. "Where was this?" he asked.

"Near the sanatorium on the Chusovaya River."

"Are you serious? On the bluff overlooking the village?"

"That's the one."

"I've been there!" Sasha said. "We went once in the fall when the leaves change color. We rented out one of the rooms for the weekend."

"It's good for that," Max said.

"Well, you'll miss the leaves this year, for sure," Roman said and Sasha's head dropped.

"Don't worry," I said. "They'll be there when you get back."

"That's ok," Sasha said. "But I'll really miss the ice castle in the city center this winter. I always helped cut the blocks from the river and haul them up to the square."

"I'm an expert at ice castles," Roman said and Max snorted.

"What does that mean?"

"It means I know how to build them."

"You should see the one we built last winter," Sasha said. "A hundred meters long. Walls, towers, a slide from the tallest tower for the kids. We hollowed out some of the blocks and strung lights inside. At night it sparkled. Took us a whole week. You should see it."

Sometimes we talked about Afghanistan, but Dima was the only one of us who knew much about it. He wanted to be a teacher and he could read German and a little French.

"Teach me to read French," Sasha said to him one night. "You never know—I might need it when we get to the mountains."

"If you like," Dima said without looking up from his book.

"Maybe you could teach me to speak a little Afghan too," Sasha went on. "That might be better."

"No," Dima said, still without looking up from his book.

"Why not?"

Dima sighed and looked up. "There's no such language as Afghan. I thought even you knew that."

"What do you mean? The bandits can talk can't they?"

"Sure, but not Afghan."

"Well, what do they speak?" Sasha said.

Dima closed his book and tossed it aside. "Pukhtu, some speak Dari," he said. I had no idea if that was true, but Dima sounded like he knew what he was talking about.

"All right then," Sasha said. "Teach me to speak Pukhtu."

"I hope we're not there long enough for that," Dima said and we all laughed, even Sasha.

"I'm cleverer than you think," Sasha said. "You'll see."

~~~~

At the beginning of our second week in camp, after we settled into a routine, a transport arrived from Novosibirsk one morning before the political lecture. We grinned and elbowed each other while we watched the new recruits being manhandled into ranks on the tarmac. As the escorts did their work, an officer stood by waiting to address the newcomers.

When we returned to the barracks after dinner, we found three new boys assigned to our company. One of them had taken the empty bed next to Sasha and was busy arranging his uniforms and equipment on Sasha's bed.

"Hey, hey, what's this?" Sasha said to him in a loud voice.

The new boy looked up and blinked "What's the problem?" he asked.

"What's the problem? Whadaya think's the problem? That's my bed and now look at the creases, you've ruined them."

"I won't be long," the new boy said.

"No, you won't," Sasha said. His ears were getting red and I was watching the door to give the alarm if the sergeant was coming.

"When I'm …" the new boy started to say, but before he could finish, Sasha grabbed one side of his bed and lifted it up, spilling the gear and uniforms onto the floor. It occurred to me that Sasha had just done far more damage to his creases than the new boy's gear had done, but now wasn't the time to say so. The new boy had been cheeky to use Sasha's bed without asking and he needed to be set straight about how things worked around here. I was sure there would be blows. But then the new boy just shrugged and grinned.

"Sorry," he said. "Didn't mean anything by it. I couldn't tell if your bed was made up or not." He stooped down and picked his things up from the floor and dumped them onto his own bed. Sasha glared at him, but his ears weren't so red anymore and after a moment he let the matter drop and started to make his bed up again.

One of the other new boys from Novosibirsk took the bed next to Oleg.

"That wasn't a very clever thing your friend did today," I said to him later.

"Who, Maerko? He's no friend of mine."

"His name's Maerko?" I asked.

"Yeah, Stepan—Styopa—Maerko. I had to sit next to him on the flight. I was glad when it was over."

"He doesn't seem so bad," I said. "A little cocky, but Sasha can be a hothead."

"Humph … you'll see," he said.

A couple of days later, before lights out, I was sitting in bed relaxing and the others were getting their gear ready for the next day. Styopa had stepped outside the barracks for a smoke. Sasha was lying in his bed staring up at the ceiling and he sat up when Styopa closed the door.

"I'm telling you—watch out for that one," he said to no one in particular. Several of us looked at each other.

"Who?" Oleg said.

"Who do you think? Mr. big-mouth Novosibirsk," he said and Oleg rolled his eyes.

"Forget about that. He said he was sorry. And he was right—I couldn't tell if you'd already made it up." Roman and I laughed.

"I'm not talking about my bed," Sasha said.

"Then what are you talking about?" Oleg said. The rest of us were listening. Sasha glanced toward the door.

"Those stories of his. You've heard 'em," he said. "He thinks we're idiots."

"What stories?" Max said.

"About his family and their big flat and fancy friends. Says his dad is some big professor of something."

"The space program's in Novosibirsk," Max said.

"Doesn't prove anything," Sasha said.

"Physics," Dima said.

"What?" Sasha said, turning toward him.

"Physics. He said his dad's a professor of physics. At the Budker Institute."

Sasha raised up his arms. "You see," he said.

"See what?" Oleg said. "Maybe he is."

"And maybe my father's a Hero of Socialist Labor," Sasha said.

"Ok, you can be a hero too—you can pull my kitchen detail tomorrow," Oleg said and we all laughed.

"I don't know who his dad is and I don't care," Max said.

"It's a lie, I'm telling you. If he's a big rich professor in that place, he could get him a deferment like that," Sasha said, snapping his fingers. "He'd never let him end up here, getting ready to go where we're going."

"It doesn't matter," Roman said.

"It does matter," Sasha said. "Think about it."

"I don't care about his people—whoever they are—and neither do you," Oleg said.

"Oh really? Let me ask you—do you believe him?" Sasha said to Oleg. "Well?"

Oleg sighed and sat back on his bed. "Maybe, maybe not," he said.

"That's my point," Sasha said. "Think about it—what else will he say that you're not sure about? Well?" he asked, looking around at the group of us. "I'm not going into the mountains with somebody like that."

Sasha was making his case against Styopa pretty well, raising points I hadn't thought about. I admit I was troubled. The others looked troubled too and Max was about to say something, but then Dima motioned for us to be quiet and Styopa came back inside.

~~~~

The time was coming for me to learn to jump out of an airplane in flight, something I never dreamed I'd ever do.

In our fifth week, Sergeant Pryamilov greeted us one morning with an odd little smile on his face. I noticed it right away and it set my nerves on edge because he never smiled like that unless he had some new misery in store for us.

"Today is a special day for you," he began, still smiling. "Get ready for the greatest thrill of your life. I hope all of you survive." He laughed at his own joke, which made me feel even edgier.

After breakfast the sergeant marched us to a building next to the airstrip filled with nothing but long wooden tables. One table was set apart from the others at the end of the room and next to it, standing very straight with his arms behind his back, was another sergeant. Sergeant Pryamilov went and stood beside him.

"Gather 'round," Sergeant Pryamilov said and we formed a circle around the two men. On the table were two canvas bundles with straps, one smaller than the other.

"This is Sergeant Kozyrev," Sergeant Pryamilov said, introducing the other man. "He'll be your jump instructor. I don't need to tell you to listen to him carefully."

He nodded to the other sergeant who stepped over to the table and picked up one of the bundles. "These are parachutes," he said "This is the main chute and this is the reserve. In the next days you will learn to use them. First, you will learn to pack them properly and then you will learn how to operate them in descent without killing yourselves and wasting state property. If you can't learn to do that, you won't be in the Airborne Forces for long."

Oleg gave me a crooked smile.

The sergeant dropped the reserve chute onto the floor and slid the main chute to the middle of the table.

"Watch carefully," he said.

We watched while he opened the pack, pulled out the contents and arranged the tangled lines and canopy material on the table top. When the canopy and lines were free from the pack and stretched out, he pointed to two wooden handles, each connected to a short line.

"These are the brakes," he said. "They are toggle lines connected to the rear of the canopy. You use them to raise and lower the canopy rear, changing it's shape—like the way flaps on an aircraft wing move up and down, changing the wing's shape and its lift capabilities. Everyone understand?"

"Yes, Comrade Sergeant," we all said.

"When you change the shape of the canopy, you change the speed of the descent—in other words, you put on the brakes."

It all seemed easy enough in the calm of the demonstration room, but what would it be like while I was falling through the air?

He stretched out the lines and ran a finger down the length of each one to make sure there were no tangles. "You do this to prevent a line from looping over the top of the canopy and destroying its ability to catch the air. I don't need to tell you what will happen if the canopy can't catch the air, do I?"

"No, Sergeant," we said.

"Good."

He picked up the canopy material, pulled it clear from the lines and began folding it. "This is called 'flaking'," he said. He laid the folded material on the floor and sat on it after each fold to force out the air trapped inside. When he finished, the material was in the shape of a long, flat tube that he folded tightly back into the pack. Last into the pack went the bridle, a nylon belt attached to the canopy, followed by the pilot chute and finally the pin. He held up the repacked chute for us to see.

"If you've done this properly, when you pull the pin, the pilot chute will catch in the air and pull out the canopy," he said. I was concentrating on everything he said, trying hard to remember it all, but then Sasha leaned over to Roman.

"You get all that?" he whispered.

"I'll practice with yours," Roman whispered back. Sasha started to laugh, but then Sergeant Pryamilov looked at him and he was instantly silent.

"I'm glad you're enjoying this," Sergeant Pryamilov said to us all. "But if you don't get this right today, you won't be laughing tomorrow."

Sergeant Kozyrev gave each of us a packed main chute and told us to lay it on one of the tables. And then for the next several hours, each of us packed and repacked his chute while the sergeant walked the room from table to table watching and correcting. In no time I discovered the sergeant had made a tricky, frustrating job look easy. It was simple enough to untangle the lines, but as soon as I started flaking the canopy, the lines crossed and I had to start all over again. On my fifth try I finally was able to fold the chute back into the pack. But I couldn't shake the thought that one of the lines might have crossed. If so, I'd find out the hard way at five hundred meters in the air.

~~~~

The next morning, we assembled on the airstrip. The sun was up and the sky was still and cloudless. Each of us was strapped to two chutes, a main and a reserve, and we each wore leather headgear—like one of the old open-cockpit pilots.

Precisely at 07.00 we walked to three waiting Tupolev TB-3 transports. As I approached the nearest transport, the first of its four turbine engines, the outer engine on the starboard side, coughed and whined and then started to spin its four-bladed prop, sluggishly at first and then faster and faster until the blades vanished in a whirling blur. Then the pilot repeated the ignition procedure with each of the other three engines. Dust swirled up from the backwash.

I mounted the steps into the aircraft and took a seat on the metal bench that ran the length of the fuselage. When we were all seated and strapped in, the door shut and the Tupolev's engines roared as the pilot added power. Soon we were rumbling down the strip and in another moment we lifted into the air. For the next half hour we circled the camp until the other Tupolevs took off and joined us in formation for the flight to the drop zone.

I shifted in my seat, checking and rechecking my chutes and adjusting my straps.

When we neared the drop zone, the pilot descended to our jumping altitude of five hundred meters. We leveled out and the jump light blinked on and we were ordered to stand and make ready. Each of us hooked a static line to our main chute and then the door opened and the cabin filled with light and sound and cold, rushing air. Oleg was ahead of me in line and he turned and yelled to me.

"I won't wait for you on the way down," he said. I laughed and watched him move to the open door and without any hesitation, jump out. Then I was standing at the door, looking down at the valley. I put my toes up to the edge of the floor and a nerve shock coursed through my limbs. It was like the shock when you lose your footing for an instant on a high ladder.

My eyes bulged and then ... I stepped out.

Nothing seemed real. The broad plain below looked like a photograph, distant and unconnected to me. I was falling like a stone and the air whipped past me. My body tingled. My pilot chute trailed out and behind it, the main canopy. The canopy caught the air and snapped open and I jerked upward. I saw the camp in the distance and beyond it, the mountains.

I drifted down.

All around me, and above and below, the sky was filled with canopies and I could see some of the others already on the ground fighting with their lines to bring their chutes under control. Some had gathered up their chutes and were walking to waiting trucks.

Then the ground was suddenly under my feet and I bent my legs to roll and absorb the shock. But when I hit I knew at once I'd kept my legs too stiff. My teeth clattered and I collapsed and fell forward onto both knees. My breath rushed out of me and I gasped and struggled for control of the lines because the canopy was still up and full of air. It was all I could manage to work myself into a sitting position to wrestle the lines, but then a gust of wind caught the canopy and the lines tightened, toppling me over onto my stomach. The chute snapped taut and dragged me. Dust coated my lips and clogged my nose.

Then I heard a voice from behind me.

"Take it easy. I'll get it," the voice said. I couldn't find the breath to speak, but I nodded.

"Hold on."

It was Styopa with his chute tucked under his arm. He reached up, grabbed my canopy at the edge and brought his arm down in a wide arc, flinging the material to the ground. My lines went slack.

"Thanks," I whispered as he walked away toward the trucks, but he didn't answer. I sat up and put my head between my legs and breathed slowly several times. In a few moments I got to my feet.

Sergeant Pryamilov was waiting for us at the trucks and when he had counted all of us, he pronounced the jump a success. No one had frozen in the door of the plane or broken anything on the ground.

On the ride back to camp, we laughed and congratulated ourselves and swapped stories about how it felt to jump out into space. This jumping business wasn't so bad after all.

That night, after I finished a letter home, I went outside for a smoke before bed. Styopa was sitting on the barracks steps.

"Um … thanks again," I said. "No telling how far it would have dragged me."

He nodded. "It looked like it might be getting away from you."

"It was getting away from me," I said.

"Well, you weren't the only one. Next time will be better." We were quiet and smoked for a time.

"Nice out tonight," I said.

"Very," he said. The sky was still and clear. It was that brief time each evening when the setting sun illuminated the snow tops of the mountains in the east, transforming them into sparkling white crowns atop the dark rock.

"Finish your letter?" he asked.

"I was telling them about the jump today," I said. "D'you think the censors will mind?"

He shrugged. "Nothing very secret about that."

I nodded. "I didn't think so either. What did you think of the jump?"

"It's what I came here to do," he said.

"What do you mean?"

"I mean where else can you do what we did today? It's the reason I joined up."

"You were called up," I said.

"I would have come anyway."

"You wanted this? You're nuts." I said and he smiled.

"You sound like my dad when I told him I was coming here and wasn't going to university."

"He was surprised?"

"More like shocked. He had to sit down."

"I think I'd rather be in university," I said.

He stretched out his legs and leaned back on the steps on his elbows. "Too bad I didn't know you then. You could have taken my place."

"Yeah, too bad. I would have taken it," I said.

He turned and looked at me. "You don't look like the pencil pusher type."

"I dunno … university sounds pretty good."

"Now you really sound like him."

"Is it true, about him being a professor?" I asked.

"For the last twenty-two years. And he's just like all the rest of them—thinks he knows everything. I had to get away from all that, it was making me crazy."

"Some of 'em are saying you made it up—about your dad, I mean."

"You mean Sasha," he said.

"Some of the others too."

"That's ok. They can think what they like."

"It's just hard to believe you'd come here if you didn't have to."

He laughed. "Just what dad said. You must have been listening to our little talks."

"He wanted you to get out of your service?"

"Of course. He said it's 'your duty to use your talents, not throw them away out there. There are other fools for that.'"

"So he thinks we're fools?"

"Sorry. He thinks anybody who doesn't see things his way is a fool. But he thinks I'm one too if that makes you feel better."

"It doesn't bother me," I said.

"We went for a long walk one afternoon, twice all the way around Zayeltsovsky Park, where we used to go when I was a kid. I think he was expecting me to thank him or something when he told me about the 'arrangements' he made for me. 'I've found you a substitute,' he told me."

"And you refused?"

"'I don't want your substitute' I told him. 'I'm going myself.'"

I couldn't think of anything to say.

"Like I said, he was shocked. You should have seen his face—it got bright red. That's when he said we were finished."

I remembered how Father had hugged me close at the train station and kissed me on the cheek.

I was trying to think of something to say but then Roman flung the barracks door open and sat down between us.

"Kolya," he said, putting two fingers to his lips—his usual signal that he wanted to "borrow" one of my smokes.

"I don't have any," I said and he looked at me and smiled.

"That is a lie—a lie—and you know it," he said. He reached into the pocket of my tunic and pulled out my smokes. I shrugged.

Roman lit up and the three of us spent those last few moments before bed retelling stories about the jump as the mountains in the east faded into the night.

CHAPTER 12

 ❧

There isn't much more to tell about my time in training camp. Along with parachute training, I learned to read a map and to use a compass, to use a radio and, of course, to use knives, pistols, rifles, heavy machine guns, grenade launchers and when necessary, my hands and feet. I liked the nine millimeter pistol and became quite a good shot with it. Sergeant Pryamilov even taught us the technique of throwing a sharpened spade. That wasn't officially part of our training, but he'd learned it from the *spetsnaz* during his last tour in Afghanistan and he liked to show off. He could bury the spade's steel tip into a wood target from fifteen paces every time.

"Aim for bone. Always aim for bone," he told us. "The skull, the breastbone, the neck. If a spade hits the belly, it just bounces off."

For me the worst part of training camp wasn't the training at all—it was the waiting for what would come next. Moscow issued duty orders twice yearly, at the end of March and again at the end of September, and I knew our orders were coming.

In September the days in the Fergana Valley grew shorter and the air cooler and at the end of that month, the orders finally came.

"The orders are here," Dima said one day before supper and we all gathered around him.

"Who says?" someone asked.

"When will they tell us?" someone else asked.

"Pryamilov was talking about it with the other sergeants," Dima said. "They'll tell us tomorrow."

"Good," Styopa said. "I'm going nuts in this place."

"It's good if you want trouble," Sasha said.

"You'd rather stay here?"

99

"I'd rather go home," Sasha said.

"Well, that's not going to happen," Oleg said.

"Who knows? The whole thing might be over in another month. The longer we stay here the better," Roman said.

"The war isn't going away next month," Max said.

"Sooner or later we go. It might as well be now," Oleg said.

"We might even like it there," Styopa said and then Sasha told him he should have his head checked.

"I mean it," Styopa said. "How bad can it be? We'll see something new. We'll get out of this place. Kolya, what do you say?"

They all turned and looked at me.

"Oh … well, I don't know," I said. "We're done with training. What else is there to do here?"

"Exactly right," Styopa said.

"Well, whatever happens, I'm staying close to Kolya," Sasha said. "His luck is the best."

"I'll be right there with you," Roman said.

~~~~

Early the next morning, Sergeant Pryamilov confirmed the rumor about the orders when he addressed us at formation. We would hear a long, windy speech at the political lecture that day about doing our duty, but it was the sergeant's few words that I remembered.

"I know you've heard about the orders. Nothing stays secret in this camp for long. Your orders are here and you leave this afternoon. Have your gear packed before dinner. When you get in country, remember your training—and don't think about going home."

After I finished packing that afternoon, I went out to the barracks steps for one last smoke and a look at the mountains. The wind had begun to blow across the valley floor from the east and the mountain tops were hidden in clouds. The air smelled like rain. Oleg came out and sat with me and for a while we watched the sheets of rain advance across the valley.

"This place hasn't been so bad," he said. "It could have been worse."

I felt a drop and we moved up under the barracks roof.

"We'll make it back, won't we? Back home, I mean?" I said.

"I think so. Most of us anyway. Just watch what you're doing."

Then I told him about Sergei. I'd been thinking a lot about him lately, and about Kaari and Mikhail Petrovich and the birds.

"Ummm ... bad luck for him," Oleg said.

"You think that's all it is—bad luck—just being in the wrong place?"

He squatted down on his haunches, his favorite stance when he wanted to relax. "Sure, what else could it be? There's no great ... there's no great purpose to all this. You don't believe that do you?"

"Do you?" I asked and he shrugged.

"What was the purpose of your friend getting himself blown up?"

"I didn't say he was blown up."

"Whatever it was that happened to him."

"I don't know. I guess I can't think of any," I said.

"Because there isn't. Nothing is ... arranged. It just isn't. It couldn't be."

Rain, like a gray curtain, was making its way toward us across the valley floor, hiding the mountains.

"Babulya said there's a purpose," I said.

"So, what'd she say about your friend?"

I hesitated. We were getting into things I never discussed outside the family. "It was pretty simple," I said.

"Ok, what was it?"

"There's a purpose in everything. We just don't know what it is yet," I said.

He smiled and leaned back against the barracks wall. "A convenient answer. There's a reason, but you can't tell me what it is."

"We don't know what it is," I said.

"What we're doing here is part of some plan, is that it?"

"I guess."

The rain shower reached the edge of the camp, drumming on the metal roofs.

"So, what's the plan for you?" Oleg said. "She told you didn't she? There must be one—if there's a plan for everything—right?" He pushed my shoulder and smiled.

"Maybe, I dunno," I said.

"Well, what'd she say?" he asked and I hesitated again.

"There's a plan for me," I said.

"Ok ... what is it?"

"I don't know yet. I'll find out one day."

He snorted. "Find out how? Voices talking to you, something like that?"

"I hope not."

"When?"

"She didn't tell me that, either."

He laughed. "Not much to go on, is it? You believe her?"

"Nothing's happened yet."

He stood up and stretched his legs. "Well what about me, what's my future, then?"

It was my turn to laugh. "Do I look like a fortune teller?"

Then the rain reached us and came down hard, driving us back inside with the others.

~~~~

The rain poured down for the rest of the day and soaked us as we stood in queues, loaded down with equipment, to board the An-12 transports that arrived after dinner to ferry us over the southern mountains to Afghanistan. Everyone was quiet. There was no ceremony or celebration. Officers and sergeants stood about in groups in their weather gear, slick and drooping with rain. Sergeant Pryamilov was there, but he said nothing more to us. He just watched as one after another, we climbed the steps to the transport and disappeared inside. I paused at the top step and took a last look at the camp through the drizzle and stepped through the door.

On board we stowed our gear and strapped in for the flight. Soon the four turbine-powered propellers of the Antonov were in motion, pulling us down the airstrip and then lifting us into the swirling air.

We were on our way.

Each of us was quiet as we climbed and bounced through the clouds. I knew this was one of those transforming times—like tearing through a veil into something hidden and unknown. I thought about my home and family, but then decided it was better not to think about anything at all. I tried to make myself comfortable to get some rest.

After a steep, bumpy climb, we broke through the clouds into clear sky. Sunlight streamed in through the small windows on the starboard side of the long fuselage. A short time later we leveled out in flight and some of the boys slept while others read newspapers or magazines or played cards. I dozed for a while until a voice woke me.

"I don't believe this!" someone said and then I felt a tap on my shoulder. Roman stuck his wristwatch in front of my face.

"It stopped," he said and he shoved the watch closer to me. "Look."

I looked at it. "You're right," I said. "It stopped. You woke me up to tell me that?"

"I wound it twice and—nothing."

"That's what happens to watches eventually, they stop," I said.

"Well, not this one, not yet. I just bought it before I reported. He guaranteed it for five years."

"Bought it where?" Sasha asked.

"A street vendor."

"If you told him you were about to report, then you are a fool," Sasha said. "He'd tell you anything. How much did you pay it?"

"Twenty rubles."

Sasha pulled Roman's wrist over for a closer look. "It's junk," he pronounced after examining it.

"It's not junk."

"It's cheap," Sasha said. "Anybody can see that."

Roman was shaking his wrist, trying to coax the device back to life. "Then he'll give me a new one," he said.

"Forget it," Sasha said. "You'll never see him again."

"Who was he?" Max asked.

"A Chechen, or maybe an Ingush, I don't know, one of those. He had a booth near Izmailovo Park. I'll find him."

"Only an idiot would buy from a Chechen," Sasha said.

"Only an idiot would buy from an Ingush," Max said.

Dima leaned over and spoke into Roman's ear. "I guess that makes you an idiot either way."

"You'll never see him again so don't worry about it," Sasha said and Roman turned to him.

"Don't keep saying that! It's bad luck," he said.

"I was just trying to make you feel better."

"Well, that won't do it."

"Relax," Sasha said. "I didn't mean it that way. You'll get the chance to go find him if that's what you really wanna do."

"Most of us probably won't fire a shot," Max said. "Who knows, they might even make you a cook. Who ever heard of a cook getting shot?" He punched Roman on the shoulder.

"A cook? Really?" Roman said. "You know, I like to cook."

"You can't cook," Sasha said.

"I can cook lots of things."

"Like what?"

"I … I'm really good with eggs. Anything you want with eggs in it."

"Eggs, huh?" Sasha said.

"I think you should be our cook," Oleg said.

"Maybe I will, maybe I'll ask for that," Roman said.

"You're perfect for it," Oleg went on. "I can see you now, charging up the mountains with your pots and pans." I smiled.

"Why would I do that?" Roman said. "We'll have transports."

"Oh, I don't think so, not for pots and pans," I said. "You'll have to carry those."

"No, I wouldn't," Roman said. "Why would I have to carry them?"

"I think we should say something to the officers about this," Dima said. "We should tell them we want Roman to do our cooking—Roman and nobody else."

104

"I think all of you need to keep your mouths shut and let me worry about it," Roman said. "If I wanna be a cook, I'll ask to be a cook. You're all laughing now, but eat rations for a month and you'll beg me to make you something. You wait."

"Well, what else can you make besides eggs. I don't like eggs," Oleg said.

"I can make *chuch-elle.*"

Oleg grimaced. "Too sweet and I'm not eating anything you can roll up and carry from your belt," he said.

"You know," Dima said. "If you're really good, the officers will want you for themselves. Think about it—maybe they'll post you to the embassy in Kabul."

"You think so?" Roman said.

"Who knows where this could lead—and all because you're good with eggs."

Everyone laughed, Roman too.

~~~~

Later we took turns at the windows. The plain far below stretched into the distance. Our ancestors had once roamed that ground in great mounted troops, creating an empire that was their legacy to us. And now it was our duty to defend it—or at least that's what they drilled into our heads day after day in the political lectures.

Styopa took a turn at the window after me. He squinted at the horizon in the west.

"There's a shimmer out there. There—see it?" He stepped away and I looked.

"No," I said and he stepped back and squinted again.

"All along there," he said, pointing. "It's water, just at the horizon."

I looked again. "I don't see anything."

"Your eyes aren't so good," he said.

"My eyes are fine, but I don't see any water out there," I said.

He looked again. "It is water. I'm sure it is. It's the Caspian Sea."

"Whatever it is, it isn't the Caspian Sea," I said.

"How do you know?"

"You're not too good with maps are you? Because that's hundreds of kilometers from here," I said.

"Well, how far can we see from up here?"

"I don't know, but it's not hundreds of kilometers."

He stared out the window and sighed. "You're probably right. I guess I hoped it was water. I've never even seen a big lake."

One of the flight crew came through the cabin. "The Oxus in five minutes," he said to us.

We were coming to a range of tall mountains which meant we would soon pass over the Oxus River—Amu Darya the Afghans called it—out of Soviet airspace and into the airspace of Afghanistan.

And then we crossed the great river which from that altitude was just a thin, brown line snaking along the ground. I did my best to look relaxed as the engines of the Antonov droned on outside in the clear, thin air taking us into alien country.

A few minutes later we approached another range of mountains, the Koh-i-Babas, rising up five thousand meters to form part of the mountainous spine of Afghanistan. The white peaks stretched away as far as I could see to the west.

"Very pretty," Dima said, taking a turn at the window.

"Not if you're down there on foot," I said.

"Maybe," he said, pursing his lips. "Others have done it. We can too."

At Fergana they had lectured us about the succession of armies that had come here: Alexander; then Asoka, king of India, who followed fifty years after Alexander; then Genghis Khan, fifteen hundred years after Asoka; and later still, Tamerlane and Baber, the first of the Moguls. The last before us were the British. None of them had stayed. Now it was our turn to try to tame this country.

After we passed over the highest peaks, the Antonov began a long, steady descent into Kabul, the capital, and we crowded around the windows. I expected a dark and forbidding place, but there were green valleys and fields laid out in squares with rows of crops, probably poppies and late wheat. Animals grazed in alpine pastures and when we came in close over the lower mountains, I saw open meadows, mulberry and tangerine groves and acacia, walnut and oak trees against a backdrop of white snow. The war, wherever it was, hadn't gotten here yet.

But as we came closer to Kabul, into lower country, the land turned to brown—brown hills, brown valleys and dust.

Our approach into Kabul International Airport, after two and a half hours of flight from Fergana, was smooth and undelayed and took us over the fortress of Bala Hisar. The old citadel had been built to guard the city against invaders, but now it sat silent on a hill top. Troops camped in its shadow.

The transport's wheels screeched when they touched the runway. In the months since leaving Kursk, I had thought often about this day, my first in country, and I expected there to be fighting and confusion all around. But after we taxied to a stop near the control tower and the pilot cut the engines, all was quiet. While the sun dropped behind the mountains in the west, we loaded onto a bus that took us to a barracks on the airport grounds for the night. Our escorts fed us a hot meal of something like porridge, showed us our beds and told us to sleep.

There was no war yet, just more waiting.

~~~~

The next morning they fed us again and took us to an assembly hall near the barracks to receive our postings to one of the four regiments of Airborne Forces deployed in country. Three regiments were in or near Kabul and the fourth was at Bagram airbase, north of Kabul at the foot of the Hindu Kush mountains.

A steady stream of officers came to the hall over the next hours and left with groups of recruits. Our training company stayed together, our gear strewn at our feet, and we watched the hall gradually empty. The airport was a busy place, filled with the sound of trucks, helicopters and more Antonovs landing and taking off.

"I think it'd be good to stay here," Sasha said.

"In this room?" someone asked.

"Here in Kabul. There're lots of our people here and I want to stay where there're lots of our people."

"Lots of us means lots of us to shoot at," Styopa said.

"It's as good a place as any," Sasha said.

"You don't know anything about this place," Styopa said.

"The bandits are in the mountains. I imagine that's where we'll be too, and soon," Oleg said.

"Well, the main thing is to stay together," Roman said.

"Don't count on that," Max said.

From what I saw of the selection process—if you could call it a process—I guessed Max was right. Most of the officers seemed to select people more or less at random. They would pick one recruit here and another there, sometimes consulting the lists, but just as often not.

All through the morning the officers came and went and then a little before noon, when the hall was nearly empty, a lone officer, a lieutenant, walked up to our group. He pushed up the visor of his field cap and put his hands on his hips.

"Well boys, welcome to Afghanistan. I hope it's everything you expected."

We snapped to attention.

"Good morning, Comrade Lieutenant," some of us said.

He held a wad of folded papers in his hand and from the top sheet he read off about twenty names, including mine. When he finished, it looked like Roman would get his wish because the lieutenant had called everyone in our little group from the Fergana barracks. We stepped forward and dressed ranks. After a quick inspection, the lieutenant looked satisfied with what he saw.

"I'm Lieutenant Martynov. Welcome to the 345th," he said. "Tonight you'll sleep at Bagram field, your new home. Now let's get going."

He pointed to the door. "Outside is a bus. Climb on and take a seat."

As I picked up my gear, I took a moment to study this officer. He looked much like the officers at Fergana—fit and suntanned—but he looked weary and his uniform was dusty and faded. He seemed a decent enough fellow, almost avuncular, and I thought maybe things here wouldn't be so bad after all.

With the lieutenant watching, we walked to the waiting bus and climbed on. A transport landed on the runway and all around us men and machines were on the move. The airstrip was surrounded by Airborne troops in sandbagged positions and in ASU-85 armored vehicles.

Lieutenant Martynov followed us onto the bus and took a seat behind the driver, next to a political officer who was reading papers on his lap. The political officer didn't look up at us. When we were all on board, the lieutenant nodded to the driver who put the bus into gear. We were on our way to Bagram, an airbase forty-five kilometers north of Kabul along the Salang Highway. The highway was the main north-south artery and it continued past the base, through the Salang Tunnel and into the Hindu Kush to Doshi, Pol-e-Khomri and points beyond.

Oleg and Dima sat in the seat behind the lieutenant. After a few minutes Oleg cleared his throat. "Comrade Lieutenant, may I ask a question?" he said.

The lieutenant turned his head. "Yes?"

"Why are we being bused? I mean, why not just fly into the airbase?" he said.

"Your flight was scheduled to arrive at Bagram," the lieutenant said. "But we had a little … ah … activity there yesterday and so they sent you here," he said.

"Activity?" Oleg said.

"Nothing to worry about," the lieutenant said. "And now you'll get a little tour of the countryside."

The bus pulled away from the airport, toward the west to pick up the Salang. Everyone was quiet. I was trying hard to concentrate, to accustom myself to the sights and sounds and smells of this place. I knew my survival depended on developing an instinct for what was around me—and doing it quickly.

"Think we'll go into the mountains today?" Sasha asked.

"Hope so," Styopa said. "Better to start right away."

Some of us nodded.

"Well, I hope we see some girls here in the city," Roman said. "It's been, what … four months?"

"Forget about it," Dima said. "It's forbidden for strangers to see their women. And you're definitely a stranger. They're covered in cloth. You won't see a thing."

"Is there room inside there for two?" Sasha said. He was grinning.

"Sure—for you and her and the knife she'd cut your throat with," Dima said.

"Just for looking?" Roman said. "They wouldn't do that."

"Wanna try?" Dima said.

"Styopa can go first," Roman said. He punched Styopa on the leg.

The bus moved along the Bibi Mahroo toward the center of Kabul. Our cities at home were laid out in good order with wide streets and sidewalks. Our people walked on the sidewalks and our vehicles obeyed the traffic laws, most of the time anyway. The streets here were wild confusion; people and vehicles—trucks, buses and swarms of brightly-colored, three-wheeled motor scooters—going in every direction. The words on the buildings and streets were written in bizarre, unreadable script. Dust was everywhere, blowing back and forth with the wind.

Near what looked like the city center, we passed an open market of ramshackle stalls leaning against a row of mud-colored buildings. People wearing garments like rags were selling goods and animals, alive and dead, while hundreds of others milled about in front of the stalls and in the street. Some of them watched us with sullen faces, but most ignored us.

On many of the street corners our troops watched the crowds from atop parked T-54 tanks, their rifles at the ready. The crowds seemed to ignore them too. In every direction the city was scarred by burned and crumbled buildings and dark holes blasted into walls and pavement.

"Still want to stay here?" Oleg asked Sasha.

Soon we passed through Pushtunistan Square, where the lieutenant pointed out the People's House Palace and the Kabul Hotel. Then, as we were turning onto the Shara Ra Road, a boy, maybe ten or eleven years old, ran out of the crowd and heaved a rock straight at Sasha. It bounced off the window with a loud crack, breaking the glass in a spider-web pattern. Sasha lurched back and swore.

"There he goes!" Roman yelled as the boy ducked back into the crowd.

Our driver stomped on his brakes and I slammed into the seat in front of me. The boy darted through the crowd and for a moment I lost sight of him. But then he had the bad luck to run straight into two soldiers walking in our direction. One caught him by the arm and started to drag him back toward us. Their uniforms showed they belonged to Marshal S. L. Sokolov's 40th Army. The boy twisted and thrashed, waving his arms. Then he reached up and scratched the soldier across his face and eyes. The soldier yelled but held his grip. He tossed his rifle to his companion and keeping a tight hold on the collar of the boy's tunic, unhooked his belt. Then he started to beat the boy across the shoulders and back. The companion stood back, pointing his rifle at the crowd that had formed in a circle around the struggling pair. People screamed at the soldiers in guttural, unintelligible words. The boy shrieked and the soldier threw him to the ground, striking him over his whole body with his belt and fists. A blow to the boy's face split his lip and blood splattered over his tunic. Then the companion yelled to him to stop. He landed one last solid blow and then stood over the boy, breathing in and out. The crowd watched him, their dark eyes and faces radiating hatred.

I looked around at the faces of my companions. Even Oleg was pale. When the two soldiers walked away, leaving the boy whimpering on the ground, the lieutenant rose from his seat and turned around to us.

"Like I said, welcome to Afghanistan."

From there we proceeded west onto the Karte Mamoorin which we followed for about a kilometer before we met up with the Salang Highway. We turned onto the highway and followed it north into open land. Low brown mountains became visible to the west and to the east. To the north were the peaks of the Hindu Kush.

After about five kilometers, the bus slowed and pulled off the highway onto a dirt path and Lieutenant Martynov stood up again and faced us.

"There's something we want to show you," he said.

We drove into a narrow valley, a cloud of dust trailing behind the bus. When we came around a rocky hill, the driver stomped on his brakes again.

"Everyone off and follow us," the lieutenant ordered. He and the political officer stepped out the door and set out at a quick pace around the hill. We jumped off and followed them, picking our way over rocks and between small boulders until we came to a massive column, more than sixty meters tall and a good ten meters around at its base, rising up from the valley floor. Then the political officer spoke to us.

"Alexander's soldiers built this," he said in a reedy-sounding voice. "Look at it, look closely."

I looked up.

It was built from rough mud bricks, but it was gracefully shaped and tapered inward near the top, and at its crown was detailed masonry that looked like sculpted stone. It towered over us, stark against the blue sky. It was magnificent.

"This has stood here for twenty-three centuries," the political officer continued. "The Greeks built it to proclaim to anyone who should ever pass by that they had been here."

I moved slowly around the column's base, inspecting it from every angle. How they could have built this was a mystery because there wasn't so much as a twig or branch for ladders and scaffolds. The political officer must have been reading my thoughts.

"Their journals tell us they built it by piling up mounds of dirt, higher and higher as they went," he said. "When they reached the top, they cleared away the dirt, leaving what you see."

We took photos of the column and of each other standing next to it. I tried to imagine the men who had labored on this. I tried to imagine them camped here. What sustained them in this emptiness, so far from home?

"For all their glory and might, this is all they left behind," the political officer said. He looked around at us. "You will be different. What you leave here will endure. You will change these peoples' hearts and minds."

His eyes were wide as he spoke and his voice cracked once. Lieutenant Martynov stood behind him saying nothing, his hands in his pockets, poking at rocks on the ground with the toe of his boot.

Back out on the Salang, our bus joined up with a convoy of trucks and continued north. At the lead and rear of the convoy were

six-wheeled BTR-60 PB vehicles, each looking like an armored bee-
tle, manned by rifle troops from the 40th Army. An Mi-24 gunship,
bristling with rotary cannon and side pods of 57 millimeter rockets,
escorted us overhead. It prowled up and down the convoy.

As we journeyed farther from Kabul, the hills became higher and
steeper and the highway twisted through gorges whose rocky sides
sometimes shot up almost vertically. We'd learned at Fergana that
places like this were perfect for the bandits' ambush tactics. First they
would knock out the lead and rear escort vehicles with mines or rockets, and then they'd rain machine gun and mortar fire down on the rest
of the convoy trapped in between. I took comfort from the gunship
escort. It would be suicide to strike at a convoy with a gunship nearby.

Continuing north, we passed waves of refugees coming down
from the mountains toward the border with Pakistan in the south.
They led animals pulling carts loaded down with children, old people and bundles of belongings. Many were bent over by bundles they
carried on their backs. The animals looked lean and tough, like the
people, and there was always a sinewy, predatory-looking dog or two
following along. Some of the children were missing limbs, usually a
forearm or a leg below the knee. They ignored us as we passed, but
twice, when our jets flew low overhead, they paused to watch them
disappear over the hills. Then they resumed their march, their heads
down. The lieutenant stared ahead, his arms folded across his chest,
while the political officer read over more papers from his carrying
case.

Later we came to a place where a stream emptied into a clear pool
beside a stand of oak trees set back from the road. An Afghan family
sat on the ground in a circle near the pool, talking and eating a meal,
an old man with a long beard stretched out on his back beside them.
Parked nearby was a BTM vehicle. Its crew was out leaning against the
armor plating, smoking and talking.

The spires of rock and ice of the Hindu Kush loomed behind.

"Are the Urals like that?" I asked Max.

He shook his head. "Nothing like that."

The lieutenant turned around in his seat. "They're beautiful like
poison flowers," he said.

"Are there rebels in this area, Comrade Lieutenant?" Sasha asked.

The political officer looked up from his papers. "They're bandits—*dushmani*—not rebels," he said.

The lieutenant laughed. "You've been watching them along the road," he said.

"Really? Which ones?" Sasha said.

The lieutenant gave him a tired smile. "If I knew that, I'd be a general. We're dealing with a ghost army here—get used to that. A few are full-time fighters, but most just fight for a time and then go home and raise their crops and come back the next year and fight us again. Some do it for extra money. They've been watching you."

"We should arrest them," Sasha said.

"Arrest who exactly?" the lieutenant said.

"I don't know, all of them."

"Our jails aren't that big."

"Then we just let them go?" Oleg asked, rather too pointedly I thought, but the lieutenant didn't seem to mind his tone.

"Look at them," he said, nodding toward the windows. "If we find a village giving aid, we destroy it. That works pretty well, better than trying to arrest the whole country."

"And the ones who fight back?" Oleg asked.

"Well, we kill them, if we can find them. The rest melt into the hills. There aren't many battles here, just quick jabs and the fight's over. The trick is to feel when the punch is coming, get ready for it, and punch back, harder."

"Sounds like boxing," Max said.

"Boxing is a sport," the lieutenant said.

"Where are they going, Comrade Lieutenant?" I asked about another group along the roadside.

"Hard to say," he said. "Some of them imagine things will be easier in Kabul or Pakistan, poor fools. Some keep on the move to smuggle."

"Smuggle what?" Oleg asked.

"Weapons, anything they can steal from us, or opium."

"And we permit this?" Oleg said.

"The weapons we confiscate. The opium? Well, if it isn't being shot at us or it won't blow us up, we don't bother too much with it."

He nodded again toward the windows.

"You'll get to know these ghosts soon enough. They come from places like that," he said as we passed the remains of a village, a *kish-lak*. Its fields had once been terraced up a hillside, but now there were holes blown in the earthen bulwarks. Most of the huts were ruined, either missing walls or a roof, and their doors hung open, exposing empty interiors.

"If they can't eat, they can't fight," the lieutenant said. "So we've started hitting their fields. Other than the trouble around the base yesterday, this sector has been quiet lately. Most of the real troublemakers have moved on. Let's hope it stays that way."

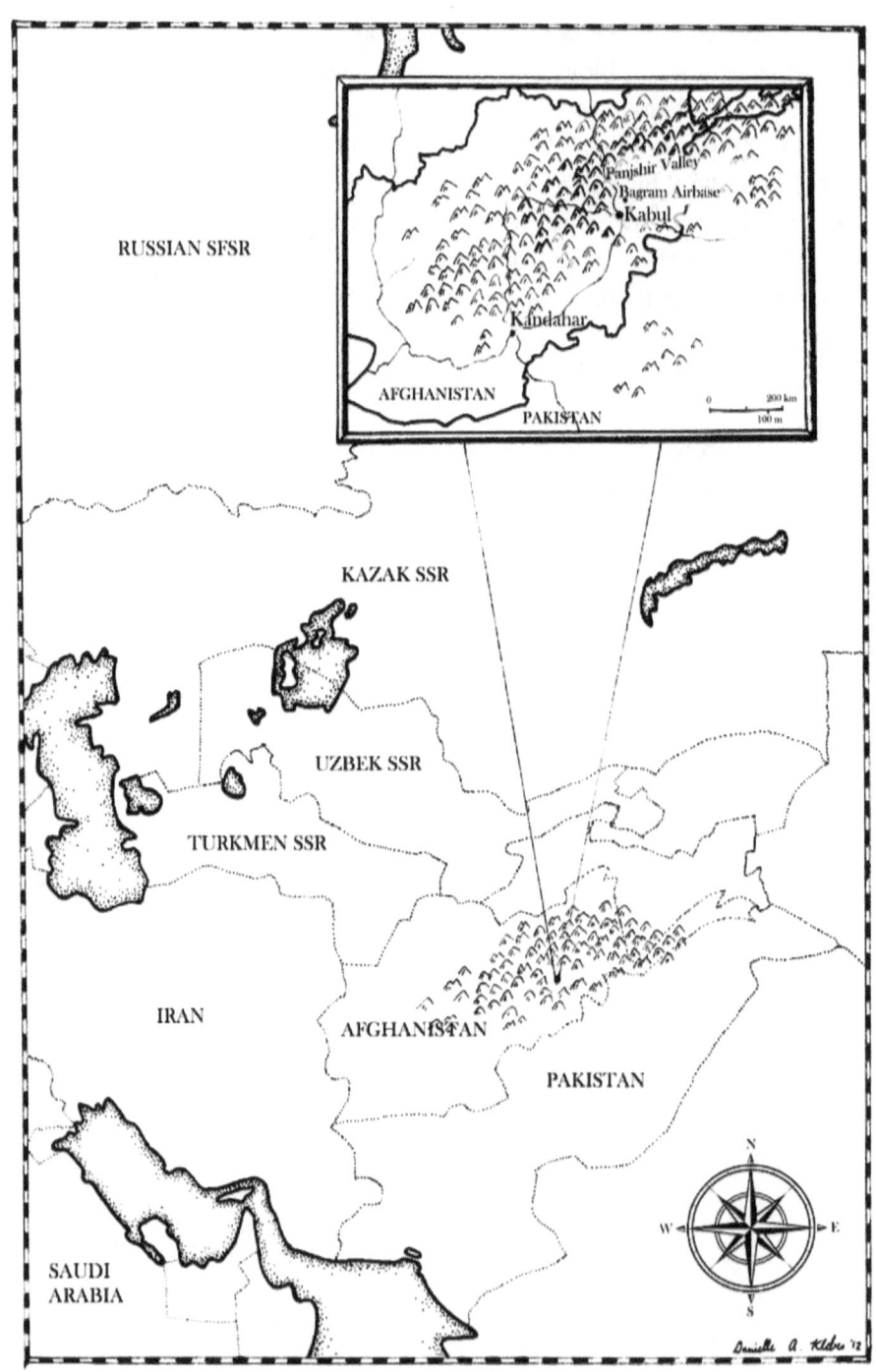

RUSSIAN SFSR

Panjshir Valley
Bagram Airbase
Kabul

Kandahar

AFGHANISTAN
PAKISTAN

0   200 km
100 m

KAZAK SSR

UZBEK SSR

TURKMEN SSR

IRAN

AFGHANISTAN

PAKISTAN

SAUDI
ARABIA

N
W   E
S

Danielle A. Kidrs '12

CHAPTER 13

❧

*T*hree weeks later I woke in the morning chill on the day of my first mission into the mountains. I'd slept little and my mouth tasted sour. I rolled out of bed and pulled on my coveralls. They'd been new and fresh when they were issued to me but now they were sweat-stained and dusty. Anyone who has been to Bagram remembers the dust. The dust in Kabul is bad, but it's nothing like the dust at Bagram. It blows in constantly from the Shomali plain and covers everything—buildings, tents, trucks, aircraft, uniforms—giving the whole camp a lunar look.

The Shomali lies at more than two thousand meters elevation and it rises up on its edges to meet the foothills of the Hindu Kush. It is furnace hot in summer and bone-numbing cold in winter.

The new day revealed the still-sleeping base outside my window. There were rows of parked bombers—TU-16s and SU-24s—and beyond the bombers, MiG-21 fighters, Mi-6 heavy transports, Mi-8 light transports and camouflage-daubed Mi-24 gunships. The machines were sleeping now, tethered to the ground, but soon they'd awaken for another day and another flight into the mountains.

Our barracks was at the center of the base, well inside the perimeter wire, about two hundred meters from the front gate. But that gave us little comfort because the bandits were becoming proficient with the 82 millimeter mortar which had a range with accuracy of up to three kilometers. One of those rounds on the barracks at night and we'd never know what hit us.

When we got to Bagram, Lieutenant Martynov gave us our platoon assignments. Oleg, Styopa, Roman and I went to first platoon which was returning from a mission. Our new comrades were just boys like us, but they had an air about them. They spilled out of their transports, dirty and tired-looking, and dragged themselves into the barracks without a word to us.

Dima, Max and Sasha went to second platoon where Dima and Sasha were told they were the new minesweepers.

To my thinking, the minesweeper was the key soldier in the platoon. Ask any *Afghantza* what he remembers about Afghanistan—other than the dust and fatigue—and he'll tell you about mines. They were in the mountains, in the valleys, around villages, even laid out in a perimeter around Bagram to seal us in. The bandits used whatever they could get their hands on, big Italian mines that could blow apart an armored vehicle and little English mines made to maim, not kill, because a maimed soldier is a greater drain on resources than a dead one. They were so much a part of our life that in no time I acquired the distinctive *Afghantza* walk—head down, eyes focused on the ground ahead, alert for telltale signs of disturbed earth or a suspicious-looking mound.

Without a minesweeper along to clear the way, a whole company could be paralyzed in the field, every soldier frozen in his tracks, fearing his next step might mean a foot or a leg gone, or worse. The minesweepers often paid the price for everyone. The week before we arrived, a sweeper from second platoon was blown to pieces disarming an anti-tank mine outside the base.

Dima was patient and careful and he was a good choice for the exacting work of locating and disarming the beastly devices. I wasn't so sure about Sasha.

"What do you think about when you're taking one of those things apart?" I asked Dima.

"Nothing," he said. "If you start to think about things, you start to worry and if you worry you make mistakes."

Later, I understood that because there were times out there when my mind just shut off, like when bullets were chipping at the rocks and ground around me, and I acted purely on instinct.

As the light outside my window increased, I made up my bed, which the regulations required us to do every day. The regulations were very specific about making up the beds, about how the corners should look and how the blanket should lay on top. The beds were inspected every morning and woe to anyone who didn't comply with the regulations. Styopa was awake and dressed and making up his bed, but he was doing a poor job of it. There were lumps on the top and the corners were round and slack.

"Styopa," I whispered. "Do it right."

He looked at my bed and then at his and started over again.

Our company sergeant, Gleb Kuznetsov, checked the barracks every day and threatened punishment duty to anyone who didn't keep his personal effects and bed area in good order. Some of the veteran boys called him a weasel, but he didn't put too many of us on punishment detail and he went into the mountains as often as any of us. The sergeants in some of the companies were always harassing their people with stiff punishments for petty infractions and some were expert at making excuses for not going on missions into the mountains. Yes, we were better off than most companies, but it wasn't good to push Kuznetsov too far; this bed-making business was a nuisance but regulations were regulations.

"All right, there," Styopa said when he finished. This time the job was better, but it bothered me that sometimes he was so careless.

Oleg and Roman were already sitting at our table outside the barracks and one of the boys from the kitchen detail was putting out our usual breakfast of bread, canned meat and tea. The sun was coming up and the veteran boys were still sleeping, one of their many privileges.

"We'll go today," I said when I sat down.

The weather was getting colder and there weren't as many missions as in summer, but I was sure we'd see action before the winter lull in the fighting. Sergeant Kuznetsov had told us twice to get ready for the mountains, but each time the mission was scrubbed at the last minute.

"Been talking with Kuznetsov this morning, have you?" Oleg said.

"I just think it's today."

"You sound like you're happy about it," Roman said. He poured tea for us and passed around the bread.

"Kuznetsov'll play with your mind," Styopa said.

"I haven't heard anything," I said. "Just a feeling."

"Another one of your feelings," Roman said.

"A good one or a bad one?" Styopa said.

I shrugged.

"It's a bad one," Roman said.

"I didn't say that," I said.

"You didn't have to. This is going to be a bad day. I can feel it already, a baaad day," he said.

"I didn't say that," I said. "But here, maybe this'll help." I put a package of chocolate in front of Roman. "From Deda, yesterday."

He grinned and snatched it up and tore open the wrapping. "Thank you, Deda," he said as he took a bite.

"We'll all thank him one day—in person," Oleg said. "Now can I have some?"

"I hope you're right," Styopa said. "Sitting around here, it's worse than Fergana. Let's see the mountains."

"You sound like a tourist," Oleg said.

Roman washed his chocolate down with tea. He looked at his cup. "You know, last night I dreamed this would be beer. No, really I did," he said. Oleg rubbed his hair. "Why would I do that? I don't even like beer."

"Well, that's it," Styopa said.

"That's what?" Roman said.

"The proof."

"What are you talking about, what proof?"

"The proof your mind is gone. It was just a matter of time, but I didn't expect it so quick," Styopa said. Roman threw a piece of bread at him.

"It was real," Roman said. "As clear as we're sitting here."

"How'd it taste?" I asked.

"You don't want to know."

"What else is there to dream about?" Styopa said through a mouthful of chocolate and bread.

"Maybe it's a sign, a sign I'm about to get leave," Roman said.

"I don't follow that," I said.

"You won't get leave unless one of your parents is dead and maybe not even then," Oleg said.

"Don't say that."

Some of the veteran boys came out of the barracks and sat down at their table. They ignored us.

Styopa lowered his head and leaned closer. "Where is there to go on leave out here, anyway?" he said.

"Maybe Kabul," Roman said.

"Kabul's off limits—if you could even get there," Oleg said.

"I said 'maybe Kabul.'"

"Or maybe some kishlak. You'd have a fine time there, lots to do, lots of girls," Styopa said.

"They keep us here with nothing to do but drill and march and clean our weapons until we beg for a mission, that's what they're doing," Roman said. "Well, not me. If they want me to drill for the rest of the war, that's fine, I'll do it."

"You think that's the plan, do you?" Oleg asked.

"I do and it's working. Listen to all of you."

"So, what's the news from Moscow?" I asked. Roman had gotten a letter from his mother the day before.

He poured himself more tea. "Not much. First snow was last week. Dad has a cold and he's in a bad mood—but that's not news. And the papers are full of Andropov—the rumor is he's sick again."

"A waste of ink," Styopa said. "Another old man. How long will this one last?"

"Who do you think'll take over when he's gone?" Roman said.

"Somebody from Moscow for sure. Maybe somebody you know," Styopa said.

"That would be a good thing for you," Roman said.

"How's that?"

"A good job for me and you could be my driver."

"Thanks."

"Sure."

"That sweeper from second platoon …" Styopa said.

"What about him?" I said.

"I was just thinking. Sasha said he was good—clever and careful."

"I guess careful isn't enough."

"Think he ever knew it? I mean when it happened?" Roman said.

"He never knew a thing," Styopa said.

As the sun floated up, the base stretched itself awake. The transport and bomber crews were out on the tarmac, running through their preflight checks.

After breakfast Sergeant Kuznetsov came to the barracks and ordered us to assemble outside in thirty minutes with full field equipment.

"This is it. I told you," I said.

"So, Kolya, where are we going?" Styopa asked.

"For a little ride," I said.

As ordered, first platoon assembled outside the barracks. Lieutenant Martynov, our platoon commander, arrived with Sergeant Kuznetsov and Captain Narumov, our company commander. The captain carried a rolled-up map under his arm and his notes from the morning's briefing by the regiment's intelligence staff. We gathered around as he spread out the map.

"We have information that weapons are stored in these villages here and here," he said pointing to two spots on the map, many kilometers distant from the base.

"Today we'll deal with this one," he continued, pointing to the more distant village. "A motor-rifle unit will go in the front, here, and you'll hold these points here and here in the rear." He tapped two fingers on the map.

The lieutenant asked if there were any questions and one of the veteran boys asked about the rifle unit and about the bandits' strength.

"The rifle unit will be company strength. We have no reliable information about the bandits," the captain said.

"We assume the weapons will be guarded, that's all we can say," the lieutenant added.

The captain looked at his watch. "Transports will be ready in fifteen minutes. Anything else?"

As missions went, this one would be simple enough. Afghan informers had given us the information about the weapons and now our response would be swift and severe. We would go to this place with utmost speed, capture any equipment or supplies, and liquidate anyone who got in our way. There were no more questions.

"All right, then," the captain said. "Here we go."

~~~~

Aleksandr Sergeyevich Narumov, our captain, had made quite a first impression on me. On our first day, each of us "greens" was chosen by one of the veteran boys to do his chores—to be his personal slave really—yet another one of the veterans' many privileges. The veterans—the *deds*—used us to do anything they didn't feel like doing themselves. We fetched their tea, mended their clothes, pulled their guard details, cleaned their rifles, cleaned the barracks, washed out the toilets, anything at all, we did it with no questions. We didn't dare ask questions because this system of servitude—*dedovschina* it was called—existed in every unit in the 40th Army and in most *decantniki* units. Anyone who bucked it had a good chance of ending up in hospital. In some units the abuse on the greens was so bad, beatings with belts and shovels and more, that some finally killed themselves to escape it.

My *ded*, Gleb Golovin from Kiev, picked me out as soon as I got off the bus from Kabul. I started immediately in his service, mending a torn tunic, before I even put away my gear. I took the bunk between him and Alex Trostorff, a veteran from Minsk. I told myself to just follow along, do whatever Golovin told me to do, and take whatever came my way.

As bad as it gets, I can take it.

But the next day, after morning exercises, Sergeant Kuznetsov appeared at the barracks door.

"Attention!" he yelled and we dropped what we were doing and stood rigid beside our beds, eyes forward. In the instant before I came to attention, I saw an officer, a captain, standing beside the sergeant.

The captain came in and walked the length of the room, then turned and walked back to the door, looking at each of us. Then he went and stood in the middle of the room.

"You older ones know what I'm going to say," he said. "But I think it's useful to repeat it, for the new people and to make sure nobody has … forgotten anything."

He resumed walking up and down the room as he spoke.

"You know what's expected of you in this company, don't you?" he asked and for an instant I thought he wanted an answer. But none of the veteran boys uttered a sound.

The captain waited a moment.

"Well, I'll tell you. You're expected to do two things, just two. You're expected to do what you're told and you're expected to make me look good."

He stopped in front of Vadim Yanov, one of the toughest-looking veterans. Yanov's bed was directly across from mine.

"Now, I understand how things are," the captain continued. "You older ones have been here and done your duty and you have your privileges, I understand that."

His face was maybe half a meter away from Yanov's. Yanov stood at attention, staring straight ahead. The captain kept talking, in a voice loud enough for us all to hear.

"But remember this. If any of my new people have … accidents, if anybody can't report for duty, that makes me look bad."

None of us said a word. The captain paused and then stepped away from Yanov.

"And if somebody makes me look bad, I will find out who is responsible. And he will regret it."

He paused again.

"Now … is this clear?" he asked and this time I knew he wanted an answer.

"Yes Comrade Captain!" we all bellowed together.

"Good," he said. He looked again at Yanov, square in the face, and then he walked out with the sergeant in tow.

As soon as he was gone Yanov swore and kicked his locker. "One day …" he said.

Trostorff laughed and threw a shirt at him. "One day, what?" he said.

Yanov swore again and let out a long, vile stream of insults about the captain.

"Yeah?" Trostorff said. "Well go ahead, do something about it."

Yanov threw the shirt back and then snatched up a towel and went out the door toward the showers.

"A long cold one," Trostorff yelled. He laughed again. Most of the other veterans were laughing too.

"Who was that?" I said.

Trostorff and Golovin looked at each other. "Fool, don't you know your company commander?" Golovin said.

"I just got here," I said.

"Captain Narumov," Golovin said. "He's the law around here, and you'd better remember it."

"What was that all about with Yanov?" I said.

Trostorff was squatted down, sorting out his locker. "Oh, last year a green was out for a month, a broken leg," he said. "He never would say who did it, but ... I guess the captain has his ideas."

"Did he do it?" I asked—before I could catch myself.

"Did who do what?" Golovin said.

"Forget it," I said. "Anyway, Yanov didn't look too happy. Maybe the captain should watch his back." I'd heard stories about veterans bullying and even beating up officers.

Trostorff and Golovin looked at each other again and laughed, loudly.

"Man, I'd pay money to see Yanov try," Trostorff said. "The whole base would turn out for that."

"Just listen and keep your mouth shut," Golovin said.

Trostorff shut his locker and stood up. "The captain's on his second tour here and in between he was at Fergana. I was there with him. He was better than the instructors in hand-to-hand."

"Get it?" Golovin said.

"Yeah," I said. "I get it."

"Well, but that's just half of it," Trostorff said. "His father's a general."

"A general, what kind of general?" I said.

"Oh, you know," Golovin said. "The kind with lots of medals—what are you, an idiot?"

"And not just any general," Trostorff said. "Ever heard of S. G. Narumov? He commanded the Trans-Baikal district and now he's commander of soviet forces in Germany."

"Even the base commander is polite to the captain," Golovin said.

"So, do us all a favor," Trostorff said. "If the captain tells you to do something, do exactly what he tells you."

"Ok, ok," I said. "I get it."

~~~~

The rotors of the two Mi-8 transports were whirling as we loaded on, ten of us in each one. We lifted off with two gunship escorts and headed northwest, flying just high enough to avoid small arms fire. American missiles weren't usually a problem in those early days of the war.

We flew swiftly, following the valleys, bobbing up and over the ridges. There were no landmarks in this country, only more red-brown hills whose rocky sides and summits rose up higher as we went north. Twice we passed over the remains of villages, now empty and abandoned.

In this mountain war our tactics were simple: get to the highest ground and get there first. It was the only way to fight and win out here. The British, in their Afghan wars, called it "cresting the heights"—only they didn't have transports to carry them up to the high spots. They walked up and then they walked back down when the fighting was over. They fought three wars here and I can tell you from my time in those mountains that they didn't lose their empire because they lacked for good soldiers.

More landscape passed below and then, about forty minutes after we lifted off, Sergeant Kuznetsov gave the signal. I checked my equipment again and tightened the chinstrap of my bush hat.

The transports dropped down and I saw a village in a narrow valley. Approaching from the south, along the valley floor, was a column of rifle troops riding in trucks and in four BTR-70 armored vehicles. People were running out of the village in every direction.

Two hills rose up behind the village. A side valley leading deeper into the mountains separated the hills. Our transports paused for a moment, well back from the hills, and a yellow flash erupted from a rocket pod on one of the gunships, followed by an explosion on the nearest hilltop. The rotary cannon from the other gunship opened up and chewed the other hilltop, sending up plumes of dust and rock. Then the transports swooped down, one landing on each hilltop. Kuznetsov was on his feet, yelling for us to get out. I was second out the door, behind Golovin, and when my *kimris* hit the ground, I lunged for the first cover I saw, a pile of rocks twenty or thirty meters away at the rim. Golovin was maybe two paces ahead of me. When I reached the rock pile, I threw myself stomach first onto the ground. I winced from a stone that found its mark between two of my ribs. I pushed my bush hat up and saw I had a clear view down to the village. The nearest higher ground was behind us, easily a kilometer away, and that was good—no small arms fire from that direction.

Oleg, Styopa, Roman and the others were prone on the ground to my left in a line along the rim of the hilltop. The transport on the other hilltop finished offloading its people and we watched it lift off. Then our transport lifted off too. The landing had taken about forty seconds. My ribs ached but excitement and energy flowed through me.

Sergeant Kuznetsov gave us the signal to dig in.

Down below there was panic and confusion. Our squad and the boys on the other hilltop were positioned behind the village to pre-vent escape westward into the mountains. Then one of the gunships came in low over the open ground at the north end of the village and dropped hundreds of PMF-1 "butterfly" mines. The mines twirled to the ground on their little green plastic wings, like sycamore seeds, landing in clusters. They created an instant minefield and blocked any escape in that direction. The villagers were trapped as the rifle troop column rumbled closer from the southeast.

"Get ready," Kuznetsov called out.

Golovin turned toward me. "They'll try this way first," he said.

I raised my rifle and sighted toward the open ground between our hill and the village. Then it was just as Golovin predicted—there was no escape to the south or east, or through the mines, and so about twenty villagers came running in a mass in our direction, toward the side valley and the mountains beyond. The boys on the other hill started firing at the ground in front of them. Some aimed higher and two villagers dropped. One looked dead, but the other clutched his side and rolled back and forth. The boys on my hill were firing too. I let off two bursts, but my aim was high, well over the villagers' heads.

The gunships circled overhead and the villagers turned and ran in the opposite direction, toward the east. The firing from our line and from the other hilltop stopped. Smoke from our rifles drifted up and the last of my spent casings fell, clinking on the rocks. My ribs throbbed.

"Kolya," someone called out. I turned and there was Oleg, several meters away on his belly. "Ok?" he asked.

"Ok," I said. I counted ten or twelve spent casings. I didn't think I had fired that many. A wind blew down from the mountains, pushing away the smoke. I realized for the first time the air was cold, much colder than at Bagram.

"Did you shoot?" I asked Oleg.

"I missed," he said.

"Me too."

The rifle troops rounded up the villagers and put them on the ground beside a stone house. The gunships stopped circling and withdrew to hover and watch from about one hundred meters away. One of the gunships hovered slightly below and behind the other to give flank protection.

Two old villagers were brought forward to speak with two rifle troop officers. A fast-moving stream, coming down from the mountains, ran past the village. The water had piled up stones, large and small ones, along the banks. The stones were worn smooth by the water and baked white by the sun. The sun was shining and the water sparkled as it ran past the stones.

One of the officers sat down on a stone near the stream and questioned the two villagers through an interpreter. They looked like headmen—members of the village *jirgah*. I couldn't hear what they were saying, but one of the headmen was waving his arms and shaking his head as he spoke. The officer kept his seat on the stone. The headman talked for several more minutes and then the officer rose from the stone, drew his pistol and shot him. The weapon jumped in his hand from the recoil and an instant later the sharp report reached us on the hilltop. The headman dropped backward.

"Agahh," I muttered. Up and down our line everyone was staring at this scene. Golovin looked over his shoulder at me.

"He could have told us and saved himself," he said.

The other headman looked down at the corpse and then back at the officer who had sat back down on the stone, his pistol still in hand. The interpreter spoke again to the surviving headman who then pointed toward a clump of trees on the other side of the stream.

Another gust of cold wind blew down from behind us, from the higher ground. I took another look—a longer one this time—over my shoulder. Even though the higher ground was a kilometer or more distant, a missile could reach us with no trouble. Those were the worst because there was no warning, no way to prepare. You heard a streak and an instant later it hit. You were either lucky to be out of its way or you weren't.

But the high ground still looked empty.

The boys on our line were beginning to relax. I checked my rifle and sat up to get a better look at the goings-on down below. I wanted a smoke but when I reached into my pocket I found I'd forgotten to bring any. Then Sergeant Kuznetsov came down the line, checking on us. My chest still ached, but I didn't mention it to him.

"How many rounds?" he asked me.

"About twelve, I think."

"Too many. Remember, short bursts."

"I will," I said, but he had already moved on.

Down below, a squad of rifle troops with dogs was moving house to house, searching for weapons and supplies, while the villagers huddled together on the ground. Even their children were quiet. The officer on the stone holstered his pistol and a moment later two minesweepers came forward at a run, each one carrying his listening equipment—earphones and a long pole with a flat metal disc attached at one end. They stopped to adjust their earphones and then started on the far bank of the stream, walking slowly toward the trees, passing their discs back and forth over the ground in front of them as they advanced. The gunships hovered a safe distance away. Golovin propped his rifle against a rock and sat up.

"If that's where the stuff is, there'll be traps around it. Sometimes there's nothing but traps. Their idea of fun," he said.

Half an hour later the sweepers reached the trees and then started to check the surrounding ground, passing their equipment back and forth over the whole area. The officers stood well back, on the other side of the stream. The gunship rotors made the only noise.

Then one of the sweepers raised his arm up and he marked the spot with a pinch of red powder from a pouch on his belt. He moved on. A moment later he signaled again and marked another spot about two meters from the first mark.

When they finished checking around the trees the first sweeper took off his headphones and knelt beside his first mark. He slowly brushed away dirt and pebbles with his hands.

I thought about Dima and Sasha.

The sweeper worked slowly, brushing away more dirt with his open hands, until he exposed something metal. It shone in the sunlight.

"Golovin, Krepko, come with me," Kuznetsov shouted and Golovin and Oleg jumped up. When we landed three of our boys set up a line of fire at the back of our hilltop to protect our rear. Kuznetsov put Golovin and Oleg alongside them.

Maybe he too was uneasy about the high ground.

With our rear strengthened we had an even circular perimeter. Down below, the sweeper was still on his hands and knees, moving dirt away, digging out a small crater around the mine. Everyone was quiet as cold wind blew down from the mountains. The rifle troops and their dogs continued their search of the village but so far, nothing—no weapons, no supplies and no bandits—just mud and stone houses and terrified people. Styopa stretched out next to me and laid his rifle down.

"What do you bet there's nothing here," he said. "They got us all the way out here just to play with us."

He might have been right, but it made no difference because if there was any chance there might be weapons out here, especially rockets, we had to check. I rubbed my ribs again and started to relax.

Then there was a blast from down below.

Styopa rolled onto his stomach and grabbed his rifle. My body was taut again. I raised my rifle to my cheek, sighted toward the village. I looked toward the trees, expecting to see the sweeper's body on the ground, but the blast hadn't come from there. The sweeper was still on his knees, patiently at work on the exposed device in front of him.

Smoke was clearing in the butterfly field at the north end of the village. Kuznetsov crouched beside me, looking through his field glasses at a man on the ground in the middle of the field, gripping what was left of his right foot.

"The fool," Kuznetsov said. "He'll never get out of there."

A donkey stood on the far side of the field, braying loudly. The man on the ground must have gone into the field to stop the animal from wandering in. It was a crazy thing to do because nobody in his right mind would try to pick his way through a butterfly field. You just can't do it.

Then another butterfly mine exploded and when the smoke cleared the man lay still. Two rifle soldiers walked up to the edge of the field, but they didn't go in. A gunship circled over the body, hovering like a giant inquisitive insect. One of the soldiers threw a rock, hitting the body. When it didn't move, they walked back to the village.

The sweeper kept at his task, never once looking up. A few minutes later, he rose to his feet with the mine in his hands and carried it slowly to a boulder about fifty meters beyond the trees, away from the village. He laid it on the ground behind the boulder.

"Now he'll check for another one," Kuznetsov said. "Sometimes they put a shell or another mine underneath the first one to boost the blast. If there's a another one down there we might have found something."

The sweeper was back at his little crater and in another few minutes he pulled a mortar shell from the hole. Everyone was watching, but he seemed oblivious to us. He placed the shell alongside the mine behind the boulder and then he went to work on the second dye mark. Half an hour later, it too yielded a mine boosted by a mortar shell.

"Now we'll see what sort of fish we've caught," Kuznetsov said.

With the second mine and mortar shell safely behind the boulder, the officer with the pistol crossed the stream and inspected the two craters. He directed a squad of soldiers with spades to dig a big circular pit around them. The soldiers started digging. The body in the butterfly field lay still in the sun.

When the pit was about two meters deep, the officer with the pistol jumped down for a closer inspection. Then he jumped back out and the digging continued. In another hour six crates of URAGAN rocket launchers were lifted from the earth. They were our own weapons, buried here to await the right opportunity to be used against us.

The rifle troops loaded the crates onto their trucks and then one of the gunships turned its rotary cannon on the mines and mortar shells behind the boulder. They exploded with a roar and a cloud of dust.

The mission was a success.

As the rifle troops remounted their vehicles, our transports returned and collected us from the hilltops. The villagers remained together on the ground, clinging to each other. But today we just packed up and left.

I sat next to Golovin on the trip back to the base. "That's strange," he said. "If we find something we always destroy the village—always."

"Maybe the headman was enough," I said.

"Maybe."

"What else could it be?" I said.

He shook his head. "Doesn't make any sense. I guess somebody just felt bighearted today."

CHAPTER 14

❧

*T*here were fewer missions in the winter because on most days a low ceiling of leaden clouds hid the mountains and grounded our flights. In the late afternoons, as night came, the wind picked up from the northwest, stirring up little swirls of dust which would appear around us suddenly and then vanish like dancing apparitions. The wind blew steadily most nights during that first winter at Bagram. A loose piece of stripping on the wall outside my barracks window flapped back and forth and sometimes late at night I listened to the flapping and imagined it was tapping out tunes I remembered from my youth.

Most of the bandits had gone back to their villages or south to winter camps in the hills toward Pakistan. We spent our days at the base marching and drilling and killing time and then marching and drilling again and then servicing our weapons and then more marching and drilling while we waited for spring and the offensives we knew would begin when the warmer weather arrived. There had been spring offensives every year since the war began, sometimes over the same ground as the year before, and we knew this spring would be no different.

Then, in March, the winter quiet in our sector ended with the suddenness of a slap to the face when the bandits ambushed and wiped out a fuel convoy on its way back to Bagram from the north. The attack hit just south of the Salang Tunnel, near Charikar, at a spot where the highway coils back on itself giving a fine 270 degree field of fire from the rock mound jutting out between the coils. Convoy raids were nothing new, of course, but this one was different. It struck a nerve with us because it hit so close to the tunnel and we all knew the logistical nightmare we would face if we ever lost the tunnel. Without it, our supplies and equipment too heavy to move south over the mountains by air would have to move through Herat, nearly six hundred kilometers to the west, and then through Kandahar. The delays and trouble would be horrendous.

But there was a more personal reason for our interest in this particular raid. One of Oleg's pals at the base, a boy attached to one of the bomber crews from Tartu, was on the convoy, returning from a trip to Doshi to pick up salvaged aircraft parts. Lucky for him that in the first few minutes of the ambush a bullet clipped the back of his neck and he bled enough to look convincingly dead.

"We didn't have escorts," he told us later. "I had a bad feeling about that."

"Whoever sent you out without gunships should be ordered onto the next convoy," Oleg said.

"In the lead vehicle," Golovin said.

"How many were there?" I asked.

"I don't know. I remember a blast when the first rocket hit, then mortars and machine guns opened up. It didn't last long and then they came in checking the bodies, going through pockets. They're all thieves, you know. They found two others playing dead, like me. Those boys cried and begged. The bandits talked and one of them laughed and then they shot them—right there on the ground." His voice was husky and then it cracked.

I pictured the scene and shuddered. Boys like us—crying, begging, dying.

"You think about that," he croaked. "Laying there, waiting for them to get to you next. What do you do? Just wait for your turn? I thought about jumping up and helping the others, but I didn't. I just laid there."

We cursed the bandits and swore to get even. And then, as if the officers had been listening to our brave-sounding barracks talk, we got our chance. The intelligence officers at the base wanted to know who was responsible. They wanted to know if the bandits from the Panjshir Valley had done this because they'd been waiting for another outbreak of trouble from those devils. They wanted to know if this was the start of it. And so our company was ordered to send out night patrols around Charikar beginning in the second week in March. Our orders were to locate them. After that, our bombers and gunships would do the rest.

For three nights we ventured out into the cold darkness, but found nothing. And then, on the fourth night, our luck changed. The clouds rolled away revealing a moon that lit up the landscape and in no time at all, we found the bandits.

Or rather, they found us.

We walked straight into an ambush. There was a quick, nasty fight and Roman took a wound in the upper arm. He lost so much blood that by the time we got him into the transport, he was barely conscious. The medic told us the bullet probably nicked the artery and if we'd stayed in the field another five minutes, he would have bled to death. But he was lucky—we got him back to the base in time.

Later, when he'd recovered enough to have visitors, I went with Oleg and Styopa to see him in hospital. We got there at the start of visiting hours and found an orderly sitting at a desk inside the front door. The orderly looked up at us from his paperwork.

"Who?" he said.

"Davidov, Roman," Oleg said.

He glanced through his papers and then looked up and shook his head. "Sorry, he died," he said and then he leaned back over his desk.

The three of us looked at each other.

I was stunned. NO, no, no! How can this be? And how can he sit there and just say that to us—like it means nothing to him?!

"Dead, no no," Styopa said. "Roman Davidov, from Moscow. He can't be, he was ok yesterday, getting better."

The orderly leaned back in his chair. "I'm sorry. He died," he said.

Styopa leaned over the desk. "But that's impossible! Look again, find out what happened."

The orderly sat forward into Styopa's face. "Impossible—impossible?" he said. "What are you talking about, don't be stupid. People die out here all the time."

Styopa slammed his fist down on the desk and the paperwork jumped. "That's right, they do. They go out on missions and get shot while you sit around in here nice and pretty."

The orderly stood up. "That's it, get out! Clear out of here!" he said. "I'll call the guard."

Styopa drew his arm back but I caught it before he could land the punch. The orderly stepped backward. "Look," I said. "Just ... just check on it. See if there's a mistake."

"Everybody says that. There's no mistake."

Then Oleg joined in. "This doesn't make any sense. When—when did it happen?" he said.

"Yesterday."

Oleg reached across the desk and scraped the paperwork off. Sheets scattered across the floor. "Then you don't know what you're talking about," he said. "Our sergeant saw him this morning and he was fine. Davidov, First Company, Second Battalion. Find out."

I was still holding Styopa. "Captain Narumov is our company commander," I said.

"And now we're going to tell the captain one of his people died in this place and he wasn't told," Styopa said.

The orderly frowned. "I'm ... I'm sure the captain has been informed," he said.

"We'll find out, won't we?" Oleg said. "What's your name, so we can tell him who to talk to?"

The orderly stooped down and picked up his papers. We waited while he put them back in order. "Wait here," he said and then he disappeared through a door behind his desk.

"You can let go now," Styopa said to me.

"You're sure?"

He pulled his arm free. "If I was going to break his face I would have done it."

"Yeah, then we'd be visiting you," Oleg said.

"It'd be worth it."

A few moments later the orderly returned.

"Ah ... sorry, there was another Davidov ... he had an infection. Your Davidov wasn't on the list. He's in the second ward," he said.

The officious fool.

He held the door open for us and Styopa glared at him when we passed.

We found Roman in bed at the end of the ward, his arm and shoulder wrapped in a wad of bandages. Tubes ran into his other arm from glass bottles dangling from a metal frame. The ward was a long and narrow room with a row of beds along each wall. It was clean and quiet and there were even curtains in the windows. And it didn't stink of medicine too much. All in all, it looked like a decent place to be. Roman was the only patient and I marveled again that the orderly could get his information so wrong with just one patient. We pulled up chairs around the bed and sat down and Oleg greeted Roman with a few words in very bad Pukhtu.

Roman gave him a thin smile. "Is that supposed to be funny?" he said. "You just said 'how do you eat?'" We all laughed. I was glad to see Roman was still Roman, even if he did look a little puny.

It was my first look at him since we brought him back to Bagram aboard the transport, his tunic soaked in the bright red arterial blood that was splattered on each of us and coated the transport floor. When he lost consciousness in flight I knew we were losing him. We were all screaming at the medic to do something and Styopa even raised his rifle and threatened to shoot if he didn't do something. Styopa sounded pretty convincing. And so the medic wrapped a rubber cord around Roman's arm, just below the shoulder, put his knee on Roman's chest and pulled—as hard as he could. The sticky flow finally stopped.

Now, in the quiet of the ward, he looked like he was mending. He was definitely thinner and paler and his hair had grown out so that his cowlicks stuck out at funny angles. I hadn't noticed the cowlicks before.

"They told us you were dead," Styopa said and I turned and stared at him. What a thing to say to a comrade in a hospital bed. Sometimes Styopa just didn't think, but Roman didn't seem to mind.

"Even funnier," he said.

"Maybe you shouldn't talk too much," I said.

"It's okay, the bullet didn't hit my throat."

"Well, that's good," Styopa said. "Wouldn't it be terrible if you couldn't talk to us anymore."

Roman looked tired around the eyes, like he still needed rest, but there was something else in those eyes too. The eyelids flickered and his gaze darted back and forth. It was almost … a hunted look. Yes, that was it, a hunted look.

"We brought you some reading," I said. "When you're up to it." I put a stack of newspapers and magazines on the bed.

"I'm up to it now. What'd you bring?"

"Ah … let's see," I said. I flipped through the stack. "The latest issue of *Izvestia* …"

"How about *Evening Moscow*?"

"Yup, a couple of issues, but not any recent ones."

"We'll bring you the new ones tomorrow," Styopa said. "They're all the same—you won't notice the difference."

"How about *Young Guard*," Roman said.

I looked through the stack again. "Sorry, I don't see it," I said.

"You shouldn't read that stuff anyway," Styopa said. "It clouds your thinking—and your thinking is pretty cloudy to start with."

Roman smiled again. "I like *Young Guard*. It's good," he said.

"It's reactionary," Styopa said.

Roman shifted in the bed. "Put them over there." He pointed to a table against the wall.

"Well, it looks like you have it pretty good here," Oleg said. "Lots of rest, no dust or petrol fumes."

Roman held up his arm with the tubes. "If this is what you call 'pretty good,' then yeah, it's pretty good," he said.

"Seems pretty good to me. It smells good in here too," Styopa said. "Like apples, maybe."

"Apples?" I said.

"Yeah, ripe apples, or cherries maybe, something like that."

"It's cleaning solvent for the floors," Roman said. "And if you think that smells like apples, your nose needs cleaning out."

Styopa grinned and tapped his nose. "There's nothing wrong with this nose. It can smell out all kinds of things," he said.

"An intelligence officer came to talk to us yesterday," Oleg said. "I imagine he'll be around to talk to you too, when you're feeling better."

"They told me one came by yesterday—while I was sleeping," Roman said. "I wondered about that."

"Have you ever wondered why they call them 'intelligence' officers?" Styopa said. "Think about that."

"What would you call them?" Roman said.

"Lots of things, but not that," Styopa said.

"He had a lot of questions," I said.

"He's a fat little guy with bumps on his face. It's like you're talking to a toad," Styopa said.

"What does he want with me? I don't remember anything," Roman said.

"There were two bandits. Kolya got one of them with the RPG and the other one ran," Oleg said.

"I remember the RPG," Roman said.

"We went back later and found the body," Oleg said. "He looked like a Tajik."

"Hmmph … that's funny," Roman said.

"What is?"

"They were Tajiks, I'm sure of it. One of them yelled to the other in Dari. Funny, I thought I'd dreamed it."

Oleg and I glanced at each other. The intelligence officer hadn't told us much, but I guessed he thought the bandits from the Panjshir Valley had done the convoy raid and ambushed us too. Roman probably just confirmed it—Dari was an old form of Farsi, the dialect of the Tajiks who lived in the northern part of the country, many in the Panjshir Valley. From those people came the *moutariks*, the mobile, professional bandit fighters who had been giving us fits since the beginning of the war. They knew tactics and weapons and they'd learned well from their mistakes in the first years of the war. They were skilled and tough—a formidable foe even for a *decantniki* unit with gunship support. Sergeant Kuznetsov's favorite souvenirs were a pair of black Czech-made boots and a black woolen cap he had taken from a dead *moutarik* near Kohistan. If they had ambushed us, our little patrol had been lucky to run into just two of them.

"You were the only one close enough to hear them," I said.

"And they won't leave you in peace until they ask their questions two and three times," Styopa said. "Are you sure there were just two? Why set up an ambush at that spot? What do you think they were doing there? Were there more of them? Are you sure about that, blah, blah, blah?"

"I don't know any of that," Roman said.

"It won't matter. They'll ask anyway."

"Just answer the questions," Oleg said. "Who knows, there might be a decoration for you in all this."

Roman looked up at the ceiling and took a breath. "Why should I get a decoration? I got shot, that's all."

He laid his head back on the pillow and closed his eyes. Until then he had seemed ok—weak and a little somber maybe, but still himself—but then his balance seemed to slip a bit. He opened his eyes and stared up at the ceiling again as two sparkling tears welled up and rolled down his face.

"I don't want a decoration," he said. "I just want to get out of here—out of this whole place." Then he covered his eyes with his hand and started softly weeping.

I looked down at my lap while Oleg and Styopa studied the floor and their sneaker tips.

We'd pushed him too far. He's weak and we pushed him too far. Stupid of us—all this talk about the ambush while he's still in here, hurting.

Oleg leaned over and patted him on his good arm. "Steady, buddy, it's ok. We all want to get out of here. That's just good sense."

"You should get a decoration," I said. "You didn't panic, you kept your head and you survived and now you have useful information. That's all any of us could do."

Roman looked at me through his green, bloodshot eyes and nodded. Styopa and I stood up.

"We'll come back tomorrow," Styopa said. "Now rest up."

"That would be good," Roman said, wiping his face.

"*Dosvidanya*," I said and I turned to leave. But then Roman reached out and grabbed my arm in a firm grip. His eyes were still bloodshot, but they were bright.

"I'll be back soon—back to the platoon," he said. "You'll be there when I get back, won't you?"

"Unless we're in the mountains, where else would we be?" Styopa said and laughed, but Roman held his grip on me.

Those eyes again, that hunted look.

"Promise me you'll be there when I get back," he said to me.

"I promise. You know we'll be there."

"We'll have a little party for you," Styopa said. "You can order the food and drinks." But Roman didn't seem to hear him.

"You know, I've been thinking about things in here," he said.

"Good, that's good," Oleg said.

"You know, you understand things better when you've had time to think about them. I've never had time to just think. Well—I've had time, but not like this." His eyes were still bright, his face still wet with his tears. I sat down again.

"Thinking about what, exactly?" Oleg asked.

"I'm not sure. I mean … it'll sound … it'll sound crazy."

"That's ok, we're listening," Oleg said.

Roman looked up at the ceiling again and chewed on his lip. Oleg and Styopa sat down. A long moment passed before Roman continued.

"I've had dreams," he said finally.

Styopa shrugged. "We all have dreams."

"Not like these, at least I hope you don't."

"You mean dreams at night?" I asked.

"Sometimes at night, sometimes in the day. Sometimes while I'm trying to think—they're suddenly just there."

"Dreams while you're awake?" Styopa asked. He looked over at me.

"Dreams … visions. I don't know what they are."

"Well, what did you see?" I said.

"Things you'd never imagine," he said.

"Tell us, talk to us," Oleg said.

"Things about what it's like after you die."

"Well?" Styopa said.

Roman was still staring at the ceiling. After a moment he shuddered and shook his head. "I can't talk about it," he said. "I thought I could, but I can't. Just promise you'll be there when I get back."

The three of us looked at each other.

"Sure, sure," Styopa said.

"We'll be there," I said.

We said goodbye and walked back to the barracks.

"It might be a long time before that boy comes back," Styopa said. "Maybe it's all that blood he lost. I think it starved his brain. Did you see those eyes—spooky."

"He's had a shock," Oleg said.

"I'll say."

"I don't know," I said. "I'm not sure that's it."

"Well, what is it?" Styopa said.

"I don't know exactly, but I don't think it's the shock—I mean losing all the blood. It's something else. Maybe he really did see something."

"Like what, like ghosts?" Styopa said.

"I don't know. What did he say—something about after you die, being dead? Is that a ghost?"

"He probably saw that idiot orderly coming for him," Oleg said. "That would do it for me."

We had a good laugh about the orderly, even Styopa who just an hour before would have liked nothing better than to get his hands around the boy's neck.

~~~~

Over the next weeks, I visited Roman nearly every day, bringing him more magazines and newspapers and things to eat so he wouldn't have to subsist on hospital food—'sewage on a plate' he called it. Slowly his body healed and his spirits revived and in April the doctors pronounced him recovered. He came back to us, seemingly the same old Roman, as good as new.

CHAPTER 15

᠈ᴥ

*I*n April word filtered down to us that the spring offensives would begin soon. It had been confirmed that the Panjshir Valley gang of bandits was behind the raid on the fuel convoy in March and now it was time to root them out of their nests, once and for all.

And so, at 15.00 hours on a cloudy Friday, Captain Narumov gave the order for the company to assemble. We filed out of the barracks and sat in a tight circle on the ground. I was glad to finally get some reliable information about what was ahead of us.

The captain, Lieutenant Martynov and Lieutenant Firyubin, the commander of second platoon, waited for us to be seated. Then, while the captain looked on, Lieutenant Firyubin crisply summarized the operation. The work down in the main valley would be done by 40th Army troops, using armor support and following a textbook battle plan—a column would push north up the valley's central road while another formation would deploy by air into the north part of the valley and push south, crushing everything in between.

"Like glass between a hammer and anvil," the lieutenant said.

While the lieutenant talked, the captain studied our faces. Looking for what? Fear? Indifference? I hoped I showed neither.

Then the lieutenant came to our part of the operation. The *decant-niki*—units from Bagram and from Kabul—would disperse into the mountains ringing the valley to guard the columns' flanks and to cut off the bandits' retreat. He gave us the order of battle from Bagram and from Kabul in detail, unit by unit.

"Ok, this is what you've trained for," he said. "If we don't get them out of there, we'll have a convoy raid every week. We can't let that happen, you can't let that happen."

I was feeling primed for action.

The plan the lieutenant described sounded simple enough, but things out here were never really simple. The Panjshir is a majestic, beautiful place undoubtedly, but it's a deadly one too, and its beauty can lull you into forgetting where you are and what you're there to do.

This was also going to be an exhausting trip. The main valley floor lies at 2500 meters elevation, in thinning air, and the rugged mountains around it rise up another 4000 meters, an altitude at which even the strongest of us would collapse from fatigue in minutes. Those mountains might look pleasing from a distance, but anyone who has been in them knows they are a mind-boggling maze of side valleys, gorges and canyons where a man can hide for years, as the bandits had proven to us.

No, whatever our officers might say, this would be no simple operation.

Then the captain propped up a blackboard on two chairs and sketched the Panjshir with a piece of chalk.

"Here's the main valley," he began. "And here's Anawa, here's Rokha and here's Khenj." He marked the valley towns with his chalk. Then he marked a spot on the western edge of the main valley, about halfway from north to south, and he drew a line from there running west.

"This canyon runs to the west for thirty kilometers," he said. "It's deep and it's wide and level at the bottom—good for an escape. If they try getting out, this is probably where they'll go. It'll be our job to stop them."

He paused and studied our faces again.

"First platoon will drop in here, about three kilometers from the main valley. I'll be with first platoon. Second platoon will drop in here," he said, marking a spot farther west. "We'll meet up along here in the middle, on the south rim, dig in and wait. From there we should have a good view of this whole section. Nothing will be able to come through here without us seeing it."

He paused again.

"Some of you are thinking 'why not drop in on the rim?' and it's a good question. The answer is we need to check these slopes," he said.

He rapped the end of his chalk on the blackboard. "There may be caves with weapons, food, medical supplies, who knows what. This is our chance to find them. We'll start at the bottom and work our way up."

Several of us nodded. It meant a lot of hard walking, but it made sense.

"It's not fancy, but it will work. Questions?"

Trostorff was sitting next to me. "Sir, the elevation?" he asked.

"At the floor or on the rim?"

"I'm sorry, Comrade Captain. On the rim."

"About thirty-seven hundred meters."

I raised my hand and the captain pointed at me. "Any fortified positions?" I asked.

"Photos from the air show nothing, but those are just photos."

Oleg raised his hand. "Sir, will we coordinate with any of our units?"

"Nope, we'll be alone—except for the radio. Lots of solitude."

Yanov raised his hand. "How many bandits in the area now, Comrade Captain?"

The captain smiled. "Oh probably not many," he said and everybody laughed.

There were more such questions and the answers told me we really had no idea what we were getting into. We might be rooting out the bandits, but just as easily it could be the other way around.

The captain put his chalk down and nodded to the lieutenant.

"Pack your full kit," the lieutenant said. "We'll be in the canyon for at least three days. Eat a good supper tonight."

I looked at Styopa. Isn't that what they tell condemned prisoners on their last night?

The lieutenant said we were dismissed and we jumped to our feet as the officers left us.

~~~~

Back in the barracks there was talking and joking as we got our gear together and checked our weapons—even though the odds were good some us would never see Bagram again.

"Kolya," Styopa said. "Would you mind carrying my blanket?"

"No problem, your rifle too?"

"That would be great, thanks."

"Whatever you like."

Styopa leaned over to one of the new boys who'd joined the platoon in March. "You were lucky to be assigned to this platoon," he said "People here will do anything for you. It's great."

"Really?" the boy asked and several of us snickered.

"Anything you need, just ask."

Vasily Tenin, our minesweeper, was listening to Styopa. There was a smirk on his lips. "It's good you feel that way," he said and he patted Styopa on the shoulder. "I'll need some help on this trip. I can count on you, yes?"

Styopa just blinked at him and the rest of us grinned.

"Give us plenty of warning before you let Styopa near those things," Golovin said.

"I didn't say anything about that," Tenin said. "Somebody needs to look after the dogs."

Styopa threw a sneaker at him. Tenin caught it and threw it back and hit Oleg who was packing his gear.

"Do you mind?" he said.

Back and forth the banter went for the rest of the afternoon, at supper and into the night. Everybody gave the appearance of being relaxed even though there was serious business at hand. If you couldn't do that, you were no better than a useless green.

~~~~

The next morning at 09.00 the battalion queued up to board the transports. It had come as welcome news that we would go to the Panjshir by air transport instead of by convoy. The boys from Kabul would come by convoy, a gritty trip where everybody but those in the lead vehicle would eat dust the whole way up.

By 10.00 the battalion was in the air, aboard a swarm of transports moving forward in formation like a dark cloud toward the Panjshir, ninety kilometers to the northeast of Bagram. The air was clear and smooth and we covered the distance in just minutes and then, gaping open before us, was the wide, southern mouth of the great valley surrounded by towering blue and white angular mountains. This end of the valley had once been a place of thriving villages and orchards, vineyards and fields of summer wheat. Now the fields were empty, the orchards were bare trunks and branches, and the people—those with any sense—had long ago packed up and moved on. Everyone, that is, but the bandits. The cursed *moutariks*, and their local defense cells, the *sabbets*, had declared to us by word and many bloody deeds that they would never go. And so we returned here year after year on missions like this.

Soon we passed over the 40th Army's forward staging area around the town of Anawa at the valley's southernmost end. We proceeded past it and up into the valley proper. The wide expanse of the valley floor stretched out ahead of us for more than one hundred kilometers. Below us, the main assault force, a line of trucks, artillery, personnel carriers, fuel tankers and T-54 and T-64 tanks, moved up the central road. Already the going was slow and expensive because burned-out and crippled vehicles littered the sides of the road, testimony that we would be made to pay for every bit of ground.

Then I saw a flash up ahead and seconds later I heard the rumble of bombing. An SU-24 jet had just dropped a load into a position on a high ridge and was circling for another pass while his wingman approached to let loose his load. Farther ahead, a pack of four Hi-24 gunships flew in tight formation.

Minutes later, our transport armada broke up, dispersing our *decantniki* units to the points selected for our attention. Our transport turned west to our objective, an empty, nameless place in the middle of nowhere.

We passed out of the main valley and into a canyon with a wide, flat bottom. The walls were steep and tall. As we came down lower, broken cloud cover obscured the tops of the walls on both sides. Below was a meadow of early spring grass covering the canyon floor. There were no people or animals here, just meadow and rock walls receding to the west.

We dropped lower and then came the signal to get ready. Usually a squad of scouts would go in ahead of the main force on a drop like this, to secure the landing zone, but today we wanted surprise.

Our two transports carrying first platoon touched down on the south side of the meadow and one after the other, we leaped out, heads down, running for cover. Full field equipment and ammunition weighed a little over forty kilos and I felt slow and clumsy. A gunship escort circled above to give us cover, but there was no shooting from the canyon walls and so the ship held its fire and watched. Only time would tell whether we had achieved surprise or whether the bandits were holding their fire just to toy with us.

Then the transports lifted off and rose to one hundred meters, turned to the east and vanished back toward the main valley. The gunship paused for one last look and then followed the transports. The noise from their rotors, which had filled the canyon, faded, leaving only the sound of the wind.

We were alone.

Wasting no time, we took up positions behind rocks and under ledges along the south wall and waited while Captain Narumov and Sergeant Kuznetsov scanned the canyon heights with their glasses. I braced myself for incoming fire, but there was only the sound of more wind. At that altitude—I judged about 3000 meters—the air was thin and cool and the wind pushed the clouds swiftly along the faces of the canyon walls high above us.

The captain put away his glasses and divided us into two squads for the day's march. I could see our meeting point with second platoon near the highest ridge along the south wall, about five kilometers distant. This would be a tough march. But at least the captain had made a good choice about the ground we would fight over. When we met up with second platoon, we would have a commanding view of that whole stretch of the canyon, nearly all the way back to the main valley. It would give us a good position from which to cut off a retreat and it was good high ground to defend. But getting there would be the trick; five kilometers by line of sight was barely half the distance on foot.

It was after noon when the first squad started out. First in our line of march was Tenin, to clear away any mines in our path, followed by

Oleg and our Afghan interpreter. Then came Sergeant Kuznetsov. I followed in the middle of the line and Roman and the lieutenant were at the rear. The second squad, with the captain, was to follow us along the same path in thirty minutes. We gathered around the captain to hear his final instructions.

"Stay alert and stay at least five meters apart. And drink your water, all of it. Any last questions?"

There were none.

"Ok, first squad, get moving."

I checked my gear and then we moved out onto a footpath that started about two meters up from the canyon floor. We had to hoist ourselves up before we could start walking.

At first the path took us up at a very manageable incline, with good footing, and after the first hundred meters or so, I started to pick up the rhythm of the march. I'd been on enough of these mountain marches to learn the secret—never think about how far you'd come or how far you had yet to go. Think only about your next step, the next rock, the next ledge. It helped to pass the time and keep you focused and alive.

~~~~

By mid afternoon we had gone about two kilometers, maybe a little more. A walk in the mountains might sound like a pleasant thing, but as the day went on, the march became a real strain. The cloud cover blew away, exposing a sun that was bright and hot. The footpaths—which really weren't paths at all in many places, just wide ledges—grew steeper, sometimes more than forty-five degrees, and they were littered with loose rocks so that you had to watch every step. A wrong step up there could mean a twisted or broken ankle, an injury you might not survive. And with me constantly was my fear of attack from snipers, rockets, mortar rounds or DshK heavy machine gun fire. The DshKs—called 'dashakas'—were especially loathsome. Most had been made in the USSR in the 1930's and 1940's and since the early days of this war, they had turned up in surprisingly large numbers in the hands of the bandits. We suspected they came from old Chinese stocks but we could never prove it. I hated the *dashaka*. It was a great heavy gun which fired a massive, maiming slug. You couldn't actually "aim" one of those beasts, you just pointed it in the general direction and squeezed the trigger, and whatever you hit was just plain unlucky. We had a joke that the only thing slow enough to hit with a *dashaka* was a mountain.

But mines were the worst. Tenin's eyes were good, but there was always the chance he would miss a sign and then with no warning, a blast would randomly claim one of us farther back in line. And so we kept our eyes fixed on the ground, oblivious to the vistas from up there.

For most of the day Kuznetsov stayed near the front of the line, but sometimes he would fall back with the rest of us.

"Rest," he called out every half hour or so. The instant I heard his command, I dropped to the ground in the nearest rock shadow and guzzled from my canteen. Roman sometimes could catch a few minutes' sleep. Flat on the ground with his bush hat over his face, he could be snoring almost at once. It was amazing, his one true talent we told him. Then, a little rested, we pressed on again, always watchful for signs that the bandits had passed that way.

But today there was nothing in this remote place—no people, no animals, just rocks and more rocks, hot sun and more hot sun, and moaning wind.

By 15.30 the canyon was in the shadows of the peaks to the west and I knew we had to reach a campsite near the rim before dark. Our survival through the night depended on that and so we picked up our pace, climbing and then descending, and then climbing again.

As dusk came I was becoming weary, dangerously so, and I don't mean just aching legs and an aching back. I was falling victim to an especially insidious enemy—the slackness of mind that creeps up and steals your concentration. When that enemy appeared, you were in trouble because concentration was everything out there. And so I willed myself to concentrate on the path in front of me, watching it turn left, then turn right, then go up and then down and then up again.

Man, how far down is the drop over that ledge? You could fall for ten minutes before you hit bottom. How far down would that be?

Hundreds of meters, it must be, hundreds. And how far across the canyon is it from here? Now there's a question. You'd have to be a bird to know that. That's right, a bird—a bird could tell me. What ever happened to Sergei's birds? I should be back home now looking after them, not wandering around out here. Man, isn't that the truth, there's nothing out here. Why would the bandits hide here? There's nothing out here for them—or us. Let's all just agree to give this place up and go home. And there's that ache in my foot again. What is that, a pebble in my sneaker maybe? I'd better stop and get it out. If I don't get it out I'll wear a hole right through the sock and then I'll need new ones when I get back to ... to Bagram. Did I almost say 'home'? I think I did—I almost said 'home.' Well, it is home, isn't it? It's starting to feel more like home than ...

"Hold," someone called out from up ahead in the line and I snapped out of my fog.

Stop it. Concentrate, stay focused.

"Hold," someone behind me called out as the command was passed down the line.

I planted my feet and switched off the safety on my rifle. Tenin had stopped up ahead and he was crouching down, studying the ground. Kuznesov stepped out of line and made his way forward while the rest of us waited.

I took a long pull from my canteen and then scanned the surrounding heights. Nothing—still just rocks and wind, but now that we were in afternoon shadow, the air was much cooler. Up ahead a discussion was taking place. Tenin had risen from his crouch and he, Oleg, Kuznetsov and the Afghan interpreter stood together in a circle looking at something Tenin held up between his thumb and forefinger. Then they turned their attention to the high ridges, looking back and forth along the canyon wall. There was nothing up there but rocks as far as you could see. After a few moments, Kuznetsov passed the word down the line for us to stay alert and then he gave the order for us to move out. Our line started ahead again. Kuznetsov stood to the side of the path and a moment later I came up alongside of him.

"What was it?"

"This," he said. He handed me an unspent round. I held it in my palm. It was a 5.45mm, the ammunition for the AKS-74 Kalakov, the standard weapon of the *decantniki*, a lighter weapon than the Kalashnakov. The round was still shiny.

"Ours?"

He looked around at the canyon walls again. "Not sure. Our people haven't been in this area since last year. It might be from them, but …"

Our rifles were always the first thing the bandits stole from our dead. "The *moutariks* love the Kalakov," I said.

"Yes, they do. Just one means it probably fell from a pocket."

Then Styopa came up and passed by me. He was watching his footing and sweating. I was sweating too, even as dusk approached, but the sweat dried quickly, leaving me coated with a salt film that I tasted at the corners of my mouth. The band inside my hat still felt damp and clammy.

As Styopa went by, I saw a squadron of our bombers flying high above, heading southwest toward Bagram, their white vapor trails sharp against the azure sky and tinged golden orange by the late sun.

My ammunition pouch sagged across one side of my chest and I pulled the straps tighter. My tunic was damp under the pouch.

"Kolya," Styopa said. He pointed up to the rocks where a mountain ram stood, like a statue, staring down at us with an expression of detached curiosity. The animal showed no alarm, just faint interest in these strange intruders into his domain. We often glimpsed these noble-looking creatures, usually high up at dusk when they came out to feed on plants growing in the rock crevices. They would watch us for a time and then withdraw into the rocks.

Night would come quickly at that time of year and no one with any sense would wander along those paths at night, especially just after dark before the moon rose. For a few fleeting minutes, the low-angle, late afternoon light gave us a spectacular show as it shined iridescent oranges and pinks on the sunward peaks to the east and along the top ridges of the far side of the canyon.

There wasn't much daylight left and we had to make camp soon.

A short time later, Kuznetsov found a wide, flat section of ground near an overlook into the canyon and he ordered us to set up a perimeter. I peeled off my field pack and chest pouch and sat down to await my orders for the night watch. Two-hour watches were standard and I hoped mine would be last so I could get some sleep.

Then Tenin tapped me on the arm. "Kolya, give me a hand with the wires?"

I was tired and my feet ached, but you never refused a request for help unless you were nearly dead. Besides, giving Tenin a hand would help to pass the time.

"Sure." I slung my rifle and picked up one of his canvas bags. He picked up the other.

We walked ahead along the path for a distance while he studied the ground. Then he chose a level spot with a small rock pile on each side of the path.

"This'll be good," he said. "Far enough to give us a good warning."

"It's about sixty meters," I said.

"Umm … more like seventy-five."

We set the bags down and he pulled a length of line from his tunic pocket. Then he lifted a MON-50 mine from one of the bags. The MON-50 is a shrapnel mine that explodes in a hammering, focused blast.

"How many of these have you set?" I asked and he smiled.

"Enough to know the thing is to remember where you set them."

I was starting to sweat again.

We set two of the charges to face forward along the path, one on each side, and we ran the line from one to the other about half a meter above the ground.

"Ok, hold yours still," he said. While I held one charge, he gently pushed the other backward into the rocks. When the line went taut it was nearly invisible.

We set more charges around the camp and we rigged lines to each one from different directions. A few minutes later, on schedule, the second squad and the captain arrived. When they were inside our perimeter, we set charges along the path behind us so that when we were done, the camp was sealed inside an invisible web of killer sentinels.

By the time we finished, the sky had deepened from azure to indigo and most of the boys were already stretched out on the ground under their blankets.

Kuznetsov gave me the watch at 04.00 and so I sat down to eat a supper of rations. Starlight soon illuminated the landscape and I sank back into the shadows of the rocks to wait.

CHAPTER 16

ﾞ✥

*N*ight in the mountains was a time for myself.
　After my meager supper, I spread my blanket on the ground and laid down, looking up at the stars while I listened to the hushed conversations of my comrades. You always spoke in whispers or low murmurs at night in the mountains because a full voice could carry a long distance in that emptiness. Some of the boys said it didn't matter if we kept our voices down because the bandits had night vision equipment from the Americans and could see us relaxing in our camp, even in the deepest dark. I didn't know if that was true, but I was too tired to worry about it. All I could think about was a few hours of sleep.

A little later the moon rose and the wind picked up and I crawled under my blanket and slept.

~~~~

At 04.00 the boy on watch ahead of me touched my shoulder. I awoke instantly, shook off the sleep, stretched and rolled up my blanket. Then I took my position at the north end of our perimeter, squatting among the rocks, watching the canyon floor. The others were sleeping under their blankets, indistinguishable from the rocks in the moonlight. I listened for sounds of fighting in the main valley, but all was quiet. I thought about Kursk and what must be happening there. My family had been good about writing often to tell me the news from home but in time it all seemed less and less connected to me. In my letters I never mentioned the Korennaya chapel. I was tempted to, but I didn't. Most of the boys in my class were now in service, some of them maybe in this campaign. If I weren't here, beside these rocks, making sure the others could sleep in safety, what would I be doing in Kursk? Anything really useful? Probably not. It was just as well to be here.

I thought about Father.

Did he still sit in the evenings on the benches under the trees outside our block? I hoped so. He always enjoyed that. Maybe now Mother comes down from the flat and sits with him. Does she still go to the lectures at the *Dom Kultury*? They used to last through the winter, stop in March, and then start up again in April through the summer. Or did they start in May?

Things from home were becoming faded, less clear. Life was here now—in this platoon, in these mountains.

The light began to increase in the east, behind the mountains, announcing the end of my watch. The others were still sleeping. At dawn, Kuznetsov rolled out of his blanket and came to my side.

"Anything?" he said.

"Canyon and more canyon." He scanned the canyon floor and then the heights on both sides with his glasses.

"Go wake Tenin. We'll move before it's full light."

I found Tenin sleeping soundly under his blanket. I shook him just once and his eyes popped open.

"It's time," I said and he grunted. He sat up, rubbed his eyes, took a drink from his canteen and then spit it out. Two or three of the others were now up and packing their gear. Tenin nodded to me and we started out up the path to the trip lines we had set ahead of us.

The trip lines and MONs in our rear and off the path would be left in their places because they might get the chance to do their work on the bandits later.

"How many have you gotten with these?" I asked him as we knelt down beside one of the mines.

"I don't know. You never know for sure. Truth is, I don't really want to know." He tapped the stock of my rifle.

"How about you?"

"Not sure," I said. I don't think he believed me, but it was true. I had fired only at fleeting figures from a distance and I had no idea if my marksmanship was good.

"You don't keep count?"

"No."

"Never anyone up close?"

"Never," I said and he nodded.

"That's good."

"Is it?"

"I think so. That's the way I want it anyway—at a distance, or with one of these," he said as he opened up his bag. "It doesn't get inside you so much that way."

I knew what he was talking about. I'd seen it in some of the others, especially in Styopa. There was something in him now that I hadn't seen before, something that took pleasure in the worst parts of this business, like finishing off wounded bandits with his knife. He always said he was just following orders—that we didn't have provisions for prisoners or boys to spare to guard them—and that was true. But I feared he actually liked cutting their throats, feeling his sharp blade slide slickly through their windpipes. Does he ever think about that when he's alone? I've never asked him.

Tenin unsheathed his knife and cut the line across the path. Then he slowly, carefully lifted the two MONs, one at a time, from their rock cradles. I watched, not exactly holding my breath, but not breathing easy either. He unscrewed and pocketed the firing pins and then repacked the disabled mines into his bag.

Our forward line of march was now open again.

When we got back to the camp the rest of the boys were eating breakfast and the captain was speaking into the radio to Lieutenant Firyubin, giving our position and our direction of march for the morning.

The sun hadn't yet broken over the peaks in the east and a mist covered the ground along the canyon floor. As the sun rose higher the mist would start to burn away. The captain gave the order to move out. Today the whole platoon would go together.

The air was cool and I felt rested and well.

We traded equipment to carry on this leg of the march and so I picked up a bag with two ammunition drums for the grenade launcher and fell into line. The round drums weighed about ten kilos each and with all my other gear I was soon sweating again. Styopa was in line ahead of me and I concentrated on his steps, doing my best to place each of my steps where his had been. I noticed he walked on the outsides of his *kimris* and had worn the soles down.

On we went all that morning, along the walls and slopes of the canyon, around large rocks and over uneven ground where the path disappeared and then reappeared later. When we weren't watching the ground, we watched the heights for signs of trouble. The sky was clear and I saw more white vapor trails of our jets against the blue sky high overhead and far off in the distance. We stopped often for water and rest. More mountain rams watched us from the rocks. In places the canyon floor opened up into more broad meadows, but we saw no villages, no crops, no livestock, no signs at all that this land had ever been put to any useful purpose. It was timeless.

~~~~

A little before noon, we came to a place where the canyon wall began to curve gently inward. At first it was barely noticeable, but the curvature continued for several hundred meters, forming a great sweeping crescent, as if a giant spade had scooped out a section of the wall. The grade of the wall flattened out a bit to about forty-five degrees. Our rough path followed the curvature. Tenin and the Afghan interpreter and then Oleg, in the lead of our line, followed the path into the crescent.

We were making good time.

I plodded after Styopa. The path had good footing and the canyon floor opened up to its widest expanse yet, giving the best view of the day. The floor was level and green with new grass and was cut through in the middle by a rushing stream, full to its banks.

I was enjoying these sights, and I said so to Styopa.

"Sure, sure," was all he said.

Then something began to feel odd—not quite as it should be. I'd been in the mountains long enough now to have a sense about places and situations, and a sense when something wasn't quite right. It would come over me without any warning, like an itch from my tunic or a pebble in my shoe. Suddenly it was there and it bothered me.

This gentle crescent looked ordinary enough, but once I was inside, I saw exactly what it was—a vast field of fire from the rocks and ledges above us. Any spot on our path could be fired upon by at least a dozen positions.

Kuznetsov stepped out of line and stood back from the path, scanning the heights up above us. He motioned for me to stop.

"Kolya, set up here and give us cover until we're all out," he said. I stopped and dropped the bag with the grenade drums.

It was part of our training that whenever we stopped in our line of march, we were to immediately sweep the area around us, three hundred and sixty degrees. It was a procedure usually honored in the breach and after so many marches, I rarely followed it. But this time I did.

Maybe I was bored or maybe I was daydreaming again, but my training just took over.

I placed the metal stock of my rifle against my shoulder, sighted down the barrel and pivoted slowly around. Captain Narumov had stopped in line behind me and as my rifle barrel swept toward him, a bandit stood up from behind a rock, not twenty meters from where the captain stood. He was taking aim at the captain with his rifle. The captain was looking down, facing away from me, adjusting the pistol holster on his belt.

I'd never seen a live bandit, only dead ones after a fight.

I couldn't believe he was real.

Some of our boys called the bandits by the more respectful name 'dukhi'—ghosts, because they seemed to appear and vanish at will—and it flashed into my head that I was seeing a ghost now.

How could a mere man come from nowhere into the middle of our line?

But whatever he was, man or ghost, he was calmly, deliberately, seizing his chance to take out one of our officers. In another instant he would succeed unless I stopped him.

As my rifle barrel swept past the captain's head, the bandit came into my sights and my finger pulled back on the trigger. A burst of fire spit from the barrel. The recoil dug the stock into my shoulder.

The bullets flew past the captain's head, within centimeters of his right ear, finding their mark on the bandit's shoulder, neck and jaw. He went down as the captain's head jerked up. While the bandit crumpled to the ground, the captain spun toward me and our eyes met. I had a vague impression that words were forming on his lips.

If so, I never heard them.

All I heard was a hissing sound, like the sound when you break the cap on a bottle of gassed water. Then a pink flash enveloped me. A shockwave lifted me off my feet and threw me toward Kuznetsov.

There was no sound, only light and the punch of the blast that knocked the wind out of me.

They told me later the rocket hit behind me, just behind a boulder which took most of the force.

"Another meter to the left and you wouldn't have a head, boyo," Styopa said. "Before you hit the ground, they opened up on us."

~~~~

Lying prone beneath the ledge where Styopa had pulled me, I slowly became aware of sound—loud, unrecognizable sound—ringing in my ears. Dirt and fragments of rock were mashed into my neck and cheek. My head pounded. I kept my eyes tightly shut, afraid to open them, afraid to discover terrible wounds, as yet unfelt. Moments passed as I mustered the courage to begin an inventory of my body parts. I stretched and flexed in a rolling wave from the bottom up—toes first, then feet and legs, then gut, chest, fingers, hands, arms and neck— checking to make sure I was all still there. To my relief, everything was still there and it all seemed to work.

I let out a long breath.

Then I think I lost consciousness again. When I came to, I tasted warm salt from my nose bleeding down into my mouth. Someone was rolling me over onto my back and yelling in my ear.

"Kolya! Kolya! Look at me," It was Styopa.

He grabbed my chin and shook it from side to side. My eyes started to focus and I lifted my head to look around. I sat up. My hat and rifle were gone and I smelled burnt cloth from my collar.

"You're ok," he said. "Get your rifle."

I peeked out from under the ledge.

All along the length of the crescent our boys had taken cover and were returning fire up into the heights above us. The fire coming down on us was a continuous barrage and bullets churned up the ground. Two of our boys with RPGs were sending rockets up to the high ground and the explosions punctuated the din from the rifle fire and brought small flows of rock and dirt down onto us. Red, acrid smoke from smoke bombs drifted down the line.

The bandits had the high ground and they probably outnumbered us.

"You hear me?" Styopa yelled. "Get your rifle, we need you." He turned and directed a stream of fire upward.

"Where ... where is it?" I managed to say.

"Over there."

I saw it, about five meters away on the ground. I was useless and exposed without it.

"Go ahead," he yelled as he loosed more bullets.

My head was clearing. I jumped up onto my haunches and sprang out from under the ledge on my hands and knees. I grabbed the barrel and rolled back to cover. A bullet nipped through the loose material of my trouser leg, but it missed the flesh. My head still ached, but I felt better—at least now I had my rifle.

Kuznetsov was about ten meters away, squatting behind a rock, yelling into the radio. I couldn't see the captain anywhere.

"I don't believe we were this stupid," Styopa said. He drew a magazine from his breast pouch and slapped it up into his rifle. "Like a bunch of greens." He swore.

Then a mortar round exploded down the slope from us. It was an 82mm and it wouldn't take the bandits long to find the range on us, maybe just a round or two more. When that happened, the rocks would be useless as cover.

Another mortar round hit, still down the slope, but closer. It threw up a geyser of rock and dirt that pelted us as it fell back to earth. The air was becoming unbreatheable from smoke and dust.

Then one of our rockets found its mark and a high-pitched shriek echoed off the canyon walls over the rifle fire.

"We've got to get out of here," Styopa said. "We stay here and we're dead."

"They'll cut us up if we move," I said.

"They'll cut us up here. I see 'em moving around to the right—better crossfire."

I looked out from the ledge. "The mortars'll get us first."

One of our boys pitched forward to the ground from his position just ahead of Kuznetsov. He would be the first of many if we didn't get out of there.

Styopa threw a rock at Kuznetsov. "We can't wait, we've got to pull back, we've got to get out of this pocket!" he yelled to him.

"Maybe go forward," Kuznetsov yelled.

"We don't know what's up there," Styopa yelled back. "Backward, it's got to be backward!"

Another mortar round hit, still below us, but closer. It rained more dirt and rock down on us.

Kuznetsov raised his glasses and looked ahead for a moment. Then he nodded. "Ok, we'll go back," he yelled. "Get ready to cover them."

He put his fingers in his mouth and gave a loud whistle. Trostorff was about twenty meters ahead, behind another rock. He turned and Kuznetzov gave him the signal to pull back and to pass the word up the line.

Styopa and I squatted together under our ledge.

"I don't know," I said. "It's too far. They won't make it, they've got to go forward."

"No way we can split up. We're cooked for sure if we do that."

"We're gonna lose good people," I said.

He pushed another magazine into his rifle. "I'm down to three. You?" I hadn't fired yet, but I checked my pouch anyway.

"Six," I said.

"Good, give me two," he said and I handed him two full magazines.

162

The mortar fire was still coming rapidly, but now it was directed farther up the line. Kuznetsov was talking into the radio again. Then he gave the signal to me and Styopa to give covering fire.

"Here they come," Styopa said.

At the far end of the crescent Tenin and the interpreter leaped from behind their rock cover, firing their rifles on the run. The rest of us directed our fire up above us with everything we had. Bullets hit all around Tenin and the interpreter, but they ran fast, dodging and weaving, and somehow they both made it to cover alongside Oleg. Now the three of them would fall back to the next pile of rocks where Trostorff crouched.

Styopa laughed when he saw them make it to Oleg.

"That was good."

"It won't work," I said.

"If you've got a better idea, I'm listening." Then he pointed down the slope. "What about down there?"

I scrambled out to the edge of the path on all fours and then back under cover.

"It's no good. Too steep and no cover on the way down."

"Then we all go back the way we came," he said.

More mortar shells hit, two back along the path from where we'd come—where I'd last seen the captain—and the bandits' rifle fire intensified.

That's when it started to come to me that this was it—the end, the finish for me and for all of us. We might fight on here for a time, but in the end we wouldn't make it, none of us would. We were having a bad piece of luck and soon we'd pay the price for it. In the times ahead, other *decantniki* would talk about us and swap theories about how we let this happen. Today would be held up as a lesson, an example of the kind of mistake that gets good people killed. We'd be sneered at and as I sat there under that rock ledge, I cursed the bandits for blackening our names.

We were good soldiers. We'd been careful and watched for the signs, I knew we had.

It was just that this cursed crescent was one superb trap—unseen until you were snared and then it was too late. But I supposed that's probably so with all good traps. Still, we should have seen it.

Then Styopa tapped my leg. "Okay, get ready. They're coming."

Tenin raised his arm and waved it once, the signal he was ready to move. We lifted our rifles. Then he bolted. He dodged back and forth along the path. Styopa and I stepped out from our ledge and sprayed bullets up to the high ground. I emptied a whole magazine. Tenin dodged and weaved, bullets hitting all around him.

And again he made it to cover. He dived to the ground beside Trostorff.

We ducked back under the ledge and I took a long pull from my canteen. Sweat rolled down my face, streaking the dirt and soot on my forehead and cheeks. Dust and smoke hung in the air.

"Here." I offered Styopa my canteen and he took a long drink and handed it back. It was almost empty.

Now it was Oleg's turn. I could see him crouched low to the ground, his rifle and bush hat in his hand, waiting. When Kuznetsov waved to him, he sprang forward, running, head down. I kept my eyes on him.

Come on, come on.

He weaved along the path, following Tenin's track. Once he stumbled, but he caught himself and kept coming.

Don't stop, don't look up, keep coming.

He was almost back to Trostorff. I held my breath, willing him to stay low and to keep moving. Through the blizzard of bullets, he kept coming.

Then it happened. His time arrived.

When he was just meters from safety, he was hit, many times, in the back. I knew in an instant he was finished because he stopped. He stopped and stood straight up, his face a mask of shock. Blood erupted from the front of his tunic as he staggered another step forward and then collapsed, face down. Once on the ground, his body kept twitching, like from convulsions, from the impact of many more bullets.

Kuznetsov swore and yanked off his hat and threw it to the ground. I heard Styopa swearing and the next thing I felt was my own voice rising in my throat.

"NOOOOOO!!! MURDERERS!! NOOOOO!!!"

I lunged out from under the ledge. I just wanted to get my hands on one of them.

You'll pay for this! I swear you'll pay!!

But Styopa dived and caught my ankle and pulled me to the ground and back under the ledge.

"Are you crazy?! He's gone!" he screamed at me.

I thrashed backward and forward and side to side, struggling to break his grip. He locked his hands together at the back of my neck. The tighter he held me the more I kicked and thrashed. I tried to bite him and I made sounds you'd never believe a human being can make.

He kept his lock around me and squeezed so tight I couldn't breathe. I coughed. "You're killing me," I croaked.

"I will if you don't stop," he said into my ear.

Finally my strength left me and I laid face down in the dirt, breathing heavily, crying, with Styopa's full weight on top of me.

He let go of me, but my tears kept coming.

Oleg was the best of us. He was my friend. If he had fallen, how could the rest of us possibly go on?

How long I remained in that state I do not know. I was still foggy from the rocket blast. The fury of the battle rolled over and around me and swallowed me whole. This was the end and I would simply wait for it and accept it when it came.

The battle raged on—more mortars, more rockets, more rifle fire.

But then everything changed.

Kuznetsov was yelling into the radio again and Styopa turned to me with a popeyed stare. He held up a dirty hand, two fingers extended. At first I didn't comprehend, but then the fire from above us subsided as if a thick curtain had been dropped between the bandits and us.

From down in the canyon came a faint pulsating sound.

"HA!! Yes! Yes!! YES!!!" Styopa yelled.

He turned toward the east. "There! There!" he shouted an instant later. The sound became distinct and two gunships appeared, following the middle of the canyon floor. We waved our rifles and cheered. Joy and relief washed over me.

When gunships reached us, the lead ship hovered about two hundred meters from the face of the canyon wall, his wingman behind him. Then the air was filled with rockets, more than I could count, blasting apart the canyon walls above us. The explosions became a continuous roar, up and down the length of the crescent. Rock and dirt poured down onto us, but still we cheered. When the rockets stopped, the wingman moved forward and riddled what was left of the wall with his rotary cannon.

When the cannon stopped, a quiet spread across the canyon as the echoes trailed away in the distance. There was no more firing from above us.

~~~~

In time transports arrived and landed on the canyon rim and we limped our way up to them, carrying our wounded and the bodies of our dead. Four of our boys, including Oleg, were gone and six had serious wounds. I carried Oleg, slung across my shoulders. I was surprised at how little he weighed. I laid him onto the transport floor and brushed away the dirt from his face. I smoothed down his matted blonde hair.

My hair was burnt and I still had blood trickling from my nose and ear and so the lieutenant ordered me back to Bagram aboard the transport with Oleg.

When I got back to the base, I ripped off my tunic, still sticky and heavy with Oleg's blood, and burned it.

I never returned to the Panjshir.

CHAPTER 17

❧

*T*he door to the flat opened and I heard people.

Roman spoke first. "Where is he?"

"Bedroom," Styopa said. Then they came into where I was resting. There were at least three of them.

"Kolya, we've brought Dr. Vronskaya to look at you," Roman said.

"No doctors."

"Don't start that …" he started to say, but Styopa interrupted him.

"I don't know if you're out of your mind or what, but you're going to be looked at. I don't care what you say."

No doubt the colonel had been the one to arrange for a doctor to come to my flat. Then the doctor spoke. She was all business.

"Sit up please," she said. "Raise your head and look straight ahead." She gripped my head on both sides. With her thumbs she raised my right eyelid, then my left eyelid.

"He said he saw a light," Styopa said.

"What kind of light?" she asked me.

"I don't know, it was … it was bright, really bright … and …"

"And what?"

"I don't know. I've never seen anything like it, the color."

"What color?" she asked.

"White … but …"

"Has this happened before?"

"Never."

"Have you been ill?"

"I've been fine."

"He's never sick," Styopa said.

"Any blindness in your family?" she asked.

"I don't think so."

"Do you have any sensation of the light?" she asked a moment later and I understood she was shining a light in my face.

"No."

Then Ksusha spoke. "He hasn't gotten any better. What is this?"

"Difficult to say," the doctor said. "Have you taken any drugs, pills?" she asked.

"No."

"Too much to drink, maybe?"

Roman laughed. "He won't even drink watered-down beer with us."

"Strange," the doctor said after she let go of my head. "Your pupils react to light, but you say you see nothing. It may be pressure in the brain against the nerve, or maybe a virus or even a shock. There could be many reasons. My best guess right now would be a shock."

"You could say that," I said.

"So what can you do about it?" Styopa said.

"I won't know until we do some tests."

"And for that you'll go to hospital," Styopa said.

I heard the doctor putting away her implements.

"Have you slept at all?" she asked.

"Not much, off and on, I think. I don't feel tired."

"You look terrible," Styopa said.

"That doesn't help," Roman said.

"I'll give you something to help you sleep for now," she said. "Tomorrow we can have you moved."

"I don't want anything—no drugs," I said. "I want a clear head, I need a clear head."

"Kolya, for once do what you're told," Styopa said, and then someone gripped my arm and held me while the doctor rolled up my shirtsleeve. I felt something wet and cold on my arm and then the prick of a needle. She withdrew it after a few seconds and almost at once I felt warmth in my arm and my mind began to drift ...

PART THREE

CHAPTER 18

෧෨

The train wheels squealed and the cars slowed. A row of *izbu*, painted shades of ocher, red and green, came into view in my window. I smiled when I saw the delicate patterns in the wood trim around the windows and the small square plots of garden next to each cottage. Their picket fences ran up to the edge of the tracks. I had been back in the USSR for two days, all that time in Moscow, but now I was home.

Soon the buildings and streets of Kursk appeared in the early morning sunshine. It was two years and four months since I had seen this place.

Would it feel like home? Could I fit back into this life here?

I'd find out soon enough.

The car slowed again and then the station platform came into view and slid past the window. We stopped with a jerk and the brakes let off a rush of pressurized air.

I lifted my bag and paused in the compartment door to study my reflection in the corridor window. Overall it was not a bad appearance. Before boarding the train in Moscow, I changed into my best uniform and boots and I pinned on my parachute badge and campaign ribbons. On my head was a blue beret which I adjusted again to the proper angle.

Now I was ready.

As I moved down the corridor toward the car door, a man was coming toward me, boarding the train here at Kursk. When he looked up and saw me he stopped and stood to the side so I could pass. He had the weathered face and clothes of an outdoor worker. He nodded to me.

"Welcome home," he said.

"*Spaseebo*. It's good to be back," I answered him. No one had taken any notice of me in Moscow, and that was to be expected there, but in Kursk people are different, more friendly and polite.

I stepped off the car at almost the same spot where I had boarded another train more than two years earlier. As it was then, the platform was filled with people hurrying back and forth, carrying bags, waiting to board. It was early October and the sky promised a fine autumn day. Then I heard a shout and I saw Mother breaking through the crowd, running toward me. Her face beamed.

"Kolya! Kolya!" she shouted to me, waving her arm above her head. I grinned and dropped my bag and waved back.

"He's here! He's here!" she yelled to Father and Deda who were hurrying behind her.

I leaned down and she flung her arms tight around my neck. I buried my face in her hair. It smelled clean and sweet. Then the others were standing around me and we were all talking and laughing at once and Mother and Father had tears on their faces and they were hugging me tightly and kissing me on both cheeks. Deda had a hold of my hand and he was pumping it up and down. What I was and where I'd come from were plain to see from my uniform and many strangers who were passing us on the platform joined in the welcome with pats on my shoulders and words of greeting.

"Look, look at the ribbons!" Father said to Deda and to one of the strangers as he pointed to my chest.

"You must tell us what each one is for," Mother said.

"I promise."

"Does it fit?" Deda asked and I laughed as he tried on the beret he'd snatched from my head.

"It's yours," I said.

"No, no," he said. "I just wanted to try it on."

"Deda, it's yours. I've worn it enough."

Mother stepped back to look at me. "So tanned and so thin," she said.

"It looks good on him," Father said. "He looks like a man, all grown up."

Then Mother flung her arms around my neck again and cried. Father stroked her hair.

"Ok, ok," Deda said after a moment. "Let's get the boy home. You know we've prepared something for you."

"You didn't need to do that."

"It's nothing much, but you know Babulya."

When we got to 14 Parkovya, Babulya was waiting for us on the stairs outside our flat. She was dressed in her best clothes. When I came up the stairs she took my face in her hands the way she always did when I was a boy and looked into my eyes.

"I knew you'd come home," she said. "Now come inside. You have much to do."

CHAPTER 19

✿

Whatever it was that Babulya believed I must do would have to wait. First, I needed to find a job.

The sugar plant where Father worked was a rambling collection of brick buildings on two hectares of land at the southern end of the city, not far from the wooded banks of the Seym River. Hundreds of people worked there and every day during the harvest months, trucks from the collectives delivered sugar beets by the millions for processing into a sweet brown powder with the earthy aroma of the steppes. In those days our sugar was known everywhere in the USSR.

After the trucks unloaded their mountains of beets at the loading docks, the floor workers shoveled them onto the giant belts—using hand tools Father made—to run through the cleaning and slicing machines. The noise from the conveyors and the slicers filled the plant. Sparse sunlight filtered down through windows encrusted with years of dirt. Long overhead electric bulbs shone to illuminate the gloom. After the beets were sliced to pulp, the conveyors dumped them into the cooking vats, each one big enough to hold twenty standing men. When the plant was in full production, the vats were kept fired twenty-four hours each day, cooking and reducing the heavy beet sludge. On days when the wind was up, you could catch the sweet smell for many kilometers out into the country.

I'd been home for about a week when Father joined me at breakfast one morning. He pushed a copy of the plant newspaper across the table to me. On the front page was a photo of Viktor Trifonov, one of our neighbors in the block who worked at the plant.

"I'm sorry about Viktor," I said. "Deda told me."

"We rode the tram together every day for ten years. It'll be strange without him. He was the best mechanic I ever saw. If he couldn't fix it, it couldn't be fixed. It was like he was part machine."

"Sorry … a fever, Deda said."

"Cut his hand, on a piece of metal. I saw it the next day. It looked swollen."

"Did he go for treatment?"

He shrugged. "You knew Viktor—he said it was nothing. You couldn't tell him anything."

"You should have made him go to hospital."

"He wouldn't do it. A couple days later the whole arm was swollen. By then it was too late. Septic."

I looked at the photo. I remembered Viktor as a big jolly man and it captured that well. "I hope at least they gave him something for the pain," I said.

"Morphine, I think."

"Too bad."

"Yeah." He nodded. "You know," he said after a moment. "With Viktor gone, there's only Yuri Matyukh left to tend the machines."

"That's not good," I said.

"Oh, he's not so bad. Viktor taught him a lot. He's pretty good."

"If you say so."

He pushed the newspaper closer to me. "Well, what do you think?" he said.

"About what?"

"You know …"

I looked down at the paper, then back up at him. "Oh, no," I said. "No, no, I can't do that."

He leaned across the table, his words coming out fast. "Now just listen, think about it. With Viktor gone there's a position for another mechanic," he said. "Yuri will be senior and there's a spot now for a junior man to come in and help him. The way Yuri did with Viktor."

I shook my head. "I can't do that. Besides, Yuri's not much older than I am. They'll want somebody with experience."

"No, you're wrong about that. They've already said Yuri will be senior," he said. He stopped and took a breath and continued more slowly. "So … now … there's a spot for somebody junior—like you, with your training."

He studied my face.

"I don't know anything about those machines—washers and whatever else is there. They'll want somebody who does."

"A machine is a machine. And anyway, the director knows about your service and he wants to talk to you about it."

"The director knows about my service? How is that?"

He grinned. "Well, I might have mentioned it. I might have told him you were coming home. And he wants to see you—tomorrow morning."

"Yevgeny Borisovich wants to see me?"

"Yes. Tomorrow."

I pushed the paper back at him. "What is this? The director doesn't bother with who gets a mechanics job."

"Please," he said. "Just go talk to him—do that for me."

Father was watching me. I knew I had no choice—he'd mope around for days if I didn't go and talk to the man. He was still watching me.

Well … why not?

If there was really a job in this, I didn't have to take it. And as I thought about it, I was a little curious. I had a hunch about something and I wanted to see if I was right.

"*Horocho*," I said. "I'll talk to him."

Father reached over and squeezed my hand.

~~~~

And so early the next morning, I sat outside the office of Yevgeny Borisovich Kornilov, the plant director, a man I had seen many times in my life, but to whom I had never spoken a word. For as long as I could remember, at every May 1st celebration for the plant workers and at every other big event, Yevgeny Borisovich was there, presiding in his grand style, speaking to everyone, telling jokes, being the center of everything. It was Yevgeny Borisovich who personally handed out bonus pay every year to the floor leaders if the plant made its quota—which it had done every year for as long as I could remember. When officials came to the plant to discuss matters of planning and production, they spoke to him and only to him. Sometimes his picture was in the city newspapers. He knew Father, of course, Father being the only blacksmith at the plant, but we never socialized with him. We could never socialize with a man of his wealth and position.

As I waited, the collar of the new shirt Mother had bought me scratched my neck and reminded me of the words I'd had with Father that morning, about whether I should wear my uniform.

"It will impress him," Father had said. "Go ahead, wear it, it looks good on you."

"It's against regulations. I've been discharged."

"Only a week ago. Nobody will complain this one time."

"It's a bad idea."

"How is it bad?"

"What if the director doesn't like it? Have you thought about that?" I asked and his brow wrinkled.

"Why wouldn't he like it?"

"I just told you—it's against regulations for me to be in uniform. He'll probably know that. He might think I'm bragging, trying to impress him. He might not like it."

Father thought it over. "*Horocho*, you could be right. So wear your old school clothes. That'll be even better. He knows about your service and he'll think you're being modest. Yes, that's much better."

So there I sat, wearing my scratchy new shirt, waiting to see the great man.

The director's office was situated comfortably in a spacious brick structure inside the plant, along the south wall. A mousy-looking secretary sat at a desk outside the director's personal office, working with piles of papers. When I entered she looked up only once, to tell me to sit down and wait. I took a seat in the only other chair in the room, grateful for the chance to relax a moment and collect my thoughts. I wasn't afraid of the director, exactly, but I didn't want to say anything stupid or, worse, get myself into trouble by saying things I shouldn't say. I would need to be careful.

While I waited a steady stream of people came in from the plant floor and the secretary told each of them the director had an appointment and to come back later. The telephone on her desk rang several times and she told each caller the same thing, the director was busy with an appointment and to call back later. I wondered what important person was in with the director. Behind the desk, along one wall, was a long row of metal file cabinets, each one secured with a stout lock. The noise from the plant floor wasn't too bad, but I could feel the vibration from the machinery and the sweet odor from the cooking vats was strong.

Then the door opened and Yevgeny Borisovich motioned to me with two fingers to enter. I rose and followed him into the office and sat in a chair facing his big wooden desk. We were alone. I noticed he had three phones on his desk.

He leaned forward and offered me a cigarette, which I declined. He folded his hands on top of the desk.

"So, Nikolai, it's good to have you back," he said.

"Thank you, Comrade Director," I said. "It's good to be back."

"Tell me, how is it to be home?"

"Good, very good, but still a little strange."

"Nothing surprising about that," he said, leaning back in his chair. "Jumping from one world into another can't be easy."

"It took just two days to get here, but 'different worlds' is a good way to put it, Comrade."

"You'll adjust soon enough. And you look fit, ready to get on with your life."

"Thank you. I feel fit. That part of it was good."

"No doubt, the girls will soon notice you," he said with a smile.

"They haven't yet."

"Give them time and a little encouragement. Wear your uniform—that always works."

I wouldn't tell Father about that remark.

"I imagine it was pretty tough down there." He leaned back in his chair.

Careful. Remember your orders.

"It was broiling hot in the daytime and freezing at night. Even colder in the mountains, but we didn't go there very much so that wasn't so bad."

"Sounds like Moscow," he said and he chuckled.

"It was nothing like Moscow, Comrade Director."

"No, I suppose not." He thought a moment. "Learn any of the language?"

"I didn't want to get close enough to any of them for that."

"I don't blame you—savages, we hear. You were gone how long?"

"Eight hundred and fifty-three days."

He laughed. "Did you count the hours too?"

"You never do that until the end. Some say it's bad luck even then."

"I can see that. Any friends still there?" he said.

"A few, Comrade Director."

"You must be hearing that little voice calling you back."

I nodded. "You understand things very well."

He waved a hand. "Oh, there's no magic in understanding that. But you have to put all that behind you. You're here now and life goes on." Then he leaned forward in his chair. "But tell me, we hear so many stories. How is it down there—really?"

Ah, there it was at last—the question, the same question that had been put to me in one way or another, sooner or later, by just about everyone. Father took his time to get around to it, but the director's position gave him license to ask me whatever he pleased and so he had gotten to it straightaway. My little hunch was right. But I didn't blame them—they just wanted to know.

"Not really so bad," I lied. "In some places the fighting was heavy, but in our area it wasn't so bad."

"And your area was Bagram?"

"That I'm not able to say, Comrade."

"Oh, even to me in a little chat like this?"

"Even to the General Secretary as far as our orders go. Sorry. Treason is treason."

"I see."

"I'm sorry."

He sighed. "I understand." He took a cigarette from the pack on his desk, lit it and blew out a long stream of blue smoke. "You were with the *decantniki*, the 'blue berets,' right, no secret about that?"

"That's true, Comrade Director."

"You can be proud of that, they're the best."

"It was a privilege," I said. "We had the best of everything, especially the food."

That wasn't always true, but our food was much better than the stuff they fed the rifle troops.

"The news reports say the blue berets are mostly building roads, bridges, schools, things like that."

"Yes, Comrade Director," I said.

"'Yes' the reports say so or 'yes' that's true?"

"If the news reports say so it must be true."

The plant machinery was pounding away. We held each other's gaze and then he leaned back in his chair again and gave me a crooked smile.

"I understand. Well, maybe we can talk about these things again, another time."

"I'm at your service."

He nodded and then picked up a sheet of paper from his desk. "So, you want Viktor's position?"

"Well, no," I said. "Father said Yuri Matyukh will be senior and needs somebody to help him."

"Yes, yes, that's correct. I meant you want the open position."

"Yes, Comrade Director."

"Well, the position is open, for a qualified person. Whoever has the job has a great responsibility—to keep all of this running." He waved a hand in the general direction of the plant. "Can you handle it?"

"It'll take me a little time," I said. "I learned the basics at school and did some mechanical work in service, but I don't know your equipment."

"Of course, but I have no doubt you can do it—if your hands are half as clever as your father's. Matyukh will show you everything."

He rose from his chair and I rose too.

"The job is mine?" I said.

"The job is yours. Start in the morning. Rina will give you the forms to fill out. Good luck."

I thanked him and then spent the next hour with the mousy secretary, filling out the necessary papers.

Before I knew what had happened, I had a job.

As I walked to catch the tram back home, it began to drizzle. There was a crowd at the stop and the people pressed forward around me when the tram slowed and rolled to a halt. Yellow sparks flew from the shoe running along the electric line above the car and everyone boarded, filling the car to its capacity. Deda always called tram cars "germ boxes," especially in winter, and we would walk together long distances to avoid riding them. But today I stood in the middle of the car, holding on to the overhead bar, surrounded by bodies. A young woman stood so close I could smell her perfume. It smelled nice and she was quite pretty, but even with a young pretty girl flat up against me, all I could see that afternoon was dark sky and rain.

CHAPTER 20

W hen I reported to the plant the next day, I discovered I couldn't have picked a worse time to start my new job.

Like every other plant in the USSR, the sugar plant had production quotas handed down by the central economic planners in Moscow. To make sure the plant conformed to the central plan, the quota figures were checked carefully at the end of each quarter. As they were for most plants, our quota was set so high that a slowdown for even a single day could jeopardize compliance with the plan. And slowdowns were inevitable—because of equipment problems, fuel shortages or sometimes even the weather—which meant the quotas usually weren't met until the last few days of the quarter. That meant the plant ran hard during those last few days, punishing men and machines.

I started three days before the end of the quarter.

Father and I rode the tram together and joined a herd of other workers filing into the cavernous plant buildings shortly before seven o'clock, the starting hour for our shift.

"Good luck," he said as he walked off to his smithy. "Stay sharp and things will be fine."

"I'll see you at dinner," I called after him.

"Don't bet on it," he called back.

I found the machine shop with no trouble. It was another brick structure inside the plant, along the south wall, but unlike the director's spacious office, it was cramped and cluttered with tools and the remains of cannibalized equipment. I hadn't seen Yuri in years, but I supposed he hadn't changed much. People never really do.

But when I came through the door of the shop, there was no Yuri. The man waiting for me introduced himself only as the "floor leader."

"You're Razkazov?" he asked.

"Yes, Comrade."

"Well at least you're here. And on time. That's something, anyway. They never tell me anything. The quota figures go in at the end of the week. They tell me this morning I get a brand new man to get number two line running. You know what quota time means?"

"It means …"

"It means everything must be up and running—everything."

"Yes, Comrade, I understand."

"Good. I hope so. You can start on one of the slicers on the number two line," he continued. "It keeps jamming. Come on."

He walked out of the shop and I followed behind.

He was a small man and he talked in staccato bursts in a high-pitched voice. As we went along the plant floor, he pointed out things to me.

"Those are the vats. See 'em?"

"Yes."

"Number one conveyor is over there. See it?"

"Yes."

We wound our way through the machinery and soon came to the downed slicer.

"There it is," he said. "Third time this month it's gone down. Get it going. Then grease the whole line." He pointed to the conveyor that fed the slicer.

While he watched, I looked the slicer over and found the problem with no trouble. A bent blade blocked the slicing arm from retracting, jamming the whole works. The bend was very slight, not easy to spot, but just enough.

"I think I can just bend it back," I said. "That might do it."

"Fine, go ahead."

"What about Matyukh?" I asked. "Should I wait for him?"

He shook his head. "Out sick—again. Damned inconvenient time too. Don't worry about him, you just get this going." Then he hurried away.

I looked the situation over again from every angle and decided the simplest solution was the best. I grabbed the blade with my hands and bent it very slightly, back into its proper alignment. I made a few small adjustments to the joint that retracted the arm and then greased the joint. When I hit the button, the machine started up and ran smoothly. Then I went back to the shop to get another grease can and I spent the rest of that day on my back under the belts, applying the thick yellow lubricant everywhere I thought I heard metal grinding on metal. It took all the rest of the day to grease just one conveyor line.

I'd been inside this plant many times before with Father, but now I saw it with new eyes—the eyes of a prisoner who has paced off his cell in every direction and knows it to the last centimeter.

That was the first day.

~~~~

On the second day, Yuri returned.

He was waiting for me in the morning in the machine shop. He looked basically like I remembered, except his hair was cut so short his head glistened, even on that cool morning. The beginnings of the fleshiness around his middle and in his face from too much drink were unmistakable. He was leaning back in a chair, one foot propped up on a piece of pipe. He gave no hint of our prior acquaintance.

"Ah, good, you must be Razkazov. I've been waiting for you," he began, with what was evidently his idea of a greeting. "I've wanted to meet the lucky one."

"Lucky one?"

"You—the lucky one."

"Why am I lucky?"

"A dozen people wanted this job, maybe more, and it went to you. That makes you lucky, wouldn't you say?"

I shrugged.

"Some with pretty good qualifications too—experience with this equipment. What's your experience? Nobody told me."

"A little instruction in school, and some mechanic work in service," I said.

He stared at me as if there should be more. "That's it?"

"That's it."

He sighed. "Well, come on, let's see what you can do."

He stood up and pushed the chair aside. "Follow me."

We left the shop and went through the maze of the plant floor, along the conveyor belt of line number one. Sound pulsated from the slicers and he shouted to me over his shoulder.

"There's a problem with one of the cooking vats."

"What kind of problem?"

"Don't worry, you shouldn't have any trouble with it."

When we reached the vat, he dropped down onto one knee and pointed to the mechanism at the base that tipped and emptied the huge bowl. An access panel in the outer housing had been removed and it was lying on the floor. Assorted tools were strewn about and a box of more tools, some rusted and others caked with grease, was open on the floor nearby. I squatted down beside him and peered into the open side of the housing. Two teeth of the main gear were broken off and I knew at once the repairs would require removal of the whole housing, gearing and axel, and replacement of the broken gear.

"You've worked with this kind of assembly before, right?" he said.

"No, but I've worked with gearing."

"Good. This is simple enough. There's the new one," he said, pointing to a shiny new main gear lying on the floor.

I peered again inside the housing. "How can I find you if I need help?" I asked.

"Hard to say," he said. "I'll be busy this morning, very busy, but I'll check on you later." Then he turned and walked back into the maze of machinery. I took off my jacket and began to consider my plan of attack.

I quickly discovered what kind of job this really was. To remove the housing required me to first loosen the heavy bolts that fastened it to the floor. These were placed at such inaccessible angles that I wondered what kind of cruel joker had designed this thing. There were eight bolts in all and each one took nearly half an hour of straining and contorting my body to loosen and remove. But, by working steadily, I managed to remove them all by late morning. By then my knuckles were raw and bleeding from the many times my wrench had slipped, slamming my hands into the cold metal of the housing or onto the floor.

By noon the broken gear was fully exposed. In spite of the morning chill, my shirt was soaked through around my neck and armpits
and my hands were covered with greasy dirt that smeared onto my face
when I wiped away the sweat. Now I could start removing the axel
from the main gear.

Just before the dinner whistle blew, Yuri returned and watched
me, neither offering assistance nor commenting on my progress. He
stood there with his arms crossed, watching me. Then he looked at his
watch.

"Go ahead and work through your dinner hour," he said. "The
floor leader wants this finished by four o'clock." Then he went back
into the machinery.

I swore at him under my breath, but I knew there was no point
in complaining. He was going to give me a proper introduction to my
new job and as the senior man, that was his prerogative.

By two o'clock I was tired and hungry, but the job was going well.
I had removed the axel and the broken gear and I judged there was
plenty of time to install the new one and reassemble the housing by
four o'clock. I'd been working since early morning without a break and
I decided there couldn't be any harm if I went and got my pail and ate
a quick dinner before finishing. So I headed off to the machine shop.

When I returned, I wiped my hands clean and sat down on the
floor. I wolfed down one sandwich and was munching on a second
when I saw it—or rather, I didn't see it.

The new gear was missing.

I jumped up and went over to where the gear had been lying.
I stared down at the floor as if it might magically reappear. Then I
searched the whole area—under the conveyor, behind the other vats,
around all the washing and slicing machines. Everything was just as
I had left it—the pieces of housing, the other gears, the tools—they
were all there. But not the shiny new gear.

And so I searched again, this time making a wider inspection of
the plant floor, all the way back to the machine shop.

Still nothing and now it was close to two thirty.

I went back to the vat and then back again to the machine shop,
this time in search of Yuri. He might be able to help, but he wasn't

there and so I walked the floor for a time, searching for the gear and for Yuri and taking care to stay out of sight of the floor leader who would surely ask about the job if he saw me. The time was nearing three o'clock.

A valuable hour had been wasted.

At three-fifteen I returned again to the job and when I got there, my growing suspicions were confirmed. The new gear was there, on the floor where I last saw it, and Yuri stood a few feet away, his arms akimbo, looking over my work.

I was right—people never change.

He was shaking his head and he started to speak, but then the floor leader came from behind me and Yuri's words died away. For a long moment the floor leader stared at the disassembled mess around us. His face was dark and he looked at his wristwatch.

"Do you see the time! What has been happening here all day!?"

Yuri and I looked at each other, neither of us speaking up. When we didn't answer, the floor leader slapped me solidly across the face with his open hand. I stepped backward, arrested by the sting and the affront of the blow. Yuri started to laugh, but then the floor leader turned from me and in one fluid motion, crossed the few steps to where Yuri stood and slapped him so hard that I heard the smack over the machine noise. All the while, the man was spewing out swear words at us as quickly as he could think of them—faster perhaps, because much of what he said seemed automatic, almost instinctive.

Yuri and I stood there mute and in a few moments the floor leader regained sufficient control of himself to interrogate us.

"I asked what has been happening here. Why is this still in pieces?" he said. Yuri was still rubbing his jaw and didn't answer.

"I want an answer!" the floor leader screamed, this time so loudly that two other workers came to investigate, but finding trouble, retreated back into the machinery.

"The work was coming along fine until he hid the new gear," I said. The floor leader blinked, at first not seeming to comprehend me.

"Hid the gear? What are you saying? Who hid the gear?"

I pointed at Yuri whose expression betrayed his surprise that I hadn't kept his antics a secret—as if there were some understanding between us about that. Then Yuri recovered himself.

"That's a lie," he said.

"You hid it? Why?"

"It's a lie."

"Did you hide it or didn't you?"

"I hid nothing. It's there, where it's been all day. He's a lousy mechanic and he's slow. And now he's making excuses."

I was struggling to keep cool and I pointed to the housing cover and the exposed gearing. "All that was done before two o'clock," I said. "The job would be finished if he'd left me alone."

"He's a liar," Yuri shot back. "I came back here a few minutes ago to check on him and this is what I found."

The floor leader's face was red and his neck muscles bulged.

"All it would take …" Yuri started to say.

"Enough!" the floor leader shouted. "I'll decide later what to do with you fools—both of you." He looked at his watch again. "You'll both put this back together—now—and you have exactly one hour to do it. Do you understand?"

He glared at us.

"Yes, Comrade," I said.

"Yeah," Yuri said.

He stalked away, leaving us alone in awkward silence. Yuri was still rubbing his jaw.

"Well, he's right about one thing," I said.

"And what's that?"

"You are a fool."

Yuri snorted. "It was a joke."

"Funny."

"If you'd kept your mouth shut everything would be ok."

"And take the blame for you? I don't think so. Why'd you do it, anyway?"

"If you'd kept your mouth shut, all he could say is you're slow. You could say the job was too big. I would have backed you up."

"Who knows what he'll say now—maybe that we stole the bloody thing—did you think about that?" I said.

For the soviet worker, to be inept was forgivable, but to steal or misuse property of the state was another matter altogether.

"You deserve it if he does," I said and he groaned.

"You mean we deserve it, pal. He'll report us both, d'you think about that? You're the fool."

"You haven't answered my question," I said. "Why'd you do it?"

He shrugged. "A little fun, no harm in that."

"Like being out sick yesterday?"

He grinned. "I like to watch him squirm—quota time always gets to him."

"He can see there's nothing wrong with you," I said, but he just waved a hand at me.

"He'll forget about that—he always does—and probably about the gear too. You'll learn—about getting along around here."

More talk was pointless. How could I reason with that kind of thinking? Besides, we were wasting time and so we went to work. With both of us on the job, it didn't take long and we had the vat running by four thirty. The floor leader came back at four thirty-one. He watched for a few minutes and then left without a word.

Over the next few days it seemed that Yuri's prediction was right—the floor leader said nothing more about the gear business and I settled into a tolerable routine. But I couldn't help wondering how soon it would be before I needed that kind of "fun" to get me through the day.

There had to be more than this.

But what?

CHAPTER 21

ᴈ᷎

*I*n time Yuri and I learned to coexist. He was never cordial, barely civil most of the time, but at least he didn't bother me with any more idiotic stunts like the one he pulled with the cooking vat. We helped each other only when absolutely necessary, but otherwise we stayed out of each other's way. That was just fine with me. Gradually, I took over more and more of his duties because the drinking sickness steadily tightened its grip on him. He missed a lot of work and sometimes on weekends I saw him and his associates at their favorite pastime of "four on a bottle" in the middle of the day. Once I watched them down a full liter of vodka in under five minutes. He wasn't yet thirty, but he looked ten years older. His craziness when he was drunk got so bad that once he tried to snatch the cash from a kiosk while two militiamen were on break not twenty meters away. He spent eighteen months in jail and came out with one eye beaten shut and a pronounced limp. And he drank as much as ever.

Should I have tried to help him?

I decided not—his problems were of his own making. It was none of my business and as the years passed, I watched him wither like a fly trapped between panes of window glass.

~~~~

After his discharge from service, Roman returned home to Moscow and found work maintaining the quarters of the Ministry of Light Industry and Textiles on Kirov Street. He worked long hours at the tired old glass and concrete building keeping its mechanical systems in working order. He lived with his mother, Irena Davidova, in their flat on Taganskaya where he had grown up. I stayed in touch with him because there was a regimental reunion every year in June in Moscow and I had an open invitation to stay at his flat whenever I came to the city.

For the first few years I stayed away from the reunions, but later, as memories faded, I came to look forward to them. They were a chance to see old friends and to hear the news about how the war was going from the boys just recently back. One of them first told me the rumor that our troops would soon withdraw back across our borders, leaving the Afghans to themselves.

At first I refused to believe it.

How could we withdraw when our business there wasn't finished, when the bandits were still roaming free in most of the countryside? And what of all that talk about securing our southern border? Didn't that matter anymore?

I was sure it was just another story, but then, a few months later, the first withdrawals were announced in the news and we began to pull out.

What had been the point? What did we get for losing Oleg and so many others?

~~~~

Whenever I came to Moscow I always telephoned ahead to Roman to tell him when to expect me. He always said the same thing—come whenever you like, this is your Moscow home. But once, he added something else.

"I've got some news for you," he said.

"Ok, what is it?"

"When you get here."

"Why not tell me now?"

"I'll tell you when you get here."

"It sounds like trouble," I said.

He laughed. "No, no trouble. It's good news."

"You know I don't like surprises."

"This one you will. We're having a little celebration tomorrow night and I want you here. I really want you here."

That was all he would say and he rang off.

When I arrived the next day, we went into his kitchen and I sat down while he made tea for us. We talked a little about my trip and I told him the trip had been fine, as always.

"So, what's this big news?" I asked after we'd gotten through the small talk. He sat down across the table from me.

"I'm getting married," he said.

At first I didn't know what to say. He was the handsomest one of our group from the Fergana barracks and there was no doubt he could have any girl he wanted—which to me seemed like a good reason not to get married.

"I don't believe it," I said.

"I knew you'd say that. But it's true. We agreed to everything last week."

"Well ... that's good, I guess ... if it's what you want."

"It's what I want."

"Ok, well, who is she, then? You haven't said anything about any special girl."

He coughed. "I haven't known her all that long."

"How long?" I said.

"Her name's Oksana Zarzhetskaya—everybody calls her 'Ksusha'—and she lives here in the block, upstairs. Her father's an engineer, a very good engineer. They moved here from Baku. He had the top engineering job at the Deepwater Platform Station."

"Are you marrying the girl or the father?"

"Will you just listen, I'm trying to tell you about her."

"I'm sorry, go ahead."

"They're Moscow people and so they came back here a few months ago."

"How many months ago?"

"Two or three."

"Three months?" I said. "And now you're marrying this girl?"

"I know what you're thinking, but wait 'till you meet her."

I sat back. "Sounds like you've got it pretty bad."

"I'm telling you, you'll see what I mean. They're coming over tonight."

"You're serious about this," I said.

"Of course, I'm serious."

"Have you ever had a girl friend, a real girl friend, before?"

"Well …"

"And now you're going to marry the first one?"

"I told you—you'll see what I mean," he said.

There he was again, the old stubborn Roman I recognized so well. This was the girl for him and that's all there was to it. Nothing I could say would make any difference.

"Ok, I'm waiting for you to tell me something about her," I said. "So far, all I've heard about is her dad and Baku."

He got up to make us more tea. "She's a university student—she's studying mathematics and logic."

"Logic—logic?" I laughed. "That's big trouble for you, my friend. You're about the most unlogical person I know."

"Look, Kolya," he went on. "There's a reason I want you to meet her."

"What's that?"

"You can't guess?" There was a twinkle in his eyes.

"Ah … I don't think so."

"I want you to stand with me as my witness—at the wedding."

I'd never been a witness before. In fact, I'd never been to a wedding. "I've never done that before," I said.

"It'll be easy, you won't really have to do anything, just hold the ring and don't lose it—ha! Her friend Yelena Trofimova will stand with her. It's only right you should be the one to stand with me. If it weren't for you there wouldn't be a wedding."

He watched for my reaction.

"Please," he said.

The truth was I thought the whole thing was ridiculous, his getting hooked up with a girl this way, but I couldn't refuse him and, after all, a university student with a bigshot engineer for a father wasn't a bad catch—I had to admit that.

"Sure, my friend, for you, of course."

"Good, good!" he said and he slapped me on the shoulder.

That evening at suppertime the doorbell chirped and Roman hurried to the door to greet his guests. There were five of them and he made the introductions all around. Boris and Gennady, Ksusha's brothers, looked to be young enough to still be pupils. The father was an ordinary-looking man who was introduced to me as Viktor Vladimirovich. The mother was Alyona. Ksusha was maybe five or six years younger than Roman and I could see right away why he was so taken with her. She was quite lovely—slender with dark hair cut short and an easy smile that showed perfect, white teeth. When we were introduced she held out her hand and I took it and her grip was warm and soft and very pleasing. For an instant I was sorry when she let go of my hand to embrace Roman around the neck.

The brothers were laughing and congratulating Roman as Irena Davidova pushed us all toward the meal she had laid out for us on her best table in the parlor. We pulled up chairs around the table and sat down. The brothers sat on the floor. The talk was happy and excited.

"We've heard all about you," Boris said to me.

"Have you?"

"But I didn't know you'd be here tonight."

"Well, I just telephoned Roman yesterday."

"You flew up today, then?" Boris asked.

"No, by train."

"All the way from Kursk, just to be here tonight?"

"Well ..."

"Roman said you saved his life in the war," Gennady said. They were all looking at me.

"Oh ... one of Roman's stories," I demurred.

"A story? Was it really a story?" the boy asked Roman.

"Kolya doesn't like to brag," Roman said. "You'll see when you get to know him. But it's no story. Your sister wouldn't be here with the man of her dreams if it wasn't for my friend here." Ksusha pushed him gently on the shoulder.

"Tell us," Boris said to Roman.

"The whole story," Gennady said.

"I'd like to hear it," Viktor Vladimirovich said.

"So would I," Alyona said and Roman took that as his cue to retell the events of a day like no other.

~~~~

It was true—I had saved Roman's life, but it was just a fluke, really. It was in the morning before the sun came up and we were returning to our pick-up zone from a night patrol. Winter wasn't yet fully over and the night was cold. We were spread out in a single line along a rocky path and a full moon was still up over the mountain peaks, making the night seem like day.

And we walked straight into an ambush.

Two bandits, one using an old British.303 Lee Enfield and the other using one of our own 7.62 millimeter *snaiperskaya vintovka dragunova*, dropped two of our boys with their first fire. The rest of us scrambled for whatever cover we could find. I was lucky because when the shooting started, I was maybe five meters from a boulder that gave me good cover from both bandits' fire. Golovin was behind me in our line and he fell to the ground beside me. Roman was about twenty meters ahead and wasn't so lucky. His only cover was a small overhang of rock just off the path and he pressed himself up into it as far as he could fit. More shots rang out and bullets chipped the rocks around me and Golovin. The bandits were above us in the rocks with a good field of fire. We were pinned down and it wouldn't take them long to pick us off one at a time after the sun came up and we ran out of water. Golovin and I sat up beside each other behind our boulder.

"Can you see 'em?" he said while he unslung the RPG-7 rocket grenade launcher he carried on his back. I pulled myself up and peeked around the edge in the direction of the shots.

"Nothing," I whispered, but then I saw a muzzle flash against the dark rocks and another shot rang out. I pulled back.

"I see one," I said. "Didn't see the other."

"Where is he?" he asked as he snapped up the sight on the RPG. I leaned my head back against the rock. My heart was pounding; my breath was short and shallow.

"At two o'clock, about sixty degrees up."

"Ok," he said and he turned over onto one knee and brought the tube to his shoulder. He stood up, stepped out from behind the rock, and aimed the tube up toward the shots. But at that instant a shot rang out and he collapsed to the ground beside me. The bullet had gone cleanly through the shoulder. The RPG clattered on the rocks.

"Ahhh," he groaned. There wasn't much blood, but he'd never be able to aim the RPG.

Styopa and Trostorff had taken cover behind us and were returning fire, but their little AKS-74 rounds were useless against the bandits' dug-in positions. The bandits fired again and I crouched low. The weapon that had hit Golovin was definitely a Lee Enfield, probably fitted with a night scope, which meant the bandit could spot us easily. Then there was another crack and a cry of pain.

"Ahhgghh!!"

It was Roman. I peeked around the rock and saw that the bullet had found the fleshy upper part of his arm. It was a bloody wound and if he stayed in that spot, half exposed, the next few shots might take the arm clean off. If he ran he would be cut down in a second.

"Kolya!" he called out. There was panic in his voice.

"Roman! Stay where you are!"

"I can't! I've got to move!"

"Don't! Stay where you are, I'll come get you!"

I had no idea about what to do next. Then I saw the RPG lying in the dirt, out in the open. I sprang out, grabbed it, and sprang back behind the rock. Another shot rang out from the Lee Enfield and a bullet thudded into the dirt close to the toe of my sneaker. I looked down at the tube in my hands. I was nowhere near as good a shot as Golovin with one of these. I snapped the sight back up and looked through it down the barrel. I took off my bush hat and held it up. A shot rang out and I stood up, pointed the tube and squeezed the trigger.

"Whhhoooosh!"

The projectile leaped from the end of the tube and raced up the face of the rocks. An instant later it found its mark with a flash of bright light followed by the thud of the explosion. The tube had been loaded with an HE-frag round for extra punch and I heard nothing more from the Lee Enfield. For several long minutes we waited for more shots, but there were none. The other bandit had fled back into the hills.

~~~~

Roman's supper guests listened in silence. I had heard him tell this story before and it always made me uneasy.

"Roman exaggerates," I said.

"You see," Roman said. "Kolya never brags."

"Why do you say he exaggerates?" Ksusha asked.

"Because it was pure luck I hit that bandit. I couldn't have hit him again in a hundred tries," I said and she laughed.

"But that's not the point. Surely you see that."

"I'm not sure I do. What point?"

"It doesn't matter whether your aim was good or bad. What matters is you took the shot. That rocket didn't launch itself," she said, smiling her pleasing smile. I demurred again.

"It took courage to do what you did—that's the point," she said and the others around the table nodded.

"I wouldn't call it courage exactly. I didn't think about it. I just did it," I said and she laughed again.

"Are you always so hard on yourself?"

"Well …"

"If you had thought about it, would you have just left Roman out there? Is that what you're trying to tell us?"

"Kolya, I should have warned you," Viktor Vladimirovich said with laughter in his eyes. "Never argue with Ksusha."

"We're not arguing, are we Kolya?" Ksusha said. "I'm just trying to show him what he said makes no sense."

"Thanks," I said.

She turned back to me. "The rocket was out in the open, on the ground?"

"That's right."

"And you made a choice to go get it."

"I didn't think about it."

"Of course you did," she said. "You're not a machine. We do things because we choose to do them. Maybe you didn't think about it for long, but you chose to go get that rocket."

"Here we go with that again," Boris said.

"And you did it not once, but twice," Ksusha continued. "You chose to stand up in the open and take your aim. You might have been killed, but you did it anyway."

"I hoped he wouldn't kill me," I said.

"Exactly. You must have thought about it long enough to hope his aim would be bad or that he wouldn't see you. You knew the risk, isn't that so?"

"She's just complimented you," Roman said.

"Is that what that was?" I said.

"Well, whatever he thought, we're thankful for what he did. Let's drink to that," Viktor Vladimirovich said. He reached for the bottle of vodka on the table and filled his and Roman's glasses and then raised his. The rest of us reached for our glasses of tea.

"To comrades," he intoned.

"To comrades who took care of each other," Ksusha said.

Then Viktor Vladimirovich and Roman knocked back their shots and the rest of us took a sip of tea.

We set our glasses down and Boris turned to Roman.

"What's it like to be shot?" he asked. "Did it hurt, I mean really hurt?"

"It hurt."

"They should have given you a medal," Gennady said.

"They did."

"Which one?"

"The Veteran of The Afghan War badge."

"With the blue ribbon? Can I see it?" Gennady asked.

"No, not the blue ribbon. It's the red and gold cross," Boris said to his brother.

"They should have given you a medal for bravery," Gennady said.

"Or maybe even the gold star?" Roman said and smiled.

"You think so?" the boy asked.

197

"No, I'm just teasing you," Roman said. "They don't give out that one just for getting shot."

"Show us the scar," Boris said.

"That's enough," Ksusha said.

"It's ok, I don't mind," Roman said and then he unbuttoned his sleeve and pulled it up, exposing the fiery red welt.

"You see," he said to Boris. "It was no story."

CHAPTER 22

♒

Two months later, on a hot August afternoon, Roman and Ksusha presented themselves before the city authorities and paid the three ruble fee to register for a date at the Wedding Palace at 33A Leningradskiy Prospekt. They were assigned a time slot on a Saturday in September at three o'clock in the afternoon.

On the wedding day I was back in Moscow, asleep in Roman's parlor in the early morning when I heard water running from the tap in the kitchen. It was Roman, up early, making tea. I sat up and stretched.

"Put on enough for me," I called to him.

"You're awake," he called back. "Good, we can go over a few things."

I let out a sigh. We had been over everything at least twice—some things three times—the night before, but now it seemed we would do it yet again.

"You're sure you told the car to be here at one fifteen?" he went on.

"I'm sure."

When I hired the taxi to take us to the Wedding Palace, I gave the driver specific instructions to be down on the street outside Roman's block early enough for me to do the decorations. I had ribbons and a toy bear ready to go. Roman had insisted on a toy bear to mount on the taxi's front grill—instead of the girl doll Ksusha wanted.

"I want sons," he had said. "Girls will do, but only if we can't have boys."

He brought me my tea and we sat together on the floor. He always made his tea strong, nearly black, and he loaded it with sugar, the way we used to do in service. Two big gulps and I was wide awake for more of his endless instructions about the arrangements for the day, starting with the decorations for the taxi.

"Make sure the ribbons are tied back across both sides of the hood," he said in a serious tone. "It's bad luck if there's ribbon on just one side."

"I've never heard that," I said.

"It's true. If there aren't two ribbons it's bad luck—it means the baby's life won't be, you know … complete."

"Where do you hear this nonsense?"

"He would never marry, or have kids, something like that," he said and I rolled my eyes.

"Tell me you don't really believe that."

"I'm not taking any chances. Do you have enough ribbon?"

"I have enough," I said.

When the taxi, a Volga, arrived later in the day after we finished our dinner, the driver and I spent nearly half an hour with the decorations, doing our best to give Roman exactly what he wanted. First, we wired the toy bear securely to the front grill. Then we attached two white ribbons to the bear and, as Roman had insisted, ran the ribbons back across both sides of the hood, fastening one to the driver's window and the other to the front passenger's window. I felt a little foolish—how often do you see two grown men working on a toy bear— but when we were done I knew Roman couldn't have done a better job himself.

By ten minutes after two, Roman and I were dressed in our black suits for the ceremony. Mine was borrowed, but he had bought his. I didn't ask how much it cost, but I was sure it was a lot because it was made of fine, soft cloth and it was well-tailored to fit his frame. He actually looked quite elegant. I stepped back and admired him.

"You look good," I said. "She won't recognize you."

He laughed a little at my joke, but I don't think he was really listening.

"That's good enough," he said and waved my hand away when I started to straighten his tie. "We've got to go."

At two fifteen we left the flat and started up the stairs to Ksusha's flat. But then he stopped on the stairs and turned around.

"The kvass, we forgot the kvass!" he moaned and then he started back down the stairs. I put my hands out on his chest.

"The driver has it. I took it down with the decorations."

"I didn't see you give it to him."

"He has it, I'm telling you."

"It's bad luck if we don't have the kvass."

I pointed to my watch. "It's bad luck if you miss your wedding," I said and he looked at his watch again and then turned and bounded up the stairs.

We rang Ksusha's bell and Alonya opened the door with Ksusha standing behind her. Alonya smiled at Roman and stepped aside so he could claim his bride.

I've never been much for women's fashion, but Ksusha looked enchanting. Her cream-colored dress fell almost to the floor and the long sleeves were made of delicate lace that matched her gloves. She held a bouquet of pink and white flowers and when she smiled at Roman, his powers of speech deserted him. He just gaped open-mouthed. I suppose he couldn't believe that in a short time this beautiful, refined creature would be his. I could scarcely believe it myself. Ksusha's friend Yelena was there too, in a pale blue dress that matched her eyes. Then Viktor Vladimirovich, Boris and Gennady crowded into the doorway behind the women.

"Ksusha, you look beautiful," I said after a long moment when Roman had said nothing.

"Thank you," she said with her perfect smile. Then Roman recovered himself.

"Yes, beautiful, wonderful! You look wonderful!" He took her hand and kissed it. Viktor Vladimirovich and the brothers slapped Roman on the back and then Viktor Vladimirovich looked at his watch.

"You see the time? You'd better go," he said and so I pulled Roman's arm, he pulled Ksusha's, Ksusha pulled Yelena's and the four of us hurried together down the stairs.

As I had instructed him, our driver was waiting out on the street with the pitcher of kvass, the traditional, fermented nuptial beverage.

"You'll like this batch," he said. "There's a little kick."

Roman took it and quaffed a huge swallow. With a big, wet grin he handed the pitcher to Ksusha who took a long drink while Yelena and I and a small crowd of passersby stood around them in a circle and clapped. Then Yelena finished it off and we all jumped into the Volga. I sat beside the driver and the others crowded into the back seat with Ksusha in the middle. The driver gunned the engine and the Volga nosed its way out into the street.

We were on our way.

The traffic was heavy for that time of day and we drove for a time in silence. I could feel Roman tapping his toe on the floor and his fingers on the window. He looked at his watch, then again, then again, then again.

"Just relax," I said to him.

"You look very nice," the driver said to Ksusha as he looked up at her in his rearview mirror.

"Thank you," she said. "You're very kind."

"Yes, very nice. My daughter got married last year. You remind me of her. She has the dark eyes like yours."

Then Roman leaned forward over the seat. "Listen, will we get there on time?" The traffic was still moving slowly.

The driver looked up at him in the mirror. "Oh sure, no problem," he said. "I drive for weddings all the time. No problem."

"We have about thirty minutes," Roman said, looking at his watch again.

"No problem, Mr. Bridegroom. Just relax. I've driven for fifty weddings, fifty, and I've never been late."

"Fifty?" I said.

"Maybe more. Once I drove for the Mayor's daughter. She was very nice. They were all very nice."

"Do you remember them all?" Yelena asked.

"Who?"

"The fifty weddings?"

"No, darling. Not all of them, but I'm sure I'll remember you."

Then we slowed to a stop in the traffic.

"This won't work, we're going to be late," Roman said and he leaned forward again to speak into the driver's ear.

"Turn right here at Prospekt Mira," he said. "You can go around Frunze Park and over to Novoslobodskaya. It'll be quicker."

"I don't think so, Mr. Bridegroom," the driver said.

"Do you see the time?"

"Just sit back," he said. "Fifty weddings and I've never been late."

Roman started to say something, but then the traffic started moving again. We made good time for the rest of the trip—without taking Roman's roundabout directions. The Volga pulled up in front of the Wedding Palace at two fifty-seven and the tires screeched when we stopped. The four of us jumped out and ran up the front steps.

"Gorko! Gorko!" a man walking by called out to us. A woman walking with him laughed and clapped.

"What's that mean?" I said.

"He wants Roman to sweeten his bride's lips with a kiss," Yelena said.

"Not yet," Ksusha called back to them over her shoulder.

We stepped through the front doors of the palace and ran down the long hall to the double doors that led into the ceremony room. On our way down the hall, we passed a couple on their way out. They looked happy—and relieved. Other couples were standing about outside the ceremony room fixing their hair and clothes and talking in hushed tones as they waited for their turn inside. Our timing was perfect. We stopped outside the doors to catch our breath precisely at two fifty-nine. Ksusha and Yelena straightened each other's dresses and I tried again to do something with Roman's tie. Roman gave his name to the attendant. She looked at her book and her watch and then stepped into the ceremony room, closing the doors behind her. A moment later she came out again, nodded to us.

I took a deep breath and we entered the chamber.

The room was spacious with a high ceiling, fine decorative moldings on the walls and around the doors and a brightly-polished wood floor. A crystal chandelier hung on a chain from the ceiling over a marble-topped table in the center of the room. Vases of white flowers stood on each end of the table. Soft light filtered into the room through tall windows covered with sheer curtains. A recording of classical music played from speakers in the ceiling. To the left of the table stood a bust of Comrade Lenin and a wreath of fresh white and red flowers laid around the base of the bust. Roman took Ksusha's hand.

"Ready?" he whispered to her.

"Ready," she whispered.

When the doors closed behind us, the wedding director, a small elderly woman, rose from her chair behind the table and beckoned us to come closer. She wore a long, lavender gown and a wide, red sash—the badge of her office—across her chest. As we approached the table, she nodded to an assistant and the music stopped. Then she reached down onto the table, picked up a piece of paper and started to read from it.

"Good afternoon," she began from her script. "I am authorized by the ruling authorities of the City of Moscow of the Russian Soviet Federated Socialist Republic to register this marriage between Roman Dmitriyevich Davidov and Oksana Viktorovna Zarzhetskaya on this day." Then she set the paper down on the table.

"Are you Roman and Oksana?" she asked.

"Yes, Comrade," Roman and Ksusha said together.

She smiled. "Are you ready?" she asked Ksusha.

"Yes Comrade," Ksusha answered in a clear voice.

"And you?" she asked Roman.

"Ready," he said.

"Then please step forward and sign the document." She pushed the wedding paper across the table and picked up a pen and held it out. Without any hesitation, Ksusha took the pen, leaned over the table and signed her name in a quick, neat hand at the two required places. When she finished, she handed Roman the pen and he scrawled his name above hers.

I looked over at Yelena and winked.

"The witnesses will now sign," the wedding director said and Yelena and I took our turns with the pen. When we finished, she took back the document and examined the signatures.

"The rings please," she said.

I stepped forward and handed her two gold bands. She inspected them and then asked Roman and Ksusha to step forward again.

"You will now exchange the rings that will symbolize this marriage and the duties you undertake today to the state and to each other," she said.

Ksusha and Roman turned to each other. He took her slender hand and fixed the ring in place on the third finger of her right hand. Then she did the same for him and they smiled at each other and turned again to face the wedding director.

"This is a great and important day for you and for the state," she said. "Do you both understand the obligations you take on here today?"

"Yes, Comrade," Roman said.

"Yes, we do," Ksusha said.

"The state requires you to be strong and productive and I urge you always to help and encourage each other and always to act together as one. This will bring you happiness. Always be there for each other."

She paused a moment and then smiled again.

"I declare now that you are married," she said. Ksusha and Roman turned to each other and embraced and kissed lightly on the mouth.

It was done. The music began to play again, this time a lively, dancing tune. We thanked the director and her assistant and the assistant handed Roman and Ksusha their passports, showing them where she had registered their marriage. Roman pulled an envelope from his jacket and handed it to the director. She took it with a slight nod. We left the chamber and I glanced at my watch; the whole affair had taken exactly ten minutes.

Outside in the hall, where the next couple was waiting their turn, Roman was himself again. He smiled widely.

"I thought I was going to faint," he said, throwing his arm around Ksusha's shoulders.

"From what, marrying me?"

"No, no, from saying the wrong thing and then her saying 'Oh, no, this won't do—the whole thing's off.'"

"That's better." Ksusha stood up on her toes and pecked him on the cheek.

"And I was sure Kolya would fumble the rings," he said. He gave me a little push.

"How'd I do?" I said.

"Well, you didn't drop them."

Our driver was waiting for us out on the street and as we came down the steps, he doffed his cap to the newlyweds and bowed low.

"You see, fifty-one weddings and never late," he said and we all laughed.

We got back into the Volga and sped away to Red Square for photographs. Ksusha and Roman stood together on the steps at Lenin's Mausoleum while Yelena and I took turns taking the pictures. We took dozens, from every angle.

"Roman," I said as I looked at him through the camera lens. "I think your color is finally back." We all laughed again. A group of shoppers who had come out of *GUM*, the state department store, called out a greeting as they crossed the square. We waved back at them. They walked away past St. Basil's Church.

The celebration was already underway when we arrived back at Ksusha's flat. Roman loosened his tie and tossed his jacket onto a chair. Ksusha disappeared into a bedroom and emerged again in a few minutes wearing a stylish, short blue dress. The flat was filled with neighbors and friends eating zakuski and drinking vodka and champagne and dancing to music from a record player. They stayed late and I finally retired to Roman's flat after one in the morning. On my way out the door, I glanced back and saw Roman and Ksusha dancing together in the middle of the room, cheek to cheek, to the slow melody of a Georgian love ballad.

CHAPTER 23

❧

*R*oman's was the only soviet wedding I ever witnessed because the next year brought the end of the USSR—with no more warning to us than a thunderclap. Our great state vanished like ground mist in the morning, or as Deda put it, like wood smoke from an *izb* chimney when the wind catches it. It was there and then it was gone. And with it went our jobs, our positions, our pensions, everything we had depended on for our security.

And as bad as that was, it was worse that the reasons remained a mystery. We watched television, we read newspapers and we talked—to our neighbors, to our co-workers, to our supervisors—but no one had answers.

It was inexplicable. How could we be a world power one day and bankrupt the next?

Father and Mother have never adjusted to the new ways and I don't suppose they ever will. Why, there was even talk that they would be forced to move out of the flat at 14 Parkovaya unless they bought it from the new government. The notion was incomprehensible to them. A monkey could more easily grasp the principles of electricity. Deda showed more equanimity. He had outlived Babulya and most of his friends by that time and he said he was just too old to make much of a fuss about it. Life would go on for him pretty much like before.

I understood how Mother and Father felt, but I embraced the changes. For me they meant new possibilities. I even allowed myself to imagine I could get my hands on a Moscow *propisku*—a residence permit—that golden piece of paper that would be my ticket out of Kursk to a new life.

CHAPTER 24

꩜

*T*he next October I was again visiting in Moscow, staying at the flat with Roman and Ksusha and Irena Davidova. It was late in the afternoon and we were waiting for Roman to get home from work. He had phoned to say he was working late, repairing one of the pipes from the pumping station that brought steam into the ministry building. The day had brought the first chill that fall and he had to make sure the pipes were in good order for the real cold ahead. Near suppertime, when there was still no sign of him, I decided to go over to Kirov Street to meet him when he finished his shift.

The sidewalks were crowded with people carrying their shopping packages, their collars turned up against the wind that had started to blow. I stopped on the front steps to button up my coat. As I fastened the last button, I noticed a figure leaning against a light post on the street, watching the crowd, his hands in his pockets. I just glanced at him at first, but then I took a second look. He was familiar somehow. I squinted and walked down the steps.

It couldn't be.

He seemed lost in his thoughts until I was just a few meters away. Then he turned and saw me.

Styopa?

He stood up straight and smiled. He pulled his hands from his pockets and opened his arms wide. "Hello, boyo," he said.

Styopa!

I threw my arms around him and we hugged and kissed each other and laughed.

"I don't believe it!" I said.

We called each other a lot of not so nice names, loudly enough that some on the street turned to see if there was trouble.

"I thought for sure you were dead," I said.

"Who else would wait for you out here in this cold?"

I'd said goodbye to him here in Moscow after our flight home from Bagram, before he went home to Novosibirsk, and I hadn't seen him since. For a time we wrote, but the letters had stopped years ago.

"Waiting? For me?"

"Who else? I called your flat and your mother gave me this address, but she didn't have a flat or telephone number. You really should give her those, you know. So, I came and waited. You or Roman had to come along sooner or later."

"How long have you been here?"

He shrugged. "I landed at Domodyedovo this morning."

"I mean out here on the street?"

"Long enough to get a stiff back."

I stepped back to size him up. "Let me look at you. You look awful, too thin. Come up to the flat and let's get some food in you."

"Ahh … not just yet."

"Come on, you still eat, don't you?"

"I have a better idea. Let me buy you supper—somewhere where we can talk, just us."

"Buy me supper? So you're a big spender now, with money for restaurants?"

"I can manage to feed you, I think." He pulled his gloves from his pocket and started to put them on.

"Well, sure—if that's what it takes to find out what you're doing here," I said.

"I told you, waiting for you. Let's go."

"Ok, but come up to the flat first so I can let them know not to save me a place. Roman'll want to see you. He's married now, you know."

"Your mother told me."

"She's charming, a lot better than he deserves."

"I'll wait here. I don't have a lot of time on this trip and I want to be sure we have time to talk."

"Ok," I said. "Stay there."

And so after I told Ksusha not to hold supper for me, Styopa took me straightaway to one of the new "foreign" restaurants that were popping up around the city.

The Starlight Diner was a big silver tube—like an obese metro car—at 16 Bolshaya Sadovaya, set back from the street in a small wooded park across from the Chinese embassy. Styopa said it was supposed to be a replica of an American diner, down to the red and yellow plastic condiment bottles on the tables. I'd heard about it. It catered to foreigners who wanted to eat western food while they were in Russia and to the "new" Russians who wanted to show off their money. In those days people like me jumped at the chance to work at places like the Starlight as cooks and servers because they paid western wages. They also charged western prices that I could never afford. A meal at the Starlight cost more than I could earn at the sugar plant in a week.

There was a line to get inside, but Styopa spoke to someone inside the door, passed some money, and we were let inside. Customers sat on metal stools at a long counter, eating and drinking. Sweaty cooks in white aprons worked an open grill behind the counter, calling out to the servers when their orders were ready. The servers, all of them pretty young girls, hurried back and forth, taking food and drinks to customers sitting in booths along the walls. The place was filled with cigarette smoke and the sounds of clattering dishes and talking people.

A hostess took us to the small bar in the back where Styopa greeted a petite blonde woman with a hug. He told me she was the manager.

"This is my good friend, Kolya," he said to her. "Treat him right, it's his first time in here."

She held out her hand. "Pleased to meet you," she said in good, but accented Russian.

"Pleased to meet you too. Your accent, you're English?" I said.

"American. Ever been there?"

I laughed. "No. Where exactly?"

"Satellite Beach—Florida, why?"

"Just curious. I've never met an American before."

She smiled and opened her arms. "Am I what you expected?"

"Umm … I guess."

Styopa laughed. "You're not what I expected, not mean enough."

"Well, I'm glad you're here," she said to me. "I hope we'll see you again."

Then one of the servers called to her and she and Styopa said a few parting words in what sounded like passably good English.

"When did you learn to speak American?" I asked when we sat down at the bar.

"English," he said.

"Right, that's what I meant."

"Oh, I don't know much, but in our business, it's starting to come in handy. I've got some tapes and she lets me practice on her."

"Your business?"

"We'll get to that. So—what'll you have?"

The mirrored wall behind the bar was fitted with shelves filled with bottles of expensive-looking liquor with foreign labels. He turned to the barman.

"Beer—Heineken." The barman nodded and looked at me.

"Just tea," I said.

"Ah, my Kolya, always the sober one."

I shrugged. "No taste for it, you know that."

"Yeah, I know that. Something strange about it."

"Remember what my grandmother said."

"I know, I know, 'it's God's hand' on you."

"That's it. You haven't forgotten."

He smiled. "Well, if you ever get a taste for it, I think you'd be a Scotch whiskey man. There's Glenlivet," he said, pointing to a bot-tle on one of the shelves. "That's a single malt. And that," he said, pointing to another bottle. "That's Glenmorangie. Eighteen years old. A bottle of that would cost you maybe fifty British pounds. Half a month's wages in Moscow. A whole month's I would imagine in Novosibirsk or Kursk."

"You can have mine," I said and he shook his head.

"Truth is, I don't really like the taste."

"For somebody who doesn't like the taste, you know a lot about it."

"If our clients like it, I want to know about it."

"So you have clients now too?"

He nodded. "I do indeed."

"Ok, my friend, what is this? Your 'business', your 'clients', what are you up to?"

He reached up and put his hand around my neck. "How long has it been, six, seven years?"

"Eight."

"Really?"

"Yup ... why'd you lose touch?" I said.

"I dunno, why did you?"

The barman set our drinks down in front of us. While Styopa paid, I looked him over more closely. He was definitely thinner and there were lines around the eyes now. And overall he looked like times were good for him—the bar was filled with prosperous looking people wearing stylish clothes and Styopa fit right in with his soft brown leather jacket and matching gloves that I couldn't afford with six month's wages. I felt shabby in my plain jacket and trousers and scuffed-up shoes. A Russian couple sitting next to us was joined by friends who spoke what sounded like German and one of them bought drinks for the whole group and paid with notes he peeled from a thick wad. Styopa watched me take all this in with a smirk on his face.

"Like this place?" he asked.

"I'm glad you're paying," I said and he laughed.

"You're my guest."

"How often do you come here?"

"Whenever I'm in town."

"I didn't know you'd been in Moscow. You should have called, we could have met."

"I meant to, I really did, but there's never much time. I'm here for a day or two and then I leave."

He downed his beer and motioned to the barman to bring him another.

"You're still at the plant, right?" he asked and I nodded.

"How is it?"

"You know how it is," I said.

"I can imagine. Still—it's a living."

"I guess."

"Well, you could look for something else."

"I don't know how it is in Novosibirsk, but at least it still pays, on time even. Wages at the tractor plant are six months behind, other places worse than that."

"True, but there're new ... let's say 'opportunities' these days," he said.

"They haven't found me yet."

"'Yet' may be the key word, my boy."

Before I could ask what that meant, the call came that our table was ready. Styopa laid a nice tip on the bar and then a hostess took us to a booth in a corner of the dining room. It was big enough for six people. The menu was in English and Styopa ordered us both a supper of western style eggs with roasted potatoes, bacon, toasted bread and coffee.

"So, what brings you to Moscow this time?" I asked after the server left us.

"I'm moving here soon," he said.

"Really? When?"

"In a month or so. There are a few details to work out yet, but soon."

"That's outstanding," I said "We'll get to spend some time together—with Roman and Ksusha too."

He leaned toward me. "The truth is, I do want us to spend time together—that's why I came to find you."

"Well, you found me."

"You see, my business is moving here too, and that's where you come in."

"What does that have to do with me?"

He picked up one of the condiment bottles and started to slowly turn it on the table. "You know, I was just like you," he said.

"How's that?"

"Oh, doing nothing, waiting, waiting for something to come along. Know what I mean?"

"I knew you'd never go to university," I said.

He kept turning the bottle. "Actually, I did go, for a year. It wasn't for me."

"You knew that before you started."

"Like I said, I was just waiting."

"And you think that's what I'm doing?"

"Aren't you?"

"I have a job."

He sat back and looked at me for a long moment. "I finally understood things would never get better if I just waited for something to happen. I had to make it happen."

Now it was my turn to sit back and take a long look at him. "Is there a point to this?"

"Are you tired of waiting?"

"I get the feeling I'm being recruited for something," I said.

He put the condiment bottle back in its place. "Possibly."

When we finished the meal he paid and we left the diner and stood together outside under the trees. It had gotten colder and he zipped up his jacket and pulled up his collar. The tree tops rustled from a small wind. He pulled a folded piece of paper from a pocket and pushed it into my hand. Then he hugged me again.

"Come to this address tomorrow morning. It'll be worth your time." I looked at the address. I didn't recognize it, but I knew the neighborhood.

"What's this about?" I said.

"I've kept in touch with some old friends and we need someone with your … ah … experience."

"My experience? Doing what, oiling rusted gears?"

"We'll explain tomorrow. I'm just here to see if you'll talk to us."

"How could I not talk to you, my friend?"

"I hoped you'd say that. Tomorrow morning at 10, then. Someone wants to see you."

He walked away.

CHAPTER 25

𝕊tyopa's puzzling invitation took me the next morning to a neighborhood on the Sparrow Hills—*Vorob'evy Gory*—a line of high bluffs fronting the Moscow River, five kilometers southwest from the Kremlin. The sweeping view from those heights—of the Novodevichy Convent, the Moscow River, and the skyline beyond—is the best in the city. I couldn't help feeling expansive and optimistic whenever I went there. On weekends the park along the ridge is filled with newlyweds toasting each other and posing for photos. I tried to persuade Roman and Ksusha to go there for their wedding photos, but Roman didn't want to spend the money for the extra taxi ride.

The address Styopa gave me belonged to a flat in a small, modest-looking block set far back from Aleksei Tolstoy Street, well concealed behind a screen of birch trees and a burdock hedge. I'd been to that neighborhood before, but I'd never noticed this block. In soviet times, when it was built, quality things were always hidden. To the unobservant, it was completely ordinary, built with common white brick, but if you looked closely, you'd see the workmanship was very fine. Someone had leveled the rows of brick with care and any excess mortar had been neatly smoothed away. Instead of the exposed, rusted metal balconies like ours at 14 Parkovaya, the balconies here were sealed with what looked like fresh paint and were set back into the walls. The darkened glass windows were double caulked. And out in front were weeded flower beds and a trimmed lawn of winter grass. I was sure there was electronic security, but I couldn't spot it.

I punched the code he had written out—*sem, sem, shest, dvah*—into the keypad mounted on the wall next to the front door. The heavy door clicked open, giving me entry into a tastefully furnished lobby.

I got into the lift and it carried me swiftly to the top floor where I stepped out onto a spotless landing illuminated by soft light from bulbs recessed into the ceiling. I reached up to the wall beside the only door and pushed the button once. A bell rang inside the flat and a moment later Styopa opened the door, looking freshly bathed and shaved and wearing creased grey slacks and a soft sweater the deep color of red wine from the Caucasus. He wore his dark hair slicked straight back like some sort of film actor.

"You're early. I knew you would be. Come in, come in," he said, opening the door wider. I smelled his cologne when I passed by him into the spacious foyer. He took my coat and gloves.

"This way. Let's be comfortable," he said and he led me into an enormous parlor appointed with fine wood furniture and colorful, gilt-framed paintings on the walls. Beyond the parlor was a kitchen filled with shining appliances. Rich carpets covered the wood floors. In one wall of the parlor a wood fire crackled in a fireplace.

I was stunned.

I had always imagined there must be flats like this for the very top people, but I never expected to see one. For me, such places as this were like the moon—they existed, but they simply had no connection with me and they never would.

We sat down opposite each other in big, cushioned chairs near the fire. Styopa looked relaxed as he played the part of the attentive host.

"How about some tea, or maybe something to eat?"

"No thanks, nothing. I had a good breakfast." He said.

"I knew you'd be early, I knew it."

"I wanted to make sure I could find this place."

"Sure. No problems then? Finding the address, I mean."

I shrugged. "No problems."

"Good, that's good."

What I wanted much more than food was an explanation. I wanted to get my old friend talking and I knew from past experience that shouldn't be too difficult.

"Well, my friend," I said, "It looks like the new ways have been good for you."

"Business is good."

"It must be. So this is your new home?" I said and he laughed.

"Business is not quite this good for me, not yet anyway. No, this is the colonel's flat, one of them. He lets me use it when I'm in town."

"The colonel?"

"An associate."

"Looks like a good kind of associate to have," I said.

"You're right about that. It was his idea to invite you here."

"His idea?"

"Well … I mentioned your name and he agreed we should have a talk with you."

"Well, where is he?"

"You'll see him soon, I hope."

I settled back into my chair and looked around at my surroundings. Styopa watched me with the expression of someone studying products on a store shelf.

"I wish Roman and Ksusha could see this," I said. "They'll think I've made it all up."

Styopa sat up in his chair.

"Actually, I'd prefer you not mention this to them," he said. "We want to keep this between us—for now."

"They know we had supper. They know I'm here this morning."

"Sure, that's ok, but just keep the details between us. It's best right now."

"Look, Styopa" I said. "I haven't heard from you in years and now you turn up and dangle all this in front of me. What do you want?"

He laughed. "You sound like a state prosecutor."

"I mean it, what's this about?"

"Tell me, how do you like it here in Moscow?" he said.

"Well enough."

"Better than Kursk?"

"Yes—stupid question," I said and he laughed again.

"I agree, but I wanted to hear you say so. You'd like to live here then?"

"I have a job in Kursk, remember?"

"You could call it that."

"It's decent," I said.

"For some maybe, but not for you. Remember who you're talking to. I know your ... talents."

"You're forgetting I don't have a residence permit," I said and he leaned back and shrugged.

"Don't worry about that," he said. "We can arrange one."

"Can you?"

"No problem at all."

"And why would you do that?"

"Now who's asking the stupid questions? To get you here to Moscow, of course."

"Styopa, what do you want?"

He eyed me for a moment. "Like I told you last night—we need someone with your training."

"Go on."

"Reliable people—people with good sense and judgment— aren't easy to find, especially these days. We need someone like that. I thought of you."

"You're flattering me."

"I know better than that."

"You're doing it anyway—and who's this 'we' you keep talking about?"

"The colonel—and our other associates."

"Go on," I said and he paused, like he was deciding whether to cross over a line.

"Here it is," he said. "We work for the Defense Ministry. After the old government dissolved there have been demobilizations. You've heard about that, I'm sure. Equipment and supplies must be assembled and stored. Arrangements must be made to locate and account for it—and to transport it all to storage depots. You can imagine, the job is huge."

"Doesn't the Ministry have people in active service for that?"

"It does and we're not involved in that end of things, actually. The truth is, it's impossible to store it all and so the Ministry has licensed a few groups, like us, to sell the excess. We get a commission, a very nice one."

He paused and the fire popped. I understood at once where this was going.

"All of this comes from a few extra rifles?" I said about our surroundings.

"Those 'few extra rifles,' as you put it, have been more than enough to equip three battalions, and we're just getting started. And there's new product to sell too. Our license includes that."

"Who are these 'groups' who are doing the selling?" I asked.

"Oh, people who know where the clients are. People like us."

"So what's this got to do with me?"

"We need somebody who knows the equipment. Somebody to check the condition, make deliveries. And some of our clients want demonstrations and so we need help with those, too."

"You can do all that," I said.

"True, but I need help and you're a mechanic, too. I'm not. We have trucks to maintain."

"There must be thousands of mechanics in Moscow."

"I'm sure there are, but can we trust them? That's the question."

"Trust them with what?"

"Kolya, you know what I'm talking about. Look, there's money at stake here, a lot of money. I know you, we can trust you, and you're perfect for this. We want you to join us."

He sat back, watching me. Then he leaned forward again to the edge of his chair.

"This is a chance for you to finally do something—and to make some good money. It's perfect for you. Come with us, we'll be together again. It'll be like old times."

It sounded so simple and there was no denying the grand flat we were sitting in or Styopa's evident prosperity.

"Which systems are we talking about?" I asked.

"Only the lighter stuff. It's less complicated, politically, and it's cheaper, which means a bigger market."

"Which systems exactly?"

"Well, the Kalashnikov and most of its derivatives. Most of that new product comes from the Ishmash plant in Izhevsk."

"Which models?"

"Mostly the 101s and 102s. Most of our clients want the 5.56 millimeter cartridge."

"That's NATO spec ammunition," I said.

"Very good, you're remembering."

"The 5.45 does more damage," I said as memories flooded over me. Instead of piercing through like the heavier rounds, the 5.45 millimeter tumbles when it makes contact with flesh, turning whatever it hits into a bloody mess.

"Don't we know it, but most of our clients still prefer the heavier round."

"Do you deliver the weapons with original serial numbers?"

"Certainly. We couldn't remove them if we wanted to. They're struck down to .2 millimeters into the metal."

"So this is legal?"

"Oh, who's to say what's strictly legal in Russia these days."

"Is that all?"

"Is that all we get from Ishmash? Oh, no. We sell the Nikonov assault rifle and the Bizon submachine gun. And the Dragunov sniper rifle is very popular too—you'd be surprised who some of our clients are for that. Like I said, though, just the simple stuff."

"If you're doing so much business with Ishmash, why move to Moscow?" I asked and he smiled, like a fisherman who'd just set his hook.

"To be close to the used stocks at the Tula airbase. Tula will be bigger for us than Ishmash ever was and there are fewer headaches getting the product out and over the border to Poland. There are decent roads from Tula to Moscow and rail links from Moscow all the way to Brest and Warsaw."

"Which weapons from Tula?"

"All the normal equipment for the *decantniki*, and new product from the Instrument Design Bureau—the Kornet-E and Metis-M missile systems will probably have the biggest market."

"I don't know those," I said.

"Portable anti-tank weapons, like the RPG. You won't have any trouble with them. Oh, and from the Tula Arms Plant, we also sell the new compact assault rifle with silencer. You'd be surprised about the clients for that, too."

"I imagine I'd be armed."

"I'm afraid so—a necessary precaution these days with all the criminal elements on the loose."

"Have you had any of that kind of trouble?"

"None at all and we don't expect any. We have good protection from a roof here in Moscow."

"A roof?" I said. "Thugs, you mean. Why would the Defense Ministry need a roof?"

"Everybody needs a roof these days, even the Ministry."

"Why not use the Federal Security Service or officers from the Interior Ministry?" I asked and he shrugged.

"We'd rather not involve them. They … complicate things."

"I hear a roof costs money, a lot of money."

"It's manageable. You can't believe how much money there is to be made. We couldn't sell all the product in ten years and we'll be retired long before that."

He sat back and studied me again.

"Well, then, is everything clear?" he asked and I nodded. Everything said and unsaid was very clear.

"Then what do you say?"

"You brought me here to show me how much money there is in this?"

"We wanted you to see for yourself the … fruits of our labor, so to speak."

He would insist on an answer, but why did I hesitate? Hadn't I been desperate all these years for just this kind of opportunity? Well, here it was on a golden plate. These were troubled times and something like this was just what I'd dreamed about. The currency had been wildly unstable that summer, the price of a loaf of bread jumping from 3000 rubles to 5000 in just one month. Plants were closing and people were going hungry. Even if I kept my job at the sugar plant, there was no guarantee it could still pay my wages next month or that the wages would be worth anything if it could pay them. And then, as if by a miracle, here was a way out. What was I thinking—of course I would take it!

"What else can I say? Ok."

"Excellent, excellent!"

He jumped up and hugged me around the neck.

"You won't be sorry about this. You'll see," he said.

Then he lifted the receiver of the telephone on the table next to his chair, dialed a number and said I had agreed. A short time later the colonel arrived at the flat. After I'd gotten over my surprise the three of us talked over the many details of my new employment until dinnertime. My head was spinning and I declined their offer to stay for the meal. I left, determined to find a quiet spot where I could sit and ponder it all.

From Aleksei Tolstoy Street, I wandered down to the fence along the ridge of the Sparrow Hills. At the bottom of the steep wooded slope, the Moscow River bends back on itself in a wide arc. A line of river barges, linked end-to-end like sausages, motored slowly forward, foam swirling back from the bow of the lead vessel. Inside the river's arc was the athletic stadium, empty and quiet at this time of year. Beyond the stadium, along the river's east bank, a few solitary figures strolled in Gor'ki Park.

Down the fence from where I stood were the ski jumps for the Moscow State University and state team jumpers. The jumpers were out that day and I watched them slowly climb the stairs up to the high launch platforms. They carried their skis in bundles over their shoulders. A small crowd gathered near me to watch. The first jumper, strapped into his skis, slowly approached the edge of the platform and stood there for many long seconds, motionless. All eyes were fixed on him. Then he pushed himself forward onto the jump and plummeted downward. Seconds later he rocketed off the end of the jump and into the air, his head forward, the loose material of his garments fluttering in the wind. He was suspended there for an instant and then he disappeared behind the trees and down the hill. From the steep upward angle of his trajectory as he shot off the jump, I was sure he had no idea where he would land.

Then it hit me and I smiled and shook my head.

"Perfect," I said out loud.

CHAPTER 26

*T*he next day, Styopa and I met again, this time for supper in the dining room in the tower of the Hotel Rossiya. We sat next to a window with the westerly view toward Krasnaya—Red Square—and the red, crenellated walls of the Kremlin. He was leaving that evening for Novosibirsk and we talked about my affairs in Kursk and how soon I could wind them up for the move to Moscow. Before he left, he pushed an envelope across the table to me. There was amusement in his eyes.

"More of your surprises?" I asked.

"Look inside and see," he said, watching me over the rim of his teacup. I tore open the envelope and found a short stack of crisp new notes in foreign currency.

"Swiss francs," he said.

"For what?"

"You can't keep staying with Roman. This'll help you get your own flat."

I counted the notes, making sure the server wasn't looking. It was a lot of money, more than enough to lease a very decent flat for a year, with plenty left over for furniture.

"I can't pay this back," I said and he smiled.

"Pay it back when you can. You might be able to sooner than you think."

I fingered the notes again. They had a fine, smooth feel.

"What about the currency laws?" I said. "There'll be questions about how a nobody from Kursk could get Swiss francs."

He set his cup down.

"Oh, I don't think so. Who's going to report you? Everybody needs money these days and as long as these are genuine—and they are—there won't be any questions."

Of course, I accepted his generosity and in a few weeks time I moved into a two-bedroom flat near Serpukhovskaya, on the south side of the city. It had big windows that looked west and unusually good water pressure in the pipes. Best of all, it was near our garage and warehouse which were out on the southwest stretch of the outer ring road, about a kilometer from the M2. It was an easy trip to the garage from my new flat—the metro from Serpukhovskaya to Prazhskaya and from there, a short bus ride to the ring road. Later, as our business grew, I moved into much better quarters on Mokhovaya Street.

Business often took me away from the city, sometimes for days and sometimes even for weeks, but when I was home there was time for relaxing and general loafing. Whenever Roman and Ksusha asked me about my business with Styopa, I made vague references to "used equipment."

~~~~

The spring and summer after the end of my second year in Moscow were busy times for Ksusha. She was in her last year of graduate studies at Moscow State University. She wrote stories for *My iz MGU*, the Students' Union newspaper, and she worked on the committee that planned the Lomonosov international conference for that year. The conference was held in April and more than a thousand university students from all over Russia, Belarus, Ukraine, Latvia and Estonia attended to hear lectures and present papers. I never knew what the lectures and papers were all about, but the event must have been special because she got a letter from the university Rector himself congratulating her on the committee's great achievement.

"A lot of hot air," Roman said to me.

"Have you told her that," I said.

"Are you kidding?"

In the summer, after classes ended and the weather turned warmer, Ksusha said I needed to get out a bit.

"Really, Kolya, all you do is work or sit around your flat," she said.

"Or come over here to eat," Roman said.

"Kolya's always welcome to supper. But really, have you seen any of the city?"

"I've ridden the metro," I said.

"That's not a serious answer."

"I will—when I get some time."

"You should show him," Roman said to her. "Before classes start again."

"After you get done with whatever it is you do in the morning," he said to me. "Just make sure you're back in time for my supper," he said to Ksusha.

"That's too much trouble," I said.

"It's no trouble," she said.

"Kolya, just go," he said. "She needs something to do and I'd rather have her with you than a bunch of puffed-up students."

She leaned down and kissed him on the top of his head.

So every day for a week Ksusha took me around the city. She took me to see the grand residences of the czarist patricians at Kropotkinskaya, the old buildings painted pastel pinks, greens and yellows, and then we walked in the shade of the trees along Gogolevsky Boulevard. I especially liked Old Arbat Street where we looked through the shops and stopped on the promenade to listen to the musicians and to a storyteller who performed every day at three o'clock at the corner of Znamenka Street. We ended most days sitting under the maple trees at Manege Square eating ice cream we bought from one of the street vendors, women dressed in white coats like hospital workers. It was sweet and cold and the perfect way to finish a warm day.

"So what do you think, so far?" she said.

"I feel like a tourist."

"Well, in a way you are. And we've just scratched the surface. There's still the ballet, museums, the theater …"

I held up my hand. "One at a time, please."

My ice cream was melting and I took a big bite. "Really, thanks, thanks for showing me. I do appreciate it. It was good of Roman to loan you to me."

"Oh, is that what he did?"

"Just kidding." I took another bite of ice cream before it could roll down onto my hand. The sunlight shone off her wedding ring. "You know, I'm happy for you two."

"Thank you. I'm very happy."

"I can see he is too. I had my doubts, you know."

She smiled. "You and everybody else. But he's so gentle and kind—and not just to me. I love him very much."

"It shows. He's a fine boy—man, I mean."

She laughed. "There's a lot of boy there too." She finished her ice cream and then wiped her hands against each other. "He loves you like a brother, you know."

"I feel the same."

"When we were dating it was always 'Kolya this, Kolya that.' Sometimes it felt like there were three of us."

"You mean, the two or three weeks while you were dating?"

"Three and a half months, thank you."

"Just kidding—again. We went through a lot together."

"He'll never forget it. It's one of the reasons he wants to stay close to you. He says you have a kind of power."

"That's ridiculous."

"It's what he says. I don't mean he says you can change things. No, it's … it's something else."

"He says that, does he?"

"Is he right?"

"I've never thought of it that way."

Then a band of Hare Krishnas came down the sidewalk, dressed in sheer, flowing robes in rainbow colors. They shook tambourines and beat on drums to accompany their wailing voices. Leading the little parade was a young girl in a red robe and pointed slippers who leaped, twirled and twisted to the music. The crowd watched with perplexed looking faces and parted to let them pass.

Each day I brought Ksusha back to the flat in the early evening where Roman was waiting. And each day he invited me to supper. Ksusha was an excellent cook, and there was no one waiting for me at my flat, and of course I accepted.

On the evening of our last outing, a Saturday, we got on to the subject of the sugar plant. Roman and I were sitting at the table while Ksusha fixed our supper, a dish of noodles and sausage, Roman's favorite.

"Beets? Really? I didn't know they made it from beets," she said. "We always had a package in the kitchen, but I didn't know that."

"What did you think it's made from?"

"I don't know—sugar cane."

I laughed. "This isn't Cuba."

"Beets. I'd like to see it," she said.

"The plant? No you wouldn't. It's dirty and noisy and there are people there you wouldn't like too much."

"What was his name?" Roman said, snapping his fingers.

"Yuri Matyukh," I said.

"That's it."

It was strange—I could go for months without ever thinking about Yuri and then, for no reason at all, he would pop back into my head.

"Who is he?" Ksusha said. She handed Roman a steaming plate. I told her a few of the things Yuri had done to me. To tell everything would have taken the whole evening.

"I know what I would have done," Roman said.

"You would have let it go," she said. She handed another plate to me. The food was piled high and it smelled of hot grease and spices.

"I don't think so," Roman said while he twisted a mouthful of noodles around his fork.

"Yes, you would have."

"Tell that to Kolya—he hasn't let it go." He took in a mouthful.

"Kolya knows that."

"I might have lost my job," I said.

"Maybe, maybe not. If you did, so what?" Roman said.

"I needed that job." I took a bite of sausage. It was hot and it burst open and juice ran down my chin.

"You should have taught him some manners," Roman said. "You were just back from the war, in top shape. You could have waited for him after work and … you know … taught him some manners."

"Maybe," I said. "I hated him enough, that's for sure."

"Nothing too serious. If you broke a bone or two—little ones—that would be ok."

"That's a lot of rubbish and you know it," Ksusha said. "Kolya, don't listen to him, he doesn't mean it."

"I know," I said.

"But you have to let it go, Kolya. If you don't, it just hurts you, not him."

"I don't follow that."

"All these bad thoughts you've been carrying around about him."

"I don't think about him that much."

"It's like you took a big drink of poison and now you're waiting for Yuri to die," she said. "Does that make any sense? Who has the problem?"

"I don't know what you're talking about."

"Let it go, Kolya."

"I can't."

"Forgive him," she said.

"Just like that?" I said and I snapped my fingers. "Everything's fine."

"I didn't say 'forget.' I said 'let it go'—forgive, not forget."

"Why should I do him any favors?"

She laughed and sat down at the table. "You're not listening. It's for you, not him."

"What is?"

"Forgiveness," she said.

I shook my head. "I don't get what you're saying."

I looked at Roman but he was busy shoveling more food into his mouth.

"She's not making any sense," I said to him. He just shrugged and cut another piece of his sausage.

"Forgive him, Kolya. It'll lighten your heart, not his."

"Impossible," I said.

It seemed we were at a standoff. She pursed her lips and studied me for a moment with an expression like she was trying to decide how much she should say.

"What are you doing tomorrow morning?" she asked.

Roman laughed. "Now you've done it."

"Hush," she said to him as she put her hand on his shoulder.

"I don't know … I might be busy," I said.

"You're such a lousy liar," Roman said.

"On Sunday morning?" she said.

"First tell me what this is about," I said, but Roman would only smirk at me.

"Meet me here at six and you'll see," Ksusha said.

~~~~

The next morning I was in a deep sleep when the ringing began. It was far away and faint, but it persisted and it grew louder and closer, like it was following me, or coming at me. I wanted it to stop, but I couldn't tell where it was coming from. And it got louder and louder and then … I snapped awake. It was the telephone beside my bed. I groaned and looked through bleary eyes at my wristwatch. It was early, very early. I reached for the receiver and put it up next to my ear while I laid flat on my back with my eyes closed.

"Da?" I said, weakly.

"Kolya!"

It was Ksusha and she sounded wide awake. Then I remembered. I groaned.

"You aren't still sleeping," she said.

"What time is it?" I asked with my eyes still closed.

"It's almost six, get up or we'll be late."

I sighed and sat up and passed the receiver to my other ear.

"You really want to do this?" I said.

"Get up and get dressed. We don't have much time."

I groaned again and stretched. I wanted to stay in bed and relax. The last thing I should be doing at that hour was getting up in the dark and going halfway across Moscow on what was sure to be a fool's errand.

"I'll go next time, I promise," I said.

"You'll go today—like you promised last night, now get up."

"Take Roman."

"We've been over this."

She had me in a corner and we both knew it. I did agree to go with her, but only because she'd caught me at a weak moment. It must have been the food. I sat there in bed trying to think of an excuse, but nothing came to mind, at least nothing I thought she'd listen to. And so I sighed, loudly.

"Ok," I said. "I'll be there."

"There isn't time for you to come to the flat. Be at the metro in forty-five minutes," she said and the line went dead.

Forty-five minutes later, I met her on the platform at the station at Taganskaya. There were a few other people standing about, but not many.

Anybody with any sense was sleeping.

After a few minutes, the train pulled in and stopped and we boarded. The car was about half full and we stood together near the rear doors. The doors shut and we pulled away into the dark of the tunnel. We held on to the bars overhead as the car gained speed and rocked from side to side. The wheels pounded over the rails. There was nothing but darkness outside the windows. A short time later we emerged into the light of the next station where more people boarded, nearly filling the car. We were packed in and the doors were about to close, when half a dozen gypsies, stunted and filthy, crowded on together. One of them, a woman, carried a grimy, sleeping infant in a harness on her back. Everyone in the car stepped back and gripped their belongings. The doors closed and we accelerated back into the tunnel.

Almost immediately the gypsies picked out one of the passengers, an old man carrying a wrapped package, and they circled around him.

"*Nyet! nyet!*" he said sharply, waving them off, but his words had no effect. They closed in around him and ran their dirty hands up and down his clothes, feeling for his pockets.

"Get your hands off me!" he yelled as he pulled the hands away. His voice was full of outrage—and fear.

"Shouldn't we do something?" Ksusha whispered to me. The old man started to twist and step backward to escape the probing fingers.

"Quiet," I said.

The old man backed down the length of the car with the pack tightly around him. The gypsies were speaking rapidly to each other in their strange-sounding speech. The other passengers pressed themselves into their seats and against the walls and watched.

"If we do anything they'll be after us," I said in a low voice. "We'll get off at the next station."

I looked out the window for the lights of the next station and when I turned back around, one of the gypsies, a boy, was standing in front of me. He ran his hand up the sleeve of my jacket. Meanwhile, the old man was twisting and swatting at his tormentors and his package fell to the floor where it was scooped up by one of the pack and dropped into a greasy-looking cloth sack. Then another filthy boy broke away from the old man and joined the waif confronting me. There was loud murmuring and shuffling by the other passengers. They shrank farther back into their seats and closer to the walls.

"*Nyet!*" I yelled, hoping to startle the boy, but it had no effect on him. I pushed him across the car and he fell into the lap of a young woman who sprang up and away as if I'd dropped a hot iron into her lap. Ksusha tried to pull the hands of the other boy off my jacket, but then he started to run his hands over her. The old man came toward us, bringing the pack with him. They were jabbering to each other and when they got to us, the woman with the infant reached up and snatched Ksusha's beret from her head. The infant woke up and its high-pitched wail added to the growing pandemonium.

I'd seen gypsies at work before, but never like this—out in the open on a metro car.

Then we came into the light of the next station and the car stopped. The doors beside me opened. I pulled several pairs of hands away and jumped out onto the platform. I reached back in and pulled Ksusha out after me.

"Help me!" the old man yelled, looking at me with panicked eyes.

He was standing near the doors with a half dozen pairs of hands still working through his clothes. The doors were about to close and so I reached in and grabbed him by the front of his jacket and pulled him out onto the platform where he fell to his hands and knees. The doors closed and the car rolled away down the tracks.

Ksusha and I were breathing heavily and she leaned down and helped the old man to his feet. He didn't look hurt but his package was gone and his clothes were pulled askew. He steadied himself.

"My gloves, they got my new gloves! I stood in a queue an hour for them!" he shouted. I assumed he was talking about the package that had disappeared into the gypsies' cloth sack.

"Are you hurt?" I said, but that only seemed to goad him. He pulled himself up to his full height and pointed a finger at my chest.

"You don't see it do you? None of you do."

"See what? And why are you yelling at me?" I said.

"In my day if those animals had dared do that they would have disappeared. Phhhffttt!!" he said, flicking his hand wide open. "They'd be gone. But not now—now there's no order, no control of anything—and this is what we get."

"Steady," I said. "It wasn't our fault."

He looked at me with his watery eyes.

"Of course it's your fault."

"What are you talking about?" I said.

"I just told you. You don't listen, none of you do." His voice was loud.

"I am listening—to an ungrateful old fool who isn't making any sense," I said, but then Ksusha put her hand on my arm.

"Kolya, don't," she said.

The old man looked at her and then back at me.

"Listen to your girl there and keep quiet. We had a great country. We were strong. There was order and discipline. We had laws. Those animals wouldn't have lasted five minutes when I was your age. But that wasn't enough. All of you had to have more—money and useless trinkets. That's all that matters to people now. And look what we've come to." A drop of his spittle hit my chin and I wiped it away.

It seemed that things bottled up inside of him, maybe for years, were all coming out.

"I'm going to report this, but a lot of good it'll do," he said. Then he turned and strode off, down the platform toward the escalator to the street. He walked with his head held high. Ksusha and I watched him go.

"Are you ok?" I asked her.

"*Horoscho.* Ok."

"I'm sorry about that, about your hat. I'll get you another one."

"You don't need to do that."

"And you shouldn't ride the metro alone anymore. I've never seen it this bad. It isn't safe. I'm going to tell Roman not to let you do it."

I turned and glimpsed the old man as he disappeared up the escalator.

"And you? Are you ok?" she asked.

"I'm fine."

"What he said wasn't all wrong, you know."

"I know, but he didn't have to be so obnoxious. Somebody should teach him some manners."

"Like Yuri?" She smiled.

She'd done it again.

"Well ..." I said. "No ... not exactly, I dunno."

The next train came sliding into the station and the doors opened. "Let's get going, or we'll be late," she said.

We boarded the car and rode out to the Chamovniki district where we got off and went up the stairs to the street. It was still early and the street was deserted except for a man sleeping in an alley. The alley smelled damp and musty, like early morning.

The Chamovniki is one of the old living districts in Moscow, a place where you can still find a few of the old-style wooden blocks of flats. We passed by several with their carved window frames and curtains tightly drawn. We walked several blocks and then came to a tall brick wall. Parts of the wall were worn down and crumbling at the top and it was nearly covered over in vines. We passed through an open gate in the wall into a green park. In the center of the park was a church. Its grey walls were finely decorated with round arches and geometric designs in shades of red, blue and gold. I looked at Ksusha.

"It's the Church of Nicholas the Miracle-Worker," she said.

"I can see that, but why are we here?"

"Services start in twenty minutes and I want you to go with me."

"You didn't say anything about going to services."

"Would you have come if I had?"

"I don't know, maybe."

"I'm not sure I believe that, but 'maybe' is good enough for now. Let's go, it's almost time."

What else was there to do way out there at that hour?

"Sure, why not?" I said. "We're here."

Morning sunlight lit up the gold domes atop the church. A cross rose up from the center dome. The church door was propped open and two old beggar women, dressed in shapeless mounds of clothing and each holding up a cup for alms, sat on chairs outside the door. Ksusha took a scarf from her bag and covered her head, knotting the scarf under her chin. When we passed by the beggar women on our way into the vestibule, she dropped a kopeck into each cup.

Inside we sat on a wooden bench along a wall in the vestibule to wait for our eyes to adjust to the low light. I leaned back against the wall and crossed my legs. Immediately, a young man dressed in a military uniform rose from a bench along another wall, came over to me and without a word, knocked my ankle off my knee.

"I'm sorry, I forgot," I whispered to him, but I doubt he heard me because he was already going back to his seat. He sat down again, but he kept an eye on me.

"Sorry," I said to Ksusha.

"Don't worry, you're not the only one. There are a lot of newcomers here these days."

"A military uniform—in church? I don't believe it."

"Ready?" she asked.

My eyes had dilated to the light. "Sure."

We rose and I followed her from the vestibule through the center arch, into the sanctuary. The experience was just as I remembered it—like stepping back into a mystical time. There were no seats or benches and the worshippers stood in groups facing the iconostasis. A choir, hidden from view, chanted a hymn, the voices echoing from the stone floors and walls. Muted, colored light filtered through a stained glass window high above the floor of the nave. Light from hundreds of flickering candles bathed the room in a golden glow. Beyond the halo of candlelight, the room was in deep gloom as groups of worshippers shuffled about, moving first in one direction and then in another, like currents and eddies in a river. Some were softly chanting. The room smelled strongly of incense.

"Will you get me a candle?" Ksusha asked and I dug out two kopecks from my pocket and handed them to a deacon standing in a corner. He gave me two candles and I handed one to Ksusha. Then I followed her to an alcove. On the wall, gazing out at us, was an icon, the face of one of the saints, painted generations ago but still vibrant from the candlelight reflecting from flecks of gold and silver in the paint. Ksusha made the sign of the cross and knelt before the icon. Then she leaned forward and kissed it and placed the candle in a holder on the floor. I lit my candle from hers and placed it on the floor. Then she rose and stood beside me.

"Do you know him?" she whispered.

I studied the face. "Give me a hint."

"The crusader against wealth."

I thought a moment, trying to remember. "Zlatoust, John Zlatoust?"

"That's right."

I looked back at the face. "I used to know them all."

Then the choir finished the hymn and all eyes turned toward the iconostasis for the celebration of the Eucharist. It was painted in deep hues of gold, green and blue and covered with icons that regarded us through serene, almond-shaped eyes. A moment later the priest emerged through the royal door in the iconostasis. He was dressed in purple vestments brocaded with gold thread that sparkled in the candlelight. A single reader followed him. Behind the royal door, heavy curtains hung from a rod to the floor, concealing the altar.

As the priest came through the door, he began chanting out the Enarxis, starting with the Litany of Peace, followed by Psalm 102 and then the Little Litany. His voice was deep and melodious and evocative of traditions from centuries past. The congregation and the reader answered him antiphonally. The words were spoken in Old Slavonik, but they expressed the hope of millions of worshippers in many lands down through the ages. Unconsciously, I joined in the chant.

"You know this?" Ksusha whispered to me.

"Some of it."

"Who took you?"

"My grandmother."

Later in the service, during the Prokimenon, as the priest swung the chalice, releasing clouds of sweet, incensed smoke into the room, I studied the worshippers around me more closely. This congregation was decidedly different from the small groups of the faithful I remembered from the services I attended as a boy. Then there were only old women, most of them poor, but here there were young people, men and women, some of them in stylish clothes, and military men in uniform, even a few officers.

After the Prokimenon, the priest began to call out the morning petitions of the congregation.

"O Lord, give Thy blessing on all that we do and say to others this day."

"*Gospody Pomiluy*—Lord, have mercy," the congregation answered. Many people bowed and crossed themselves as they chanted.

"Guide us in all things."

"*Gospody Pomiluy.*"

"Teach us to remember that Thee and Thy Will are sovereign and that Thy purposes work in all circumstances."

"*Gospody Pomiluy.*"

"Give us the strength to meet this day and all that it brings."

"*Gospody Pomiluy.*"

"Be with those who are sick, those who are lonely, those in need."

"*Gospody Pomiluy.*"

"Grant Thy blessing on our country and restore order and tranquility."

"*Gospody Pomiluy.*"

"Let Thy Spirit go abroad again in our land and bring renewal."

"*Gospody Pomiluy, Gospody Pomiluy.*"

When the service was over, Ksusha and I walked back through the park to the metro station.

"How did you know I'd know the name of that saint?" I said.

"A hunch. I thought you might."

"It was a long time ago."

"But you remembered."

"It just came to me."

We passed through the gate in the old stone wall, out of the park. "I suspected as much," she said.

"What?"

"You knew what I was saying to you last night, admit it."

"Maybe."

"So, what'd you think, about today?"

I walked along with my hands in my pockets. "It … it brought back memories."

"Good ones?"

"Well, sure … not bad ones anyway."

She laughed. "I guess that's a start." We crossed from one side of the street to the other. Two street sweepers were at work with their long brooms. "I hope you'll go again," she said.

"We'll see," I said.

"What does that mean?"

"It means I don't get much out of religion."

She laughed again.

"What's so funny?" I said.

"It's a worship service. It's not about what you get out of it. You're there to give, not get."

We reached the stairs down to the metro station. The man in the alley was still there, snoring. Ksusha took her cape and put it over him. He coughed, snorted and then rolled onto his side, pulling the cape up over his shoulder. A woman was unlocking the doors of a kiosk at the top of the stairs. Once inside, she started to stack her wares on the shelves.

"You made the sign of the cross with two fingers, not three," I said.

"It's the way of the Old Believers."

"My grandmother was an Old Believer. But that wasn't one of their services."

She shrugged. "It's God's house."

"Who took you?" I asked.

"My father."

"Viktor Vladimirovich? But he was a Party man."

"For his job, never in his heart."

"How did he manage that?"

"We were careful—we had to be. We never went near a church, only services in flats. But we stopped when I started school. I suppose he thought I would say something, get us into trouble."

We went down the stairs to the platform.

"Roman knows about this?"

"Oh, yes."

"Then why wasn't your wedding in the church? Lots of people are doing it nowadays."

"We had our wedding."

"You could have another one. People are doing that now too."

She shook her head. "Roman won't even talk about it. It's the only thing we've argued about." Then she laughed. "Can you imagine Roman arguing? He was really upset."

"He'll do it. He'd marry you again on a rooftop if it's what you really wanted."

"But not in the church. He won't talk about it."

The headlights of the train were approaching down the tracks.

"Talk to him again."

"I … I'm not sure I want to. It was so strange. There was this look in his eyes. I've never seen it before—or since."

I turned to face her. "Tell me what you saw," I said.

"I don't know. I can't describe it …"

"Try."

She looked up at the ceiling, then at me. "It was … there was fear … I don't know, that's all I can say."

Could it be—after all these years? Was that possible?

The train stopped and the doors opened and we stepped on board.

"The truth is, I hoped you might know something," she said. "I've wanted to talk to you about it."

I reached up and grabbed the hand rail as the doors shut. "I don't know. Sorry."

"You're so close, I just thought you might know something."

The train pulled into the tunnel and we rode in silence back to Taganskaya. When we got off, I said goodbye to her on the platform.

"Can I ask you—when you were kneeling before the icon, what were you praying for?" I said.

"For Roman, of course. And for you," she said. "That you'll find what it is you're looking for—or it will find you."

CHAPTER 27

I was gone all the next week on business, but returned to Moscow on Saturday in the morning. I unpacked and was relaxing in my flat, reading the papers and watching a little television, when the telephone rang. It was Roman and there was a zip in his voice.

"Let's get out, let's do something today," he said.

"Sure," I said. "I don't have any plans."

"Good. There's a concert this afternoon at the Phoenix Center." I could hear him rattling a newspaper.

I frowned. "What kind of concert?"

"It says here Teryushnova, the mezzo-soprano, accompanied by Ostroukhova on piano ... selections from Mozart, Verdi and Bizet. What do you think?"

Roman owned dozens of recordings of symphonies and concertos, and operas sung in German or Italian. There was always a piece playing in their flat.

"You know, you're a snob about music," I said.

"Thanks. Well, what do you say?"

"I say I don't like that stuff."

Then I heard Ksusha speak up in the background and Roman put his hand over the mouthpiece. I heard muffled speech. A moment later Ksusha came on the line.

"I have a better idea. Both of you come with me to the church this afternoon," she said.

"A service on Saturday?" I said.

"I told you—forget it," I heard Roman say.

"Not a service, it's a lecture," she said. "And it's not in the church, it's out in the park. You won't have to go inside."

"A lecture about what?" I said.

"Come and find out."

I'd slept through enough political lectures to last a lifetime, but it would be good to get out—and just about anything sounded better than one of Roman's tedious concerts.

"A waste of time," Roman said.

"No it's not," she said. "I want you both to hear this. It won't take all day, it starts at three."

"Well, tell me what it's about," I said. "At least tell me who's giving it."

"Father Yarlov," she said.

"Father Yarlov? Dimitri Yarlov?"

"That's right."

"Father Yarlov is coming to that little place."

"That's what I said. You've heard of him?"

"Very funny. I watch TV every now and then."

The truth was, unless you'd been in a coma for the last several years in Russia, you knew all about Father Dimitri Yarlov. He was one of the few to speak out in those days against the corruption in the government and growing power of the criminal gangs. That took courage because if you spoke out, the odds were good you'd meet up with a bullet. One shot to the back of the neck, in a car park, was the usual method. But Father Yarlov kept talking and the more he talked the more attention he got from the newspapers and TV reporters.

"Are you kidding? He's a troublemaker," I heard Roman say. "We're not going near there."

"He'll probably be our next saint," Ksusha shot back at him.

"No," he said.

"Please, do this for me," I heard her say. "Please."

"Anything else, but I can't go near that place, I can't," he said.

Then there was silence on their end for a long moment.

"Ksusha," I said.

"Yes."

"Put him back on."

Roman came back on the line. "So, are we on for the concert?" he said.

"I'll tell you what—if you go to the lecture, I'll take us out for a nice dinner after its over."

He was quiet a moment. "I … can't go in there," he said.

"You won't have to. Ksusha said it's in the park. We'll go, listen and then leave and you won't have to go inside. We'll have a nice meal together."

"On you?"

"On me."

"Where?"

I tried to remember the names of the some of the swanky new places in town. "How about the Amadeus Café?" I said.

He laughed. "The next best thing to hearing his music, I guess."

"Well?"

"I don't know … going to that place …"

"It's not a service and it's outside."

He was quiet again. "Ok … I'll go," he said finally.

Then Ksusha came back on. "So we're going?"

"I bribed him. When do I meet you?"

"Two o'clock—at Taganskaya."

This time we had no gypsy trouble on the ride out to the Chamovniki district and we arrived shortly before three at the little church in the park. Gathered on the lawn outside the church doors were two or three hundred people—students, workers, pensioners, military men, mothers with their children—all milling around, talking and waiting.

At first we stood back from the crowd looking things over and then Ksusha said we should get closer to the front. We maneuvered our way through the crowd to a spot about a dozen meters from the church doors. It was as close as Roman would go. By that time the crowd had swelled to many dozens more and it was growing steadily larger. Most of the people were quiet and respectful of where they were. But some had been drawn there, to the excitement, like moths to a light. They huddled together in groups of threes and fours on the fringes of the crowd, drinking from bottles they passed among themselves, talking and laughing.

Ksusha turned and glared at them. "What are they doing here? Can't they show any respect?"

"They're just bored," I said.

"Well, I'm going to stop it," she said but before she could move, Roman reached over and grabbed her by the wrist.

"No, you're not. If they bother you that much, we can leave."

"Isn't that what everybody says these days—if it's wrong, just ignore it?"

A group of the rowdies broke out into more loud, vodka-soaked laughter, one of them laughing so hard he fell to the ground. Another threw an empty bottle against the church wall where it shattered into pieces. Ksusha stared at the ground, her lips pressed tightly together while Roman held her wrist.

Then, with no announcement, the church doors opened and out came Father Yarlov, waving a hand at the crowd as he mounted the steps onto a small platform on the spot where the two old beggar women had sat the week before. The crowd pressed in around him, some sitting on the ground in a circle at his feet. A deacon brought a chair up onto the platform, but the priest ignored it and stood there for a long moment looking over the crowd.

He was easy to recognize from his pictures on television and in the newspapers—the heavy gold cross hanging from his neck onto a wide chest, and the photogenic face, especially the full brown beard and dark, liquid eyes.

I took a step closer to him.

Two or three of the rowdies were still laughing, and one was yelling something at the others, but the priest didn't seem to notice. He seemed to be sizing up his audience, waiting for the right moment to begin.

Roman was staring at him. He let go of Ksusha's wrist and held her hand. He looked pale.

Then, without preamble, the priest launched straight into his talk, like a man with much to do and little time left to do it.

"I want to tell you about something," he began. "Something important, so important I've been traveling all over this country talking about it."

The noise from the crowd died away.

"I want to tell you about the knock, the knock at the door that each of you will hear one day." He paused.

"What does that mean?" Roman whispered.

"Sshhh," Ksusha said.

"But the truth is, I'm here to do more than just tell you about the knock—I'm here to warn you about it."

"Let's go," Roman whispered.

"Be quiet and listen," she said.

"Oh, I know many of you don't believe what I'm telling you is real. Or you think it will never happen to you. But hear me out. God knocks at the door of each of our hearts, asking us to let Him in. The knock will come. Some of you may have heard it already."

I took another step toward him.

"But when it will come, what form it will take when it comes—those aren't the real questions for us."

He paused again and smiled.

"The real question is how we respond when it comes."

There was murmuring from the crowd and more laughter from the rowdies. As I turned to look at Roman and Ksusha, a peculiar look flashed on Roman's face, a look that was faintly familiar. It was an odd expression—of both fear and pain—and it was there for just an instant. Ksusha put her arm around him and squeezed his hand. I was about to ask if he felt ok, but then a man with a snow white beard standing beside me raised his hand high above his head and started waving it back and forth. He was trying to get the priest's attention. His clothes smelled like mothballs and he was a little unsteady on his feet.

Another drunk.

"Father Dmitri, forgive me," the white beard called out. "But I have a question for you."

He spoke in a clear voice, using good diction and grammar. I looked at him more closely and saw his hollow cheeks and the circles under his eyes. I realized he wasn't drunk at all—he was ill and maybe hungry. Many in the crowd turned and frowned at him, but the priest gave the man a gentle smile.

"What is your question, my son?"

The white beard took a deep breath. "Father Dimitri, you are a famous man, an educated man. You know many important people. Please tell us who is responsible for all of this?"

There was more murmuring from the crowd.

"All of what, my son?"

"The way things have become in this country."

The murmuring grew louder and some were nodding at the question. The priest nodded too.

"I've been blessed with an education, that is true, but I'm an ordinary citizen, as you are," he said.

I wanted the priest to get back to his talk, but the white beard persisted.

"But you know people in the Duma, in the Federation Council. You've traveled, you know things. We've read the things you've said. Tell us who is responsible? We must know. They must be brought to justice."

The smile faded from the priest's face.

"You want names?" he asked and the white beard nodded.

"Yes, names!" another called out.

I didn't see anyone taking notes, but it was a good bet news reporters were present.

"Whose names do you want exactly?" the priest asked.

"Those who have destroyed this country, who've brought us to where we can't earn a decent living," the white beard said.

Now even some of the rowdies were listening—between drinks.

"And what would you do with the names?"

"Bring them to justice," someone else said and the murmuring grew louder still.

"Justice? Justice, you say? Is that it really?" The priest stared at us for a long moment. "No, I don't think so—I don't think its justice you want. I think you want revenge."

"That is justice for the criminals who have done this," the white beard said. "The criminals who've made themselves rich while the rest of us go hungry. The criminals who've stolen our resources and ruined our savings so that everything we've worked for is gone. You know

246

what I'm saying. Just look how they've looted Gazprom and Unified Energy Systems, how the arbitrazh courts are riddled with bribes, how arms from our military are stolen and sold on the black market—and on and on it goes. Tell us who is doing this."

Whoever he was, the white beard knew what he was talking about.

The priest seemed lost in his thoughts. Then he replied. "You are correct. I do know who is responsible," he said.

"Then tell us!" someone called out.

"Give us the names!" another said.

"You won't like the answer," the priest said.

One group of rowdies started shouting and one of them tossed a pebble up at the platform. The priest held up his hands.

"You think it's only those you call the criminal groups that have done this?" he asked.

I was listening.

"Yes, they're involved, but they're only the tip of it. Others are just as responsible, maybe more so."

"Then tell us!" many said together.

The priest waited a moment. His sense of timing and drama was superb.

"The truth is—I am responsible," he said and then there was silence, silence followed shortly by confused voices, at first just a few and then many.

"That's nonsense," a man called out.

"You're mocking us," another said.

The priest held up his hands again.

"I tell you from my heart this is not a matter to joke about. I am responsible—I am. And you are responsible. Each of us is responsible."

His brown eyes passed over us.

"You think others have caused these problems? Well, what about each of you? What have you done?"

The white beard shook his head and took a step forward. "You ask what have I done?" he shouted at the priest. "I'll tell you what I've done—I've done what I must do to survive in a country they have ruined. So now you judge me for that?"

The priest shook his head.

"I don't judge you, I don't. But listen to yourself. Your answer is the answer millions would give. Isn't that so? Don't we all believe we have our reasons for doing what we do? And what has that brought us? I'll tell you—a country of people doing as they please."

"I won't listen to this," the white beard said and he turned and started to walk away through the crowd.

"Listen to me," the priest called after him. "How many of you have helped yourself to things that aren't yours? How many? Maybe some food, maybe other things? How many of you have paid a little blat to an official for a favor?" He paused. "Aren't these the things you accuse others of—the ones you call criminals?"

The priest had been moving back and forth across the platform as he spoke, aiming his voice at different sections of the crowd. But then he stopped. His gaze was steady.

Is he looking at me? Can't be.

The white beard came back to where I was standing.

"You compare me to the animals who shoot people down in our streets?" he said.

"I compare you to no one. But I say all of us, myself included, have missed the mark of what we were intended to be. And that is the root of our troubles. These economic and legal matters you speak of are symptoms, nothing more," he said with a wave of his hand.

"But if you won't speak out and name the criminals, who will?" a woman called out.

"I understand what you're saying and the time may come—soon— when it's necessary to speak out against certain people. But I tell you, that won't solve our problems. Those people will be replaced—by others like them. The answer is not through the police, or the courts. The answer is in our hearts. Change our hearts and you'll change our country. Believe that. If you answer the knock when it comes, your heart can be changed and all these other matters will take care of themselves."

"Come on, we're leaving," Roman said to Ksusha and he started to pull her away. Now his face was flushed red.

"You can go, I'm staying," she said.

Then a man in front of me spoke up. "But things have been done, terrible things. Do we just forget about that?"

Father Dimitri seemed suddenly tired and he sighed and sat down in the chair and folded his hands in his lap. I stood on my toes to see him.

"Listen to me, all of you. You know my story. I spent five years in the camps and I confess I went there an angry man, angry at my jailers, angry at myself, angry even at God. It gives me great pain to admit that now, but it's true. Bitterness had taken root in me and I was filled with despair. I even thought of leaving the church. But in time, God's grace brought me back, led me to understand that He uses our troubles to shape us into who He wants us to be. He gives us the tools to live an abundant life, but it's our choice to pick up the tools and use them."

Many were nodding in agreement.

He's looking at me again—I'm sure of it.

"In time I thanked God for putting me in those camps. But there were many who never let Him into their hearts. They lived only for revenge and in time they became just like those who put them there, some of them worse. Are you asking for that?"

This time there were no more questions. After a moment, the priest stood up and went back into the church.

The crowd began to break up and we went back to the metro and rode back into the city. We got off at Kievskaya and walked to the Amadeus Café in the Radisson Slavjanskaya Hotel on Berezhkovskaya Naberezhnaya. We were a little early for supper, but already the dining room was half filled with talking, festive people.

I should have been one of them. After all, I was with my two dear friends, about to eat a fine meal, but by the time we were seated at our linen-covered table in the middle of the room and Roman was intently studying his menu, I wanted only to be left alone to think.

"I love places like this," Roman said. "Especially when rich friends like Kolya are paying."

I was staring down at my menu, not seeing the print.

"Kolya?" Ksusha said to me.

"Sorry," I said. I smiled at her.

"You're being quiet."

"I was just thinking."

"About all that rubbish this afternoon?" Roman said without looking up from his menu. "It gave me an appetite, I'll say that."

"What rubbish was that?" Ksusha said.

"That old man with all the questions."

"I thought you meant Father Dimitri," she said.

"No, I didn't mean your precious priest. I meant all those questions. They sounded rehearsed, didn't you think? Kolya? Maybe the priest put him there to keep things interesting. I wouldn't be surprised."

Ksusha pushed his arm. "That's ridiculous."

"You never know."

Then Roman leaned over toward me and snapped his fingers in front of my face. I'd been staring at my menu again.

"Hello, Kolya. Are you going to join us?"

"Sorry," I said. "I was thinking … about the priest."

"What about him?" Roman asked as he went back to his menu.

"I thought he handled those questions pretty well."

Roman looked up with a frown, but then nodded.

"Oh, right, I see what you mean. Tell them something, anything, just to shut them up."

"That's not what I meant."

"He didn't 'handle' the questions," Ksusha said. "He spoke the truth and I hope you were listening. We can complain all we like about the way things have become, but if people don't change, nothing else will change either."

"Who's complaining?" Roman said. He snapped his menu shut. "I like the way things are." He leaned back in his chair with a grin.

"And he wasn't just talking about the criminal gangs," Ksusha said.

Roman stopped grinning and looked around the room. He leaned in closer to us. "Keep your voice down. You don't know who's here." He signaled to the server to bring us drinks.

"Who is it exactly you're calling 'criminals'?" I asked.

Roman looked around again. "I dunno, but not us," he said.

"Don't be so sure," Ksusha said.

"Now you're starting to sound like the priest," Roman said. He reached for a slice of bread from a basket the server had put in front of him.

"Maybe he was right." I said. "Who's to say who's a criminal and who isn't."

Roman frowned again. "If you kill people, that makes you a criminal. If you steal things, that makes you a criminal. If you don't do those things, you're not a criminal. What's complicated about that?"

"Nothing," I said. "Nothing at all."

"Then your priest should concentrate on the people doing those things and leave the rest of us alone."

"You'll never get rid of them," I said.

"I'm glad one of you was listening," Ksusha said.

Roman smiled and shrugged. "Come on, forget about all that and let's enjoy ourselves," he said.

CHAPTER 28

❧

*T*he next day, Sunday, Styopa called me at my flat in the afternoon. "Ok, pal, time to earn your keep," he said. "We have a little job to do."

"Sounds good, what's up?" I said.

"A delivery, from Tula … and you'll never guess who for."

"Ok, I'll never guess."

He waited a moment. "Koeppel," he said.

"Really."

"Yep."

"When did this happen?"

"The colonel got a call yesterday. It's just a sample—to see the quality, but … if it all checks out, who knows how much they'll want."

"I imagine he's excited—how long have we been waiting for this?"

"You have no idea. He's called me three times today already."

"Zurich?"

"Warsaw—which is one reason he's on edge. 'There can't be any foul ups and we can't be late.'"

"Sounds like him."

"The meeting's Tuesday afternoon."

"We're never late," I said.

"We better not be this time. I'll meet you at the garage. See you at eight." Then he hung up.

And so I rose early the next morning, packed two extra changes of clothes in my travel bag and started out for our garage on the ring road.

You wouldn't think much of the garage if you saw it from the street, and that was just the way we wanted it. It was a plain, brick building in an ordinary neighborhood of flats, but it suited our purposes. We had equipped it with steel doors and stout locks and we bricked up the windows. Inside were three Gazel trucks, each one painted drab grey, coated with grime, and looking generally dilapidated. I kept them looking that way because the last thing we wanted were shiny new trucks that might draw attention. But under the grime, these vehicles were in fine working order. The tires had good tread depth, the bearings were lubricated and the engines were clean and carefully serviced. They were each good to go a thousand kilometers at a moment's notice. The newest Gazel was my favorite. The gears shifted smoothly and the suspension was so good that you felt only the deepest road holes. I always used it for delicate loads.

My working days in Moscow followed a set routine. In the mornings, I started up the engines and drove each truck a few kilometers out on the ring road to keep the batteries charged. Then I would start to work on the wooden crates that were stacked in neat rows, five deep and four high, in the storage room at the back end of the garage, well away from the doors and moisture from the outside. The contents of those crates—either decommissioned small arms or new ones fresh from the plant—were the lifeblood of our enterprise. We left it to others to tackle the complicated business of selling the expensive, hi-tech systems. Ours was just a simple old trade with a limitless market. We sold Makarov pistols and Kalashnikov automatic rifles—AK-47s, AKS-74s, and sometimes the AKSU, the short-barreled model of the AKS-74—and, of course, abundant ammunition for all these weapons. In the last six months, Styopa and I had taken apart and serviced enough of these to equip two battalions. We checked and oiled each bolt, adjusted the trigger pull to the proper resistance and replaced the firing pin if it showed even the slightest wear. The manufacturer's grease was removed from the new weapons and all were then carefully repacked into the crates for shipment to whomever would pay.

I arrived at eight, ahead of Styopa, and tinkered with the Gazel engines. All looked good. He showed up a little after nine o'clock, carrying a zippered nylon bag and his old leather haversack slung over a shoulder.

"How many crates does he want?" I said.

"Ten, no more."

"Then do we really need both of us? I can be back by morning, no problem."

"I know, but he wants us both on this. 'No foul ups,' remember? When we get back, it's straight on to Nurzec if we're going to get there by Tuesday."

A journey to Tula, back to Moscow, and then straight on to the little town of Nurzec, deep in the forests of eastern Poland, meant a long, tiring trip ahead.

"Do we stay in Nurzec or go on to Warsaw?"

"We meet the client in Warsaw, but we can stay over a few hours to rest up if you like."

"It doesn't matter. You decide," I said. The accommodations in Nurzec were basic, but adequate, and we'd be ready for a rest by the time we got there.

"Let's draw."

"Fine," I said, and he took a packet of matches from his pocket, drew out two and then turned his back to me. He turned around and held out his hand with the two matches between his thumb and forefinger.

"Short match, Nurzec; long one, Warsaw."

I reached out and plucked one of the matches. It was the long one.

"Warsaw it is," he said.

I shrugged because it really made no difference. Nurzec was ok, but Warsaw fine too. It had a comfortable feel for me, enough like Russia to feel familiar, but with enough of the newness of the west. On our first visit there, I'd taken time off for a coach tour and a walk through Old Town—through the Castle Square, to King Sigismund's Column and through Old Town Market Square, which really wasn't old at all, having been obliterated in the war and then rebuilt afterward. I especially liked the Royal Castle, that gaudy, gilded, fairy-tale palace of the old Polish kings that sits grandly in the middle of Old Town, a reminder of the days when Poland was a player in the world.

"Someday you should take a girl there, on holiday," he said. "No more romantic place than Old Town at night. A good supper, then a walk to the Barbican or through the Royal Baths. She'd be putty in your hands." He laughed.

I adjusted the clutch on the newest Gazel, filled the petrol tank and checked the oil and other fluids. I loaded six full cans of petrol into the rear because we would never risk a stop at a petrol station when we were carrying product. Then I unlocked the steel cabinet we kept at the back of the garage and we each drew out a Makarov pistol. I checked to make sure the clip was full and I slid it into a holster on my belt under my jacket. It felt solid and its weight rested comfortably on my hip. Then I drew out another Makarov, checked its clip, chambered a round, and slid it into a holster I kept hidden in the rear of the Gazel, inside the drop gate.

Styopa climbed into the driver's seat carrying the nylon bag, a pair of good field glasses in a case and his haversack into which he had packed sandwiches, a length of cooked sausage and a bottle of cold tea. He started the engine and I opened the doors and the truck rolled smoothly out onto the street. I closed the doors and secured the lock. A few minutes later we were out on the ring road, heading east for the junction with the M2 which would take us south to Tula.

"So how's the colonel?" I asked.

"Totally focused on this meeting—he's dropped everything."

"I can believe it."

"This is a big step for us, Kolya." A truck cut over in front of us and Styopa blew the horn.

"This Koeppel, do we trust him?"

"You know who he is. We can't ask too many questions."

"Mmm ... well, I guess the colonel knows what he's doing."

"This is our big chance. We can have all the product in the world, but without a network abroad, it's just so much scrap—you know that."

"We've done pretty well so far."

"We've been lucky so far. Now we need more than luck. He could take us up to a whole new level."

"Or down a few."

"Koeppel has the contacts to take everything we can give him and more."

I shifted in my seat. "So what's with this sample, on three days notice? There's no mystery about our stuff."

"A test, I guess. I don't blame him—all kinds of people say they can deliver product, but doing it reliably is something else."

"We are reliable," I said.

"We know it, but he needs to see it."

We continued south on the M2. Traffic was heavy as we passed the exits for Podolsk, Klimovsk and Chechov, but later, near Serpuchov, it thinned as the road took us through open country. Then, for a time, we drove through a birch forest, then the forest broke and we were in broad open country again, then again in forest, and later again in open country. The sun was shining in a clear sky. It was a good day for a drive.

Late in the afternoon we passed through Jukovlevo and Zaoksi. As we went further into the country, we passed through many villages, each one like every other, rows of cottages huddled closely together along the shoulders of the road in the thick grass. Behind the cottages the great open steppes stretched away. There was no warning to the approach of these places; abruptly in the middle of the openness they were there and then, just as quickly, they were gone.

In midafternoon we passed a cottage that was twice the size of the others, painted mustard yellow with a ribbed metal roof. The dormers atop the roof were painted fresh white. Along the western side, running the cottage's full length, was a wide, covered porch, a pleasant-looking place to sit at the end of the day to watch the sun set across the fields. Pigs wallowed in a wire pen in the side yard. One of them looked up from its slop to watch us pass, pushing its snout against the wire. A young girl, her head covered with a red scarf, stood ankle deep in the grass, turning the crank of a well next to the pigs' pen. She too turned to watch us pass. I waved and she waved back.

"Who's worse off, eh, the girl or the pig?" Styopa said. When I didn't respond he shook his head. "Really, think about it. Think of being stuck someplace like that."

"I don't know, it doesn't look so bad. I wonder if it has a name."

"Kolomenskoie."

"How do you know?"

"When I came through here last year, their sheep were spread out all over the road, half a kilometer—it was a mess. One of the women told me." He rubbed his chin. "Seems like she said it once had a Tatar name but they changed it. Can't remember what that was."

"You stopped and talked to her?"

"Sure. Nothing else to do."

"And what would you say if I'd done that?"

"So, who's she going to tell, a bunch of sheep? Anyway, you wanted the name of the village and there you have it."

I watched the rooftops of Kolomenskoie shrink away in the mirror outside my window.

"It's a good place," I said. "A good place to build a dacha, spend some time."

He looked at me as if to say I should have my head examined.

"I mean it," I said. "That big place with the porch. Very relaxing. You want a place to relax some day, you've said so."

"I plan to do a lot of relaxing, but not in a place like that."

"Show me something better," I said.

"That's easy—Zhukovka. Now, there I could relax."

Zhukovka—I should have known sooner or later he would get around to it. The colonel had once taken him to meet an associate at his dacha at Zhukovka and Styopa never got over it. It was just thirty kilometers from Moscow but from the way Styopa talked, you'd think it was Shangri-La. It was a place of fine country homes on the bluffs over the Moscow River, an unapproachable sanctuary in soviet times where the top Party people, musicians, scientists and important academics—all the people with money and power—insulated themselves from the rest of us. In the new Russia, where enough money could get you anything, it had become even more insular, if that was possible. It was a place of quiet pine and birch forests and privileged solitude. It was the magical prize for all Styopa's labor.

"That's where I want to be. A man can relax there, forget about things, enjoy himself."

"Doing what?"

"Anything he likes—a little fishing, a little gardening, walks in the woods."

"Fishing, gardening? You?" I chortled. "Maybe a little fence mending, and some laundry?"

"You can laugh now, but you wouldn't if you saw it."

"Right now I'm thinking about getting to Tula and back—without any trouble. Tell me again about this job."

He rolled his window down and the wind blew in. "I've told you what I know. It's a sample and—oh, I forgot—the client wants a demonstration before he places any big orders."

"You didn't say anything about that—where? Warsaw?"

"Probably Nurzec, but I imagine we'll do it on the moon if that's what Herr Koeppel wants."

"If there's going to be a big order, we should get it all on one trip."

"There isn't time." He looked over at me. "Relax, my friend, relax, you worry too much."

"And I think sometimes you don't worry enough."

He laughed. "And that's why we're so good together." He slapped me on the shoulder.

Later, when we were still north of Malachovo, we came up behind an open bed truck carrying a dozen or so workers journeying home from a day in the fields. They huddled together in the bed of the truck, their tools laid out beside them. Two of them, a teenaged boy and girl, kissed passionately, clinging tightly to each other. The others ignored them and stared back at us with slack faces.

"Imagine having that kind of energy," Styopa said. "Work all day in the sun and still ready for love. Wonderful."

"That truck's probably the closest they can get to any privacy."

"I'm sure you're correct," he said in mock earnestness. "But you're not feeling the passion of life. That's the trouble with you, my lad. You analyze things too much. Learn to let life carry you along. It's more exciting that way—and easier."

"Don't get too close to them," I said. "And try to stay on the road."

South of Malachovo we left the M2 for the Tula road as the sun was dipping in the sky into dusk. The Gazel had been running well all day, very smooth and quiet.

An hour later, we entered Tula and Styopa steered the truck onto the long, straight boulevard that runs past the power generating plant and the main gate of the Airborne Forces base, home of the 106th Guards. A line of vehicles waited at the gate, their drivers holding their entry papers out the window, ready to present them. We passed by the gate and then turned off onto a dirt and gravel road that we followed through thick woods around the eastern and southern perimeter of the base to a small clearing about a hundred meters outside one of the unmanned and rarely-used rear gates. Styopa pushed on the brakes and switched off the engine and we waited in the quiet, listening for sounds of pursuers. After a few minutes, when we were satisfied we were alone, he took the nylon bag from under his seat, climbed out and went into the woods. He returned without the bag and climbed back into the cab. We sat in the quiet and waited, munching the sandwiches and sausage and drinking the tea from his haversack.

By eight o'clock, the sun was low, but there was still enough light to see the gate. I took out the field glasses and studied the tall wire fence that ran the length of the perimeter around the base. Then I studied the gate and the trees beyond the gate inside the base. The gate was closed and secured with a heavy chain and lock. The narrow road leading away from the gate to our clearing was obscured by tall weeds, giving a good overall impression of disuse—just as we wanted it. I passed the glasses to Styopa.

"Let's hope they're on time," he said. "We've got to get going to make the train in the morning." He swept the glasses along the fence in both directions from the gate.

"If they aren't, it'll be a long night."

"It'll be a long night and a long day either way, my friend," he said, still staring through the glasses.

It was more than an hour before our meeting time with our colleagues from the base and so I killed time smoking and taking a few turns around the truck. Then I walked for a distance along the road into the woods and back again. It was a pleasant night, cool and clear, and a gentle wind sometimes stirred the pine trees along the edge of the clearing. More time passed and I smoked more cigarettes. A little after nine thirty, I put out my last smoke. I fidgeted. There was nothing exciting about this part of the business.

At ten o'clock we were still alone in the quiet woods. Minutes passed and we strained to listen for any approaching sounds.

"They've missed it," I said.

"Give 'em another five minutes."

The five minutes passed and we were still alone. Now there was no question about it—our colleagues from the base had missed the meeting time at ten. We could only guess at the reason—maybe trouble, but more than likely just some goings-on at the base that delayed them. Now we'd have to wait for the backup time at eleven. Styopa let out a big breath and ran his fingers through his hair.

"It's gonna be tight making that train," I said.

"We'll be ok—if we drive fast."

"That's a good way to get stopped."

He lit up a cigarette while I finished my sandwich and drank the last of the tea. Styopa stared blankly ahead through the windshield, tapping his two fingers with his cigarette on the steering wheel.

"How much longer before you can relax?" I said.

"I'm relaxed now."

"I don't mean now. Back there on the road you said you're going to build a dacha, relax a little."

"Soon, if business stays so good—if we don't foul up this job."

I nodded. "Forget about Zhukovka," I said.

He looked at me. "Why?"

"You'd never fit in there."

He shrugged and looked out through the windshield.

"It was a joke," I said.

"It's ok. Nobody really fits into a place like that, you know. They buy their way in. Anyway, that isn't why I do this."

"Why do you do it?"

"Same reason you do."

"And that is?"

"What else is there for us?"

Then I thought I heard a sound. "Did you hear that?" I said. I looked down at my watch.

He held his hand up. "Quiet."

The time was ten thirty, long after our friends inside the base should have abandoned any attempt to contact us at the first delivery time. I listened to the night, but there was nothing. Maybe I was mistaken, or maybe it was just noise from the paved road that carried into the woods in the stillness. Several minutes passed and I started to relax, but then I heard it again, sharp and clear this time.

And this time there was no mistaking what it was—the sound of a vehicle approaching, slowly, in low gear.

We looked at each other and then climbed out of the truck, quietly closing the doors. The sound came from inside the base, from beyond the line of trees inside the fence. We stood still, listening, and I felt for my pistol. It was there, in its holster, and I switched off the safety.

"A security patrol?" I said.

"Not now, out here."

"So what do you think?"

He looked at his watch. "We wait."

The moon had come up and he took the glasses and studied the gate. "It must be Anton, it's got to be," he said, lowering the glasses.

The sound kept up its steady approach, sometimes faint, sometimes clear, but growing louder as it drew near from behind the screen of the trees.

Then, there it was, a lone truck, and it stopped inside the gate. It was running dark and in the moonlight we saw a spectral figure jump down from the cab and work the chain at the gate. The night air amplified the clanking of metal chain running through metal fence. Styopa raised the glasses again.

"Anton?" I said. I couldn't make out the man's face from that distance.

"I can't tell … but who else could it be?"

The driver pushed the gate and it swung out in a wide arc. He hoisted himself back into the cab, shifted into low gear and drove slowly toward us, leaving the gate open. The night remained quiet and still. The truck came into the clearing and stopped about thirty meters in front of us. Gravel along the overgrown road crunched under the tires. Moonlight reflected off the windshield, obscuring the driver's face. Then the driver switched off the engine and hopped out onto the ground and I breathed out. It was Anton Brekhunov, a *decantniki* lieutenant posted to the base.

Styopa stepped forward to greet him. "So what's this?" he said. "You lose your watch or d'you just have better things to do?"

Anton patted Styopa on the arm and then lit a cigarette. "Sorry. Couldn't come sooner and maybe couldn't come later. So I came now."

"That must mean trouble," I said.

"Ah, you could say that. Visitors from Moscow yesterday and again today. Inspections."

"Who?" Styopa and I asked together.

"A team from the Procurator-General."

"That's not good," I said.

"Watchdogs," Styopa said.

"And another tomorrow—from the Duma Defense Committee. A full inspection and inventory."

Styopa rubbed his brow while we took a moment to let this news sink in. "We haven't heard anything about this."

"Neither had we, but they're here and they mean business."

"Because of the deployment?" Styopa said. Two battalions had departed from Tula a week ago for Chechnya. There were stories about it in the newspapers and on television.

"Maybe," Anton said. "Whatever the reason, security is pretty tight right now."

"Where are they?" Styopa asked.

"Sleeping, I imagine, otherwise I wouldn't be here. Anyway, we need to be quick so let's get unloaded."

"Where's Slava?" I asked.

Anton shrugged. "Only five crates, so I didn't bring him."

Styopa nodded. "Ok, well, let's see them then."

We went around to the rear of Anton's truck and he shined his light over the crates laid out in a neat row in the bed. Each had its lid pried open and was packed with twelve Kalashnikov rifles. I took two from each crate, pulled back the bolts and shined the light down the barrels. The mechanisms worked well and they were clean and overall in good condition. I nodded to Styopa. Then Anton and I carried the crates to the Gazel and lifted them into the bed and covered them over with a tarpaulin. When we were done, Styopa went into the woods and came out carrying the nylon bag. He handed it to Anton. Anton took it and dropped down onto one knee and shined his light inside at the neat bundles of small denomination Swiss francs. He thumbed through the bundles while Styopa and I looked on.

He stood up when he finished counting and I looked at my watch; it was nearly eleven.

"Let's get going ..." I started to say, but then I heard a noise behind us, the sound of a boot scraping gravel. I turned and standing there, pointing a rifle at us, was Slava, a sergeant in Anton's platoon. Styopa and I looked at each other and then back at Anton who had drawn his pistol and had it leveled at my chest.

For a long, tense moment no one spoke. I swore to myself at our carelessness. After all, wasn't this what you had to expect sooner or later in our business? Only a fool didn't take precautions. Well, Styopa and I had just proven ourselves to be first class fools, blundering into this situation like a pair of greens.

Then Styopa swore at Anton. "Have you lost your mind!" he shouted at him. His voice boomed in the still night.

"I've never felt better," Anton answered him. "And now drop your pistols on the ground, both of you." He moved his pistol from me to Styopa.

Neither of us moved.

"Now!" he shouted.

I complied slowly—very slowly. Anton seemed calm and in control of himself, but he had to be out of his head to be doing this. And Slava's rifle barrel wavered back and forth between Styopa and me and his breathing sounded short and uneven.

A dozen questions assaulted me. Were they drunk? Was this a careful plan or something they'd cooked up tonight? And what was the point? Styopa was right—this was insane. Surely they weren't launching off into this madness just to steal enough money for five crates of rifles.

But whatever their reasons, it was clear they would shoot us where we stood if we didn't do exactly as they said. So I reached under my jacket, unhooked the holster from my belt and dropped the holster, with the pistol inside, at my feet. Styopa pulled his pistol by the butt and flung it at Anton's feet. Keeping his pistol pointed at Styopa, Anton stooped and picked up the Makarov and fired a round from it into the ground at his side. Then he pointed both pistols at us.

My mind was racing. They had to know how ugly their future would be if they crossed the colonel. Were they really that crazy, or desperate?

"I always thought you were clever," Styopa said to Anton. "This is the stupidest ..."

"Shut up!" Anton said, raising one of the pistols to Styopa's face.

"You're dead men, both of you, you know that don't you," Styopa said.

"Shut your mouth," Slava growled.

Those were the first and last words out of Slava that night because then Anton fired Styopa's Makarov again. The loud crack reverberated through the woods and the bullet found its mark, high in Slava's chest. His rifle fell to the ground and he dropped, dead instantly. Styopa and I looked at each other.

What is this!?

Anton pushed his own pistol into his belt, keeping Styopa's Makarov pointed at us.

"Kolya," he said to me. "Hand me the rifle, stock first and very slowly." He kept the Makarov pointed at Styopa. "And if you try anything, he dies."

I did as he ordered. I took four slow steps over to Slava's body, leaned down and gripped the rifle by its cold barrel, lifted it from the ground and handed it to Anton, stock first. He kept his eyes fixed on my face and the pistol leveled at Styopa's chest.

"Going into business for yourself, are you?" Styopa said to him. "Now I know you're an idiot. How long do you think you'll stay alive if you kill us?"

"How long if I don't?" Anton answered. "And besides, who's to say I killed you?" Then he laughed as if he'd just heard a good joke. He pointed Slava's rifle at us and dropped the Makarov on the ground.

"I'm sorry about this, I really am. But this inspection is serious," he said. "Two more officers from the Procurator will be here tomorrow. Something had to be done and this makes the most sense. It had to be."

"And you keep the money," I said.

He smiled. "I guess I could leave it here, but what's the point of that?"

"Of course," Styopa said.

The smile faded from Anton's face.

"Okay, get your petrol cans and put them here on the ground. Leave one in your truck," he said. Again neither of us moved.

"Get the cans now or I'll shoot you where you stand," he said.

I remember what happened next only dimly, as if I'd seen it all through a blurred window. It was easy to guess at what Anton had in mind for us and if Styopa and I didn't act quickly we were finished. And so we took our only chance to survive.

I backed slowly toward the rear of the Gazel, but Styopa stood his ground, glaring at Anton, so that the distance between Styopa and me grew to where Anton couldn't keep us both in his line of fire.

"Stop there—" he started to say, but he never finished. Styopa sprang at him, low to the ground, with a sweeping kick that caught him sideways at the left knee. Anton's leg buckled beneath him. As he fell he fired a burst from the rifle, but his aim was high, well over Styopa's head. Anton hit the ground and Styopa pounced on him, grabbing for the rifle. But Anton was a trained *decantniki* officer, even if he did look a little out of condition, and he pushed Styopa away and rolled to his side, yanking the rifle with him, away from Styopa's grasp. He rolled over twice and came up on one knee with a clear shot at both of us.

But the one or two seconds Anton took for his body rolls were all the time I needed. As he was hitting the ground after Styopa's kick, I was already at the back of the Gazel, reaching for the Makarov concealed behind the drop gate. As he came up onto his knee, I found my target. I aimed for the mass of his chest. Finding it, I squeezed the trigger twice and felt the pistol leap from the recoil. The bullets struck close together in the middle of his chest and he fell backward. In an instant Styopa was standing beside the body, kicking the rifle away. The woods were quiet again.

For a long, tense moment we stared at each other in mute alarm. Half a dozen shots had been fired, more than enough to summon any nearby security detail. My head reeled from another torrent of questions. What had just happened here and why? And what was this inspection all about? Was Anton lying about it? Were the inspectors already out looking for us? We had just narrowly escaped Anton and Slava, but would there be others after us? The questions just kept coming.

"We need to call the colonel—now," I said.

"He'll be boarding his train at six, leaving his flat for the station probably an hour before. We'll find a phone box."

"I saw one near the power plant."

"Ok, let's get out of here."

"What about them?" I said, pointing to the bodies at our feet. "And the truck."

Styopa looked at the gate, then down toward the paved road. "We need to go."

"Put them in the woods," I said.

He looked at his watch. "There isn't time—we'll miss the train."

"We'll get the next one. If we take 'em into the woods, it'll give us the most time."

He looked again at the bodies and then at the open gate into the base.

"They'll be missed," I said. "Somebody's going to come looking."

He picked up the nylon bag and then looked at his watch again. He threw the bag onto the ground. "We're gonna be LATE!!" he screamed at the woods. He stood there with his hands on his hips looking at the ground.

"It's not our fault," I said.

"Yeah, great."

"We can't just leave all this out here."

After a moment he grabbed up the bag and nodded. "Ok … ok, let's do it." He stopped and looked at the woods and then pointed to a spot at the edge of the clearing. "I think we can get the truck behind those trees there."

And so we started, but right away Anton's truck was a problem. It was impossible to drive it into the trees at the first spot we tried because the undergrowth was too dense. We tried two other places along the edge of the clearing with the same trouble. By that time we had spent a precious hour, but thankfully there was still no sign of a security detail.

Finally, we found a break in the undergrowth near a small gully and with the truck in its lowest gear and its differential scraping the ground, I managed to drive it about thirty meters into a stand of sapling pines where it was screened from the clearing. With the truck hidden, I closed the gate, rethreaded the chain and fastened the lock. We followed the truck's path from the gate back to the woods, rubbing out the tread marks with our shoes. It wasn't perfect, but I thought it would give us at least a day's head start, maybe more.

Then we hid the bodies. We couldn't carry them because the chest wounds were still seeping. It wouldn't do to show up the next day at the station splattered with blood. So I grabbed Anton's body by the ankles and dragged it deep into the brush in the opposite direction from the truck. Styopa followed behind me dragging Slava. The body was heavy and I needed both hands to drag it. Leaves and small branches swatted and scratched my face as I ducked and twisted through the brush.

We found an open patch of dirt about a hundred meters from the clearing and we set about digging a wide, shallow grave. The ground was soft, but the digging was hard work because we had only a screwdriver and a jack handle from the Gazel to loosen the dirt and our hands to scoop it away.

But it kept me from thinking too much about what we'd just done. We barely spoke as we worked.

It was about one when we arrived back at the Gazel. We brushed the dirt off each other, policed the area, picking up the shell casings and covering over the bloody places with dirt. When we were satisfied we were leaving behind no obvious signs, we climbed back into the Gazel. We were now more than two hours behind schedule. We would miss the morning train from Moscow to Warsaw. The next train departed Moscow at six thirty that evening.

Styopa switched on the engine, put the Gazel into gear, and drove us slowly back to the boulevard. It was empty in both directions when we emerged from the woods. He switched on the headlights and turned onto the pavement toward the phone box near the power plant. We passed the main gate of the base and this time the entry road was empty and the security buildings were dark.

"I see it," I said when the box came into view.

He pulled up next to the box and stopped and I waited in the cab while he got out and dropped in his tokens and dialed the number. He glanced twice at his watch as the connection was made. Already at that early hour the two tall smokestacks at the power plant were spewing out thick, grey smoke in tall plumes into the sky. A fresh morning wind pushed the tops of the plumes away to the south. Then Styopa gently placed the phone back on its cradle and climbed into the cab. He was frowning.

"No answer—strange."

"He wouldn't leave this early for the station," I said.

"Maybe he went last night."

"Or?"

He looked over at me and started the engine. "I'll call the hotel in Warsaw when we get to the station. That's all we can do."

"If the train's on time tonight, we'll be about twelve hours late," I said. "That shouldn't be a problem."

"Let's hope not." He put the truck into gear and we pulled out onto the empty boulevard toward the M2.

CHAPTER 29

࿏

*B*elarus Station, Moscow, on the Leningradskiy Prospekt, is a teeming, man-made anthill. The pale green station buildings were built in Czarist times and are choked at every hour with crowds of shouting people hefting baggage and running and queuing to board trains. Vehicles queue up outside in an unending flow in the concentric traffic lanes. From early morning until long into the night, trains depart to the west. Ours would travel through western Russia, across the border into the Republic of Belarus, through its capital at Minsk, beyond to the towns of Baranavichy and Byaroza and then to the Polish border to Brest, once the westernmost city of the USSR.

We pulled into the station a little before noon. I was tired and hungry and we both needed a shave. There were dark bags under Styopa's eyes.

We loaded our crates onto baggage carts and rolled the carts along the platform to the baggage car at the rear of our train. Styopa showed our tickets to the attendant and paid the extra charges for our crates of "tractor parts." Then he passed the man an envelope that disappeared into his coat pocket.

"How many altogether?" the attendant asked as we rolled the crates up the ramp to the car.

"Five," Styopa said. The attendant stepped up into the car and counted the crates and then wrote on his manifest.

"Any going over the border?" he asked. He meant the border of Belarus with Poland.

"All five to Byaroza, none to Poland," Styopa said. The attendant nodded and scribbled his approval for the extra load on Styopa's ticket. Then he moved on to the next passengers in the queue.

We put the Gazel into a car park and then found our compartment and settled in. It was an eleven hour trip to Byaroza, time enough for some decent sleep. Styopa took the top bed and I took the bottom one.

"Are we leaving on time?" I asked the car attendant when she came down the corridor.

"Twenty minutes," she said.

"Time enough for me to get some food?"

"Twenty minutes."

"I'll be back in ten," I said to Styopa.

"Bring me some herring. Make sure it's fresh."

"You'll get sausage if you're lucky."

"And a bottle of wine," he called after me as I started down the corridor.

I jumped back onto the platform and pushed my way through the crowd to a kiosk near the ticket window. It had a good selection of wrapped foods and drinks, but there was no herring in sight. I bought sandwiches, a box of cookies and two bottles of gassed water. Kiosk food wasn't the best, but it would have to do. My stomach was already making noises and there wasn't time to go hunting for anything better. On a whim I bought an ice cream on a stick, tore open the wrapper and finished it in two bites.

When I got back to the compartment, Styopa wolfed down one of the sandwiches, drank most of one of the bottles of water and then belched.

"Best herring I ever had."

A few minutes later, the train pulled out of the station on time at six thirty. We were twelve hours behind schedule and we were bone tired. I slid the compartment door shut and locked it. I must have been asleep before we crossed over the outer ring road. I slept dreamlessly as we traveled west through the night.

We stopped at the border with Belarus and a security officer knocked on the compartment door. Styopa slid it open and handed out our passports. The officer, a dark silhouette against the corridor lamp, shined his light on the documents and then turned the light on us. He stamped the passports, thrust them back into Styopa's face and slid the door shut. I slept again, awaking only once, when we were shunted off onto a side track at Minsk to let another train pass. The next thing I remember was Styopa shaking me awake.

"Kolya ... Kolya, Byaroza in thirty minutes," he said. His voice jarred me out of my sleep. It was still pitch dark in the compartment.

"What ... time is it?"

"A little after five."

The car rocked along the tracks for another thirty minutes until, on schedule, we slowed and stopped alongside the empty platform and stationhouse at Byaroza. It was still dark when we hopped down onto the platform. We walked back to the baggage car and knocked on the door. A moment later the attendant turned the lock, slid back the bolt and rolled the door open from inside.

"I'm alone on this trip, so you'll have to come up and unload it yourselves," he said. He yawned.

We climbed up into the car and found our crates where we had left them, stacked in a corner. The attendant looked at his wristwatch and made a note of our offload on his manifest. We had paid to ship the crates all the way to Brest.

"You're a couple of businessmen, are you?" the attendant said through another yawn.

"In a way," Styopa said while we lifted one of the crates.

"You'd do better in Brest."

"Byaroza will do," Styopa said.

"I'd go to Brest."

"What's special about Brest?" I said.

"They have money to pay for things. Nobody here has any money. You should know that. What kind of businessmen are you?" he said and laughed.

"We'll do fine here," Styopa said.

"Ok, it's none of my business."

The hour might have been early, but we were alert enough to understand the meaning behind this conversation. Styopa, always prepared for such things, handed him more cash which disappeared into the same pocket as the envelope.

"Thanks," he said. "I hope your business is good."

We stacked the crates on the platform while a few other passengers detrained and disappeared into the morning darkness. A light burned inside the stationhouse, but the stationmaster never emerged. When the last of our crates was out of the car, the attendant slid the door shut and locked it. The train rolled away down the tracks.

"You have the key?" Styopa said and I felt my jacket pocket.

"Got it."

"Good, hurry it up. It's damp out here."

I left him on the platform and went around the stationhouse and into the empty streets of Byaroza, a quiet little town with a park near the station. It was just daybreak as I passed through the park. The children's swings and the chess boards where old men play in the afternoons were empty. A small bust of Lenin on a slab of polished stone in a shaded corner watched me pass through the park. In backwater places like this, people hadn't bothered to tear down these relics—they just ignored them, except in this little out-of-the-way park, someone had painted Comrade Lenin's nose cherry red. I smiled when I saw it.

I emerged from the park onto Octobers Street and went two blocks to a small garage. It was much like the one we kept in Moscow—no windows, steel doors secured by good locks and overall, unremarkable. Across the street was a food store where I'd hoped to find some bread and cheese, but it was closed. I inserted my key into the lock, turned the tumblers and the lock snapped open. I let myself inside where I found three more Gazels.

I went to the newest truck, lifted the hood and checked the battery connections and the hoses. I checked the petrol and the fluids and tested the air pressure in the tires. Everything looked good. I started the engine and it idled smoothly. I opened the door and drove out onto the empty street. I closed and locked the door and then drove slowly back to the station. I found Styopa sitting on the platform with his back against the crates, calmly smoking a cigarette. It was getting lighter.

"Everything ok?" he asked.

I nodded.

"Good, no problems here either. The whole town sleeps," he said with a flourish of his hand.

I backed the Gazel up to the platform and we loaded the crates into the back and covered them over. The light in the stationhouse was dimmer in the brightening morning, but still there was no sign of the stationmaster. With our load secured, we drove away from the station, through the town, and out onto a country road that would take us northwest toward the border crossing near the Polish village of Klukowicze.

It was six thirty when we were finally out into open farm country and the last of Byaroza fell behind us. I was driving and Styopa was reclining on the seat beside me. He looked at his watch.

"We're in good shape," he said. "The first bus crosses the border at nine. There's no need to hurry."

"Time for something to eat?"

"Let's get across the border first."

I thought again about Anton and Slava. Things were becoming clearer to me after a night's rest.

"Have you been thinking about those two?" I said.

"All the way from Tula."

"You haven't said anything."

"Neither have you."

"I wanted time to think."

"So," he said. "You've had time. What do you think?"

We came around a curve in the road and up to a tractor pulling a load of hay. The hay was wet and packed high on the trailer. Stalks dropped off onto the road. I pulled out and passed. "I didn't want to do it—shoot him, I mean. I didn't want to do it."

"He was going to kill you. And me too. Two very good reasons to shoot him. And he was a lying dog—another good reason."

"I didn't want it to be like this."

"Ah, well," he said. "You made that choice when you joined up with us, didn't you?"

"It still doesn't make any sense," I said. "They should have let the colonel handle the inspectors. That was their best chance."

He shrugged. "People do stupid things when they panic."

"Anton didn't look panicked to me."

"You think they had some kind of plan?"

"Maybe."

"And the plan was?"

"Kill us, keep the money and put the rifles back before they were missed."

Styopa lit a cigarette, blew out the match and rolled down his window. "I don't think so. A full inspection would turn up a lot more than just this load. And that would lead back to them—eventually. Those inspectors aren't stupid. Nah, those two boneheads just panicked, I'm sure of it."

"Giving the inspectors just us wouldn't be enough. Anton knew that. He had to give them an inside man too," I said.

He pursed his lips and nodded. "Maybe. Slava—a dead Slava—who could tell them nothing. Maybe, but any way you look at it, it's made us late."

At seven we passed through Pruzhany on our way west and now there was more traffic on the road and people out walking along the streets. No one took any special notice of us. I hoped things would go smoothly at the border because the last thing we needed now was a problem from customs or security—on either side of the border. We didn't expect any trouble on the Belarusian side because things were usually pretty lax there, but you could never tell about the Polish side. The Poles were getting very particular, as bad as the Germans. But we planned these crossings carefully and it was no accident that we would cross at a nowhere place like Klukowicze.

"These things are really pretty simple, if you understand people," Styopa had once explained as he schooled me in some of the finer points of our tradecraft. "First, you choose a crossing at a place out in the country or at a small village. People whose lives are going nowhere are always posted there, on both sides of the border. Then you just let human nature do the rest."

"Meaning?"

"Greed, my friend, greed, our greatest ally. Look, here's how it works. You pick a little crossing out in the country. There are dozens of them and they change the security and customs people every few months. You pay a discreet visit to the head of the security detail—always a junior officer—and you offer him twice what he makes in a year. Just to let a few harmless boxes pass through. To show your good faith, you pay half of it to him, in cash, then and there. And you promise the other half when the first shipment crosses over."

"That simple, huh."

"It always works. After the first shipment, he belongs to you because you can expose him and he knows it."

"What about the rest of the detail?"

"You give him a little more money to spread around so his people cooperate."

"How do you know he gives it to them?"

"We've never had a problem. They always find a way to make sure their people cooperate. We really don't care how they do it."

"And that's it."

"Sometimes they have a little bout of conscience after they take the money. They want to be sure what we're bringing across isn't so bad, and so they want to inspect the goods—personally—the first few times we come across. That's actually quite helpful. They can see for themselves it's just a few rifles and pistols. What harm is there in that? They keep the money, they feel ok about it, and they wave us through. It's the same with the customs people."

"And you go through this every six months, on both sides of the border?"

He laughed. "This business does require some work, you know. And we've been lucky. Some of the security details haven't changed in a year."

After Pruzhany we kept to the smaller roads on a more south-westerly course through the rolling Belarusian farm country that stretches westward until it is swallowed up by the green forests of eastern Poland. Mounds of yellow hay shaped like the tops of toad-stools, piled up to dry in the sun, dotted the fields on both sides of the road. We passed through Brody, then Kamenets and at eight fifteen, through Vysokoye. We were making excellent time.

At eight forty-five Styopa pointed to a flat patch of grass off the road and I pulled over and switched off the engine. A rusty tractor passed by us on the road, heading back into Vysokoye. The driver kept his eyes on the road, never even glancing at us.

A few minutes later, on schedule, the morning bus from Kobryn in Belarus to Bielsk Podlaski in Poland passed us, heading for the border. As it passed, I cranked the engine and we fell in behind it, about fifty meters back. Even with all of our careful arrangements with customs and border security, it was always best to have a little diversion when we crossed.

The bus trundled westward, blue smoke pouring from its exhaust pipe. The sun was fully up and it was a bright morning when we arrived at the border. The bus slowed and then stopped in front of the wooden arm of the road barricade and we slowed and stopped behind it. A Belarusian border guard, dressed in a grey tunic and cap, his rifle slung over his shoulder, barrel pointed down to the ground, stood to the side of the road with his hand up. When the bus stopped and its doors opened, he climbed up inside. Styopa and I waited. A few minutes later the guard jumped back down onto the road and two customs men boarded. We could see them through the rear bus windows walking up and down the aisle, questioning passengers and peering under seats and into the luggage racks. Some of the passengers were ordered to stand and turn out their pockets. About half an hour later, after the customs men had finished their poking and prodding and had stepped off onto the road, the border guard raised the barricade and waved the bus through.

I put the Gazel into gear and drove slowly up to the barricade and then stopped. The guard walked up to my window. He was a young sergeant with greasy blonde hair sticking out from under his cap.

"Documents," he said, holding out his hand. Styopa leaned over and handed our passports and visas out the window to him.

"*Dobroe ootre*," Styopa said. "Good morning."

The guard didn't answer, but recognition flickered in his eyes. He took our documents and opened my passport first, stopping at my photo and then looking up at my face and down at the photo again. He opened Styopa's booklet and turned through several pages, pausing to examine the many entry and exit stamps. When he finished, he closed it and handed our documents back to Styopa and walked back toward the barricade. Then a customs man came up to my window and I handed him my declaration form.

"Heavy equipment parts?" he asked as he glanced over the form.

"That's right."

"New or used?"

"All new."

"Any currency?"

"About ten thousand rubles, each of us. It's on the form."

"Any art objects, jewelry, icons?"

"No, nothing like that."

"Ok," he said. He nodded to the guard who then raised the barrier.

"*Spaseebo,*" I said.

"*Pazhalusta.*"

I put the Gazel back into gear and drove slowly onto Polish soil, coming up again behind the bus which was stopped at the checkpoint for Polish border security and customs. We arrived just as two Polish customs men were ordering the passengers off the bus.

"They love this," Styopa said. "It's their one bit of fun out here."

"Maybe they just need a smoke," I said.

"Very funny."

The passengers lined up along the side of the road. Then the customs man gave a sharp command and packages of cigarettes magically appeared out of pockets and from underneath shirts, trousers and dresses. They tossed the packages onto the road into a pile which grew into a tidy little mound. The customs men stood back and watched.

"A pretty good catch," I said.

"Mmm, probably about half of what's really there."

If Styopa was right, the passengers would make out all right on this trip in spite of what they handed over to customs. Smuggling cigarettes was a small potatoes business, but it was all some of these people had. Just a few cartons could fetch enough on the Polish market to feed a family for a week or more. In those times the average monthly wage in the towns and villages in Belarus was about twenty rubles. For the customs people, this was a kind of cat and mouse game, but they had the decency to take only enough to make a good show and leave something behind. One of the customs men scooped up the packages into a plastic bag and the passengers filed back onto the bus. A moment later, it drove off into the verdant Polish countryside for Klukowicze, Nurzec, Moloczki, Kndrydy and finally, Bielsk Podlaski.

Then the border guard waved to us and I drove slowly forward and pushed on the brake pedal when we came up beside him. He stepped to my window and Styopa again leaned over and handed out our documents. This time there was no sign of any recognition. The guard was polite enough, but he wore that impenetrable mask worn by security people everywhere—distant, humorless, in complete control and therefore very much at ease. He leafed through the pages of our passports, pausing at the multi-entry visas, but barely glancing at the photos.

"Your first trip to Poland?" he asked me in Russian with a heavy Polish accent. He could see from my passport and visa that it wasn't.

"No, I've been here before," I said.

"The reason for your visit to Poland?"

"We're bringing over the parts in the back," Styopa said. "For a trade show."

"Where will that be?"

"At the Exhibition Center in Gdansk, the day after tomorrow."

The guard nodded, handed our passports back and told us to wait. He moved on to another truck that had pulled up behind us. We waited and then the customs man we'd seen bagging the cigarettes from the bus came up to Styopa's window. Styopa handed him our declaration form and he took it with his free hand and glanced over it. He was still holding the plastic bag of cigarettes with his other hand.

"What's the value of your parts?" he asked.

"Thirty thousand zlotys, but they're for resale at the show."

"Within 30 days?"

"We hope so," Styopa said.

"You'll be responsible for sending in the notice of sale."

"I understand."

"If it's not received in 30 days the full duties are due immediately."

"Right. I understand."

"Ok," he said. "Exempt from duties at this time."

He dropped the plastic bag, scribbled his initials on the form and peeled off a copy which he handed to Styopa. Then he waved us forward and another guard raised the barricade, our welcome into Poland. The whole business—on both sides of the border—had taken less than an hour. And it all appeared perfectly correct, except when you considered that no one had ever bothered to look into the back of the Gazel. Our preparations had been very good indeed.

When we reached Klukowicze we stopped again at a telephone box and Styopa placed a call to the Warsaw Marriott Hotel where by now the colonel should have been ensconced in his room. When the hotel operator came on the line, Styopa asked to be put through and then he waited. And again there was no answer on the other end of the line.

"Maybe he's out for breakfast or a walk," Styopa said.

"Strolling the streets of Warsaw—like a tourist?"

He hung up the phone. "Right. Not likely."

"No, it isn't. Did they say he checked into his room?"

"Last night."

"Well, at least we've found him."

"We haven't found him yet."

"He'll be pretty steamed by now," I said.

Styopa pursed his lips. "Mmm."

"Look—we got here as soon as we could," I said.

"I'll let you explain it."

"Then, let's get there and explain it."

"Right. You drew the long match, remember."

But before we could explain things in Warsaw, we had a final bit of business at the border. Outside of Nurzec, one hundred and twenty kilometers east of Warsaw, is an abandoned youth camp lying peacefully in the forest. The Party built it a generation ago as a summer camp for the Komsomol. The Polish government was all too willing to take our money for a long-term lease and we paid a top price for it. No doubt the Poles thought we were just another bunch of ignorant

Russians who would never understand business. But that was just fine with us. Let them think so. We paid a top price because we got top value for our money. The camp was perfect for our special needs— a barn for our trucks and product, spacious cabins for us and our clients, a big, serviceable kitchen, and even a dining hall with wood-paneled walls and a beamed ceiling and wood floors that shined up handsomely with a little cleaner. But above all, we bought seclusion, our own little piece of the forest many kilometers distant from our nearest neighbors.

It was ten thirty when I pulled the Gazel into the barn. We unloaded the crates and checked the barn and its locks for any signs of tampering. Then we made a quick tour of the rest of the camp. Some roof stripping was missing from one of the cabins, probably from a storm, but otherwise, everything was as we had left it on our last trip. A little after eleven, we climbed into a Lada sedan we kept in the barn and started out for Warsaw.

CHAPTER 30

wo days after Styopa and I crept away from the graves in the
woods outside Tula airbase, I was standing at the window of the
Panorama Bar at the top of the Warsaw Marriott Hotel, showered
and shaved, wearing clean clothes, gazing down at Warsaw spread out
below me.

Directly below was Warsaw Central Station and to the north, the
Ghetto Memorial, the Monument to the Warsaw Uprising, and the
rust gable roofs of Old Town. The late afternoon sun lit up the haze
over the city, alchemizing it into a golden gossamer cloak over the
streets and buildings. Ripples shimmered on the Vistula River. The
streets were alive with people and vehicles, but all was quiet on my side
of the thick glass forty floors above the streets. I reached up and put
my palm to the glass. It still held the warmth of the day.

Then the serving girl came up behind me and spoke. "Kolya, nice
to see you again. It's been a while."

I turned from the window. "Hello, Aleshka. It's good to see
you too." She was a striking creature—eyes the color of the sky on a
clear fall day, creamy white skin and dark brown hair pulled back and
braided into a thick, shiny rope that hung to the middle of her back.
She was one of the many benefits of this venue.

She set a glass of water down at our table next to Styopa. She
looked at him. "For you, Styopa?"

"My usual, three beers."

She rolled her eyes. "I'll bring tea."

Then she went over to the table in the middle of the room where
the colonel was seated alone. "Colonel?" she said.

He looked up at her and smiled and shook his head. "Nothing, thank you."

She gave him a pretty smile and left the room. He watched her go and then ran a hand over his graying hair. He was looking older now, but he was still a man people turned to take a second look at when they passed him on the street. I'd seen men and women do it.

"What do you think?" Styopa whispered to me. "At least his mood's getting better."

"Yeah, from terrible to bad."

The colonel had barely spoken to us when we finally found him, sitting alone in a chair in the lobby of the hotel, reading a newspaper. He had looked up at us, snapped his paper shut, and walked brusquely past us to the lift.

"You'd better have a good explanation," was all he said.

The three of us rode the lift up to his suite and there he poured himself a glass of water from one of the bottles on the sideboard and sat down in a chair. He didn't offer us any refreshment or chairs. He looked at his watch.

"You're now exactly one day late," he said.

"Sir, we can explain," Styopa said.

"Good. Let's hear it—right now."

Styopa looked at me and then he began his account of the last day's events, beginning with our drive down to Tula from the garage in Moscow. He gave the colonel the facts of the trip in a measured way, with no embellishments, asking me from time to time to confirm some of the details. As I listened to him, the whole business again seemed unreal, like the plot of a bad film. Only it hadn't been a film; it had really happened that two close colleagues had tried to kill us for no good reason.

As Styopa talked, the colonel sat still in his chair, his gaze either fixed on us or on the glass of water he twirled gently in his hand. He asked questions to clarify a few points, but otherwise he listened quietly, taking it all in.

When Styopa finished, the colonel sat for several minutes, a distant expression on his face.

"The petrol cans?" he said finally. "What do you make of that?" It was a question I'd been pondering too. Styopa shrugged and looked at me.

"It's one of two things," I said.

"Go on."

"Anton's truck was low and needed a fill-up," I said and the colonel smirked.

"Or?"

"He was going to light us up."

"Every security man on the base would see the smoke," Styopa said.

"Anton wanted security to find us," I said.

"He could have marched us into the base."

"He couldn't do that," I said.

"No, he couldn't," the colonel agreed. "Especially if he wanted to keep the money." He was still twirling the glass in his hand.

"Security would find the rifles, three dead men, the trucks and an open gate. They'd have their thieves," I said. "He was going to torch all three of us."

"You may be right," the colonel said. "If they couldn't identify the bodies, so much the better—harder for the inspectors to tie it all back to him."

"Still doesn't explain why he didn't come to you for help about the inspection," Styopa said.

The colonel stood up and refilled his glass. "Well, that's a problem for another day. Today we have a bigger problem right here."

"Is Koeppel still in Warsaw?" Styopa asked.

"For now. He was due back in Zurich today and he wasn't happy about staying over."

"But he stayed—that's good," I said.

"I persuaded him to stay—by giving him the sample and agreeing to a discount on his first order."

I winced. It was a wonder the colonel's mood wasn't worse.

"The goods are now in Nurzec, I hope," he said.

"Yes, sir," Styopa and I said together.

"Good. Then we'll see what our friend wants to do. You can take him to the camp tonight."

"There isn't much point in that if we're giving the stuff to him," Styopa said.

"We'll offer it anyway. And if he wants the goods brought to Warsaw, we'll do that—that is, you'll do it."

"When do you meet him?" I asked. The colonel looked again at his watch.

"In three hours."

As was his habit, the colonel sat alone at his table in the bar, collecting his thoughts before his meeting. He often met clients here, in one of the bar's private meeting rooms. He liked the respectability—the veneer of worldliness—that came with doing business in a first class western hotel. And he particularly appreciated one detail about this room that any professional would notice right away—there were only two ways in and out, by the not-too-rapid lift to the lobby forty floors below or by forty flights of stairs. From this safe, pleasant redoubt high above the Polish capital we had transacted sales worth billions of rubles in those crazy first few years when the USSR was a fresh, unguarded carcass.

"Kolya," the colonel said, pointing a forefinger toward the lift.

I got up and went over and sat on the divan outside the lift doors and waited. A few minutes later, on time, the chime sounded and the doors slid quietly open and I stood up. Out stepped Reto Schneider, a solid, compact man with a square red face, and following him, Herr Otto Koeppel, looking dapper with his close-clipped grey beard and striped suit that shined when he moved. Schneider was Koeppel's head security shadow and general factotum. He looked around the room and then nodded to me. His eyes were a little too far apart, which gave his face a slightly startled look.

"*Guten tag*, Kolya," Herr Koeppel said to me in his soft Swiss accent. "*Wo ist der Oberst?*" Then he remembered himself and switched to Russian. "The colonel, please," he said.

I nodded and extended my arm, indicating the way. Koeppel strode into the room where the colonel was waiting, with Schneider and me following behind. I expected no trouble from these two, but instinctively I reached up and touched the grip of the pistol inside my jacket. The colonel stood up from his table. The two men exchanged greetings.

"Please sit down," the colonel said. "Some refreshment?"

"Thank you, no," Koeppel said. The colonel waived his hand at the serving girl who had been standing nearby and she withdrew. They sat down and Schneider and I sat down at separate nearby tables, close enough to listen and watch. Styopa stood at the door.

Koeppel shifted his weight in his chair and folded his hands on the table. He had the smooth, well-cared-for hands of one who has led a good life indoors. "Civilized" was the word that came to me. That was my overall impression of this man from our first meeting with him three months before in Zurich. The colonel rarely traveled to the west—Warsaw or Prague or Budapest were about as far from Russia as he cared to go—but he'd made the long trip to Zurich by train for the chance to meet and do business with Herr Otto Koeppel. I remembered how gracious Koeppel had been to us. He had paid for our rooms at the boutique Hotel zum Storchen, provided us with excellent meals, and when we all met in the hotel's cozy, elegant parlor next to the flowing green water of the Limmat River, he and the colonel had sipped tea from fine china cups. It was all so very civilized.

"You had a pleasant stay last night?" the colonel now asked.

Koeppel smoothed out a crease in his suit. "Comfortable, thank you. It's been many years since I was in Warsaw."

"Perhaps you'll visit again."

"Perhaps, but I'd prefer for you to be my guest again in Zurich."

"That would be my pleasure," the colonel said.

Then Koeppel smiled. "But I suppose I should give you more time for the trip," he said. "I must say, you intrigue me, Colonel. An air officer who doesn't fly."

"A retired air officer."

"Of course. Retired from one profession to begin another."

Was our business a "profession"? I hadn't thought of it that way, but that too sounded very civilized.

"That is true," the colonel said.

"As it happens, I agree with you about flying. Very disagreeable, but unfortunately, one of the necessities of what we do."

"I made a promise to myself years ago—no more rushing through life. You should try the train. Very relaxing."

"Or is it that you've tempted fate in the air enough for one lifetime, eh?" Koeppel said and then laughed. The colonel demurred. Then Schneider went over to Koeppel and spoke softy into his ear. Koeppel listened and nodded.

"So then, Colonel, your shipment has arrived?"

"It has."

"It's here in Warsaw?"

"A short trip away at one of our facilities. It would be our pleasure to take you there to inspect the goods and give you a demonstration."

"The goods are new?"

"These have seen service, but the stocks they come from have been inspected and they're in excellent condition. We guarantee it."

Koeppel raised an eyebrow. "Ah, well, it's interesting you should use the word 'guarantee' because it brings up a point we must discuss."

"Yes?"

"You'll forgive me if I'm blunt, but we can't afford to waste each other's time."

"Please, say what's on your mind."

"It's quite simple: are you really in a position to guarantee anything these days, Colonel?"

"Meaning what?" the colonel asked.

Koeppel feigned a look of surprise. "Well … just look at us here today. This meeting was to take place yesterday, was it not?"

"I agreed to give you the goods … as compensation."

"A nice gesture, which I appreciate, but unfortunately it doesn't address the issue. I don't doubt the quality of your goods, Colonel. What I doubt is whether we can trust you to get them to us when you say you will. When my clients place orders, it's because they need the goods. And they can be impatient. They don't listen to excuses."

"That will not be a problem."

Koeppel stroked his beard. "And I assume you didn't expect a problem with your sample and yet you arrived here a day ahead of it." It was a quite diplomatic way of saying Styopa and I had been late and I smiled.

"A very unusual set of circumstances this time. It won't happen again."

Koeppel cocked his head to the side. "Forgive me, but I need more than that. I told you—the clients I deal with can be very impatient."

"If you'd give us a better idea of your requirements, we could give you exact information about delivery times."

Koeppel eyed the colonel for a long moment. "A regiment-sized formation," he said matter-of-factly.

"How soon?"

"Eight weeks."

"And after that?"

"Another regiment, in another month. After that, regular orders of comparable size every three months or so for at least a year, but I don't know the exact timing of those orders yet."

"Payment terms?" the colonel asked.

"On delivery, of course."

"Currency?"

Koeppel shrugged. "Dollars, deutschmarks, Swiss francs, which-ever you like … rubles if you like."

"Not rubles," the colonel said.

"No, I wouldn't think so."

The colonel was doing well to appear calm, but I felt his excite-ment. This was what we'd been waiting for, our tap into the golden pipeline. It meant a fortune for us, many fortunes.

"Can you handle these, Colonel? Tell me now if there's any chance you can't. It will save us both much trouble."

The colonel leaned forward and folded his hands on the table. "Herr Koeppel, what's really on your mind?"

Koeppel leaned back and looked up at the ceiling. "What is the expression?—'the winds of change are blowing'? It seems they're blowing again in Russia these days. You know better than I the problems that could mean for us."

"You're speaking of the reformers?"

"Certainly. These are men of, shall we say … principles … men who are not likely to be easily dissuaded. They could put you out of business—and very soon."

The colonel waved a hand. "No one listens to them."

"Really?" Koeppel said. "Then you and I must be reading different newspapers, my friend."

The colonel was keeping his composure, but now I saw the tightness around his mouth and in his neck. To be cross-examined this way was a new experience for him. Yet Koeppel did have a point, a good one. His information was quite good too, but then that was to be expected. You don't make billions by being uninformed.

"Newspapers are good for wrapping fish," the colonel said and Koeppel laughed.

"A widely held opinion, I believe, and not just in your country. But, joking aside, Colonel, you and I both know things are getting more complicated for you at home."

"The people you refer to, these reformers, are a rabble, nothing more."

"This rabble, I believe, is right now proposing legislation in the Duma, legislation that would change everything about the way munitions are handled in your country. That's what the newspapers I read are saying." Koeppel's voice was flintier now.

"Talk about legislation is one thing, passing it is another and enforcing it, if it ever does pass, quite another," the colonel said.

"So, in your opinion, then, these concerns of mine are just … hypothetical."

"A good way to put it."

"Well, you'll forgive me, but there are developments this week that are anything but hypothetical."

"Such as?"

"The botched shipments to Armenia, for example. Hasn't the Procurator begun criminal proceedings against several parties involved? Some of your colleagues, too, I believe."

"It's an investigation, nothing more."

"Investigations have a way of leading to bigger things. Every prosecution starts as an investigation."

The colonel shifted in his chair. "Are these your only concerns?"

"Not entirely. I also understand your government is well along in creating a new state company—I forget the name of it—that will control every gun and bullet that comes out of your country."

"Rosvooruzheniye," the colonel said.

"Yes, thank you. Perhaps I should be talking to them now, rather than with you."

"Perhaps you should—if you're willing to wait—and if you want to pay state prices."

Koeppel nodded. "A fair point," he said.

"And remember this," the colonel continued. "If the Duma ever does stop its dithering and get around to setting up Rosvooruzheniye, it will have no authority—none—without a presidential decree. Whatever its so-called 'sponsors' say, it will be an empty shell unless the president gives it the authority. He doesn't give that kind of power to anybody these days. He's become ... suspicious ... in his old age."

"That I can believe," Koeppel said.

"You're much better off doing business with us."

Koeppel eyed him.

"Well ... you know your country better than I. But if we are to commit to you, and forego our other sources, then you must be able to commit to us, no?"

"Herr Koeppel, I came to Switzerland in good faith and I came here in good faith. I wouldn't waste your time and I ask you not to waste mine. If these things mean you don't want to do business with us, tell me now. Your orders will be met in full and on time. If any is a day late you can have the goods half price. Fair enough?"

Koeppel regarded the colonel for another long moment. Schneider and I watched them and Styopa watched all of us from the door.

"Very well, Colonel," Koeppel said finally. "I will accept your assurances—for the first order. After that, well, we shall see how it goes."

He stood up and then the colonel did too.

"I will send you the requirements for the first order in a few days."

"Very good. And the sample, do you want to see it?"

"I'm afraid there isn't time. You can deliver it to my representative in Siedice tomorrow."

Koeppel produced an ebony pen with a gold clip from his shirt pocket, unscrewed the cap and leaned over the table. He scribbled a few lines on a paper napkin and then handed it to the colonel.

"Here's the address. It's near the E30. You'll have no trouble finding it. Schneider here will meet you there."

"I'll send one of my men," the colonel said. "Noon tomorrow?"

"Fine."

Herr Koeppel then made a slight bow. "Thank you for a productive meeting, Colonel," he said. *"Dosvidanya."*

"Dosvidanya," the colonel answered.

Koeppel went back to the lift with Schneider and me again following behind. When they were safely inside and the lift doors had closed, I rejoined the colonel and Styopa. The colonel was standing at the window with his back to us, facing out at the city. I knew he wasn't admiring the view. We stood back, awaiting his instructions. After a time, he turned and spoke to us.

"Styopa, go to Nurzec tonight and bring the goods to Siedice," he said, handing Styopa the napkin with the address. Styopa nodded. "Then come back to Moscow as quickly as you can." He turned to me.

"Kolya, go down to the concierge and hire a car and driver. Tell them the car is to pick us up here in half an hour. We can catch up to the evening train at Brest. Wait for the car and ring me in my room when it gets here."

"Yes, sir," I said.

I rode the lift down to the lobby where I found the concierge, a small, efficient-looking woman sitting behind an ornate table. Obligingly she put aside the papers she was working on and picked up

291

the telephone to order the car. When she had the car service on the line she said it would be there as soon as I liked. I told her to have it in front of the hotel in thirty minutes. Then I went back to my room and packed my bag and returned to the lobby and waited. When the car arrived I rang the colonel and he came down immediately, carrying his travel bag. I paid our bill and we stepped into the waiting vehicle, a long, late-model Mercedes sedan, and sank back into the leather seats. The driver turned to us.

"Krakow?" he asked.

"Brest," I said. "And hurry; we want to catch up to the train to Moscow."

He nodded and then steered the powerful sedan out of the hotel grounds, over the Poniatowskiego bridge and east, out of Warsaw. We accelerated onto the E30, after a while passing Siedice and later Biala Podlaska on our way to Brest. Barely a word passed between the colonel and me for the entire trip. He stared out the window.

Sitting there in that quiet, comfortable space, I had the feeling of being safely inside as a storm gathers, knowing I would soon be called out into it.

We arrived in Brest long after dark and as we came into the city, the colonel leaned forward in his seat.

"The train station," he said to the driver. A few minutes later the car deposited us in front of the station building and the colonel paid while I fetched our bags from the boot and carried them inside.

"Set them over there and stay with them," he said to me as he headed off to the ticket window.

The station at Brest was built soon after the Crimean War, the high, airy ceilings decorated with elaborate designs in plaster that are now dark and indistinct with layer upon layer of grime. The floor mosaics are faded beyond recognition by a century and a half of foot traffic. At that hour, the central lobby was filled with people dozing on the floor and on benches, their luggage and packages drawn up around them in heaps, as they waited for the late night and early morning trains. Over the years great masses of troops from vanished empires have passed through this station, sometimes traveling east, sometimes west, but always on the move, never staying there. For decades in the twentieth century, Brest had been the western frontier of the USSR and in that time, and still today, trains running east from Brest into Russia run on tracks with a wider gauge than the tracks of western Europe and Poland. Trains running in either direction, east or west, must stop at Brest for their passengers to detrain and wait while cranes lift the cars from sets of wheels fitting one system of track onto wheels fitting the other system. It had once been a credible defense because an invading army could never just ride by rail past this point into Mother Russia. Today, in an age of missiles, it seems almost quaint, but it delayed the train from Warsaw long enough for me and the colonel to catch up to it for the trip home.

The colonel bought our tickets and ten minutes after midnight we settled into our compartment. I was still feeling tired from the strain of the long night at Tula and so I stretched out on my bed and went to sleep. I woke only once during the night and saw the colonel sitting up staring out the window. The wheels clacked rhythmically under the car.

At about six o'clock I stretched and sat up. I was thinking about getting breakfast at the next stop. The colonel was still sitting up, looking out the window. It was getting light outside.

"Did you sleep at all?" I asked.

"Not much, maybe a little."

"You should lie down a while. You'll be stiff from sitting up. Can I get you some tea?"

"Maybe later. I want to talk to you about Tula. I want you to go over it again," he said.

"What do you want to know?"

"Why do you think they were late—Anton and Slava—why were they late?"

I thought a moment. "I'm not sure. Maybe to give Slava time to get behind us."

"To come over the fence?"

"He didn't come over the fence."

"How do you know?"

"We had a clear view of it for two hundred meters on both sides of the gate. We would have seen him."

293

"Was it possible?"

"It's topped with razor wire."

"Could he have come through the gate?"

"No, not possible. We would have seen him."

"What time was it when you got there?"

"About six thirty, maybe close to seven. He couldn't have come through the gate."

"Then he was in the woods, waiting, when you got there. He must have been."

I hadn't thought about that, but it made sense. I shuddered at the idea—Slava, concealed in the woods, just meters away from where I had idly walked and smoked to pass the time, watching me with his murderous eyes.

"I guess so," I said. "Does it matter?"

"It suggests some things. I don't think they were panicked—the inspection was an excuse, a chance they'd been waiting for."

"We're rid of them."

"There'll be others. When an insect like Anton decides things are ripe for his own enterprises, things have gotten out of control. There'll be others if we don't put a stop to this."

"Yes, I see that," I said. "But, you might be making Anton out to be more than he was. It's possible he was just spooked by the inspectors."

"Can we afford to take the chance?"

"Probably not," I said.

He turned again to the window. "You're sure he said the inspectors were from the Procurator?" he asked me a moment later.

"That's what he said. And the other team was from the Defense Committee."

"Not the Quartermaster?"

"No, I'm sure about that."

"I was hoping I'd imagined it," he said.

"How bad is it?"

"Bad. The Quartermaster we could handle. The Procurator, and the Defense Committee, they'll be different."

"Maybe Anton was lying about that too."

"You think he was clever enough to make that up?"

"No."

"Neither do I. He was never that subtle. You saw that for yourself the other night."

"Then our problems are in Moscow, not in Tula," I said.

"Our problems are definitely in Moscow."

"You know who?" I asked.

"Oh, yes."

"What do we do?"

"What we should have done already—cut out this weed at its roots."

~~~~

After our train pulled into Moscow, the colonel and I parted, but not before he gave me a final instruction.

"You and Styopa come to the flat on Saturday morning. I have a job for you."

"Should we pack for overnight?"

"No, this won't take long. It's what we should have done months ago."

"We'll be there," I said and then I watched him disappear into the crowd.

CHAPTER 31

❧

O n Saturday Styopa and I called at the flat on Aleksei Tolstoy Street at eleven o'clock. The colonel answered the door and we followed him into the parlor where he had tea and a plate of sandwiches laid out for us. He looked rested from the trip back from Warsaw but his eyes had the same sparkle I'd seen in them after his meeting with Koeppel.

"Sit down," he said and after I was comfortably seated in one of his big chairs, he dropped an opened copy of *Ogonek* magazine into my lap.

"You know this man?" he asked, pointing to a photograph on the opened page. It was an old photo, but I recognized the face at once. It was an unmistakable face—the dark hair and full beard and the clear eyes that projected energy and compassion. Hanging from his neck, onto a white cassock, was a cross.

"I've never met him," I said.

"But you know who he is."

"Of course—Father Yarlov."

"Correct. And have you seen that story?"

"No, sir."

"Well, read it. It seems Father Dmitri has been talking again about his plans," he said. "Go ahead, read it."

I scanned the story alongside the photo. It reported that more than two thousand people had turned out to hear the priest at his church at Novaya Derevnya, near Moscow. I was impressed. That was many times the size of the crowd that came to hear him at the church in the Chaimovniki district. His popularity was growing, quickly.

"Do you see the subject of that particular speech?" the colonel was saying and I read farther down into the story.

"Munitions sales," I said.

"That's right."

"He's been saying these things for years, even in soviet times. There's nothing new about that."

"But now people—some influential people—are starting to listen and that is new. He's getting quite a following and that's becoming a nuisance."

"He hasn't said anything about us," I said.

The colonel sat down and poured three cups of tea from a silver pot. He handed a cup to me and then one to Styopa.

"Kolya, think," he said. "Some of the people coming to these so-called lectures sit in the Duma. The talk alone is trouble—you should understand that after your recent experience in Tula. He sees himself as some sort of national conscience and that's the last thing we need."

I looked over at Styopa who was seated in his chair, sipping his tea. I was getting the feeling he had heard this already and that what the colonel was saying now was for my benefit.

"You don't really think what happened in Tula had anything to do with this priest," I said.

"I think there's a good chance of that. I've done some checking and Anton was telling you the truth about the inspection. Those teams weren't there by accident. The Duma Defense Committee is under pressure to improve security around the bases. There are people in the Duma who are listening to this priest and all his talk."

"It might all blow over," I said.

"We can't afford to wait and see. We can't have him running around the country bringing attention to us. Unless, of course, you'd rather just shut our operation down and go back to Kursk."

Then Styopa joined in.

"He's right, Kolya. You heard Koeppel. One more slip up and he's done with us. This priest could spoil everything."

"He's just a priest," I said.

"Have you heard him?" the colonel asked. "Well, I have. He may be just a priest, but he's a very clever man and he understands how to stir up a crowd. I've seen him do it."

"He's a showman," Styopa said.

"And that story says he's going to start naming names unless the Duma does more than just talk about his reforms," the colonel went on.

"Do you think he'll do it?" I asked.

The colonel sipped his tea. "It might be just another one of his tricks to keep the newspapers interested. But we can't take the chance."

I began to see where this might be going.

"There are people in the Duma saying the same things," I said. "That it's time to put the arms dealers out of business. We should worry about them it seems to me."

"The politicians blow with the wind—and this man is the wind," the colonel said.

"Remember, this is still Russia," Styopa said and laughed. "If a priest tells you something, it must be true."

"After seventy years, we haven't shaken that off," the colonel said.

We talked on this way for another hour or more—about Father Dimitri, about the reformers and the noise they were making in the Duma, about the inspection at Tula, more about Father Dimitri—but we kept coming back to the same point time and again: the colonel was convinced the priest was a threat.

"Ok," I said. "What do you want us to do?"

"I want you two to go listen to him," the colonel said.

"We can read in the papers what he says—"

"And," he continued, "see who else is there listening." He sipped his tea again.

"When?" Styopa asked and the colonel pointed again at the magazine.

"He preaches most Sundays at his church in Novaya Derevnya. Start there—tomorrow. Tell me everything you see and hear. Everything."

He paused.

"Fine," I said and I started to get up.

"There's one more thing," the colonel said and I sat back down. "This priest must be made to understand that he's sticking his nose where he shouldn't. I want you two to meet him, before he makes another one of these speeches, and talk to him."

"And tell him what?"

"Just what I said—that he's meddling in things that don't concern him."

I almost laughed, but I knew he wouldn't see the humor. I chose my next words with care.

"Colonel, this man won't listen to any of that. It's a waste of time."

"How do you know that?"

"Because … because he believes in what he says."

"I believe in what I'm saying."

"It's different with him."

"A man of principles, is that it?"

"You could say that."

"You sound like you know him," Styopa said.

"Just read this story," I said. I held up the magazine. "Read any of the stories about him. He won't listen to us—whatever we tell him. It'll probably make things worse."

Styopa set his tea cup down. "There's no harm in talking to him," he said.

"What are we going to say?"

"Tell him we're prepared to make a contribution to his church," the colonel said. "Churches are always looking for money."

"Sir, you're not serious," I said.

"We should go early, before he gets to Novaya Derevnya," Styopa said. "He rides the train there from Semkhoz. We'll meet him before he gets on the train."

The Colonel shrugged. "I'll leave that to you."

He set his cup down in the saucer and stood up, our signal the meeting was over. Styopa and I rode the lift down from the flat to the lobby.

"I don't get this," I said. "How can he be so blind? It's not like him. What's the point in going to Semkhoz?"

"He told you."

We went out the door and stood together in front of the block. "You don't believe that. Read what the priest is saying, or watch him on TV. You know this is a waste of time."

"Just follow orders, Kolya."

"And what if there's trouble? He must have security. It'll just bring more attention to us."

"A priest, security?" Styopa looked at me through narrowed eyes. "Is there some reason you don't want to do this?"

"It's a mistake—a big one—and it's not like the colonel to make mistakes. He's not acting like himself."

"He knows things we don't."

"I don't see it that way."

He looked me in the eyes. "Kolya, be careful. There's a lot at stake here and he gave us an order."

I stared at him, wondering if I should go any farther.

"There's something else," I said. "I think I know where this is going and I want no part of it."

"He gave us an order. That's all there is to it."

"A crazy order."

"It's not your place to say that. Remember your place, my friend."

"I can think for myself." I said. "And so can you, or have you forgotten how to do that? You know where this will end."

"We're going there to talk and listen."

"Talk and listen."

"That's right."

We stood there, looking at each other. "Swear it," I said and he burst out laughing.

"Swear it? Swear what?"

"Just to talk and listen."

He looked at me for a long moment. "Ok, if you like. I swear it," he said and then he came close and flung a muscled arm around my shoulders. "Now, is that better?"

"Styopa, where will it end?" I asked and his smile faded.

"This is our business, Kolya. We will protect it. You knew that."

"And if the colonel's wrong?"

"He never is."

He reached up and put his hands on my shoulders. "My friend, are you with us on this?"

I pulled his hands away. "I'll be there," I said.

"That's not what I asked. Are you with us?"

I knew I had to answer him. "I'm with you," I said finally.

"I hope so."

~~~~

Early the next morning, a September Sunday, we waited together near the edge of a thick patch of woods outside Semkhoz. It had rained in the early morning hours and the air was damp and cold. Thunder rumbled in the distance. We'd been there more than an hour and I was shivering.

"Maybe he isn't coming," I said.

Styopa looked at his watch. "We'll wait a little longer."

"You're sure this is the right place?"

"It's the right place."

"Maybe he's already gone on to Novaya Derevnya."

"We'll give it a few more minutes."

I blew on my hands and rubbed them together. Then Styopa squeezed my arm and pointed into the woods. I squinted and then through the branches I saw a lone man walking along the path, toward us.

"Is it him?" I whispered.

"Must be. Go ahead."

I went quickly to the spot we had chosen for me to hide, about twenty meters in the other direction, behind a tree just off the path. I stepped behind it and Styopa hid behind a tree farther up the path. I watched the approaching figure walk quietly toward us and then pass the tree concealing Styopa. Now there was no mistaking who it was. Father Dimitri was walking slowly, his head down. His long overcoat was unbuttoned and open, revealing the cross hanging from his neck. I took a breath and stepped out from behind the tree and stood in the middle of the path as the priest came nearer. At first he seemed not to notice me. He kept walking, but then, when he was just a few meters away, he looked up and stopped. His face showed no surprise or fear— just curiosity—and then the corners of his eyes crinkled.

"Good morning, my son. You surprised me—you're here so early."

He must think I'm one of his parishioners. Why else would he smile at me like that?

Father Dimitri stood there, waiting for me to answer. I started to speak, but the words I'd rehearsed stuck in my throat. Next to this man, I felt coarse and dirty.

"I … I don't …" was all I could get out and then he smiled again and came closer to me.

"Don't I know you?" I felt his hand touch my shoulder.

Why is he touching me?

I struggled for something to say, but then I stopped. I saw what was behind him—Styopa approaching swiftly, silently along the path.

What's he doing? Why is he hurrying?

My eyes darted between Father Dimitri's face and Styopa.

What are you doing?

Father Dmitri lowered his hand onto my arm and he started to turn me in the direction he was walking. "Why don't you—" he started to say, but then Styopa's shoe thudded into a root. The priest spun around at the noise, saw Styopa, and took a step backward.

"Wait," I said, but Father Dimitri took another step and then his boot heel came down on a flat stone, its surface wet and slick. The boot slid from under him and he came down hard on the stony ground. His head hit with a dull thud and his eyes rolled back and closed.

I pushed Styopa. "Are you crazy! What were you doing?!"

"Oh, maaan," Styopa said. He knelt and put his fingertips on the priest's neck and then he raised one of the eyelids with his thumb. "Son of a—"

"Look what you did!" I knelt down and took the priest's wrist. There was a faint pulse.

"I didn't touch him. I was just trying to shake him up a little."

"We gotta go for help."

Styopa stood up. "Forget it, he's dead."

"He's not dead!"

"He's dead. Let's go," he said in a husky whisper. "We can't stay here."

But I couldn't go—I couldn't move. To slink away into the woods was impossible. My legs simply wouldn't carry me.

"I'm not going."

"He just fell."

"Because of you."

I put my hand behind Father Dimitri's head and I felt the warm stickiness on my fingers. I laid his head back down. Thunder rumbled again and it started to drizzle. I wiped away a droplet from his forehead.

"Father, I'll go for help," I said.

"He's gone I told you," Styopa said. He grabbed me by the collar of my jacket. I knocked his hand away.

Then Father Dimitri's chest raised up and he took a breath. He summoned the strength to squeeze my arm. The eyes opened and a trace of the smile he had given me reappeared, not frozen there, but reemerging by an act of his will.

Did he recognize me? No, not possible. He just mistook me for someone else.

Styopa grabbed my jacket again. "Get up," he said. I knocked his hand away again. Behind us, some distance down the path toward the train station, a dog barked. I looked down at Father Dimitri.

Styopa leaned down and whispered to me with barely controlled fury. "Somebody's coming. If you don't get up they'll see us. We'll be arrested! Let's go!"

The dog barked again and Styopa let go of my collar and started to run out of the woods, back toward the car.

Father Dimitri's lips started to move, at first just a quiver. He squeezed my arm tighter. I leaned down and put my ear next to his lips.

"K ... Kol, Kolya," I thought I heard him squeak. I jerked my head up and looked into his eyes. Now they were clear and focused—on me. His lips were moving again, forming words. I stared at them.

"R ... re ... restore it," he said. "Restore it." Then his eyes rolled back and closed.

I climbed to my feet, feeling the air knocked out of me, feeling the priest's blood ooze through my fingers. This was impossible. This was a dream—a terrible dream. I grabbed up a handful of dead leaves and scrubbed at my hand. I looked down the path and saw Styopa through the trees, running away.

The dog barked again, this time sounding nearer.

And then—everything changed.

The world around me tore loose from its moorings.

The air crackled, stinging my eyes. My ears popped, my skin tingled and my hair stood on end. Then the visual field of the woods intensified—something like shifting from a minor key up to a major one, but in appearance, not sound.

Oh, the sight of it—the beauty, the colors!

They brightened from the somber browns and greens of the woods to new, vibrant shades brimming with life—hues like none I'd ever seen.

My head reeled and I staggered backward as these sensations of energy and color reached a crescendo and then vanished in a burst of radiant light that erupted around me. It was so brilliant, so penetrating in its flaming purity that I dared not look on it.

My eyes shut down, leaving me in darkness.

Chapter 32

It was dawn again, three days after I staggered out of the woods at Semkhoz.

As I lay in my bed, on my back in the stillness, Babulya's words came back to me from long ago with the urgency of a siren in the night. The old woman had come often to my bedside before I dropped off to sleep and together we whispered of things—secrets shared between just us two—while she gently stroked my hair.

"Rest well, dear boy, and be thankful for the morning when it comes," she told me. "God is bringing you closer to what you must do."

"What is it, Nana?"

"He'll show you."

"When?"

"In His time."

"I wish He'd do it tomorrow."

"He'll call you when it's time."

"Will He really call to me?"

"Of course. He speaks to all of us—if we listen."

"I've never heard Him."

"Have you listened?"

I began to feel drowsy from her caresses. My eyes closed. "Will there be a voice, a voice I can hear?"

"There might be. Or He might send His messenger."

"Deda and Father say messengers aren't real."

"Oh, they are real for those with eyes to see and ears to hear." She stroked my hair with her knobby fingers. "I pray every day for them to watch over you."

"Will I know they're watching?"

She was quiet for a moment. "There might be a touch on your life, something so gentle you hardly notice it—but it will change everything."

"I've never seen a messenger," I said.

"It might just be someone you meet on the street."

I thought of the ordinary-looking people I saw on the streets of Kursk every day when I walked to school. "Messengers are good, aren't they?"

"Sometimes they tell us things we don't want to hear."

"I'll listen."

"That's good, but remember what's important."

"I know—it's what I do with what they tell me."

"Never forget that."

"Do you know what they'll tell me?"

"What God has for you—something special just for you."

"What if I don't do what He asks?"

She stopped stroking my hair.

"And turn your back on God?"

"I want to be a Party man. I want nice things for you and Deda, and Mother and Father."

"Blink your eye and those things will be gone. Only a fool turns his back on God to get them."

I was floating off to sleep in the dark room. "Nana … are we ashamed—about what happened?"

"Shouldn't we be?"

"Deda and Father never talk about it."

"One day, when you're older, you can ask them."

"Do the people still remember?"

"The people are gone, but the memories are there."

"I think God remembers."

"Yes He does."

"Why would He let that happen?"

"He planned it."

"That can't be."

"Of course He planned it."

"But why?"

"I don't know, but He planned it and in His time He'll bring good out of it."

"I don't see how."

"Nothing is impossible for Him."

~~~~

Now, remembering those words, I could see the way ahead. Everything was clear.

~~~~

Later I was up, fixing a cup of tea in the kitchen. The sky was bright blue and I pushed back the curtains from the window. Sunlight filled the room. I stirred a spoonful of sugar into the hot brew and took a sip. Then I heard a key in the door. A moment later Ksusha and Roman came into the kitchen.

"Come on in," I said. "Here, take this." I handed Roman the cup and reached up to the shelf for another.

"You can see?" Roman said. "When, how!?" He slapped me on the shoulder. "You should have called us!"

Ksusha put her arms around my neck and hugged me tight. "We've been so worried about you." When she pulled away I saw tears had welled up in her eyes.

"It's ok, I'm fine now."

She wiped her face with her hand and laughed. "I'm sorry, this has just been such a strange time. First you and then Father Dimitri, I'm sorry."

"Father Dimitri?"

"Her precious priest," Roman said.

"Oh it's terrible. He's disappeared."

"Disappeared? When?" I said.

"On Sunday," Roman said. "He left his house, but never made it to his church. It's been in the papers, on TV. There's been a real manhunt."

"The president is even calling for an investigation," Ksusha said.

Roman waved his hand. "But forget about all that. When did you get your eyes back?"

"This morning. As for how—well, Ksusha can probably tell you better than I can."

He looked at Ksusha and then back at me.

She came forward and hugged my neck again. "Oh, bless you," she said "I knew you'd do it."

Roman's brow wrinkled. "Do it? Do what? What are we talking about?"

I laughed. "I haven't done anything yet."

"Yes, yes you have," she said. "You've started—that's the hardest part."

Roman shook his head. "Wait a minute—just like that, you can see again. No doctor, no medicine, you're cured."

"There's a little more to it than that."

"Tell me this isn't some game you've been playing."

"Why would I play a game with you?"

"I have no idea—you know I've never understood you, Kolya."

"You really want to know?"

"Yes," Ksusha said. "He does."

Roman glanced at her again and then back at me. He held up his hands. "Ok, wait a minute—I see what this is." He backed up a step. "Look, I don't want any of that."

"Any of what?" I said.

He pointed at Ksusha. "Her religion, her God … I know what this is."

I stepped over to him and looked him in the face. "Yes, I think you do, my friend. I think you know exactly what this is—and I want some answers from you."

"I … I don't know what you're talking about."

"I think you do."

"This has nothing to do with me."

"It has everything to do with you. And you know it."

"I'm leaving. Let's go," he said to Ksusha.

"Roman, listen to him," she said. "Talk to us."

"About what?"

"Tell us."

"Tell you what?" a voice said from behind me.

The three of us turned as Styopa walked into the kitchen, followed by the colonel. When Roman saw the colonel, his eyes widened and reflexively his posture straightened. For a moment his mouth hung slightly open.

"The door was unlocked. Have we interrupted something?" the colonel asked.

"C … Comrade Captain," Roman stammered. "What are you doing here?"

The colonel smiled. "Relax, Davidov," he said smoothly. "And none of us are 'comrades' any longer, remember?"

We all stood there looking at each other for an awkward moment.

I cleared my throat. I looked at Ksusha and then at the colonel. "Um … Oksana Davidova," I said. "This is Colonel Aleksandr Narumov."

The colonel gave Ksusha a slight bow. "A pleasure, my dear."

"How do you do," she answered him.

"Davidov, good to see you looking well," he said to Roman.

"Yes, sir, and you too sir."

The colonel turned to me. "I thought I'd come by and see the patient for myself. So how are you? Better, yes? It seems your eyes are working again."

"Much better, sir" I said. "It cleared up this morning."

"Yes, good," he said while he studied my face. "A shave wouldn't hurt, though."

Styopa laughed. "And a bath."

The colonel looked at Roman and Ksusha. "Forgive us, we didn't mean to intrude. Did we interrupt something?" There was another awkward silence.

Then Roman found his voice again. "Kolya … has been talking with God," he said.

The colonel and Styopa looked at each other and then at me.

"Really? Talking with God?" Styopa said and he laughed again. "Was it a long conversation?"

"Long enough," I said.

"Well, tell us—what did He say?"

Yet another awkward silence.

"It's what I said that's important."

"Ok, what did you say?"

"It's over for me, Styopa," I said and his nose and mouth twisted like he'd smelled something foul.

Styopa started to speak, but the colonel reached out and put a hand on his shoulder. "I think this is a conversation we should have in private," he said. "Kolya, join us downstairs."

Styopa looked at me with an expression of amazement. "Doesn't sound like you're feeling better to me."

"Downstairs," the colonel said.

I followed the colonel down to the street where his car was parked. It was a big, new BMW. We stood alongside it.

"Maybe you're not as recovered as I thought. We need to discuss this—privately," he said.

"Please no, Colonel," I said. "We can talk, but it won't matter. I need to get out. I can't do this anymore."

He touched me on my arm, in the same place Father Dimitri had laid his hand. "I'm sorry about the priest. That wasn't supposed to happen. In fact, it's going to make things worse for a while."

"That isn't it."

He shrugged. "Then what?"

"There's something I have to do—that I've finally decided to do. I don't know if I can do it or how long it will take. Years maybe."

He pursed his lips. "I'm intrigued."

"Please, Colonel. Let me go."

"When we're getting ready to do such big things—big things you'll share in?"

"Yes."

He was quiet for a long moment, looking at me with his opaque eyes. "You know—people don't usually 'retire' from what we do."

"I know."

He regarded me a moment longer and then pulled on his gloves. He looked up at the blue sky, then at me, and he let out a big breath. "Well … I suppose I owe you that much, don't I?"

"Thank you, sir."

He got into the car, on the passenger side, and pulled the heavy door shut. Then the window slid silently down.

"I can trust you to forget everything, of course. There aren't many I would say that to."

"Forget what, sir?" I said and he smirked.

"And when your money's gone?"

I smiled at him. "It'll be gone soon, I think."

He nodded. "Goodbye, Nikolai."

"Goodbye, sir." The window slid up.

Styopa had been standing nearby. I turned from the car and faced him. He looked like he'd been slapped. "Well … boyo … this is a sad day," he said.

"Not for me, my friend."

"You'll be back."

"No, Styopa—I won't." I put my hand on his shoulder. "You can come with me, you know."

"With you? And do what? What's this about?"

"Come with me and see. You won't regret it."

He stuck his hands in his pockets and looked down, shaking his head. Then he looked up and smiled. "Humph … no … no I don't think so." He put his arms around me and kissed me on the cheek. "So long, boyo."

"Styopa, thank you."

"For what?"

"Oh, in a way, I could never have done this if it weren't for you."

He shrugged. "So long, my friend." He got into the car and started the engine and they drove away.

Ksusha and Roman were still in the kitchen when I got back to the flat. Roman looked pale.

"Kolya, I'm glad you're better, but we need to go."

I stood between him and the door. "Not yet. You're staying here."

His eyes flashed. "You don't give me orders." He swore at me and started to pull Ksusha around me, toward the door. I grabbed his arm.

"You're not leaving. You're gonna stay here and talk to me."

"I want, I want out of here," he said.

His voice quavered and when he looked at me I saw those haunted eyes I remembered from a hospital ward so long ago.

He fumbled for words. "Look ... I ... I want to get out of here."

"You're staying."

"I don't want her religion. Keep it."

"Roman, you know better," I said. "You—of all people—know better than to say that."

"I don't know what you're talking about."

"Tell us what you saw, Roman."

He stared at me.

"Tell us what you saw—that day at Bagram. Tell us what you saw."

He was as white as my bed sheets and for a long time he didn't speak. Then he sat down with a thud on a chair.

"That day in hospital at Bagram. You told us you saw something. Tell us what it was."

"I didn't see anything."

"You're lying."

"Please tell us," Ksusha said softly, her eyes big and luminous.

"It was a dream, a hallucination! I was on drugs. You saw me. I was out of my head."

"I don't believe you," I said.

The spark came back into his eyes. "Are you calling me a liar?" He licked his lips. "You don't ... you won't believe me."

"Try us."

Then the fight seemed to go out of him, like air leaving a balloon, and he sank down farther onto the chair. He leaned over and dropped his face into his hands. When he looked up, I saw that face again, the face I'd seen all those years ago at Bagram, a haunted face, the face of a man fleeing for his life from something dreadful, something unspeakable. Lines of strain pulled at the corners of his mouth and around his eyes.

"You saw something," I prompted him. "What was it?"

He leaned back in the chair and chewed on his lip. Then he began to speak to us, distantly, like he was in a trance.

"You know I almost crossed over," he said, speaking softly, as he tugged at his wedding band.

"We thought you were gone in the transport," I said.

"The ground was going by me, faster and faster."

"You were … running, flying?"

"No … no … it was more like I was still and … everything else was moving, moving past me."

Ksusha handed him a glass of water and he drained it. "It was a forest, at first trees—everything was green—but then the trees were gone and it was just rocks and sand, a desert, more like a wasteland. And then the rocks were gone and it was just sand, flat sand, white like snow—as far as I could see. The sky was white too, the same color as the sand. Everything was just blank." His face was shiny with sweat. Ksusha put her hand on his shoulder.

"Is that all?" I said.

"Then I came to the end. It was staring at me."

"What? What was staring at you?"

"It was … eternity … that's all I can tell you—eternity—forever and forever and forever, out ahead staring at me."

"What was it—what did it look like?"

"Not a person."

"Then what?"

"A … a presence; that's all I can tell you. A presence—and …"

"What?"

"There were two ways to go. That's when I heard the voices. You've never heard such joy—happiness and singing." Now he looked almost green and he leaned forward like he was going to retch. He put his face in his hands. Then he looked up. "From the others, you've never heard such … pain, sorrow." He shivered. "Hope to God you never hear cries like that."

"And then?" I said.

He didn't answer for a time. "Then I was in the bed in hospital."

313

He sat still in his chair, staring down at the floor, shaking. Sweat stood out in beads on his forehead and on his upper lip. I started toward him, but he waved me away.

"Stay back," he said and he pulled a cloth from his pocket and wiped his face and mouth. Ksusha held his hand and in a few moments some of his color returned.

"I don't want to have to tell that again—ever." He let out a long breath. "You can't imagine it."

I put my hand on his shoulder. "You were given a gift, my friend. You understand that, don't you?"

He looked up at me and nodded. "I think so. I didn't want to believe it. All those years I wanted it to be a dream or the drugs."

I picked up the cup of tea from the table and held it out to him. He took it and emptied it in one long swallow and then wiped his face again.

"It wasn't the drugs—and it wasn't a dream," I said.

"I know. I've been afraid to admit it."

"So," I said. "You're coming with me?"

He looked up at me and nodded. "Yeah ... yeah," he answered. "I'm coming with you."

CHAPTER 33

❧

Korennaya

It is summer again and the days are hot. I belong to one of the crews clearing away the rubble to make way for the rebuilding. The work progresses, slowly, but it progresses. Again there are monks in residence at Korennaya—just a handful—but a beginning. Again songs and prayers resonate across the old common.

At night I sleep in one of the old dormitories and during the day I labor for many long hours. The rubble is covered over with dirt and grass and we toil with picks and shovels to break loose the buried chunks of plaster and masonry that we load onto carts and carry away and dump down by the river. Sometimes we find pieces of masonry decorated with colored designs and I try to imagine the handsome structures that once stood here.

The thick old poplar trees standing along the front road, outside what remains of the old wall, are fully leafed out, giving us good shade for our work in the mornings. In the afternoons, when the sun is hottest, we put down our tools and walk down the hill to fill our water jugs from the spring near the river. The old legend says the spring once flowed from the roots of an immense elm tree on this spot, but if so, all traces of the tree have vanished. The cool, clear water now flows from a pipe sunk deep into the ground.

A flock of pigeons sits on the branches of one of the poplars, watching us. "That's strange, really strange," one of the locals says to me. "There've never been pigeons here before." I look up at the flock and smile.

I wonder.

Today Roman's crew is finishing the excavations along the east wall. My crew is working a mound at the crest of the bluff over the Tuskar River, at a place where the locals say a beautiful garden once flourished. Three of us are digging together to loosen the edges.

On one side of me is a local man. On the other is Yuri Matyukh. Yuri is getting stronger every day and his color is now tanned and healthy from the outdoor work. When I found him, dead drunk, his skin was the color of lead. For five days and nights I kept him chained to a tree while the poisons leeched from his body. He railed against me, shouting profane insults and hurling back at me the food I put out for him. But in time, his body and mind started to mend. When I told him he was coming with me on this project, he didn't exactly agree, but when I arrived here, he was waiting outside the old front gate.

The local man has been watching me as I work. He starts a conversation, probably just to be polite.

"Sorry, I didn't mean to stare. It's just your hair—I don't think I've ever seen hair like it. In the sun it's like … copper, polished copper. But you've probably heard that."

"Yeah—I have."

He digs a while longer. "You know, I'm beginning to believe in this project—that we can really rebuild here. I never thought it was possible."

"It's good work," I answer him.

"They say you're paying for all this."

"Well … maybe."

"Bless you," he says. "This has been a place of ghosts for so long. I never thought it could come alive again."

"If God's in it, it will come alive."

"Yes," he answers. "That is so. Just look around. He's brought you and these other young people to us to help with the work. Who would ever have believed that possible?"

"It's a privilege for us to be here."

"Who would believe Moscow people would give us money for this?"

"I wish there was more."

"Moscow has always meant one thing for this place—trouble, much trouble—and now look." He shakes his head.

"God is good," I say.

"Praise His name."

We dig together in silence for a time. Sweat runs down my face and I stop to wipe it away with my shirt sleeve. The local man is still digging.

"Do you live near here?" I ask him.

"In Rylsk."

"Sure, I know it."

"Do you?"

"I come from Kursk."

"Ah, I see. Someone said you come from Moscow."

"From Kursk."

"That's good," he says while he digs.

He loosens a jagged chunk of masonry with his pick and pries it from the grass roots. The old mortar still holds the pieces of brick solidly together.

"How long have you been in Rylsk?" I ask him.

"Always—all my life, my family too. I don't know how far back."

We dig on together in silence for a time longer.

"I am Pyotr Matveev," he says.

"Pleased to meet you."

"And you are?" he asks. It's a question I knew someone eventually would ask. But what reason could I give for refusing to tell him my name?

And so I tell him.

"Razkazov," he muses as he digs. "Not a good name to have around here, you know." He loosens another chunk of masonry from the mound.

I keep digging.

"Razkazov," he says a moment later. "Like Mikhail Razkazov, the Bolshevik? Is that right?"

317

"Yeah," I reply, wishing he would stop.

"May God rot his soul." He swings his pick down violently on another chunk buried in the grass and dirt. Then he picks up his shovel.

"Pray for his soul," I say.

"If you knew what he did here you wouldn't say that."

"Yes, I would."

"Well, you're a better man than most."

"I don't think so."

"They say Razkazov died in the camps in Stalin's time," he says a moment later.

"Yeah, I've heard that."

"Well, that was to be expected wasn't it—that eventually those dogs would turn on each other."

"I guess so."

"No ... yours is not a good name around here," he says again, but then he stops and looks up at me. "But no offense meant to you."

"I understand. No offense."

"From Kursk, you said," he says a moment later. He stops his digging and leans on the handle of his shovel. He's looking at my face.

I keep digging. "That's right."

"For how long?"

I shrug. "All my life."

"I mean before that—how long for your people?"

"I don't know. A good ways back, I think."

Now the truth begins to dawn on him. My cheeks burn in shame and embarrassment, but he seems strangely pleased, moved even.

"God be praised," he says softly and then he crosses himself. "It's a miracle!"

I stop digging. "Don't—don't say that."

"But I must say it! I must!"

"It's not a miracle," I say and he looks at me in amazement.

"It's the hand of God. Can it be anything else? First that we should be able to rebuild ... and then to have you here—a part of it. I ask you, can it be anything else?"

He drops his shovel and walks hurriedly away. He goes to a group of monks out on the common and I watch them talking together. They all turn and look at me.

Soon everyone will know.

A miracle, he called it. Is it a miracle?

I never thought of it that way. To my thinking, I'm here to repay an old family debt. But if God uses my work here—rebuilding what Deda's father destroyed—to bring hope and renewal to these people, then maybe Matveev is right—maybe that is a miracle.

Then will the eyes of the blind
be opened
and the ears of the deaf
unstopped.
Then will the lame leap like a
deer,
and the mute tongue shout
for joy.
Water will gush forth in the
wilderness
and streams in the desert.

Isaiah 35:5–6